Pigeo.

Mark Fieldse

Think you know your neighbours? Think again

Published in 2017 by FeedARead.com Publishing

A CIP catalogue record for this title is available from
the British Library.

Cover design by Mark Fieldsend
"Pigeon Street" cover font by Ollie Dupont

For Mum, Dad and Amanda

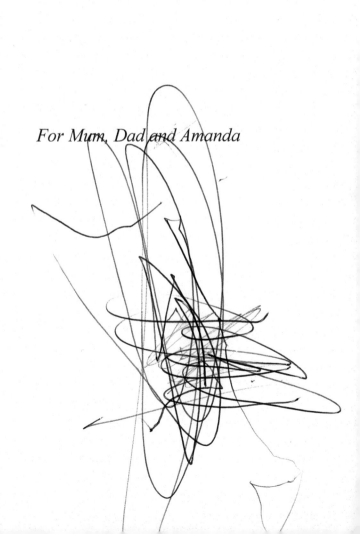

London, 2003

Closing his eyes, the waiter drew in a deep and prolonged breath, making the most of this moment of serenity amid the evening's laborious clamour. He wiped his hands firmly across the front of his trousers, the action providing only temporary relief from the moist, sweaty palms that added extra complications to an already difficult task. The waiter always savoured times like these, since he had quickly discovered from his short time at the establishment that they were few and far between.

This particular evening had been uncharacteristically quiet. A combination of a rail strike and grim weather had caused a flurry of last-minute cancellations, much to the annoyance of the manager, whose patience was wearing ever thinner with each vanishing source of income. Yet, despite the many absentees, enough diners had braved the weather and black cabs to fill the majority of tables. This created a bustling rather than hectic atmosphere, like that of an airport departure lounge.

The waiter's short period of rest was prematurely ended, as his attention was drawn to the gesturing motions of a young lady. He acknowledged her signals and promptly made his way over to her table. Even from a distance, her manner suggested some degree of distress.

Although the lady had been seated alone for some time, the presence of another plate of food indicated that this hadn't always been the case. Little of the meal she had ordered remained on the plate. In contrast, the plate of her absent companion was almost untouched; the cutlery lying crudely across its contents. The waiter offered a well-rehearsed smile.

'Yes, madam. How can I be of assistance?'

The lady paused before answering, glancing down to avoid his inquisitive gaze. When she raised her head, he noticed that her cheeks were flushed with colour.

'I'm sorry to bother you,' she said, her voice timid and embarrassed. 'It's my boyfr... er, fiancé. He left abruptly, I think to the bathroom.'

The waiter raised his eyebrows, prompting her to elaborate further.

'I-I know this sounds stupid,' she stammered, 'and I'm probably just being paranoid, but could you possibly check to see he's all right?'

The waiter nodded. This certainly wasn't the first time such a request had been made.

'Certainly, madam.'

The woman looked momentarily relieved, her shoulders lowering and relaxing, but only for a second.

'It's just for my peace of mind,' she added. 'I'm really sorry for all the bother.'

'Not at all.' The waiter smiled again. This one seemed genuine.

He strode away from the table and towards the washrooms, swanning between the chairs of other diners with great dexterity. The lady watched from afar as he pushed open the door bearing a picture of a stately gentleman and disappeared from sight.

A short interval elapsed before the waiter re-emerged, one hand passing agitatedly through his hair. Such was his demeanour that the lady was out of her seat and heading towards him before he could even raise his hand to deter her.

The antecedent serenity of the restaurant was shattered by the commotion that followed.

And the screaming.

The resounding, nauseating shrieking.

Joseph

The thin winter air burnt deep into Joseph's lungs, working its way down to the furthest reaches, where it lingered and chilled before erupting from his mouth in a billow of fog. His breathing tightened with every step, and he regretted his decision to leave the comfort and warmth of the flat for the sake of this torturous recreation. The fleecy tracksuit top was no longer insulating his chest, which had become saturated with sweat and drained the heat from him despite the exertion, and he longed for the sanctuary of home.

A short distance in front of him, and getting smaller by the minute, he could just make out the athletic figure of Iain.

'Slow down, you bastard,' Joseph muttered under his breath, grinning at the absurdity of his attitude.

Iain wasn't naturally competitive. To him, it was merely a leisure activity. Maybe this was the reason Joseph resented him at times like these, because he was only doing this for fun and yet he was so damn good at it. The plus side to this one-way rivalry was that it provided Joseph with a twisted motivation to soldier on through the harshest of conditions. If he didn't, ground would be lost, both in the literal sense and in terms of his long-term goal.

The effort of the night's run was becoming almost unbearable, but the bridge looming in the distance signalled that there wasn't much further to go. Joseph pushed a bit harder and became engulfed in the artificial amber light that flooded the streets. The dull glow highlighted the tunnel's many flaws: the racist graffiti, the pigeon shit and the stagnant puddles with their lingering smell of ammonia. Above him, among the crude metal girders, and where the light couldn't reach, roosted hordes of pigeons, lined up in what could be perceived as a giant communal pigeon toilet. Despite his tiredness, Joseph had no wish to pause beneath this structure lest a passing express train disturbed the tunnel's feathered residents.

He concentrated incessantly on each step, barely noticing the old woman he passed, who seemed to spring from the shadows with unnerving stealth. She grimaced aggressively as he darted left to avoid her and uttered drunken, disapproving curses from beneath a dirty scarf. The words were drowned out by a passing bus, which roared and hissed as it ploughed through the grime.

The return to the relative darkness of the city streets and the overflowing recycling bins marked the end of the road, and he finally gave in to his fatigue and slowed to a walk. Now that the wind was no longer in his face, his body quickly warmed up and the sweat started to build. He loped towards the entrance to his flat, where Iain was waiting, still jogging on the spot.

'Giving up so close to home?' asked Iain, tutting.

'Never. I'm just warming down,' replied Joseph, his hands on his knees.

They both chuckled in acknowledgement of the feeble bravado. Joseph heaved himself upright and made some half-hearted stretching movements with his arms.

'Same time next week then, Iain?' he uttered, sounding much more enthusiastic than he felt.

'Wouldn't miss it for the world. See you at work tomorrow.' Iain smiled and set off for his own home, a further two miles away.

Joseph was left to marvel at his friend's uncanny stamina as he perched on the cold doorstep. He always sat there after running. The warmth of the house would be overpowering if he went indoors straight away, and he was sweaty enough already.

When Joseph eventually got up, he did so a little too quickly, his vision darkening for a second. He steadied himself against the door, fumbling in his pocket for his keys. It took his weary hands several attempts to find the lock, and when they did he opened the door by leaning tiredly against it.

Joseph made his way slowly up the stairs, the door slamming shut behind him with a loud wooden crack and the heavy bolt grinding as it slid itself into place. He took the stairs one at a time rather than bounding up them in pairs with his usual vigour. The apartment was on the second floor, not far at all, although it seemed like it at times such as this.

The frustrating lock, which required a special knack to open it, offered a familiar resistance as Joseph entered the flat. He turned on the lights and prised off his shoes without undoing the laces.

'Hi, Angela! I'm back.'

There was no response.

'Angela?'

She must still be at the shops, thought Joseph, making his way lethargically into the bedroom without bothering to turn the light on.

He undressed, facing into the semi-darkness and away from the glare of the unshaded bulb in the hallway. He pulled his T-shirt and tracksuit over his head as a single item, slinging the sweaty garments into the corner to form a damp mountain on top of the clothes bin. His back groaning in objection, he pulled down his underwear and tracksuit bottoms, leaving them in a pile on the floor, along with his socks.

After fumbling around in the gloom, he found and grabbed his towel from the back of the chair and wrapped it around his naked lower body. He shuddered. It was still slightly damp and the window he had left open to air the room made it feel cold against his skin. He turned towards the bathroom, and it was then that the figure emerged from the darkness behind him.

A blow to the back of the head knocked Joseph to the ground. Before the numbing pain had even registered, he received a burning kick to the ribs. He struggled to get up, but, with the wind knocked out of him, he merely floundered on the floor, his hands scrabbling helplessly against the wall. The pain and exhaustion clouded his mind, and he fought to remain conscious.

What if Angela returns to the flat now?

His eyes darted about fearfully, his face haggard in anticipation of the next blow. It came from behind, jarring into the small of his back with agonising accuracy. Joseph arched and spun around to face his assailant. The attacker had already shifted; Joseph's tired, sluggish movements one step behind.

He received another kick, this time to his ankle, and cried out silently as the agony burrowed deep into the bone. The next strike slammed into his face. The skin's reaction was instant, his eye socket swelling up like that of a badly beaten boxer. The blood from his nose quickly followed, pouring out fast and fluid, leaving a smattering of crimson on the carpet, which quickly turned dark as it seeped into the dense green fibres.

A searing sensation developed at the back of his head as the man grabbed a handful of his hair. Joseph's head was yanked back and a shiny object slid deliberately across his face, resting against his throat. The blade felt cold against his clammy, trembling skin.

Joseph lay there, completely rigid, too terrified even to breathe properly in case his rising chest forced the knife into his neck. The pair remained in the same position for what seemed like an eternity, as if both parties were unsure what to do next.

It was the intruder who spoke first, in a low, emotionless voice.

'Get dressed, and don't make a sound,' he commanded, hurling Joseph forward again, causing him to plunge face-first into the carpet, its coarse strands like sandpaper.

Joseph crawled obediently into the bedroom, pulling himself up with the help of a heavy chest of drawers. His assailant followed behind him, remaining within striking distance. Joseph wrenched the drawer open. It was a crudely constructed wooden item that always jammed. At that moment, it felt like the hardest thing to manoeuvre in the world. He dared not look up or take his time, lest he gave the intruder any excuse to inflict further damage. Without any light to guide him, his hands blundered about in the drawer's gaping mouth, frantically feeling around for something to wear.

'Hurry up,' came the order from behind him. 'And stop crying.'

Joseph wasn't aware he had been crying. He felt the tears streaming down his cheeks, their saltiness chafing the broken skin. The realisation made him want to weep, and he battled hard against the urge to break down completely.

'Wear these.'

The intruder flicked the dirty tracksuit bottoms at his face, the legs briefly engulfing him. Joseph pulled them on, the sweaty underwear clinging uncomfortably to his legs as he did so. Turning quickly back to the drawer to avoid having to put on his other dirty clothes, Joseph found an old T-shirt and jumper, pulling them carefully over his smarting face. The blood had already begun to dry, darkening his chin and leaving a thick, sickly taste in his mouth.

'Get up.'

Joseph rose gingerly to his feet, his ankle delicate from the blow he had received during the assault. He shifted his weight warily from one foot to the other, testing the ankle's strength. The injury to his lower spine prevented him from drawing himself up to his full height, so he stooped like an old man clutching a stiff back, his other hand propping him upright against the drawers. Tentatively raising his gaze, he looked up at his assailant for the first time.

With his facial features completely obscured by the hallway light behind him, Joseph could only make out a tall, ungainly frame, the details of which were disguised by badly fitting clothes. In his left hand the man clutched a kitchen knife, the sight of which made Joseph feel nauseous. The figure stood, silent and menacing, blocking the only exit and rendering Joseph a prisoner in his own bedroom.

'Look,' Joseph pleaded, so timidly that it was almost a whine. 'Take what you want. Take anything. Please, just leave me alone.'

The man shook his head and Joseph wailed in despair, flinging himself at his captor's waist. The man side-stepped the lunge with ease and brought the butt of the knife down hard on Joseph's right shoulder. Joseph writhed in torment, his shoulder blade shattered like a broken plate.

'Shut up!' hissed the man.

Damning his own stupidity, Joseph clenched his teeth to deflect the pain, the tendons in his neck jutting out in angry ridges. Rocking back and forth on the floor, he apologised repeatedly between sniffs.

'You're coming with me,' the man instructed.

The words filled Joseph with dismay.

The hurt, the fear, they didn't matter, as long as he remained there. But outside? Once beyond the flat, he had nothing.

'Please, don't do this. Take what you want,' Joseph begged.

'You're coming with me,' the man repeated, a harsh edge creeping into his voice.

And then he walked away, disappearing down the hallway. Joseph waited longingly for the sound of the front door opening and closing. The only sounds were his returning footsteps.

'Put these on.'

He threw some shoes at Joseph's feet.

Joseph looked at them despairingly. The laces were still tied from earlier and he only had the use of one arm.

'*Now.*'

Joseph sat up against the wall and wrestled the shoes onto his bare feet with considerable difficulty. No sooner had his heel wedged itself into the second shoe than he was hauled roughly to his feet and shoved towards the front door. He limped forward and waited by the line of hanging coats for further instruction. His mind was working overtime, trying to think of a way to escape. The only hope was that he would meet someone else in the corridor; someone returning home late from work or on their way out to the pub.

Just as long as it wasn't Angela.

The man came and stood behind him, so close that Joseph could feel the moisture in his breath.

'We're going for a walk,' the man started. 'You will not call out for help. You will not try anything stupid. You will not say or do anything that suggests something is wrong.'

The irony wasn't lost on Joseph, who wondered whether his face looked as mangled as it felt. In another situation, he might even have laughed.

'If you don't do exactly as I say, I will kill you,' the man continued. 'Is that clear?'

Joseph nodded. He believed him.

'Now open the door.'

Joseph breathed deeply and pushed open the door. Much to his misery, it swung open to reveal a deserted corridor. The man prodded him forward, shutting the door gently behind them.

'Get going.'

Stepping out into the communal hallway, the material of the carpet could be heard crumpling beneath his weight. The stillness was immense. Spotlights flickered from their sunken positions in the ceiling with a barely detectable frequency, creating a repressed, dreamlike atmosphere. The serenity was so pronounced that Joseph could hear his own heartbeat, which thumped harder and faster than at any stage of his run.

From behind closed doors came a rush of high-pitched laughter, which sliced through the silence, making Joseph recoil with shock. Pausing for a second to regain his composure, he belatedly approached the stairs, taking his time so as to give his rescuers a chance to arrive. Overplaying the limp, the cause of which had numbed to a bearable level, he took small steps, fashioning the illusion of inhibited balance. Sauntering along at this speed, he deduced that it would take at least three minutes to reach the main door. Three minutes for a would-be saviour to arrive.

'Hurry up,' came the order from behind, accompanied by a prod to Joseph's wounded shoulder.

'Argh,' he started, quickly smothering his exclamation.

Given no choice, he quickened his pace. Upon reaching the stairs, he steered himself towards the left-hand side so he could cling to the banister with his good arm. It felt like his body was in danger of collapsing at any moment, and he feared what might happen if he fell. Knuckles glowing with the force, his fingers clutched the wooden rail as tightly as his aching muscles would allow. Each step seemed so far beneath him, and he had to place both feet on each one to stay upright. All the times he had denounced the flat for not having a lift were forgotten. He abhorred the prospect of being trapped in such an enclosed space with this man.

Music began to play in one of the flats, just loud enough so that only the tinny beat was audible through the walls, like the headphones of a teenager on a moving train. Another sign that others were close by, the sound was mildly comforting.

The descent passed by slowly and painfully, yet nobody came to his aid. Upon reaching the front door, the pair paused once more. Joseph could feel the coldness of the outside world radiating through the wood and drafting beneath the small crack at the base of the door. He noticed that he could see his breath, despite the efforts of the heater, which was humming away down low to his left.

'We're going to go outside now, and I'll lead you to my car.'

'Please sir, don't do this,' begged Joseph in hushed, pleading tones. 'I'll give you everything I have. Please, don't do this.'

The man chuckled, the sound so muffled it was merely the passing of air.

'Oh no. You're coming with me. I'll lead you to my car and you'll get in without putting up any resistance.'

The man grabbed Joseph aggressively by his good arm and, leaning forward, flung open the door.

The biting iciness of the December wind swiftly blasted its way through Joseph's inappropriate apparel. Browned, soggy leaves rushed past him in alarming numbers, twisting and dancing in the air like rustic confetti. He looked left and right for signs of movement, but the weather had cleared the streets of people. Nobody passed this way unless they lived in the flats. Sandwiched between the railway station and the council estate, it was hardly a popular route for a late-night stroll.

'Over there.' The man gestured towards an unwashed, neglected family saloon, parked about a hundred yards from the flat entrance.

Standing to his right with one arm across his shoulders, the man led Joseph along the pavement in the direction of the vehicle. Forlorn and despairing, there was no point even trying to resist the motion.

Bare, leafless branches dangled overhead, forcing the pair to stoop to avoid being grated by the craggy bark. On the ground, rotting leaves squelched and squirmed beneath each footfall, sliding around as a solid mass of brown sludge that would remain there for weeks until the rain washed it down into the sewers. Across the road, leaves and litter had already blocked one storm drain, resulting in a sizeable moat that rose swiftly at the slightest suggestion of rain and threatened the bikes people had left at the rear station entrance. A recent spell of wet weather had reduced the area to a squalid mess that didn't, unfortunately, inconvenience enough people for anything to be done about it. Yet Joseph now looked upon these surroundings with a sympathetic outlook, yearning to tread freely through the mire.

Without warning, the man quickened his step, propelling Joseph forward and causing him to stumble. His head shot up, scanning for the origin of this sudden alarm. Far in the distance, and getting closer by the second, was a jogger, loping towards them in a hooded grey tracksuit. Joseph's heart began to race with renewed expectation. The runner's style was clumsy but powerful, and it wouldn't be long before he reached them.

The man had to drag him hard to overcome the resistance of his feet, which were planted stubbornly on the ground. Joseph reeled forward, his body momentarily leaving the pavement, and the man had to seize him firmly to stop him crashing to the floor.

For a short time, he was free as the man frantically searched for his keys. Rather than trying to escape, Joseph found himself unable to function, overawed by his newfound position. He just stood there, staring at the man's hands as they worked the key in the lock. The realisation of the missed opportunity slowly dawned on him and he began to turn, but his attacker fixed him with such a look that he faltered and froze.

The man hauled open the door, glancing over his shoulder to assess the proximity of the approaching jogger.

'Get in the car.'

He reached forward and grabbed a handful of Joseph's sweater, wrenching him towards the car. Joseph craned his neck sideways. The jogger was so close he could read the logo on the front of his jumper and see the steam of his breath billowing from beneath his hood.

'Get in the car!' The man's voice, laced with anger, remained at a low level.

He tugged Joseph harder, still using some restraint, conscious of the way the scene would appear to any onlookers.

'N-no,' Joseph stammered, trying to back away while shaking his head and holding up his hands protectively.

Losing patience, the man leant forward against the car, with both hands on the roof. Head hidden between his arms, he spoke to the floor without emotion.

'Get in the car or I will butcher your girlfriend.'

The suggestion of any harm coming to Angela weakened Joseph more than any of the blows he had received in the struggle. Rage steamed up within him, adrenaline swamping his body like flood waters, his muscles prickling. He was frenzied with wrath, and he wanted to tear this fucker limb from limb.

But he had mentioned Angela. He could well be bluffing, but how did he even know he had a girlfriend? A lucky guess, perhaps. No, it couldn't be.

The arrival of the jogger was inconsequential. The man was in complete control and Joseph was already in the car, the door slammed shut behind him.

A potentially hazardous situation effortlessly overcome, the man walked calmly around the front of the car, rubbing his hands together briskly against the cold. He unlocked the driver's door and ducked into the car, the chassis rocking with the additional mass and the ceiling light blinking on and off. The man slammed the door shut with a shuddering bang that reverberated around the car's interior. Joseph didn't avert his gaze.

'You made the right choice back there,' declared the man, drawing no kind of response.

Unperturbed by the lack of reaction, the man proceeded to start the car, the engine coughing and spluttering before roaring into life. The heater sprang into action, blowing cold air into Joseph's face and forcing him to close his eyes, a dried-up leaf rattling about frantically behind the plastic grill like a crazed insect.

A quick glance over the shoulder was all it took for him to see that the road was empty, and the man manoeuvred the car out from its poorly parked position. Heavy metallic objects rolled around in the boot as the back end of the car swung into the road.

The man drove cautiously, in no hurry to reach his unknown destination. Joseph switched his focus to the left in order to expel the man from his field of vision. After pausing at the junction, the car passed back under the bridge Joseph had himself hobbled under not more than an hour earlier.

That fucking bridge. Twice that day he had travelled beneath it and twice he had suffered pain of some description.

Each time it got worse. Far worse.

Joseph looked out as the car trundled over Lavender Hill, passing the many estate agents that had chosen to congregate there, transforming the area into a house-hunter's oasis. Beyond the incline, the road widened and the shops became sparser. This was unfamiliar territory to Joseph, who had little reason to frequent this part of town.

An abrupt right-hand turn took them off the main road and into a narrower street lined with small, terraced houses. Occasional street lamps teased them with brief flickers of light that gave only brief snapshots of their immediate surroundings, gone before any detail could be deciphered. Redundant vehicles formed orderly queues down both sides; victims of varying levels of rust and neglect.

Without warning, the continual road transformed into a mushroom-shaped cul-de-sac and the car came to a halt at its far right-hand reaches.

'Wait there.'

The man got out of the car and strode around to the passenger side, where Joseph sat in torment, willing for the journey not to have ended. Shivering in the blustery cauldron, the man opened the door and hauled Joseph out.

He led Joseph through a warped iron gate that screeched when he kicked it open, ushering him down a short concrete path sandwiched between two patches of unkempt grass. A trio of scrawny pigeons bickered and hustled over a discarded bread crust that would scarcely provide enough food for one. It was a reckless battle, each pigeon taking a swift peck at it in turn before withdrawing quickly to avoid the other sharp, protective beaks. Inevitably, the larger of the three emerged victorious, achieving a good enough grip on the crust to sweep it up to the rooftops to be devoured in peace.

Joseph watched as the defeated pair followed after it in the futile hope that their victor would leave behind the smallest morsel, realising that he too was hungry.

There were three locks on the front door, each bigger and more elaborate than the one before it. Inside the house, the man inspected his mail as usual, unceremoniously tossing away a catalogue addressed to a previous inhabitant who had presumably left no forwarding address. Of the envelopes he opened, none provoked any response and all but one joined the catalogue in the bin. The remainder was left on the side for future reference.

Joseph inspected the house, scanning for some clue as to the background or psychology of his captor. Nothing presented itself as abnormal, or even mildly eccentric. The walls were bare, painted in a tasteful shade of apple white, and the hallway displayed no garish ornamental objects, photographs or pictures.

Darkened oak boards spanned the floor, reclining with an elegance that suggested they were of considerable quality and value. On top of this, everything was organised and tidy, the leaves that had followed them in presenting the only exception. After his morose expectations of the derelict abode such a man might inhabit, the reality was almost comforting. In fact, the house looked more presentable than his own flat, which was cluttered to a state beyond the items within it.

'Take your shoes off, please.'

'Pardon?' Joseph had heard the words, but couldn't quite accept this formal request.

'Remove your shoes.'

Joseph kicked off his trainers, positioning them neatly with his feet, which he was surprised to remember were bare. Opposite the front door, carpeted stairs led up into the unknown, and something inside him snapped.

'Where's Angela?'

The question erupted from deep within him. He had tried to suppress the anxiety in order to stay sane, but she was the only reason he was there right now. Otherwise, he would either have been safely in the hospital with the corpulent jogger or dead.

'Angela? So that's her name, is it? That's a pretty name. Pretty name for a pretty girl.'

He sounded almost sincere, but the comment sounded perverse to Joseph and it enraged him more than any threats to his own life.

He lunged at the man once more, this time catching him off guard. The man's eyes widened in astonishment and he stumbled backwards. But the attack was clumsy and he managed to parry Joseph's oncoming mass, his momentum sending Joseph skidding across the wooden floor like a playful puppy. Slipping on the polished surface as he clambered to his feet, Joseph wasn't ready for the subsequent punt to the stomach and, unlike Joseph, the man hadn't yet removed his shoes. Doubling over, Joseph gagged, coughing up a putrid mixture of water, stomach acid and blood. The multicoloured liquid sprayed onto the floor, rapidly spreading into a swirling puddle.

'You don't learn, do you?!'

The man strode forward and grabbed him with both hands, Joseph still emitting hollow, retching noises like an over-indulged drinker who had already emptied the contents of his stomach. A string of thick saliva swung from his lower lip and clung to his clothes. His eyeballs, bloodshot and glazed, bulged out of their sockets and his body convulsed in violent, spasmodic movements. Manhandled backwards, he stepped in his own vomit, which felt warm and viscous, like raw egg. Hardly able to stand due to the sickening pain in his belly, he was half-dragged, half-thrown up the stairs.

Having been shoved onto the landing, Joseph scrabbled towards the nearest door. He wanted to fling them all open, find Angela and whisk her away to safety. His outstretched arm was inches away from the brass handle when a hand grasped his wrist and brought his arm up behind his back. Joseph cried out as the ligaments in his shoulder stretched agonisingly, and he squirmed like an offender being restrained by a heavy-handed policeman.

'Not that one,' asserted the man, flinging Joseph towards the adjoining door at the far end of the landing.

'Angela!' called Joseph in a desperate wail.

'Joseph!' the reply came back, tortured and faint, but unmistakable.

The man bundled him through the door and thrust him in the direction of a chair that sat alone in an otherwise empty room. It came rushing towards him, but not so fast that he couldn't see the heavy leather straps that hung ominously from the arms and curled around the front legs like adders.

Joseph's struggling and flailing was futile against the man's brute force, and he was slammed into the chair, which rocked back on its sturdy legs. His arms were bound and his ankles belted, so that he was paralysed against his will. The door slammed shut and the light from the landing was reduced to a slender beam that crept under the door, travelling only a small distance in, as though reluctant to impose.

Under the guise of darkness, a further, final strap was slung around his neck, yanked tight, and looped around one of the ribs of the chair, garrotting him. Hyperventilating, Joseph gasped for breath like an asthmatic, the air making a wheezing hiss as it passed through his narrow throat.

'Aaaaaahhhhhhh,' he cried out, sensing his body losing control as he panicked and suffocated, straining against the pull of the gag, which only served to restrict his airway further. Water streamed from his eyes as frenzy overtook him.

'I can't breathe,' sobbed Joseph, the words choked out into a fit of coughing.

Perhaps touched by pity, or possibly remorse, the man slackened the belt a notch, granting a lifesaving extra inch of leniency. Where the coarse, acrid edges of the belt had briefly gripped his neck, there were deep, reddened indents that quickly rose up into pallid, puffy blobs. Taking prolonged, deep breaths, Joseph felt the calmness slowly seeping back into him, and the dark clouds evaporated from his mind, bringing clarity to the aberrant scene.

'Let me see Angela,' ordered Joseph as soon as his breathing returned to a state that allowed him to talk.

Seizing a fistful of hair, the man pulled Joseph's head back and drew his knife so close to his captive's neck that the sharpness of the blade could be felt against his Adam's apple, which rose and fell like a bobbing buoy in choppy waters.

'Carry on like this and you'll be lucky if you ever see her again,' the man said mildly.

'Please, I have to see her,' appealed Joseph, conscious of the risk involved in any sudden movement. 'Just let me see her.'

With a slow, deliberate motion, pressure was applied to the blade and it cut into the skin like a reckless razor. The knife-edge steered from left to right, a wound opening up across Joseph's neck, the stinging sensation like a prolonged paper cut as the skin split many layers deep. Knowing any abrupt reaction could cause his jugular to be severed, Joseph winced in response to the torment and grasped the arms of the chair, his pupils huge and deranged as they tried to look beyond his own chin at the mutilation taking place below. Blood emerged from the depths of the crevasse like crimson lava, seeping down his neck in competing trickles, its warmth amalgamating with the cold, fearful sweat that clung to his chest.

When the weapon was drawn away, Joseph finally allowed himself to scream out. The collar of his T-shirt began to cling to his chest as it became saturated with blood and sweat. He tried to raise his hands to his neck to stem the flow, his forearms straining ineffectively against the leather bonds. Instead, he lowered his head as far as it would go, the skin creasing and folding, limiting the outflow of gore.

Suddenly, the man hauled the chair backwards, so that it rested only on the back legs, which themselves sat on small, shoddy wheels that looked as though they had been stolen from the stabilisers of a child's bicycle. The room blurred past him as Joseph was swung round in a half-circle to face into its darkest reaches. The curtains were open and the night sky, illuminated by distant city lights, cast a sombre blue ambience over his sparse surroundings. The chair was released and it clattered forward into a stable position once again.

The man's footsteps disappeared behind him, the door handle clicked and the room was suddenly bathed in light again. Joseph listened hard. A door elsewhere in the house was opened and then closed.

Then there was silence.

A short period of time elapsed before the distant door could be heard opening again. The slight dimming of the surroundings signalled that somebody was standing in the doorway. It took a while to become apparent, but Joseph could detect a muffled sniffing above the sound of his own breathing.

Angela!

Joseph craned his neck in an attempt to see her. It was an impossible task. The straps held his body so rigidly that his field of vision was restricted to a little past his own shoulders.

'Say hello,' sneered the man, starting to chuckle.

'Let me see her!' yelled Joseph, stretching every sinew in his neck to its absolute limit, but gaining only a futile couple of degrees.

The laceration in his neck responded with a smarting retort, weeping dark red tears that rested upon the previous flow, which had since dried into a crusty black veneer.

'Angela!' he hollered again.

Joseph's wretchedness further humoured the man, whose mild chortle burst into an excited hoot of delight.

'Angela! Talk to me!' screamed Joseph, longing to hear her voice above the fiend's insane cackling.

He waited briefly for a response. None came; just more of the unrelenting laughter. Enraged by the brash cruelty, Joseph began to struggle frenziedly against his restraints. His body lurched from side to side like a convict in an electric chair, moving only inches at a time, and he grunted and swore with the strain. One exertion too far, he toppled the chair backwards so that he was flung flat on his back, cracking the back of his head on the wooden floor with a noise that sounded like splintering wood.

This routine brought great amusement to the man, who whooped with delectation. This time, Joseph could see him, albeit upside down, doubled over and clutching his sides, his eyes screwed shut and his mouth open wide in a silent rush of ecstasy. Standing to his left, and gagged with what looked like a tea towel, was Angela. Her expression was distraught and helpless, her body shuddering at intervals as a side-effect of her abounding tears. She wasn't physically restrained, but the anxiety kept her cemented to the spot.

'Angela! I love you,' blubbered Joseph. 'It'll be ok, I promise.'

The statement was so devoid of conviction that it offered little comfort.

'It'll be ok,' mocked the man, hooting like a baboon.

'You bastard!' bellowed Joseph. 'I'll fucking kill you!'

This was all too much for the man, who collapsed into a demented heap on the floor, holding his aching sides in elated pain. Without hesitation, Angela raced towards Joseph, her arms outstretched, the emotion exploding out of her face.

Joseph's heart sang as he realised he was about to feel the soft touch of her hands, then rapidly sank as he saw the man switch on to what was happening, and the look of loathsome intent that flashed across his face. She had only made it halfway before the man came crashing into her from behind. He never left the floor, surging forward from his lowly position. Like a pouncing beast, he swept her running legs from underneath her in a violent tackle.

Her momentum carried her forward, and for a second Angela flew, arms stretched out gracefully before her, her expression one of shock. Then she hit the ground, bouncing off the wooden boards, specks of dirt on the floor jumping up like grains of rice on the skin of a drum. Joseph felt hands being placed either side of his head, the contact accompanied by a wincing, guttural yelp that was stifled by her muzzle. The hands came together to touch his cheeks, and for a moment he felt utter bliss.

Then he saw the face of the owner: the heavy scratches on the cheeks, the swollen bruise partially obscured by her hairline, the bloodied nose, and the eyes, the pleading eyes, that had seen more baneful abuse in the previous two hours than most people see in a lifetime. They gazed deep into his own, terrified and vulnerable, yet still full of the love and compassion Joseph hoped he could transmit in return.

The couple held the stare like it was their last; brought closer by the desperation of their plight. Tears gathered at the corners of her eyelids and, as she blinked, the first of them escaped, seeping to the end of a curled eyelash, forming a droplet that grew and grew before dropping to the floor. The gentle splash was distinct in the silence.

'Angela…' whispered Joseph, his sorrow denying him further words of solace.

She moved her hands over his face and plunged her fingers into his dark, matted locks. In his mind, Joseph pictured himself lying on his back in a park, the sunshine casting a gentle warmth over the surroundings, Angela playing with his hair and talking to him about nothing in particular. The image was shattered as Angela was dragged away from him, her eyes still fixed on his and her fingers stretched out, searching for every last strand of hair to preserve the contact for as long as possible. Her features faded slowly into the darkness, eventually engulfed by the shadow of her own hair. Her traumatised gaze lingered long after the rest of her had vanished.

Joseph lay prostrate on his back as the man hauled her away, uttering the occasional cackle of laughter. A door was opened and closed twice, and this time a key was turned in the lock. It wasn't long before his own door was slammed shut, and again his surroundings were reduced to the London semi-darkness. He lay there wondering what they had ever done to deserve this. Against his better judgement, and even though it was the last thing on his mind, he blacked out, his mind shutting itself off from any further horror.

Allan

Allan awoke soon after seven with the same optimism he had been experiencing for some days, his upbeat mood unaffected by the notion that it would disappear by lunchtime in the same sudden way it always did. Having flung off the covers, he was mildly surprised to see that he had yet again slept fully clothed, the comforting warmth outweighed by their clingy, stifling dampness. But this was a mere trivial actuality that wouldn't hinder his enjoyment of this new day. Today would mark a big turning point in his life. A new beginning.

He reached across and flicked the switch on the clock radio to 'off' so it wouldn't disturb him in six minutes' time. He rolled onto his shoulders and, pedalling his legs in the air like an aerobics teacher, Allan kicked off his jeans and flicked them onto the floor. Next went the shirt, only just unbuttoned far enough to fit over his head. For a couple of minutes, he lay on the bed in his socks and underpants, eyes fixed on the cracks in the ceiling, stretching his arms to their full length, making fists and tensing his muscles, which were slower than his mind to awaken. The coldness of the duvet felt cleansing against his bare skin and he would happily have lain there all morning, except he had so many important things to do.

Allan swung his legs over the side of the bed and placed his socked feet onto the pinky lushness of the floor. He stretched again, like a tree, before meandering over to the window and flinging open the curtains. The pigeons that sojourned on the windowsill beat a hasty retreat and fled to the front garden, where they strutted nonchalantly and cooed at each other in annoyance at being disturbed. Looking down at their former residence, Allan saw they had left various gifts before departing; small puddles of brown sludge streaked with white peppered across the stones.

'What *have* you been eating?' he asked rhetorically. 'Fucking pigeons.'

He mimicked a gun with his fingers and shot them one by one, imagining their innards splattering across the grass like tinned spaghetti. He looked down again at the pools of excrement and decided to leave them there, on the assumption that rain was imminent, even though the skies were currently a vast ceiling of wintry blue. It always seemed to rain in London.

Allan wandered into the bathroom, allowing himself a self-gratifying grin at the immaculate tidiness of the house. As always, he showered with the bathroom door open so as not to restrict the steam, which would otherwise have no means of escape. The previous owners had put bars on the window, making it impossible to open. He washed methodically: shower gel for the body and face first, and then shampoo for the hair. He noticed the lightness of the shampoo bottle and made a mental note to get a new one, despite the fact there were already a couple of spares in the cupboard. Planning ahead was important.

The almost scalding water reddened his skin slightly, giving a cooking sensation that he found stimulating. Clouds of steam engulfed the bathroom and then dispersed throughout the upper floors of the house like a fog. Allan allowed himself to drip dry for a time, before stepping down onto the bathmat, thus preventing a soggy area underfoot that would annoy him every time he entered the bathroom for the rest of the day.

After wrapping himself in a towel, he inspected his chin with considerable diligence, noticing that the dark bristles were barely poking their heads through the pores. Like every other day, he shaved the right cheek first, then the left, then the upper lip, and lastly the chin. Turning on the hot tap, he quickly washed away the foamy residue before the water became too hot to touch. He dabbed his face dry, and then cleaned the mirror before admiring his rugged handsomeness for some time.

'Looking good,' he said, complimenting his reflection before walking briskly back to the bedroom, the clouds of steam parting before him as he moved.

Shutting the door to keep out the creeping moisture, Allan opened the wardrobe to reveal the sight that dampened his spirits every day, albeit only slightly. Parading in front of him, in an orderly row, was a selection of clothes more suited to a far older man. It offered a mixture of dark greens, blues and browns; devoid of style, but comfortable nonetheless. He made another mental note, this time more of a reminder, that new clothes were a priority when he had the time.

When he had the time. Would he ever have the time?

He chose a navy woollen pullover, some casual slacks and the T-shirt he had worn the day before, as he liked the softness of the material.

For breakfast, he ate two-and-a-half Weetabix, the spare half returned to the packet for the following morning. Two was too little and three was nearly always too much, so two-and-a-half it was, and so it would remain unless they made the biscuits any bigger, or indeed smaller. In such a circumstance, Allan felt that a change to the number consumed would be in order, along with a strongly worded letter to the manufacturer demanding an explanation for the change.

After brushing his teeth, Allan left the house wrapped up against the elements in a scarf, gloves and a flat cap. Because of his attire and the slight stoop he sometimes adopted when it was cold, he could easily have been mistaken for a lonesome pensioner. It was a good twenty-minute walk to the supermarket, but such was his buoyant mood that he decided to leave the car at home and enjoy the sunshine while it lasted.

The sun sat low in a sky devoid of cloud, a jet trail leaving the only taint on the magnificent blueness. Luckily, the sun was behind him, otherwise its frosty brilliance would have been dazzling. Yet every now and then, its radiance would be caught on the bonnet or windscreen of an oncoming vehicle and he would have to squint to avoid having his vision haunted by brightly coloured bands that lingered for minutes at a time.

As he walked, he reflected on how the neighbourhood seemed so much worse during the day. At night, the dark partly swallowed the rubbish and structural decay, which was now so clearly visible. He cursed his own misfortune and the price of London houses for forcing him to live in this area.

The garish greens and familiar-faced beggars marked his arrival at Asda.

'Spare any change, please, sir?' asked the first, quickly averting his gaze from the look of appalled pity on Allan's face.

The homeless gentleman appeared to be in his late twenties, although his condition prevented an accurate estimate of his age being made. His hands shook beneath fingerless gloves as he humbly held them out. The smell of vomit, alcohol and general dirtiness made Allan feel like retching.

Unaware of his own disgusted expression, Allan searched his pockets for any loose coins, but his hands only felt notes, and they emerged disappointingly empty.

'Sorry,' he muttered.

He made a hasty exit, not wanting to inhale the fetid air that surrounded this unfortunate human being for a moment longer.

Pushing the image and smell from his mind, so as not to hinder the enjoyment of his shopping experience, he grabbed a basket and entered the sterile atmosphere of the supermarket. Going against the convention set out by the store layout, he headed to the furthest aisle first, thus saving the fresh fruit and vegetables until the end to prevent them from getting crushed. The clothing section reminded him of his mental note to buy new clothes, and at the same time perplexed him, as it only catered for women and children.

Allan went up and down every aisle out of habit, even the baby care section, which contained items he couldn't possibly need. He paused at the point in the bathroom products aisle, where his usual brand of shampoo was stored, and was pleased to see that Asda was offering a three-for-two promotion on the product. However, on closer inspection, the shelf was empty, and no amount of peering behind the other bottles or looking at neighbouring shelves for the mistaken placements of a blasé shelf-stacker was going to change this. Swearing under his breath, Allan decided he would have to stop at Boots on the way home, despite it being out of the way and thus taking up valuable minutes in an already busy day.

The enjoyment of his shopping trip diminished, he grabbed the essential items he had come for – milk, bread and vegetables – and made his way to the checkout. Scrupulously scanning the rows, he looked not for the shortest queue, but for Becky. To his joy, he saw her on checkout seventeen, smiling sweetly and genuinely at each customer in turn, her adolescent beauty in no way lessened by the unflattering uniform or synthetic lighting.

Allan took his place at the back of the queue and waited patiently behind a young mother, whose trolley was filled with enough food to feed a small army. In front of her was a student who had clearly shopped using principles rather than economy. Currently being served was an elderly gentleman who had purchased nothing other than baked beans and corned beef.

Allan watched Becky go about her job with great interest. Her hands handled each item so delicately. He yearned to hold them in his own, gaze into her innocent eyes and tell her how much he lusted for her. She had a subtle splendour, a youthful sweetness combined with a mysterious air; a result of her ancestry, which Allan could never quite place. He watched her longingly, visualising how her lustrous dark hair would look flowing over her naked shoulders and pert, rounded breasts, imagining what it would be like to run his fingers through it and caress her vulnerable nakedness.

'Would you like to go first?' asked the mother, having noticed Allan's relatively empty basket.

'Excuse me?' answered Allan, snapping back to reality.

He felt his cheeks flush, concerned that his libidinous thoughts had been evident from his expression.

'Would you like to go in front of me? You don't have very much stuff there,' the woman elaborated.

'Oh, no, no. It's ok,' stammered Allan, embarrassed and flustered. 'Thanks,' he added a few seconds later when he had regained his composure.

The woman smiled at him in a condescending fashion and started unloading her shopping onto the conveyor belt. Allan went back to staring at Becky, censoring his visualisations to a tasteful appreciation of her angelic looks rather than sordid fantasies. Although he was in a rush, he was happy to have been panicked enough to reject the lady's kind offer and marvel at the checkout girl for a few more minutes.

When his turn came to be served, he waited eagerly for Becky to make eye contact and was pleased to see her smile broaden with recognition when she eventually did.

'Oh, hi there,' she said, passing his items over the scanner with divine grace.

'Good morning, Becky,' responded Allan with overstated enthusiasm. 'And how are you on this fine day?'

'Not too bad,' she replied. 'How about yourself?'

'Everything's great,' he answered. 'I have a really good feeling about today.'

'And why's that?' asked Becky, willingly taking the bait offered through his vagueness.

'I'm not sure really. You know how it is. Sometimes you just wake up in the morning knowing it's going to be a good day.'

'I wish I had mornings like that,' said Becky forlornly, 'but the thought of working here all day is enough to put me in a bad mood most days.'

Allan smiled and wondered what it would be like waking up next to her and how it would liven his spirits to even greater heights.

'What about the weekends?' he suggested.

'I'm usually hungover!' she joked. 'And besides, I'm not really a morning person.'

Allan laughed out loud to display his appreciation, masking the fact that he found the idea of this girl being one of those drunken teenage harlots he saw from time to time utterly appalling.

'That's three pounds and sixty-three pence, please,' said Becky, still chuckling slightly.

The amount was slightly more than usual. He deduced that he must have gone overboard on the carrots.

Allan handed over a ten-pound note and Becky gave him the change, quickly calculating the amount in her head before double-checking against the display.

'There you go,' she said, placing the coins in his hand.

For a fleeting second, their fingers touched. Allan felt a tingling sensation pass through his body, and at that moment he fell madly in love with her.

'I'll see you around,' he said cheerfully.

He gathered up his bags and left.

Becky shook her head and sighed at the realisation that these inane daily conversations with this friendly stranger were the highlight of her working day.

In his newfound state of love, Allan forgot all about the shampoo. He bought a cup of coffee from the hotdog stall on the way out and handed it to the tramp, who was still sitting in the walkway entrance.

'Thank you, sir. God bless you,' said the man meekly.

There is no god, thought Allan, pondering how someone so disadvantaged could maintain his faith in the existence of a divine being.

'You're welcome,' he said.

He was touched by the man's gratefulness as he beheld the warmth of the cup in his hands, grasping it like a trophy.

As he made his way home, Allan reflected that the cup of coffee would probably cause the tramp to piss in the street and wished he hadn't given it to him.

When he got back to the house, Allan saw that the postman had been. He checked his mail and was disappointed to see that none of it was for him. The majority was addressed to either Mr or Mrs Thompson, which he threw in the bin without a second look.

He took his shopping into the kitchen and unloaded the goods into their appropriate cupboards. Everything had its rightful place and his organised system made it easy to see what needed to be replenished. Today was a Friday, which meant chicken for dinner.

Allan took two chicken thighs from the freezer – representing the last of the meat in the ice box – and left them on a plate to defrost between then and six pm, when he would grill them with nothing but salt and pepper, serving them with the potatoes and broccoli he had just bought from the supermarket. He always bought exactly the number of vegetables needed for one meal and ate them on the day of purchase. Everything had to be fresh.

The plastic bags were stuffed into a drawer, joining a deluge of identical bags that had been stored for a later date, but would likely never be used. Glancing at his watch, Allan saw that it was already past eleven. The morning was almost gone and he hadn't even begun cleaning the house; something he had to do before he got on to the really important tasks of the day.

Following a cup of tea, a shortbread biscuit and a shade over fifteen minutes of daytime television, Allan started the laborious but necessary job of cleaning the house. Throwing himself into the vacuuming with a zealous devotion far beyond what would be considered normal for such a mandatory task, he marauded around the lower floor, the nozzle of the hoover probing deep into the places where the cumbersome head could not reach. He uprooted furniture, hoovering behind cushions and on top of shelves and cabinets.

Despite the thoroughness of the job, the amount of debris collected in the transparent dirt-chamber was minimal. Seeing this as a reflection of poor labour rather than the existing cleanliness of the house, Allan emptied the drum and made a second trip around, this time turning up an even more paltry amount that might simply have been the clinging remnants of his former excursion.

The fact that he had frivolously plundered another fraction of his rapidly diminishing time pool annoyed Allan immensely. The mocking face of the clock on the wall told him it was now quarter past twelve, and his anger turned to exasperation at the lack of hours in the day. Deciding that the ever-multiplying germs in the kitchen were perhaps a greater threat to his health than the dust mites lurking in the carpets, Allan re-prioritised his duties and swapped the vacuum cleaner for a mop.

Following the instructions on the back of the bleach bottle to the letter, Allan concocted the antiseptic brew that would exterminate the resident bacteria. The fluorescent glow of the bleach gave it the appearance of comic-book toxic waste, and it oozed from the bottle like a magic potion before disappearing into the water with a flurry of short-lived bubbles. Allan mopped the floor with a robotic efficiency, rinsing and wringing the mop dry after every third stroke. With no dirt to hinder its movement, the mop's dreadlocked head glided majestically from side to side, each pass leaving a dampened sweep scarcely cleaner than it had been moments earlier.

He worked backwards from the sink, and by the time he had finished, Allan was left standing in the hallway, a glistening floor laid out before him. Standing with one hand on his hip and the other clutching the mop like a weapon, Allan looked down in satisfaction at the disinfected lino.

Another battle won in the ongoing war against bacteria.

A quick glance at his watch revealed that it was quarter to one, meaning that he wouldn't have time to prepare lunch before the one o'clock news, since the floor was newly wet and walking across it now would be self-defeating.

'Fuck!' he exclaimed, pointing an accusing finger at the vacuum-cleaner sitting innocently in the corner.

The extra trip around the ground floor had cost him dearly and he was at a loss as to what to do. By the time the floor dried it would already be one o'clock, and he would miss the news headlines and the beginning of the main story. He started towards the living room, stopping halfway as his stomach gurgled at the threat of delaying its usually punctual feed.

'Fuck!' he exclaimed again.

Turning back towards the kitchen, he stopped abruptly with his toes teetering over the edge of the wooden strip that separated the hallway from the lino. He lifted a foot and made to take a step, his leg hovering in the air, wavering slightly, as if repelled by the sterility of the freshly mopped floor. He withdrew his leg quickly and took a hop backwards in case he lost his balance and was forced to step onto the lino.

'Shit!' he muttered.

He retreated to the safety of the stairs, where he sat, clutching his grumbling stomach and debating whether or not to make his lunch now, in which case he would have to clean the floor again, or wait until after the news, in which case he would suffer hunger throughout.

The big hand reached twelve and the decision was made for him. He sat and watched the news in a state of discomfort and, therefore, failed to experience his usual pleasure at finding out that the world as a whole had more problems than he did.

Allan always switched off the television set the moment the weather finished, and not a second later. Any delay and the foreign trash that followed would begin and he would be forced to watch it, since he found their tanned and superficial world inexplicably compelling. After storing the prediction for the following day's weather in a mental filing system, adding his own pessimistic slant, Allan went back to the kitchen and was granted some relief by the floor's dryness.

Friday was a vegetarian lunch day, for no reason other than that's the way it had always been. The meal was to consist of two carrots, six new potatoes and a tree of broccoli, all steamed. Rather than waste more time, Alan ate there and then, standing in the kitchen next to the stove. Inevitably, not being comfortably seated while eating his lunch restricted his enjoyment of the meal. The meatless menu was never one he looked forward to, anyway, and eating upright made it even more of a struggle to swallow the bland vegetables. It also increased the distance he had to lift the morsels from the plate to his mouth, so he had to be extra careful not to drop anything. Any falling vegetables would have led to mopping the floor a second time; something he really didn't have capacity to do.

The one saving grace was that it gave him the incentive to finish the meal quickly, as there was nothing to savour, clawing back a vital couple of minutes he had lost earlier on. Allan washed up immediately. It didn't take long, as there were no sauces to cling to the plate and no burnt bits of meat welded to the bottom of the pan. Everything wiped off effortlessly and the items were neatly left to dry on the draining board next to the sink.

Taking out the spray and sponge from the cupboard beneath, Allan scrubbed all of the work surfaces in the kitchen, then the sink, and finally the windows. By the time he had finished, it was like a showroom kitchen, and nobody would ever have known it had been used for food preparation. There were no fingerprints or traces of food. It was completely spotless.

The bathroom received a similar facelift, banishing germs that were all his own using a combination of foams, sprays and bleaches that left them no option but to roll over and die, and to hope that their friends had fared better than they had. Such was his thoroughness, it was approaching five o'clock by the time Allan finished.

Dusting was the only cleaning task left to complete. Allan always left it until last because he hated it, believing it to be a worthless exercise but diligently doing it anyway, just in case he was wrong. There was a lack of dust-collecting clutter in the house, a deliberate ploy on Allan's part to make the job easier for himself in the long run. Besides, he had little interest in ornamental trinkets, and with his holiday travels taking him no further afield than Scotland, he had never felt the urge to purchase memories in the form of aboriginal carvings or leather sculptures that adorned the mantelpieces of so many homes. He wasn't too keen on photographs either, and they, too, were conspicuous by their absence. Allan was of the opinion that he didn't need reminding of who he was supposed to care about by having pictures of their happy faces grinning at him from all angles, twenty-four hours a day. If he needed reminding of what they looked like, he would pay them a visit and then he wouldn't forget for a long time.

He would never forget.

The outcome of this downbeat attitude towards personal belongings was that he only had large, flat surfaces to dust. Of course, this didn't grant him leave to do a half-hearted job, and Allan set about the chore with the same keenness as he had the vacuuming. He found the problem with dusting was that it was very much a temporary solution to the problem of visible dirt, simply throwing the particles into the air only for them to settle back down over the next few hours, albeit slightly more spread out than before, which was why it needed doing so regularly.

In his quest to find the ultimate dusting implement, Allan had tested a whole host of utensils. In the end, he had settled for a garish pink feather duster. To aid him in his quest for cleanliness, Allan employed the help of some wood polish and an antistatic spray, neither of which appeared to do a lot, even if they smelled as though they should.

Allan did the downstairs first, allowing extra time to wipe down the items that attracted the most dust, such as the television and the hi-fi. After that, he crawled up the staircase on his hands and knees, wiping around and between each and every banister rail, filling the air with the antistatic spray as he went.

He dusted his own bedroom next, as it was the most used and therefore the most important room on the first floor. As with the kitchen, the bathroom didn't need dusting as he had already cleaned it thoroughly earlier that afternoon. That left Allan with the choice of two closed doors: the second bedroom and the spare room. The spare room had the fewest bits and pieces in it, so he decided to deal with that one first.

Duster in hand, Allan opened the door to find Joseph still lying on his back in the same prone position he had been left in the previous night.

* * *

The sound of the turning handle caused Joseph to shudder, and he raised his eyes to their farthest point in an attempt to identify his visitor. He beheld a figure he recognised as his assailant from the previous night, holding what looked like a mace or hammer.

Overcome by nausea once again, he would have been sick right there and then had his guts not been achingly drained. Fixated by apprehension, Joseph gaped at the warlike effigy that loomed in the corner, weapon in hand, voiceless and menacing, the backlighting exaggerating his size to unnatural proportions.

The man's shoulders slowly rose and fell, his head cocked slightly to one side in contemplation of what lay before him. He reached up and flicked on the light switch. An unshaded bulb blinked into life, flooding the room with a yellow haze and causing Joseph to squint. Then the man came forward, footsteps heavy like a corpulent child. Joseph closed his eyes in anticipation of the imminent assault, instead finding himself hoisted upwards at speed. Like a drunk, his senses struggled to keep up with the sudden movement and his vision swung clumsily into focus. The pounding in his head and the furriness of his tongue reminded him that it had been many hours since he last tasted water.

The man came around from behind him and looked down at Joseph in bewilderment. His expression slowly changed to a look of childlike curiosity. Arms behind his back, he slowly leant forward until his face was right up close to Joseph's.

'Boo!' he exclaimed and stood up straight again, chuckling in delight at Joseph's visible fright.

Joseph frowned, a look of contempt breaking out despite his efforts to control it. The man didn't seem to notice, although his laughter faded. They were left staring at each other again, the man from above, in his position of total authority, Joseph below, scared and vulnerable.

Joseph studied the man's features. This was the first time he had seen him in proper lighting and under comparatively calm circumstances. It almost came as a disappointment to see that he looked, to all intents and purposes, completely normal. The reason for Joseph's disappointment was hard to place. It was almost as if seeing a disfigured, horror-film freak would have made everything more comprehensible.

But the man was normal, ordinary. His hair was a deep brown, shiny and in good condition. It was styled into what a mother might call 'a sensible haircut'. His chin was clean-shaven and his skin bore all the hallmarks of a healthy lifestyle. Vacant, not unattractive eyes stared back at him, sunk into sockets that showed no signs of tiredness or sleep deprivation.

Yet, despite the man's inconspicuous features, there was something odd about his appearance that Joseph couldn't place at first. Then it suddenly occurred to him. It was his clothes. They were so out of place. He wore the attire of an old man, going well beyond conservative. The navy jumper, the corduroy slacks; the man looked dressed for a day in his favourite armchair in front of the television.

Joseph wondered how he looked in comparison and almost felt jealous about the man's apparently immaculate health. Joseph often experienced a sinking feeling when greeted by his reflection first thing in the morning. The problem was always time. Long hours in the dehydrating, air-conditioned atmosphere of the office were not helped by the long hours in smoky bars that often followed, not to mention the countless takeaways that seemed so irresistible at one in the morning. He couldn't remember the last week he had enjoyed a decent amount of sleep. Hence, when he turned on the bathroom light above the mirror in the mornings, he often saw what he had always imagined he might see twenty years down the line: puffy eyes, black shadows and visible stress. The weekly runs with Iain helped to keep him in shape, but his face told the full story, and that was all most people saw.

The man appeared to become agitated by the situation, as if he had better things to do than entertain his prisoner.

'I haven't got time for this,' he suddenly announced, moving one of his arms out from behind his back.

Joseph shut his eyes and braced himself for the impact of a heavy-ended weapon. Instead, he felt his face being smothered by a cloud of dusty softness, accompanied by the occasional scratchy prong. He opened his eyes to a flurry of pink feathers and the inane grin of the man peering over the end of the duster as he tickled Joseph on the face and neck.

Laughter was the last thing on Joseph's mind, and the flamingo feathers were another unbearable annoyance. Their dusty dryness intruded into his nostrils and mouth, like being engulfed by a swarm of fluorescent moths, shedding wing scales onto everything they touched. He did his best to avoid the colourful onslaught, but the restraints were doing their job. Devoid of humour, the tickling was almost worse than pain.

'Get off!' he yelled aggressively, unable to take any more.

The man stopped grinning and took a step back, like a scolded boy. Then he struck Joseph hard across the face with the back of his hand, each finger leaving a thick red imprint that quickly merged with its neighbours as the pain spread.

Joseph yelped in pain and lowered his eyes to avoid any further confrontation. The man's slippered feet shuffled out of sight and could be heard leaving the room, but not before he had turned the light off again. The footsteps paused outside the adjacent room and the man opened that door.

'Another one? Fuck!' he yelled, amused by his discovery.

He returned downstairs, and there was a long period of silence before the high-pitched whine of the warming-up television filled the air, quickly followed by the unmistakable theme tune of *Neighbours*.

* * *

It was more than two hours before the man returned. Joseph could tell how much time had passed by listening to the sound of the changing channels on the television. The programmes were all so meaningless as just noise. The long silences between commentary exposed the lack of content: five minutes of information or incident stretched out over half an hour; shots of wondrous yet insignificant scenery filling the gaps; interviews with people who talked at length with nothing to say; presenters whose careers were based purely on looks, serving no purpose as faceless noise.

He wished he was watching.

There was a feeling of heat in his wrists from the rawness of skin where he had wrestled hopelessly against the coarse ropes that bound him. The wounds weren't new; they were the aftermath of the morning's battle when he had been sure that his captor had left the house. An attempted escape was the natural thing to do, lying flat on his back in an empty room.

The man had done a good job on the knots. The rope was tight. Not so tight that it restricted the blood flow, but tight enough to allow only the smallest of movements. Joseph had struggled hard, the constant rubbing like holding his arms to a naked flame, so that he had been forced to give up, having made no progress. The burning of his skin matched the dryness of his throat, which felt burnt and blistered, as though he had drunk water straight from a boiled kettle.

The root of the pain was the endless calling out he had done. Shouts for Angela had produced no response and had been dishearteningly replaced by cries for help. The intensity of his own voice had reverberated through his skull and into the floor, where his head was rested, where it grew and travelled and gained bass and volume, so that the whole room was thick with the sound of his desolate cries. But there was no reaction, no reply; merely the occasional clapping of a curious pigeon.

That was before. At least he was upright now.

He no longer had the feeling of a heavy, blood-swelled head, veins jumping with each pulse of blood that pushed through his temples.

The TV flicked off and silence crept through the house once more. Joseph could just make out the man skulking about downstairs. A tap was turned on and he could hear the jangling of cutlery. There was a further period of quiet, presumably while the man dried up, as it was followed by the banging of cupboard doors and the ceramic clink of stacking crockery.

And then the man came back upstairs and headed straight for Joseph's room.

'Would you like a drink?'

'Pardon?' Joseph was slightly taken aback by the offer.

'I guessed you might be thirsty, sitting there all day, and might like a drink.'

'Oh.'

The sincerity in the man's voice made the offer more perplexing.

'Could I have some water, please?'

'Is that all you want? I've got other drinks. How about orange juice?'

'Water's fine, thanks,' said Joseph, wary of offending the man's attempted hospitality.

'Ok,' he replied, and went back downstairs.

Joseph heard him return and the thought of the water made him salivate in anticipation. He was so thirsty, having not had anything to drink since before he had gone out running the previous night. So it came as a disappointment when the man bypassed his room and went straight next door. He remained in there for a while, but Joseph could hear nothing of what went on inside. He prayed that Angela was having an easier time of it than he was.

The pain was bearable so long as it was inflicted on him and not her.

The man left the room and went back downstairs again. More running taps followed and then he returned, thankfully, to Joseph's room.

'I brought up two glasses, but she drank them both,' said the man apologetically.

Joseph said nothing, unsure how to react to the statement.

The man held the water to Joseph's lips, tipping the glass back as Joseph frantically swallowed. The flow of water was too fast and he briefly choked, spraying water across his own lap and down the front of the man's trousers. Glancing down, the man saw the dark, soggy patch on his slacks, as though he had wet himself. It seemed to bother him very little and, aside from a slight frown, he waited contently for Joseph to finish spluttering. After he was sure that Joseph had regained composure, he gestured with the half-empty glass. Joseph nodded and he watered him once again, more slowly and attentively this time, so as not to induce a further spillage.

'More?' asked the man once the glass was empty.

'No. Thanks,' replied Joseph, shaking his head.

The renewed moistness inside his mouth was so pleasurable that he felt a genuine feeling of gratitude towards the man.

'Just shout if you want any more,' said the man. 'My name's Allan. Just shout for Allan.'

'Thanks,' Joseph repeated and the man walked away, leaving the door open.

* * *

Allan journeyed back to the lounge and continued watching television. He was slightly annoyed that he had missed the first seven minutes of *MasterChef*, which meant he didn't know what anybody was trying to cook. He did his best not to let this trivial matter spoil his enjoyment of the culinary delights on show.

* * *

The end of the ten o'clock news signalled the passing of another day, with Allan having achieved precisely nothing. Admittedly, he had been to the supermarket and cleaned the house, but these were run-of-the-mill, daily activities, merely things to help keep his life ticking over. He hadn't managed to start on any of the really important stuff he had planned to do.

It would have to wait until the following day.

Allan slumped back in his chair and pondered over where all the hours had gone. He had stupidly watched the news twice, both at lunchtime and just then. Unsurprisingly, there was little difference in content. It had the same stories, just different faces. No monumental developments in world politics had taken place, and no natural disasters. There were a couple of extra murders on the local news bulletin, but that was to be expected.

There were some sick people in the world, and they all seemed to congregate in south London and small-town America. They walked among the everyday people, assaulting the occasional traffic warden, stealing the odd school kid's mobile phone or tormenting an unsuspecting pensioner.

Allan sighed and went upstairs to get ready for bed. He cleaned his teeth and inspected the healthiness of his skin in the harsh luminosity of the strip light above the mirror. While the colourless glow was enough to expose faults in even the most flawless complexion, Allan was pleased to see that he was generally blemish-free. Before retiring for the night, he returned to Joseph's room.

'Goodnight,' he called out into the darkness. 'Sleep well.'

There was a slight movement from the seated figure, but no reply. Disappointed at the lack of response, he went next door to Angela's room.

'Sleep well, Angela.'

Again, he received no reply. Feeling slightly downhearted that his guests had shunned his attempt at good hospitality, Allan forgot to get undressed and climbed dejectedly into bed. He looked over at the clock. It was ten fifty-seven, about fifteen minutes later than intended, which meant he would be tired in the morning. This would be detrimental to his plans, as he had so many things to do.

So many important things.

* * *

The radio released a mechanical click before exploding into life during the latter stages of an intrusively catchy pop song performed by prepubescent-sounding teenage girls. This was, thankfully, interrupted within less than a minute by the boisterous presenter.

'You're listening to London's number one radio station,' he said, in an anally cheerful voice. 'It's just after eight on a very wet, very cold Saturday. But it's still a Saturday! Coming up, we have...'

'Fuck off, Tarrant,' exclaimed Allan, turning off the radio in frustration.

It was less the smugness of the presenter that got to him and more the fact that he had required the alarm to wake him up. Usually, he slipped out of sleep at about five to eight and switched off the radio well before he was disturbed by the rallying call to modern-day, teenage London. The choice of station was deliberate. He loathed it. The negative emotions towards its host and listeners triggered within him were so strong that he viewed them as a danger to his personal health. Thus, by setting his alarm to this station, he was sure his body would wake him up automatically to avoid the impending trauma. He always preferred to wake up naturally.

After convincing himself that his dislike for the music was a sign of superior taste, Allan got out of bed, safe in the knowledge that he occupied the moral high ground. When the anticipated coldness of the floor never materialised, it dawned on him that he was still wearing last night's clothes.

'Not again,' he muttered. 'What the hell is wrong with me?'

He shuffled over to the curtains and flung them open, the resident pigeons beating a hasty retreat. Yet again, they had left a number of gifts to thank him for providing such a convenient windowsill. Allan looked down forlornly at the puddles of shit, then up at the depressing greyness of the skies.

The radio presenter had been right. The rain was hammering down, arrowing left and right as the December breeze swirled about the cul-de-sac like a twister. The raindrops darted about in all directions, the angle never steep enough to wash away the obscenities on the window ledge. How he detested those irrepressible pigeons; not just because they repeatedly shat on his property, but because of their whole existence.

They were vermin, good-for-nothing pests that brought joy to nobody, except for the occasional deranged tramp who insisted on feeding them and surrounding himself with a collective cloud of dirtiness.

People like that didn't count as far as Allan was concerned. They were useless pests themselves. Eyesores and nose-sores. Ear-sores as well, at times. But they were human, so there was nothing he could do about them. Pigeons were a different story. Nobody would complain if he killed a few pigeons. They would most likely thank him for it.

Pigeons served no purpose. They weren't even part of the food chain. Who would eat a London pigeon? Even the stray cats that occasionally prowled the neighbourhood turned their noses up at the sight of a dead pigeon.

Something had to be done.

Being greeted by the sight of a soiled window ledge, along with the scarpering culprits every time he opened the curtains, was the worst possible start to the day. Allan stormed downstairs, on a mission. He opened the cupboard under the stairs and started digging around in its contents. He knew the toolbox was definitely in there somewhere. He remembered seeing it a few days earlier while looking for a spare lightbulb.

Tidying the storage cupboard was something he had been meaning to do for some time, but he had never got around to it due to the hundred other things that needed doing first. Maybe if he found a spare hour or two that day he would do it.

Allan paused for a moment, his arms still buried up to the wrists in the hordes of junk.

A spare hour. That was a luxury he hadn't experienced for a while.

Allan realised that sitting there thinking about it was self-defeating, so he attacked the job in hand with greater purpose and, sure enough, it soon produced the rewards, as the toolbox was hauled out from beneath a lady's raincoat. Allan fumbled with the locking mechanism, his adrenaline getting the better of him, overcome by the possibility of finally banishing those fucking pigeons.

The lid screeched with rust as he prised it open, the sight of its contents satisfying enough to bring a warped smile to his face. Confronted with so many weapons to choose from, he selected a heavy-ended hammer, a saw and a handful of nails. He also selected a wooden shelf, which was never likely to be put up and was therefore dispensable.

He cradled the implements in his arms and carried them up the stairs, consciously not letting the shelf scrape against the walls. A nail or two broke free from his grasp and bounced noisily down the wooden stairs to freedom. Allan made a mental note to retrieve them later on to prevent the risk of injury.

He couldn't afford any casualties at this crucial stage of the battle.

* * *

Joseph woke to the sound of frantic, aggressive hammering, and to a feeling that his bladder was going to split its sides like a water balloon. The combination of the two wasn't ideal; the shock of the former almost providing an impromptu solution to the latter. Thankfully, he regained his composure before the floodgates opened and was saved from the further discomfort of sitting there in warm, damp, even smellier clothes.

It was ironic that the dryness had returned to his mouth, and he had doubts about whether to accept more water if he was ever offered it.

Who knows? It could be a sick torture method Allan was using to push him to the brink of dehydration before filling him with liquids and leaving him for days on end to wrestle with his dignity. Because it *was* torture.

How he would love to be able to just let it go. If only he was standing in the sea, even a swimming pool. Sea. Swimming pool. Water. A bad chain of thoughts.

45

The fact that he was seated only served to make matters worse. He could almost feel his bladder being pressed down by the rest of his insides.

* * *

Allan glanced across at the window.

Those pesky pigeons had blatantly returned to the windowsill as soon as he had left the room and were there to greet him when he got back, strutting up and down in a line, mocking him.

Arrogant bastards.

Allan had no time for pigeons, and the masterpiece he was working on meant he could banish them from the window indefinitely. They could go and strut someplace else, on someone else's property, as far as he was concerned.

As he hammered the final nail into the plank, he looked over at the window again and nodded knowingly.

'You'll get yours,' he chuckled to himself as he flipped the plank of wood over onto its flat back.

It resembled an instrument of torture more than anything else. The varying length of the protruding nails, combined with his erratic hammering, had resulted in a tangle of spikes boasting no obvious symmetry. It was hardly a uniform bed of nails. His shoddy workmanship annoyed him slightly, but he conjectured that it was more than adequate for the purpose of this particular conquest.

Allan carried it over to the window, the pigeons abandoning ship long before he got there. He pulled up both layers of double-glazing, noticing the difference in temperature. With great care, he positioned the plank across the window ledge, its ends protruding slightly on both sides. He shut the window, took a few steps back, sat on the bed and waited.

It wasn't long before the pigeons returned to check out the new obstruction to their favoured perch. They circled above it for a while, taking turns to swoop down, attempting to land and pulling up again at the last moment, inches away from scraping their underbellies on the pointed tips. They continued this investigation for some time, repeatedly arcing in like dive-bombers.

Stupid birds. They couldn't seem to accept the nails were there, as though they would eventually disappear if they flew around for long enough.

Allan guffawed boisterously at every attempt.

'Come on, you fuckers!' he cried. 'Take a seat. Please, it's all yours!'

His taunts caused him great amusement, and he rocked backwards onto his bed, kicking his legs in the air like a baby.

'Be my guest!' he continued. 'Don't you like your new...?'

He was cut off mid-sentence by the sight of the display on the clock radio. It was nine fifty-two.

Had it really taken him almost two hours to build that spiked monstrosity? Surely not.

But his watch read the same, which meant there were only two hours of the morning to run. This was a disaster for Allan.

He flung off his clothes and ran naked into the bathroom. He re-emerged a couple of seconds later, having forgotten his towel. Suddenly conscious of his own nakedness, Allan returned to the bedroom, covering his genitals with his hands. The window cleaners had a nasty habit of turning up unannounced, and he couldn't recall the last time they had been there, so the odds appeared to be stacked against him.

While he wasn't a particularly shy or modest person when it came to his body, a full-frontal confrontation with a man up a ladder was a situation he could see being distressing for both parties.

Once he had gained possession of the towel, he scurried back to the bathroom with his nether regions more than adequately covered.

* * *

The shampoo bottle farted at him as he squeezed it, its flatulence informing him of its emptiness. It was vitally important that he remembered to buy more shampoo that day as he was down to his last two bottles.

* * *

The slamming doors and the sound of running water were hardly music to Joseph's ears as he sat there, silently suffering. Droplets of perspiration were beginning to gather around his hairline as the physical effort of the resistance began to take its toll. Joseph wished he could sweat out all the excess water in his body so that he could sit in peace. His constraints meant he couldn't even cross his legs, a remedy that, while not particularly effective, always seemed to provide a degree of comfort.

He heard footsteps in the corridor. Allan was leaving the bathroom. Against his better judgement, Joseph called out.

'Allan?' he yelled, his words greeted only with the sound of the bedroom door closing.

Joseph waited an unrealistically long time for a reaction. Nothing came.

'Allan?' he called again, slightly more assertively. 'Are you there?'

Allan emerged from the bedroom looking utterly perplexed. Still in the process of buttoning his shirt, he shuffled towards the source of the sound, his head jutted forward as he scanned for further noises. Progress ended at the point where the carpeted landing met the darkened wood of the spare bedroom. Tightly grasping the doorframe with both hands, Allan leant forward into the gloom, not wishing to step into the room that housed this mysterious, tied-up man.

'Yes?' replied Allan timidly.

'I need the toilet,' Joseph murmured with embarrassment.

The bizarreness of the request gave Allan more courage. He released his hold on the doorframe and took a couple of steps into the room.

'The toilet?' he questioned.

'Yes,' replied Joseph. 'Please can you let me go? I'm fairly desperate.'

Having to ask permission felt like being back at infant school.

Allan looked down at his watch. The hands and digits were glowing faintly in the gloom, although the time they spelt out was hardly illuminating from Allan's point of view. This was already turning into a waste of a morning, and he didn't have time to deal with additional, unforeseen problems such as this.

'I'm sorry,' replied Allan. 'I need to go out. You're going to have to wait for a bit.'

Joseph couldn't quite believe what he was hearing, and the urge was getting stronger with every moment that passed.

'I don't think you understand,' he argued with some frustration. 'I need to go right now.'

'I'm sorry,' repeated Allan, 'I'm too busy. You can go when I get back.'

'I'm begging you,' appealed Joseph. 'It won't take long. Please.'

It had to be one of the most degrading experiences of his adult life, begging someone to free him of his binds so he could take a piss.

Further attempts were worthless. Allan had already left, shutting the door as he exited the room.

As the warmth flooded through Joseph's trousers, the relief was so profound he wondered why he had ever bothered to hold back in the first place.

* * *

An umbrella wasn't a great deal of use on a day like this. In fact, it was more of a hindrance. Allan spent most of the walk to Asda in a hotly contested tug-of-war between himself and the wind. Every time he thought he had gained the upper hand, the wind would come back with renewed vigour, and usually from a different direction, trying to wrench the umbrella from his clutches and carry it off down the street like a big, black jellyfish.

It was tempting just to give up and sacrifice the thing to the elements for all the good it was doing him. Watching it hurtle through the air before being obliterated by the number 77 bus would be quite a spectacle to behold. It would probably have earned him a round of applause from the general public had there been anybody about.

It was Saturday; the weekend, but the streets were almost deserted. The few people that had ventured out were seeking refuge from the squally conditions, huddling like cats in bus shelters and shop doorways.

These people had too much time on their hands. Far too much time. How else could they let a little rain interrupt their plans in such a way? Nobody would catch *him* cowering in a doorway to avoid getting a bit wet.

But he wasn't getting *a bit* wet, he was getting absolutely drenched. The umbrella served its purpose from the point of view that his upper body and head remained completely dry. However, the rain was coming in so steeply that his clothes were rapidly becoming sodden from the waist down. The first saving grace was that his trousers took on a uniform wetness, so they didn't give the impression that he had had an unfortunate urinary accident. The second was that the downpour had temporarily freed the streets from their dirtier inhabitants; namely pigeons and tramps. This meant the lack of change in his pockets would be less of an issue today.

Why hadn't he taken the car?

The queue of vehicles outside the car park provided the answer to his question. It would have taken him an age to get a space and he would rather have suffered the sodden clothes than sit for ten minutes in a stationary vehicle, wasting time and money.

The shoppers had brought the weather with them to the supermarket. Trails of muddy footprints merged into an expanse of dirt that stretched in all directions from the entrance, every new customer extending its reach by a few extra feet. It was in danger of covering the entire fresh fruit and vegetable section, and was perilously close to the fish counter. The limp-wristed efforts of the cleaner were doing little to help the cause.

Allan was happy to be able to leave this section until last, as there was always the hope that the youth might have bucked up his ideas by the time he returned. Saturdays always provided Allan's least enjoyable trips to the supermarket because the increased busyness was made worse by the inferior quality of staff. The reliable midweek workforce was diluted by the haphazard casualness of college kids trying to earn a bit of extra pocket money. Sunday was almost as unpleasant; the fact that everyone was on double pay making their incompetence twice as bad. The one saving grace was that Becky was a model of commitment and worked seven days a week, so at least he had something to look forward to when it came to paying.

Allan followed the same route as the previous day, snaking up and down each of the aisles in turn. To his delight, the shampoo section had been restocked and the three-for-two promotion was still valid. He triumphantly loaded his basket with six bottles, feeling a shiver run down his spine at the prospect of having a total of eight bottles in the house.

They would last for months!

Allan found himself whistling along to the Christmas songs of years gone by, their muffled melodies pumping out of the public-address system as he bounced happily along the remaining aisles, swinging his satisfyingly heavy basket as he went.

He made an extended visit to the meat section to get some chops, digging deep into the piles of pre-packed pork to find the freshest available produce. Content that the ones he held in his hands were as fresh as he was going to get, he moved on to the fruit and vegetable section.

It came as no surprise to see that the floor was still filthy. Allan gave the cleaner a stern look as he passed him, drawing no reaction beyond an apologetic smile so fake that it was merely a show of teeth. Ignoring the petty display of defiance, Allan unceremoniously gathered together his vegetables for the day and made his way to the checkout.

Conveniently, Becky was at one of the nearer tills, almost as if she had taken note of his routine and chosen a position that made it easier for him to get to her. As Allan took his place at the back of the monstrous queue, she looked up at him, a psychic link informing her he had arrived. They exchanged a smile and Allan's heart skipped a beat.

As it finally neared his turn to be served, it dawned on him that their relationship – a mere three minutes per day – could not last in its current form, and that it was time to do something about it. When it came to unloading his basket, he almost wished he hadn't got so carried away with the shampoo as, presented with six bottles of the stuff, Becky might think he had a hair hygiene problem. However, this was a small obstruction in the path to true love and he would endeavour to overcome it.

'Good morning, Becky,' he chirped. 'Although it isn't really, is it? In fact, it's pretty awful out there.'

'I see what you mean,' said Becky, glancing out of the window that ran the full length of the building. 'For once, I'm not so bothered about being stuck in here all day.'

She grinned and Allan imitated her gesture, forging a common link between them. There was a break in the conversation as he tried to think of something clever to say.

'You must love this shampoo!' Becky remarked as she swiped through the fourth bottle, noticing there were still two to be accounted for.

'It's on special offer, so I thought I'd stock up. It's not as if it goes off,' he said defensively.

'I do the same thing myself,' replied Becky as the last bottle slid down the metallic surface towards the open carrier bag Allan was holding.

So sensible at such a young age, thought Allan, pondering on how perfect Becky *really* was.

'That will be nine pounds and thirty-two pence, please. Would you like any cashback?'

'Could I have thirty pounds, please?'

That ought to impress her.

Becky handed him the receipt and a pen.

'Could you sign there, please, and initial the cashback?'

Allan did as she requested and handed them back to her. It was now or never.

'One more thing, Becky,' Allan started. 'I was thinking...'

Feeling the blood rush to his head, he struggled to find the words he had rehearsed over and over in his mind. The supermarket ceased to function and everybody turned to listen to what he had to say. He could feel their eyes bearing down on him from all angles. The room swelled around him, melting, twisting and contorting as it wrapped itself around his head, preventing him from speaking. His banging heart was the only audible sound, resonating around his temples as he slipped into a state of panic. The feeling was akin to what he had felt at school all those years earlier when he had been required to make a speech in front of the class. Back then he had frozen up, just as was doing now.

Then he caught a glimpse of Becky, a look of excited expectation in her eyes and a consoling smile on her lips. The panic vanished as quickly as it had arrived.

'I was thinking,' he repeated. 'If you're not doing anything, would you like to come for a drink with me this evening?'

He fully expected her to say no, but it didn't matter. He had said it and there was no going back.

Becky blushed slightly, aware she was now the centre of attention for everybody in earshot, the redness adding a new colour to her tanned skin.

'Ok, I'll have a drink with you. I finish at six, so how about sevenish? Where would you like to meet?'

Allan hadn't planned this far ahead and his emotions, a mixture of joy and disbelief, made it difficult to identify one. He needed to buy himself more time.

'Would somewhere fairly near here be convenient for you?'

'Sure. Anywhere will do, I'm not fussy.'

'How about The Falcon? Near the station?'

'Ok, great. Sounds good to me. I guess I'll see you at seven.'

'Yes. Let's meet inside, in case one of us is running late.'

'Ok.'

He grabbed his bags and made for the exit.

'Allan!' Becky called after him.

He stopped abruptly, his body completely rigid as if he had been shot.

'You forgot your cash.'

Allan's shoulders slumped as he relaxed again. Smiling sheepishly, he returned to the till where Becky was holding three £10 notes in her outstretched hand.

'Thanks,' he blushed, taking the money. 'See you later.'

'Yeah, see you later, Allan.'

* * *

Having received the second soaking of the day – and it wasn't even lunchtime yet – Allan entered the house in the kind of mood that can only be brought about by the British weather. He could hardly have been wetter if somebody had taken a fire hose to him for a prolonged period. It felt like he had stepped into a lake. There was rainwater everywhere. And it wasn't fresh, pure, country rain, swept over from the Atlantic by a south-westerly wind. This was London rain, condensed smog; the kind that dissolves statues; that creates more dirt than it washes away.

The droplets gathered on his scalp in vast numbers and wriggled forward like transparent maggots, sliding down his fringe before dropping onto his forehead. With the most direct route down his face blocked by his eyebrows, they split into three groups, arcing left and right down the sides of his cheeks and over the bridge of his nose. Allan had to continually wipe his sleeve across his upper lip to stop the toxic liquid running into his mouth. His sleeve was also wet, so it left an unsatisfyingly damp residue behind.

Allan considered walking about dripping dirty water everywhere akin to treading around the house wearing shoes covered in dog shit, so he decided to undress there and then on the doormat.

His coat had proved an inadequate buffer, so his cardigan was damp and saturated around his collar, where the water had run down his neck. The concentration of wetness had seeped through to his T-shirt, which clung uncomfortably to his chest.

Allan impatiently tore off the garments, using the drier bits as a makeshift towel for his hair and face. The removal of their restrictive coldness was bliss, and the warmth of the house could be felt directly against his bare skin. The occasional shudder of the door as it held fast against the wind, beating hard against its surface with unseen fists, added to the feeling of comfort. It was a further relief to remove his trousers, the fabric of which clung so closely that he feared they might become part of him if he left them on any longer. The rejected clothes sat sulking on the doormat, leaving Allan standing there in his pants; the only item to have survived the tempest.

As the temperate air of the house closed in around him, a familiar prickling, almost an itch, crept up his back. Allan reached around, running his fingers across the skin, the fingertips rising and falling at regular intervals as they felt their way from right to left and back again, moving between the rougher valleys and the smoother ridges. Looking over his shoulder, he caught a glimpse of his back in the hallway mirror and his fingers fell away.

He headed upstairs. It was tempting to take another shower, to wash away the evil fluid before it made him itch or turned his hair green.

He really didn't have time to do that. Everything today seemed to have gone against him. Sleeping in late, incontinent pigeons, awful weather, unprecedented queues at the supermarket and more awful weather. The day had reduced him to standing in the bedroom in his underwear. Shopping aside, he was almost back where he had started. In fact, he was even further back than that, given that he had been fully dressed when he awoke. Nothing annoyed him more than to witness a day sliding away like this.

Deciding that choosing what to wear would be a needless waste of time he didn't have, Allan simply put on a dressing gown and wrapped a towel around his head, like a fluffy pink turban. This would be his outfit for the rest of the day until he went to meet Becky.

Not that it was overly important. He wasn't expecting visitors.

* * *

The open door of the spare room reminded him there were urgent matters he was supposed to have attended to on his return to the house.

* * *

Joseph had heard Allan enter the house and had been waiting for him to come in and announce his arrival for some time. Not that it mattered any more, as the damage was already done. His wet, clingy trousers were a constant reminder of that.

The sight of Allan in a dressing gown and a pink towel was unsettling. It gave a certain physicality to his craziness.

'I must apologise for my appearance, Joseph,' started Allan. 'I got caught in the rain. It's an awful day out there. Really bad.'

I can see that, Joseph wanted to say.

Sitting opposite the window, he hadn't failed to notice the rain rattling against the window like machine-gun fire, and the row of trees bending and arching in all directions like a procession of spindly yoga practitioners. To make matters worse, a group of three pigeons had decided to take up residence on the windowsill and had spent the morning marching back and forth in line, in what looked to be a well-practised, regimental routine. It was horribly ironic that those mangy birds could shit at will, while he had to endure the knowledge that his lower body was covered in his own urine.

'That's ok,' replied Joseph. 'You don't have to dress up on my account.'

Allan almost smiled, but he really didn't have the time to make small talk.

'You can go to the toilet now,' he said.

Joseph found himself chuckling at the misguided timing of the offer.

'It's too late. I've already been.'

Allan jumped back as though he had been stung, his eyes widening in shock. He could see that the restraints were still in place, or at

56

least they appeared to be. Cautiously stepping forward, Allan tugged at them, one by one, with his left hand, keeping his right hand clenched in a tight fist, ready to strike at the first sign of trouble.

The ropes were still secure. He scanned Joseph from head to foot, and this brief investigation revealed the true meaning behind Joseph's statement. It was the way the trousers clung to his legs rather than their patchy darkness that gave it away. A puddle the size of a saucer was all that remained on the floor, the rest having already soaked into the woodwork. Allan shook his head at his captive's lack of self-restraint.

This presented a dilemma. It wouldn't be long before the piss went stale and started to smell, and the last thing he wanted was for the house to start smelling like it was accommodating a tramp. On the other hand, there was no way he could wash the man without releasing him. He could see this was to be an ongoing problem. Allowing Joseph to use the bathroom properly without jeopardising his own safety was a major conundrum, and one for which he had no obvious solution.

'Couldn't you have waited a bit longer?' Allan found himself saying.

'Don't you think I tried?' Joseph responded, the dry, hoarseness of his voice betraying a morning spent yelling for help.

It was the kind of husky tone one developed in a smoky bar when shouting was required to makes oneself heard above the overly loud music and the voices of all the other people shouting to be heard. Except worse. This voice was one that spoke of a morning's fear and desperation; a morning of screaming like a banshee into an abyss in the hope that somebody, anybody, might be listening and have the awareness to act upon its pleas.

Quick to recognise the symptoms, Allan acted swiftly to put an end to it. Moving with a ruthless efficiency that hadn't been evident since the calculated violence of the abduction, he swept behind Joseph's chair and hoisted it back onto its wheel-based hind legs. Buckled in and winched back, Joseph's anxiety was akin to the apprehension experienced before take-off, the muscles tightening one by one until his whole body was taut.

Allan paused, inhaling deeply and flooding his lungs with oxygen. Then he wheeled Joseph forward at pace. The acceleration seemed instant, like a cartoon character disappearing into a cloud of smoke from a standing start.

Joseph realised Allan wasn't going to stop. He would be flung headlong through the window, the mosaic of glass like a razor-sharp cheese grater against his face, which would burrow under his skin and into his eyes, the screwed-up eyelids offering only fleeting resistance.

The shards ripped through his iris and sliced through the diluted pupil, the adrenaline having turned it as large as a five pence piece. A single jagged gem journeyed further, rupturing the back of his eyeball before screeching to a halt a couple of layers further back, embedding its twinkling mass deep within the pulpy confines of his brain.

The intrusion disturbed the sensation of falling, which, although brief, was almost relaxing. The feeling of freefall was something he had felt only in dreams; the irresistible lure of gravity; the inevitable downward journey.

It was abruptly cut short by the sledgehammer blow of the tarmac hitting his chin. His own bodyweight caused the rest of his face to follow through, his lips ground into a formless triturate that resembled ketchup-covered scrambled eggs. Next came his teeth, which were obliterated like Tic Tacs. Those he wasn't forced to swallow, and that didn't mash deep into his gums, were scattered across the ground like bloodied mints. The momentum of his falling body came crashing in behind, his neck snapping in an instant. Joseph's head, pulverised beyond all recognition, was left at right angles to his torso, which spasmodically twitched like newly slaughtered livestock. All around him, the glass fell like polished hail.

Joseph watched his glorious demise play out before him. There was a certain beauty to the scene; a symmetry to the events that made it a prodigious spectacle. The initial barrage of noise, accompanied by the exploding window, was followed by a serene period of silence, where everything fell to earth at the same speed in a plummeting tableau before the magnificently savage crescendo as his body met the ground, the tinkering of the glassy storm playing out a gentle lullaby that faded away into nothing as the pieces bounced lower and lower on the tarmac. It would have been a rapid, if not entirely surprising, conclusion to the previous couple of days.

The pull of the restraints yanked him rearwards like locking car seatbelts, snapping him back to reality with an abrasive jerk. Joseph's head lolled from side to side as he accustomed himself to the new surroundings and the concept of being alive. At first, the sudden influx of daylight made him wince and he felt like an animal crawling out of hibernation, both awe-inspired and lethargic. With vast windows to the front and sides, Joseph was smothered by the daylight, which was brilliant in its greyness.

'Take a look outside,' said Allan. 'Then tell me what you see.'

There was little beyond the twisted branches of the oak tree, which formed a knotted web that partially obscured the rest of the world. A lengthy, undeviating road extended into the smog, bereft of both character and charm. Each side of the street looked like a mirror image of the other, with identical houses cloned from the same monotonous design. Trees planted opposite the bordering walls of each pair made convenient rubbish-dumping grounds for the inhabitants of the street, who were seldom seen but often heard. Their territory-marking garbage was the only evidence of their existence apart from the occasional domestic eruption, which sporadically ignited the street's otherwise inert tenor. Trash generated by trash.

The edges of the pavement were lined with patchy, overgrown grass, but the sparsity of green was hidden from view by the browns of the dead leaves and dog shit. The street was the antithesis of its creator's intention. Idealistic, American-dream suburbia didn't work in Clapham Junction.

'Tell me what you see,' Allan repeated.

'Nothing,' replied Joseph distantly.

'Precisely,' agreed Allan. 'Nothing. Why would anybody come here? It's a dump. It has nothing to offer apart from disease. And it's not even cheap!'

The words wafted over Joseph like a bad smell. All they did was confirm what he could already see.

'Do you think I live here out of choice?' Allan continued. 'Don't you think I'd move if I could?'

Joseph didn't answer, caring nothing for Allan's unsatisfactory housing situation. Then, without warning, he was swung quickly to the left and pushed forward until his knees were just inches from the wall. From there, he could see the house next door, separated from his present abode by the width of the spare room. It was clearly empty, and a 'For Let' sign stood crookedly in the overgrown front garden.

'Observe to your left the empty house,' said Allan, in the style of a scripted tour guide. 'The property has been vacant for a number of weeks now, can't think why. Most people don't even get past the end of the road. They just phone up the estate agent and cancel the viewing on the spot. And to your right...'

Allan dragged the chair backwards and swung it around in one smooth movement, so that Joseph was facing the opposite window. The view was almost identical, minus the hulking body of the tree.

'Here we have an equally crap house,' Allan continued. 'This one isn't empty, but it might as well be for all the use the owner is to you. A widow lives there. She's sick. And mad. You can listen to her, if you like. She's quite the talker.'

Allan pushed Joseph out of the alcove and over to the far right-hand wall of the room which, like all the other walls in the room, was completely bare. Allan parked the chair right up against the wall's scattily painted surface.

'Listen,' he whispered. He stood there, motionless, even going so far as to hold his breath.

Joseph strained to hear something, anything, but the only noise he heard was a barely noticeable chiming in his left ear, the unfortunate consequence of standing next to a speaker for the best part of an hour at a rock concert during his teenage years.

'I can't…'

'*Listen.*' Allan's voice had become more forceful, yet still barely amounted to a hiss.

Just as Joseph was starting to feel the beginnings of frustration at this seemingly pointless exercise – which seemed to him like trying to listen to a passing ant – a sound emerged through the paint, plaster and cement.

'Help.'

It sounded like an animal – a bleating sheep or goat perhaps – only the formation of the word suggested that the source of the noise was human.

'She's dying, I think,' Allan said without compassion. 'And she's as deaf as a doorknob.' He paused, then screeched, '*Shut up, you old hag!*'

Allan banged on the wall with open palms as he yelled at his unfortunate neighbour.

There was another silence before she responded with an identically meagre 'Help.'

Allan whooped with laughter.

'So you can shout and scream all you want, Joseph,' he said, regaining his composure, 'because no-one can hear you. And even if they can, do you really think they'll care? To them, you'll just be another nutcase on the street.'

Allan wheeled the chair away from the wall. Rather than leaving it in the centre of the room where it had been previously, he dragged it all the way to the opposing wall and Joseph was left facing away from the door and into the corner. Despite the picture of helplessness Allan had painted during his guided tour, Joseph realised he must have been reasonably concerned to keep his prisoner away from the window.

'I've got things to do, so I'll see you later, Joseph,' said Allan. 'Just shout if you need anything.'

He left the room in his customary shuffling fashion, closing the door as he went.

* * *

Learning from his mistake the previous day, Allan kept a keen eye on the clock as he vacuumed. Watching the news once on an empty stomach had been bad enough; twice would be a travesty. While doing the rounds with the vacuum cleaner, he rediscovered the pile of sodden clothes from his shopping trip and had to take a break to sling them into the washing machine before they started to smell damp. They had left a wet patch on the wooden panelling. He had caught it early, so hopefully the boards wouldn't warp, but the discolouring was likely to last for a couple of days.

Again, Allan was disappointed by the fruits of his labour when it came to emptying the drum of the vacuum cleaner, as he saw barely more than a sprinkling of dust float down into the kitchen dustbin. Yet today, more than any other day, he had no time to make a second trip around, so he reluctantly turned a blind eye to it. He would just have to clean it extra thoroughly the following day. Lunch consisted of a single pork chop, potatoes and spring greens. Allan did not get much enjoyment out of the meal or the lunchtime news because his thoughts kept slipping back to all the dust and grime he had missed while vacuuming.

Mopping was one chore Allan found unfailingly satisfying, as the results – a floor so shiny it looked polished – were there for all to see. He found that the cleaning of the kitchen and bathroom had a similarly therapeutic effect; a manufactured scent of cleanliness left by the detergent to accompany the dazzlingly reflective surfaces. By the time he had wiped the bathroom towel rail for the final time, the substandard vacuuming was all but forgotten and Allan's mood had risen out of the doldrums.

It quickly sank down again when he saw that it had taken him well over two hours to get to where he was at that moment. Allan sighed heavily. Another day gone. He had less than three hours to shower, change, have dinner and get to the pub. All the important things that urgently needed his attention would have to wait another day. It was beyond him how people managed to work an eight-hour day and still find time to do all of the tasks needed to keep them healthy and safe from contamination.

He showered for a second time, finding it even more satisfying than the first as the rain water spun away down the plughole in an ever-twisting, ever-churning spiral. It was a relief to banish the pollution from his form and let his skin breathe again. Out of habit, Allan covered his face in shaving foam after stepping out of the shower. On realising his mistake, he decided to shave again rather than waste it, a further squandering of time since it had been less than six hours since the last grooming.

Then it came to choosing something to wear. It dawned on Allan that herein lay the root of his disconcertment; the real reason for his constant distraction since returning home from the supermarket. Faced with the same shabby array of clothes he had to pick from every morning, it was manifest that no combination would lead to a suitable outfit. He had known this all along at the back of his mind, without wanting to take the time to resolve the problem. He fanned through the clothing, starting at the far left and working his way to the far right. The first sweep yielded a T-shirt; the easiest item to select since the weather was such that it would remain hidden beneath the other layers anyway.

He laid the T-shirt on the bed and made a second sweep, this time coming up empty-handed. The third passing was equally unproductive, as was the fourth. Allan sat down on the bed. There wasn't enough time to go to the shops, so he would have to make do with what he had, which meant being decisive and open-minded. Figuring that going for plain, dark colours would be the safest option, he returned to the wardrobe and plucked out an army-green woollen pullover and a pair of conservative navy slacks.

He put on the garments and stood in front of the mirror. It was hardly the height of fashion, but he looked presentable nonetheless and Becky would be unlikely to run away screaming at the sight of him. The fit, rather than the colour or style, was the main problem. The shoulders of the jumper were slightly too broad and the waist of the trousers sat a couple of inches too wide, so that a belt was needed to bunch it together and keep everything in place.

He returned to the bathroom to comb his hair and, while there, trawled through the cupboards to find some kind of scent or body spray. As he had suspected, there was nothing there and he had to go without. He went back to the bedroom to take one last look in the mirror, consigning himself to the fact that this was as good as it was going to get.

Taking even greater care than usual so as not to spill anything on his outfit, Allan prepared his pork, greens and potatoes with the same meticulous attentiveness he had displayed five hours previously. He transferred them to a plate, garnishing his meal with a generous dollop of mustard, and went through to the living room, where he switched on the television and flicked over to the news.

No sooner had he taken his first mouthful than it became evident to Allan that he would not be able to finish the meal. It wasn't that he wasn't hungry, but the anxiety had caused a nest of butterflies to hatch in his stomach and their constant fluttering made him feel nauseous. He was unable to swallow anything more than a couple of mouthfuls. Cleaning aside, he had so many things to worry about; immediate things; things that could go wrong on his date with Becky.

Chewing on a piece of pork, he found himself pouring over trivial matters such as how to greet her and what to say. He did his best to think up interesting questions and amusing anecdotes to fill any gaps in the conversation. The prospect of the date quickly diminished him to a nervous wreck and he would have gladly cancelled on Becky to buy himself more time to prepare and gather his thoughts, but this wasn't an option as he didn't have her telephone number.

* * *

Joseph listened to Allan coming up the stairs, the footsteps heavy and angry, and he envisaged with dread the possible reverberations of his maddened mood. His new vantage point allowed him an unhindered view of the top of the stairs, removing Allan's capacity to sneak up behind him, and as his abductor approached he saw him holding what appeared to be a plate of food. Allan had changed into more normal clothing since his last visit, although he was dressed in an outfit that would have looked more at home on an older man. He walked around so that he was directly facing Joseph, then presented the plate to him as though he were offering up a gift of great worth.

'I made this but I can't eat it, and I was wondering whether you'd like it.'

Joseph looked at the contents of the plate with suspicion. It smelt good. The aroma wafted up past his nostrils, causing his mouth to flood with saliva and his stomach to groan wantonly. Allan had even cut the whole meal up into bite-sized pieces, presumably so that he could spoon-feed it to him. But who knew what the sick bastard had done to it?

'That's very kind of you, really, but I'm not hungry,' replied Joseph, his paranoia winning out over his hunger.

'But I *can't* eat it,' emphasised Allan. 'It'll go to waste.'

'I'm sorry,' said Joseph, sensing his agitation. 'I would eat it, really I would, and it smells delicious, but I really don't think I could.'

'You haven't eaten for days!' bellowed Allan, the plate shaking in his hand. The fork dropped to the floor, where it bounced and tumbled, clattering loudly off the boards as it jigged back and forth between its plastic handle and steel tip. 'You must want it!'

'I'm sorry,' Joseph whimpered, his eyes transfixed on the fallen cutlery; a point of focus away from Allan; away from his rage.

'Sorry?' questioned Allan. 'Is that it? *Sorry?* You ungrateful fuck!'

Joseph winced as the plate shattered against the wall behind him. Shards of ceramic were sent scattering in the explosion, lumps of potato rebounding in all directions, the debris falling onto his clothes, onto the floor and nestling in his hair. Spring greens were left dripping from the paintwork like pond slime.

'See what you've done!' yelled Allan as he stormed out of the room, slamming and locking the door behind him.

* * *

She was late. Deliberately choosing a table that allowed him to observe all three of the pub's entrances, Allan's eyes raked the area. Becky was nowhere to be seen. It didn't help matters that he had been early. He had left the house some time before he had strictly needed to, with the intention of taking a leisurely stroll to clear his head and calm himself down. Unfortunately, the weather had not been accommodating to his plans; the shrill wind and misty rain persuading him to cut his amble short.

Instead, Allan had taken the most direct route to the pub and had landed at The Falcon a full twenty minutes early. He bought himself a bottle of beer, sat down and waited.

Time ticked by so slowly that he feared seven o'clock might never arrive. The television screens that adorned each corner of the pub were dead, and without a mobile phone to fiddle with he had only his own thoughts for entertainment. Even people-watching was problematic. The bar area was well-lit and he didn't want to appear like a psychopath by staring at everybody else. One option would have been to sit at the bar and chat to the barman, who had seemed like a friendly, good-humoured young man when he served Allan, but had Allan done so he would have lost his table. He didn't want to be left with a couple of cumbersome barstools by the time Becky arrived.

If she arrived.

Hitting him like a heavy blow to the head, Allan suddenly realised that, in his haste to get ready earlier that evening, he hadn't dusted the house. Tomorrow there would be twice as much dust as usual, making his job twice as difficult and therefore meaning that it would take twice as long. This was a catastrophe since he had pencilled Sunday in as the day he would make a start on all the *really* important duties he had been planning for weeks.

He was destined never to get anything done as something always cropped up to ruin his plans. There was only one thing for it. He would have to go home and do it right away. To hell with Becky; she had squandered her chance. Already twelve minutes late, her disorganisation had cost him enough time and he didn't have time to play waiting games while she powdered her nose and applied her eyeliner. It was an abrupt, albeit necessary end to the evening, and he would have to explain his reasons to her during his daily shop the next day.

Allan downed the rest of his beer and began to put his coat back on; a coat that still hadn't fully dried from the morning's downpour.

'Allan!'

The voice stopped him in his tracks and he turned to see Becky coming towards him from behind, her cheeks reddened and glowing from the cold outside. 'I'm so sorry, Allan, the bus was late. You must have thought I wasn't coming!'

She was out of breath.

'Have you been waiting long?' she asked, draping her coat across the back of the chair.

'No, not really. I aimed to get here slightly early to reserve a table but I got delayed, so I've only just got here myself really,' Allan lied.

'That's ok then,' she said. 'It's going to take me a while to warm up. I'm still freezing!'

Allan could see that this was true as her nipples were poking through her top like bullets. He reflected on the fact that this was the first situation he had been in where he was allowed, perhaps even expected, to look at her without feeling embarrassed or self-conscious. He welcomed the invitation with open arms, taking the opportunity to examine her in a way that would have been considered odd at the supermarket.

Without the restrictions imposed on her by her place of work, Becky's beauty had soared to new heights. Gone was the starched stiffness of the uniform, which had been replaced by a figure-hugging mixture of cotton and Lycra. The familiar buttoned-up collar had been swapped for a plunging neckline and straps so threadlike they were almost cutting into her slender shoulders. The top was designed to be worn only by those possessing the figure and confidence to do so, and Becky had both.

Free from the constraints of the regulation band she wore at work, her hair spilled down her back, the colour so vigorous that no two strands were the same shade. The artificial facelift provided by the ponytail had vanished, so that her skin was relaxed, showing a youthful plumpness that had not been evident before. Rather than detracting from her sculptured features, it exaggerated them, adding a softness to her cheeks and a friendliness to her sexuality. She looked magnificent to Allan and he was eager to get things moving.

'Would you like a drink?' he offered. 'That ought to warm you up a bit.'

'Sure. How about sharing a bottle of wine?'

'Ok. Do you prefer red or white?'

'White please… if that's ok with you.'

'Sure.'

Allan went to the bar, returning with an open bottle of Chardonnay and two large wine glasses. He filled them both, carefully topping up the first to make sure that it was exactly level with the second. Then he slid one over to Becky.

'Well, here's to a great evening!' Becky said as a toast, raising her glass.

'Yeah, cheers,' responded Allan, taking a sip.

The wine was light and refreshing, and both parties approved. With the formalities of toasting over, it was Becky who made the first stab at meaningful conversation.

'So, Allan, what do you do? Besides shopping at Asda, that is.'

'I'm not actually working at the moment,' replied Allan, 'but I keep myself busy.'

'Busy?'

Her chest rose and fell hypnotically as she breathed.

'Yeah, you know how it is. Trying to sort your life out takes time. The days just fly by. How about yourself? Besides *working* at Asda, that is.'

Allan was pleased to see Becky giggle at his attempted joke. It might well have been a fake laugh, but at least she was making the effort.

'Not a great deal, really. I'm only working there for a year to save money for university.'

'Oh really? Have you got a place lined up already?'

'Yeah. I'm going to Imperial College to study biology.'

'Wow. You must be quite young, then. You're very mature for your age, you know.'

'I'm not sure how to take that! Just kidding. I'm twenty, so not as young as you might expect. I had to resit a year,' she added.

'You didn't do as well as you wanted?'

'No, it wasn't that. My dad died during my A-levels and I took some time off to be with my mum.'

Becky lowered her eyes.

'I'm sorry to hear that. I lost both of my parents earlier this year, so I know how you feel.'

'Both? That must have been awful. Was it some sort of accident?'

'You could say that.'

'I think we should change the topic of conversation. This isn't very uplifting!'

'I think you're right!'

'How old are *you*, Allan? Just out of interest.'

'Twenty-six,' he replied, immediately knocking more than ten years off his age.

'Oh, ok. I must admit that I find it hard to judge with you. If you'd said twenty-three I wouldn't have been surprised, but if you'd said forty I still would've believed you. I'm glad you're not forty, if I'm being honest. That would be a bit weird! You've got one of those timeless faces. I expect you'll look exactly the same in ten years' time.'

'I can only hope so.'

'What's your surname?'

'Why?' asked Allan suspiciously.

'No particular reason. I'd just like to see whether your name suits you.'

'Thompson.'

'Allan Thompson,' mouthed Becky.

'So, does it suit me?'

'Yeah,' she smiled. 'I guess it does.'

The conversation continued in this inane, superficial vein for some time.

* * *

'Angela? Angela? Can you hear me?'

Joseph closed his eyes so he could single-mindedly focus on the one sense that was of any use to him right at that moment.

'Yes, Joseph.'

Barely a whimper, scarcely a squeak, the reply was debilitated, weak and drained of all vitality. The fight had gone from the owner's body, leaving a jaded wreck of a woman who dared not think too much for fear of what her imagination might have thrown up.

'Angela, it's going to be all right. We're going to get through this.'

Joseph tried to sound sincere, finding it all but impossible as he didn't hold any faith in the words himself. He heard no response from Angela, whose silent tears did not carry well through the walls.

* * *

'Do you live alone, Allan?' asked Becky.

The contents of the wine bottle had been diminished to a mere inch of liquid and the drinkers had relaxed accordingly, the nervous tension visibly dissipating as they leant towards one another as though an unseen magnetic attraction existed between them. Both had their hands on the table, ever creeping forward but never quite touching. Neither possessed the courage to instigate the physical contact they both wanted, the fear of rejection threatening greater exposure than nakedness.

'No, I live with two others. A couple.'

'That must be a bit strange!' Becky's features contorted to express her bemusement. 'I can't imagine sharing with a couple.'

'It isn't too bad. They generally keep themselves to themselves. I barely hear a peep out of them most of the time. They're like mice, those two.'

'Are they there now?'

'Yes, but they'll probably be in bed by now.'

Becky looked at her watch. It was delicate, silver and ornamental, almost like a bracelet.

'But it's only just gone nine,' she said questioningly.

'I know!' chuckled Allan. 'They don't go out much.'

'Weird couple,' pondered Becky. 'Sorry! I don't mean to insult your flatmates. I'm sure they're very nice.'

'Yeah, they are,' he confirmed.

'Well…' she smiled flirtatiously, rolling her eyes towards the exit and touching his hands for the first time, cupping them in her own. 'How would you feel about getting a bottle of wine and taking it back to yours?'

'I'd love to.'

The warmth of her caress dictated that this was the only feasible answer. He was completely at her mercy; utterly powerless.

They gathered their coats and strolled arm-in-arm to the off-licence next door. It was as short a walk as could conceivably be imagined, which was lucky as the weather had become bleaker than ever.

Allan took little time in picking out a bottle of wine, his choice limited by the sparse selection of bottles that were already chilled. He played it safe and went for one he had tried before. It was a mid-priced bottle of Sauvignon Blanc, innocuous enough to be inoffensive to anyone who wasn't a connoisseur. Allan paid for it, breaking into the last of the ten-pound notes he had withdrawn at the supermarket earlier that day.

It was still relatively early and easy to get a cab, with a queue of them already waiting by the central reservation opposite the off-license. Wrapped in each other's arms to fend off the buffeting wind, Allan and Becky jumped into the nearest one and collapsed onto the huge seat that ran along the back wall of the Tardis-like interior.

'Where to, mate?' enquired the taxi driver, peering at them through the mirror.

'Lupton Road, please.'

'That's just up past Lavender Hill, isn't it?'

'It certainly is.'

This cabbie certainly had The Knowledge, Allan thought. It seemed unlikely that the driver took many trips to that part of town.

The journey was rapid, almost over before it started, with Allan paying the bill at its conclusion. This took his expenditure for the evening to over twenty pounds, leaving his wallet heavy with coins that rattled and jangled whenever he moved. The cabbie didn't hang about for long, knowing the deserted streets would gift him no passengers for the return journey.

Becky did not appear to be fazed by the neighbourhood. She patiently let Allan lead her to the front door and stood there, huddled in against the cold, while Allan dealt with the multiple locks. The cloud cover overhead had begun to clear and the moon, shaped like a toenail clipping, was starting to shine through.

Upon entering the flat, Becky stood gazing in wonderment at its speckless state.

'Wow!' she exclaimed. 'This is far cry from what I'm used to.'

'I'm sorry, the place is in a bit of a mess,' Allan apologised. 'I didn't get a chance to clean it properly earlier.'

'A bit of a mess? You're joking, aren't you?' she laughed. 'The place is *immaculate*, especially compared to Mum's flat. It's amazing. You'd never have guessed it from the outside.'

'I know. I'm surprised you made it down the garden path without having second thoughts.'

Chuckling tipsily, they hung up their coats by the door.

'Do you mind taking your shoes off before we go through?' Allan requested. 'It's a house rule, I'm afraid.'

'Mum has the same rule,' she replied with a smile.

Mercifully, the central heating had served its purpose and the floor was warm under their feet as Allan led her into the living room.

'Make yourself at home. I'll grab a bottle opener and some glasses.'

Becky reclined on the two-seater sofa that sat invitingly beneath the curtained window on the left-hand side of the room. It had a cold, firm, unruffled feel to it, as if nobody had graced its cushions for weeks. The fabric was free from creases and had a uniform flatness, almost as though it had been ironed. Becky noticed that the extreme orderliness was a common feature throughout the room. All the objects within it had a precise location and had been deliberately placed.

The decoration of the room was plain in an empty, detached way, the character of the owners coming through not by their possessions, but by their lack of them. There was little in the way of articles adorning any of the surfaces, aside from a cluster of books on the bookshelf, and even these had a practical use: maps, encyclopaedias and a dictionary. The room had been stripped of all individuality, marked by the bright squares that chequered the walls where pictures had once hung. The surrounding paintwork had been faded by the sun and dulled by ever-increasing layers of dirt.

'Comfortable?' Allan asked, returning with the necessary implements.

'Yes, thanks. Not one for clutter, are you?' commented Becky.

Allan stood still and studied his surroundings as though he were visiting the room for the first time.

'I see what you mean. There's a reason for it. I've been meaning to decorate, but haven't found the time to do it yet. It's not so bad like this anyway, once you get used to it. It's easy to keep clean and tidy, so it has its advantages.'

'Not very homely, though.'

'I guess not.'

He sat down next to her on the sofa, awkwardly opening the bottle and filling the glasses. The glug-glug of the pale yellow liquid produced an amatory sound, possessing a marvellous bass-rich quality. There was no toasting this time as Allan and Becky each raised their glasses to their lips. Becky took a sip, while Allan lowered his glass in disgust.

'It's corked,' he scoffed.

'Pardon?'

'It's gone bad. Smell it.'

Becky swirled the glass, so that the wine swished about like a whirlpool and then sniffed at it, wincing as the aroma filled her nostrils.

'Smells like my brother's feet.'

'I know. It means it's gone off. That bloody off-licence. I'll have to take it back tomorrow.' He took the glass from her hand and put it down next to his on the coffee table, discernibly riled.

'It's drinkable. We'll just have to hold our breath,' Becky suggested.

'No way,' he said dismissively. 'I'm not polluting my body with that stuff. Look, I think I may have a bottle in the kitchen. Let me get it.'

He stood up to leave, but the touch of Becky's hand on his jumper stopped him. He turned to face her, beholding the longing countenance, her eyes half-closed, lips reaching forward. She pulled him towards her and, leaning down, he kissed her, or rather she kissed him. She placed her lips over his closed mouth; closed through fear, through unfamiliarity. She was persistent, her tongue working his jaws open, soothing them, stroking them and coaxing them apart.

She moved her hands behind his head and pulled him closer. He was reluctant at first, his body rigid and resistant. She cajoled him further, running her hands over his back and forcing him down.

He began to succumb and toppled forward, raising one knee onto the sofa to support himself. His arms moved from his side, where they had been timidly rooted, imitating the position of her own. He was fascinated by the way her flesh bulged above and below the strap of her bra. She tugged him slightly harder and he sank down beside her, their legs touching at the knees. Their forms were symmetrical, like a mirror image.

'Can we continue this upstairs?' she whispered.

Allan nodded and led her out of the room, the corked wine long forgotten and left to sit dejectedly on the table. They made their way up to Allan's bedroom and Becky climbed onto the bed. She lounged back on it, gently patting the empty space next to her, enticing Allan to join her there.

Allan dimmed the lights slightly and went over to her, stroking her silently from shoulder to thigh, all the time watching her face for clues as to what to do next. She placed her hand on his hip and slowly slid it underneath his T-shirt. He shivered, her hand still cold from her time outside in the December bitterness. He felt goosebumps jump up all over his skin, exhaling heavily as her hand traced over his body, which was fraught and tense with nervous energy.

Following her lead, he moved his left hand from her hip to her bare midriff, holding it there for a second, waiting to see whether she would repel or oppose him. There was no reaction, so he moved his hand further up her body, crawling with his fingers and burrowing beneath the clingy confines of her top, his knuckles brushing up against her bra. The material was patterned, textured, scratchy and thin, the plumpness of her breasts detectable through its lacy covering.

Here he paused, scared to go further, but she guided his hand with her own and soon they were underneath her bra, his hands cupping her breasts. His fingers were warm and clammy, fumbling and groping, making scissor-like movements over her nipples, his thumb wedged into the gap between her breasts, squeezing and fondling. They started to kiss once again, more passionately this time, their mouths forming an airtight seal, their tongues wrestling excitedly, out of sight, nostrils hissing as their lungs cried out for more air.

Allan opened his eyes to look at her face. She was too close, her features distorted and out of focus. She was like a Cyclops, her one eye closed in ecstasy, concentrating, dreaming, caught up in the moment. Becky traced the path of his stomach hair and slid her hand down his trousers, grasping his penis in her palm and working its shaft with rhythmic movements that caused Allan to writhe and contort.

He slipped his spare hand onto her waist and pulled her in close, their chests together, bellies touching. Becky lifted a leg over him, so that they had become completely intertwined in one another, a single entity. Now that she was up against him, he glided his hand down the back of her jeans, inside her knickers and around her behind, alternating between affectionate stroking and lustful kneading, unable to grasp as much flesh as he craved. He moved from cheek to cheek, lingering over the space between, fascinated and overwhelmed. Becky's other hand ran through his hair, grabbing handfuls and handfuls, her grip almost painful as they squirmed against one another, rolling over and over, changing sides and positions, their mouths rarely parting for more than a fleeting second.

'Allan, sorry. I really don't want to stop, but I need to use the toilet.' Her voice was squeaky and timid, like that of a schoolgirl.

'Sure,' replied Allan, almost relieved to have a break.

Hands were returned to their rightful owners and Becky knelt up on the bed, straightening her clothes and hair. As she pushed the henna locks away from her face, her elbows held aloft, Allan placed his fingertips on her stomach, the flatness exaggerated by her posture. She reached down and grasped his hand, raising it to her lips and kissing it adoringly.

'I'll be back for you in a minute,' she promised, climbing over him and disappearing through the door.

The intensity of the encounter having left him emotionally drained, Allan slumped back onto the bed, wondering how it was possible to have such strong feelings for someone he barely knew. Everything about Becky was perfect. She was intelligent and considerate, not to mention the most beautiful girl he had ever known. The fact that she seemed to like him back was the icing on the cake. There was nothing he wanted more than for her to return so he could cradle her in his arms and tell her how he felt.

The sound of a rattling door handle hauled him out of his amatorial dream world. He leapt out of bed like a startled hound and followed Becky's trail out of the room. He discovered her clutching the door handle of the spare room, sheepishly releasing it when she saw him coming.

'Wrong door,' said Allan, ushering her away.

'I wondered why it was locked,' Becky replied as she was shepherded into the bathroom. 'See you in a second.'

Returning to the bedroom a few minutes later, she was surprised to see Allan sitting agitatedly on the edge of the bed, his head lowered. His legs were kicking out impatiently, his arms propping him up from behind, hands facing backwards.

She sat down next to him and put an arm around his shoulders.

'So, where were we?' she murmured, kissing him on the cheek.

The manoeuvre provoked no reaction from Allan, whose focus remained on the floor, his body equally unresponsive.

'I've changed my mind. You're going to have to go home.'

She might have thought he was joking, except that his voice was devoid of humour and his body language suggested he was entirely serious.

Becky was astounded by the capricious coldness. All she could think to say was, 'What?'

'I'm not feeling right and I think it would be better if you went home,' he reiterated.

'What's the matter?'

'I don't know. Please, I think you should leave.'

'Fine!' she snapped. 'You're too old for me anyway!'

'Don't be like that, Becky. I'll walk you back.'

It was a feeble attempt at a peace offering.

'Don't bother! I wouldn't want you to put yourself out!'

She was getting more and more aggressive by the second as the sheer unreasonableness of his attitude began to sink in, the annoyance simmering violently under the surface.

'Come on, let's go,' said Allan, grabbing her by the arm.

'Don't touch me!' barked Becky, wrenching her arm from his grip.

She stormed down the stairs, fighting back the tears that were gathering in her lower lids, the whites of her eyes reddened and fiery. Allan was in hot pursuit, but remained a safe distance away.

'I'm going to walk you back to the station. It's not safe for you to walk alone,' insisted Allan.

Becky didn't answer as she was too busy putting her shoes back on. She hurriedly pulled on her coat and marched out the front door. Allan calmly prepared himself to go back outside, then followed her, jogging to catch up. They walked briskly and silently, side by side; close together but a world apart.

The walk seemed to take an age. Twenty minutes was a long time to go without speaking to one another, without even the slightest acknowledgement of each other's presence.

When they reached Clapham Junction station, Becky didn't stop. She passed straight through the ticketing barriers and disappeared up the tunnel, dodging the water dripping from the ceiling, which made it resemble a damp cave. She did not turn back to witness Allan's apologetic wave.

It was the worst possible end to the evening from Allan's point of view, having let the girl of his dreams slip through his fingers. He loitered around the ticket machines for some time, a desperate hope lingering within him that she might reconsider and return to him.

But there was no sign of her. She was gone forever.

He left dejectedly, his head hung low, and meandered through the sterile brightness of the shopping area, where everything bar the food outlets and the mini-supermarket were shut off to the outside world. Allan wished he could do the same. He wanted to pull down a corrugated metal blind so that people would know he was closed for business and wouldn't bother him, wouldn't look at him.

People came towards him in couples and groups, wearing clothes that were trendier than his, younger than his. He felt inadequate, an outsider, as though he had got off at the wrong stop and stepped into a world that didn't belong to him; an alien place built for party people.

Allan stepped out onto the street, where the flower seller's stall was also boarded up. Discarded leaves had turned to slime, the surplus petals blackening in the dirt, indistinguishable from the chewing gum that was destined for a longer stay. Strangers talked at him, trying to sell him things and give him things. Everybody wanted something. He ignored them, deflecting their intrusive gazes, turning left and heading up Lavender Hill. He hurried past The Falcon, not wishing to be reminded of the place where the torrid evening had begun.

He was stopped in his tracks by a small rat of a man.

'Excuse me, sir. I'm really sorry to bother you, but I don't suppose you could spare me some change? I'm trying to get to Oxford and I'm only a bit short.'

Allan looked down on him with disdain. The beggar was how Allan imagined a homeless person ought to be: pale, gaunt, diseased and markedly malnourished. He wasn't like so many of the vagrants he came across, who, apart from the smell and general dirtiness, didn't look particularly unhealthy. Allan always felt that if they were going to ask for money, the least they could do was look the part. He had no time for half-hearted squatters.

This unfortunate man looked worthy of some charity, so Allan dug around in his pocket, his cold fingers delving in among the loose change. He wrapped his fingers around what felt like a twenty-pence piece, but when he withdrew it he was frustrated to see that he had pulled out a pound coin. Not wanting to come across as a miser, he handed over the money with considerable resentment, smiling as generously as his irascible mood would allow.

'Thank you, sir.' The man's eyes lit up as he beheld the coin, his mouth open in a huge grin that suggested he was holding a priceless nugget of gold in his hand. 'Thank you! That ought to do it. You're a saint, sir. A saint.'

He scurried off into the night and quickly evaporated into nothingness, scampering back down the hole from which he had emerged.

Allan continued his journey with his pockets and conscience feeling slightly lighter, pleased with himself for having performed his good deed for the day. Then it started to rain. Allan stopped in disbelief. How could it rain so much in one place in one day? The oceans must have been evaporating away by the second to produce this much rain. It started to rain harder as the sky really opened up, the water coming down in torrents. Eager to avoid a hat-trick of soakings, Allan glanced across at the taxi rank in the hope of seeing a line of black cabs. There were none there; only a long line of people queuing for a sheltered ride home.

Allan dashed back to the shelter of the station, where the unlicensed operators were already rubbing their hands together with glee. Nature's damp offering had gifted them a sudden change of fortune.

'Taxi?' asked the nearest man, sensing his desperation.

'Yes, please. How much to Lupton Road?'

'Ten quid, mate.'

'Ten quid? You've got to be joking! It's only up the road!'

'Take it or leave it, mate.'

'I'll leave it, thanks.'

Allan approached the next man. All being foreign and adorning cheap, black leather jackets, the illegal taxi drivers were easy to spot.

'Where you going to, boss?'

Allan named his destination, emphasising its proximity to where they were standing.

'Ten quid.'

'Do I look like a tourist? I'll give you six.'

'Sorry, man. I'll take you there for eight, because it's raining and all, but that's my final offer.'

Allan sighed and took out his wallet. He only had seven pounds left, and no amount of searching around in his pockets was going to throw up the all-important extra pound.

'Listen, will you take seven? It's all I've got on me,' he asked politely.

'Sorry, boss. I can't go lower than eight.'

'Please. I'm going to get soaked otherwise!'

'It wouldn't be worth my while. I shouldn't even take you for eight. Ask any of these guys.' He gestured around the general area without even looking at anyone.

Allan got the message and admitted defeat. If only he hadn't given that pound to the beggar! It wound him up enormously that the scrawny pest was on his way to Oxford, no doubt travelling in comfort, while he had been left to walk home in the rain. He scanned the area frenziedly, praying the weaselly scrounger was still skulking about so he could corner him and demand his money back. But he had scuttled away long ago, dragging his filthy frame off to Oxford to sleep in a gutter like the vermin he was.

Allan slogged up the hill in a crazed fury, the rain arrowing at him in a heavy deluge. It struck him so hard that it burrowed through his clothing in seconds, each individual drop chilling his saturated skin like icy shotgun pellets. It came beating down on him, running down his face and into his eyes, blinding him, darting into his mouth and choking him, poisoning him. He had no choice but to trudge onward, muttering to himself, cursing under his breath. He hated the weather, the world and everyone that lived within it.

* * *

Irrespective of your situation, state of mind or health, there are always a few seconds as you first wake up when you feel utterly at ease; before your mind slips back into waking consciousness; before it remembers the reasons for your worries and fears. This is how Joseph felt when he was awoken the next morning by the rumbling of his stomach, a tumultuous growl that entered his dream like thunder and disturbed his sleep. For a moment he believed he was waking up at home, a whole Sunday with Angela to look forward to. It didn't matter that he was upright. He must have fallen asleep in front of the television, having had a bit too much to drink the night before.

The sensation was similar to that experienced while travelling when, no matter how attractive the destination, a passenger who is slipping in and out of slumber never wants the journey to end. During this waiting period, this dead time, everything is beyond their control. They're in transition. The feeling is one of safety and detachment. None of life's problems can be confronted from this position, so they become distant and unimportant, and the resulting mood is one of total contentment.

If only it were possible to capture this feeling and hold on to it.

But the pain, the stress, it all seeps back, bit by bit, starting as a niggling doubt and forcing its way to the forefront of the mind. By the time Joseph's eyes had readjusted to their surroundings, the dread had returned. The anxiety and physical suffering were joined by a new ailment: extreme hunger. It was more than two days since any food had entered his body, and his empty stomach had shrunk to the size of a small fist. With no source of energy, he felt fatigued and unresponsive, as though his head had been removed and attached to the body of a cripple. He was so weak it felt as if his only chance of escaping the bounds was if his starvation reached such an extent that his emaciated limbs became able to slide from the straps unaided.

And all around him lay the very things he craved: bits of meat, potatoes and vegetables. It was so near, yet so far; an infinite distance away. It didn't matter that it was cold and covered in dirt. Had it not been for his restraints he would have scooped it up off the floor and licked it off the walls, scavenging for every last morsel. Outside, the pigeons were peering in and laughing at him, parading their stomachs back and forth along the windowsill, plump and full from their morning feast of garbage and scraps.

It was lucky the window was closed or they would have entered, all three of them, and eaten the spilt food right in front of his eyes. *His* food. The food he had so foolishly rejected. They would have eaten every last bit, and shouting and screaming at them would only have held them off for so long. They soon would have realised that he couldn't harm them, not while he was tied up; that he was only capable of making noise. Then they would have pecked about his ankles, brushing their tail feathers against his incapacitated legs and cramming their already bloated bellies with more and more food, as if they would never eat again.

How Joseph had grown to despise those pigeons.

* * *

Sunday morning came and went without any incident. There was no opening and closing of doors, no turning on and off of light switches, no running of taps, no footsteps. It passed by completely undetected, so much so that it may as well not have existed.

* * *

At 14:17, a door opened to the sound of the radio and Allan loped to the bathroom, emerging after a short time clutching a full roll of toilet paper. He returned to his bedroom and slammed the door behind him, reducing the radio to a barely audible drone until it ceased altogether a few minutes later.

* * *

Allan was suffering on a number of counts. In the first instance, he regretted his actions of the previous night. Becky had not deserved to be treated in such a way. He felt he might have blown his one chance and alienated himself from his perfect partner, which was difficult to accept. He had spent much of the night running over the events of the evening in his mind, analysing each stage in turn. He considered alternative paths he could have chosen at each juncture and the likely consequences of these alternative approaches. Unfortunately, it seemed to him that any path except for the one he had followed would have led to him spending a passion-filled night with Becky.

As it happened, he had crawled into bed alone; the very bed on which he had been involved in that intimate encounter just an hour previously. The longing had returned like a fever. These thoughts had kept him awake for most of the night and when he eventually found peace, when all the possibilities had been played out multiple times, he had managed to get some rest. It was a short, tormented slumber, and when he awoke early the next morning he felt as if he had aged tremendously while he slept.

As had been the case for the previous few days, the clock-radio had woken him up. It was a different presenter and a different programme, but the same annoying radio station. However, unlike other mornings, he had lacked the willpower to reach over and turn it off. It had even been too much to aim a clumsy hand at the snooze button. Instead, he had lain there allowing it to wind him up.

Part of him had wanted to go back to sleep, which was the only way to properly regenerate himself. Another part of him had wanted to get up and make a start on all the important things that needed doing. He couldn't afford to sleep all day, especially as that would mess up his sleep pattern and prevent him from sleeping later that night. So he had done neither. He had just lain there, agonising over which would be the better option, and by lunchtime he could have counted the number of hours he had managed to sleep on one hand.

It hadn't taken long to occur to him that a lack of sleep wasn't his only problem. A pounding head and a streaming nose was adding to his distress. Allan figured the headache was attributable to a combination of the alcohol he had drunk and the lack of sleep, which essentially amounted to a hangover. He blamed the runny nose on the clouds of dust that must have been in the air as a result of his laziness the day before, the trio of drenchings he had been victim to not presenting themselves to his mind as a more viable option.

The illness was of the most annoying sort: clear mucus that trickled out with such persistence that he felt he was in danger of becoming dehydrated, interspersed with fits of savage sneezing that immersed him into a state of severe sweatiness, the salty liquid pouring from his body as though he were being wrung out. The box of balsam tissues next to his bed had receded at an alarming rate, and it was their eventual expiration that had forced Allan to leave the comfort of his bed and seek out a substitute; toilet paper being the only available option.

* * *

It was now 15:42 and the skin under Allan's nose had already begun to rub red raw. Despite being one of the softest available, the toilet tissue was not designed for the nose and its abrasive qualities soon began to take effect, the chafing beginning after the first couple of wipes. The snotty discharge kept on coming, unrelenting in its flow, and Allan had to keep on wiping, to continue inflicting pain upon himself, for the sake of his own comfort and hygiene.

It really had been an onerous day.

* * *

It is a dangerous thing to be left with only your own thoughts for any substantial length of time, as Joseph had discovered. No matter how much he resented having to work, this unexpected time alone had taught him that one of the comforts of employment was its predictability.

Friends and colleagues frequently aired their views to him about the hardships of work: the stress, the long hours, the fear of being sacked. These problems were finite and manageable. Everyone was aware that they existed and the solutions were obvious and attainable. A particularly bad day at work might potentially include such plights as a shortened deadline or a public dressing down from a superior, but a job could only be *so* bad, whereas the hardship of thinking was limited only by the imagination.

Anything that was dwelt on for too long would eventually be blown so far out of proportion that the trivial nature of the original problem became all but forgotten and escalated into a personal crisis. Bad hangovers developed into meningitis and a lack of response to phone calls or text messages was seen as a sign that the other person no longer cared. Joseph appreciated that it could also work the other way around, so that meaningless achievements could be seen in a new light and spun into personal triumphs, but it wasn't in the human nature to sit around thinking happy thoughts rather than wallowing in self-pity, and his present situation did not inspire any uplifting or spiritual cleansing.

Of the many things Joseph ruminated over as he sat gazing out across the empty room, one chain of thought occupied him more than any other. A lot of the time it would be hiding, sitting quietly and patiently at the back of the class, but every now and then it would raise its hand and ask to be heard, and every time this happened Joseph would give it the time of day and cerebrate through the issue in great detail, as if it were a new concept he was considering for the first time.

The concept was Angela. Everything came back to her. Irrespective of where his mind took him, no matter which trail he took through his own psychological maze, it would always lead back to Angela. He realised she was at the centre of all he did; the focus of all his efforts. Nothing else held any real importance. He had a good job, and while it wasn't one he particularly enjoyed, he appreciated he that had to work in order to survive, and he could have done a lot worse. The best thing about the job was that he earned enough so that Angela would never have to go without. There were other jobs, easier jobs, out there, but he primarily did it for her.

Even now, the main reason he wanted to escape wasn't for his own well-being, but for hers. Angela provided his focus. She *was* his life. Take Angela away and everything else – the job, the nice flat, his looks, his health, his possessions – became meaningless; merely an aside. Without Angela there would be nothing, and this terrified him far more than the thought of his own death.

* * *

Allan decided he had better get an early night. In fact, this was more of a decision not to get up, since he had only ventured out of bed for less than five minutes throughout the day, and then only because he had absolutely had to. The day had slipped by long ago and he hadn't even managed to make a start on the cleaning, let alone the more consequential duties that should have followed. It was a shade after 7pm and Allan mused that if he went to sleep right away he would be able to wake up incredibly early the following morning. Sunday's inactivity could be written off as an anomaly and he could get straight back to the business of sorting things out.

It had been a long day, dull and taxing, and at that moment he felt as though he could drop off to sleep at any second, so it was a relief that he didn't have to get up to pull the curtains closed, not having opened them in the first place. He had woken in the dark and would go back to sleep in the dark. Lying in the foetal position, Allan emptied his mind of thoughts and waited to drift into unconsciousness.

Two hours passed and Allan was still no closer to getting to sleep, stuck in the same state of dispiriting somnolence he had wrestled with for most of the day. During his efforts to get to sleep, Allan had adopted an assortment of positions – lying on his back as if in a coffin; on his front; and spelling out various letters on his side – each change in pose accompanied by a deep sigh as his exasperation grew. There was nothing in the world Allan hated more, nothing that made him angrier, than being unable to get to sleep. He even found dusting preferable because at least it was reasonably productive.

Another hour passed. Allan realised it was fast approaching his normal bedtime and he was more awake than ever. He slammed his fists into the pillow and kicked his legs in a mock tantrum. Three hours were gone and nothing had been achieved. Each minute that passed was a further minute he would have to sleep the following morning. Another day was slipping away and it hadn't even arrived yet. He was getting so mad he could feel his hair tingling. The more he thought about it, the more it riled him and the more awake he felt. He was stuck in a vicious circle of rage and insomnia.

* * *

Joseph couldn't sleep either, for not altogether different reasons. Like Allan, he desperately wanted to get some shuteye. What separated his need from Allan's was that sleep for Joseph was a way to shut out the pain; to experience a few precious hours of detachment. In his dreams he was free, not shackled to a chair, and there was no suffering. He didn't always sleep for long, and sometimes his head would loll forward so that the strap around his neck choked him back into consciousness. He would awake coughing and spluttering and disorientated, the lacerations in his skin smarting as the wounds reopened under the pressure. The occasions when he drifted off for many hours at a time made it all worthwhile.

Right now, he was simply staring forward into the darkness. Joseph didn't know why he even bothered to open his eyes. He had spent so long looking at the same thing the image was burnt onto the back of his retinas with such precise clarity that he could picture it vividly, even with his eyelids screwed shut. He knew where all the knots were positioned on the wooden floor and the exact location of the scuffs in the skirting board. He could map the cracks in the ceiling that snaked in all directions, overlapping each other like rivers or creases in the palm of a hand. He knew whereabouts in their tangled web the ring was screwed in, the wrought iron ring of such girth it must have once been put there to hang an item of great weight, such as a punchbag or a hammock. He could even tell approximately what time it was by the position of the pools of light that lay on the unpolished boards during the infrequent occasions when the shafts of light broke through the gloom. Joseph feared that the vision of these four walls would haunt him forever, reminding him of his prison every time he closed his eyes.

What he could hear was equally disturbing. For large chunks of the day there would be pin-drop silence, monotonous and intimidating. One side effect of this was that all other sounds appeared amplified and Joseph would be made to jump on a frequent basis, partly due to his being permanently on edge.

Every house has its own sounds and this one was no exception. The heating came on at the same times each day – six in the morning and three in the afternoon – and remained on for six hours in both cases. Ignition was marked by a deep and heavy clunk as the boiler sparked into life, followed by a series of metallic clicks as the hot water moved around the pipes. The next hour or so would be the noisiest times of the day; a concoction of gurgles and hisses bounding about the house as the radiators crept towards their target temperatures. Things would hush down for a bit as the house warmed up, then the creaking would start, the floorboards screeching and groaning as they expanded in the heat.

And these were just the noises made by the house itself. They were joined by the sounds of external elements, like the pummelling of the wind and rain against the windows. And then there were the pigeons, who buoyantly cooed and chirped in their haughty, carefree manner. And of course there was Allan, who, apart from that day – during which he had been conspicuous by his absence – seemed to be permanently pottering around, either cooking, cleaning or unloading shopping.

There was a new sound now; one Joseph had hoped he would never hear. To begin with, it was eminently faint, barely audible, and Joseph had to listen carefully to confirm whether it was there at all. But then it rose in magnitude, and, although muffled by the dividing wall, the source was clear. It was Angela crying.

Joseph's heart tore, overcome by a feeling of utter worthlessness. Usually at times like this he would embrace her, cradling her in his arms and comforting her with tender, doting kisses and soothing words. To hear her sobs and not be able to do anything to stop them was torture. Suddenly, his restraints took on a new magnitude, dwarfing his arms, which had become puny and frail from days of idleness.

'Please don't cry, Angela,' he begged.

Her weeping grew louder, the sound of his voice only serving to make things worse. It reinforced the fact that he wasn't there for her, that he couldn't help. There were no words to her crying, no pleas, just a mixture of sobs and whimpers; an agonising moan that shattered him to hear it.

* * *

Allan was close to reaching breaking point. Midnight wasn't too far away, and yet sleep was still such a long way off. On the path ascending the mountain of slumber he had yet to surmount even the lowest of foothills. Now, lying flat on his back, Allan tried a relaxation technique he had been taught by his mother as a child when sleepless nights had been an unremitting problem that eventually required medical attention.

He started to tense every muscle in his body, starting at the toes, then the legs and working up his body all the way to his face, which he screwed up as tight as it would go. He held the taut position for as long as possible, his body beginning to shudder under the strain, squeezing his fingers tighter and tighter into his sweaty palms, nails digging into his skin. His jaws began to ache as his teeth pressed together with great force, crushing the night's frustrations between his molars.

Only when he could hold it no more, when he could sense tingles of cramp threatening to wreak havoc in the arches of his feet, did he release. And, as his muscles relaxed, he felt the aggression and desperation dribbling out into the mattress, where it was absorbed and trapped by the dense fibres. He lay there like a corpse, focusing his mind on his breathing so that it couldn't wander onto other, more distracting subjects. Then he waited for sleep to take him.

It was working!

Allan stopped himself from getting too excited at the prospect of a good night's sleep potentially being salvaged and concentrated on remaining in a state of tranquil bliss. Maybe tomorrow wouldn't be such a disaster after all. He found himself content to just be lying there, listening to the sounds of the night. The eeriness was somehow comforting; dark and quiet. Clouds of steam hovered around the streetlamps, the faint glow from which was detectable even through the curtains and his closed eyelids. The sound of the occasional bus was barely noticeable as each one thundered along the main road full of drunken revellers on their way home. He heard cats prowling the streets for a midnight snack or another cat to fight with. This was the way night-time was supposed to be.

Yet he was troubled by an unfamiliar sound, one that did not sit comfortably alongside the traffic and the creaks. It was a dampened, stifled noise, like a television had been left on at high volume in another room. Allan couldn't identify its origin, so he chose to ignore it, shutting his ears to that particular frequency. Only he couldn't. It was too varied. It was constantly changing in pitch and volume, nagging at him, eating away at his patience. Soon it became the only thing he could hear. It filled his head, poked at him, got under his skin like a swarm of bugs, irritating him. It was like fleas crawling around in his ear canals, biting at him, laying their eggs, hatching out and jumping all over his face.

Allan sat bolt upright in bed, his hands buried deep in his hair. He had to find the source of the noise, otherwise it would drive him crazy. It could return at any time to plague him and then he would never sleep again.

Allan threw his legs over the side of the bed and gingerly stood up. He was fatigued, weakened by his illness, and it took time for him to adjust to the upright position, swaying like a tree in the wind as his head spun lethargically into focus. No sooner had he steadied himself on his feet than Allan set off in search of the noise, fists clenched and eyes full of fire, his rage bringing him strength as the adrenaline pumped through his veins, blood simmering like tar; hot and black.

Stepping out onto the landing, the noise grew louder, its direction muddled. It was coming from all angles, swirling around him, engulfing him. Yet in its new, amplified clarity, it was identifiable as the sound of a woman crying. He waited, motionless, ears pricked like a hunting dog, and slowly he began to lock on to the origin of the sound.

He moved towards it, tiptoeing up to the door of the spare room, where he paused and leaned against its surface, one ear pressed up against it. He had found it. The noise was coming from within the confines of this room, and it was time to put an end to it.

Allan grabbed the handle and turned it, but the door refused to open. He tried it again, the catch sliding in and out to no avail. The wailing from inside the room grew louder as he shook harder, developing from an abandoned whimper into panicked screaming, alarmed by the noise of the crazed rattling. As the screeching increased, so did Allan's urgency to silence it, and he pushed harder. The lock held fast, the frame of the door bending around it, refusing to give way. Allan began to barge the door with his shoulder, grunting like a maniac as he did so, but still it wouldn't open.

Finally, in one brutal assault, Allan stepped back and kicked out at the door, putting all of his weight through his heel. The door flung open with a loud crack, the handle smashing into the adjoining wall and leaving a sizeable dent.

Allan stormed into the room, shoving aside the rebounding door as it swung back towards him.

And there, right in front of him, sat the source of all his problems.

* * *

The next morning, Allan woke to discover that he had recovered little in terms of his health, still feeling as though he harboured a life-threatening illness. The only good news was that his nose had dried up, although in doing so it had formed an airtight seal within his nostrils that no amount of blowing would shift.

The first couple of attempts produced a satisfying quantity of phlegm that almost spilled over the sides of the toilet tissue: thick, elastic and the colour of pond water. Allan felt himself awash with an immensely pleasing sensation as he studied the sticky contents of the tissue, knowing he had dispelled such a huge quantity of filth from his body. The remnants remained stubbornly firm. Allan blew and blew until he felt light-headed, achieving only a bubbling sound and the sensation of things moving about, while his sinuses stayed well and truly blocked.

The headache still lingered in the background and there was now a sore throat to contend with. It was a dull ache in his tonsils, preferable to the type of sore throat that felt like a sea urchin had passed through the windpipe, but wincingly painful nonetheless. With the previous day wasted, Allan was eager not to let another pass without making at least some progress in the execution of his important plans. He decided to lie there and gather his strength for five minutes before getting up and going about his daily activities as if nothing was wrong.

Five minutes proved to be an insufficient length of time, as did ten, fifteen and half an hour. It was more than an hour later by the time Allan had finally summoned up enough strength to drag his sweaty, reluctant form out from under the duvet. It was cold outside the comforting confines of the covers and it required a great deal of willpower not to jump straight back in. Allan resisted the urge and instead wrapped himself in the fleecy warmth of his dressing gown, the material soft against his skin.

His first port of call was the kitchen, where he emptied three glasses of water in turn. The first couple of mouthfuls hurt his throat as he swallowed, but the coldness of the liquid soothed his tonsils enough so that the remainder was merely uncomfortable. The water felt like it was cleansing his insides as it passed down through his body into his stomach, and Allan left the kitchen feeling much better already.

A shower would help to complete his rejuvenation, so the bathroom was his next destination. It was an invigorating experience to rinse away two days' worth of grime. He imagined the dirt falling from his body in great clumps like sunburnt skin, while the fever drifted out of his gaping pores and was swept down the plughole with all the other germs. Ridding his chin of the semi-beard that had sprouted over the past couple of days was equally refreshing, the banishment of the dishevelled look giving a superficial healthiness to his appearance. Brushing his teeth was the final piece in the puzzle, and Allan left the bathroom feeling like a new man.

He returned to the bedroom and opened the wardrobe to find an outfit to wear to the supermarket. Nothing presented itself as suitable, and having to face Becky in a poor state of dress and health after such a short period of time had elapsed caused the fatigue and ailments to return. Allan retreated back to bed, cowering between the sheets, which were still dirty and damp.

* * *

The darkness crept up on him with great stealth, arriving so rapidly that Allan feared he might have blinked too hard and lost the ability to open his eyes. The hours left in the day were scarce. Lying flat on his back, Allan could feel the base of his ribcage jutting out above his shrunken stomach and realised the combination of hunger and sweating had caused him to lose weight.

This was a distressing discovery, as he knew he would need to keep his strength up if he were to have any chance of clawing back the time he had lost through illness. He needed to eat. Allan was aware that he had run out of meat, but this didn't matter. He could use milk as his source of protein and just eat extra vegetables and potatoes. The fact that he didn't have any sort of appetite seemed trivial. He would force down every last mouthful, rinsing it down with the milk if needs be.

Allan quickly found this to be easier said than done as he sat in front of the television gazing at a half-eaten meal. At first, it had been straightforward and he had shovelled the food down at great speed, his stomach murmuring appreciatively as the contents of the plate diminished before his eyes. But he soon began to slow. The saliva dried up and the feeling of the moistureless food in his mouth made it difficult to swallow. It got itself stuck at the back of his throat and made him want to retch. The milk helped at first, washing down the unchewed chunks of broccoli and carrot quickly and painlessly, but his stomach soon decided it was full and threatened to throw back anything more that tried to enter it.

Allan pressed on for some time, forcing down a few more spoonfuls between deep breaths and nauseous sighs. Eventually, he had to admit defeat. There was no point trying to stuff more down if it was just going to end up swimming about in the toilet bowl.

* * *

'I've brought you some more food.'

It made Joseph sick to see Allan again after what had happened the night before. Hearing Angela crying had chilled his soul, pushing him to the limits of despair, but what followed – the slaps, the thuds, the shouting and her tears turning to screams – had maddened him, spinning him into a state of insanity; of fitful rage. He couldn't see, he could only hear. Every sound had caused a violent image to explode in his mind; images that were worse than the reality, if that were possible.

He too had yelled and wept, begging for Allan to call off the attack, and when that hadn't worked, he had demanded that Allan cease the onslaught with malevolent threats he had no way of carrying out. When this had also failed and the beating had continued, Joseph had broken down himself, sobbing like a baby and equally as helpless, the sound of his own shrieks not loud enough to drown out the mayhem taking place in the neighbouring room.

Having Allan stand before him now caused the horrific visions to come flooding back. The visions he had fought so hard to suppress swarmed around inside his head like angry bees and his eyes glazed over with hatred.

'I've brought you some more food,' repeated Allan in an identical tone of voice, which suggested that he didn't believe Joseph had heard him the first time.

Joseph wanted to burst out of his restraints there and then and beat him to within an inch of his life, knowing it would be a futile attempt that would only serve to make him feel worse. He looked at the food. It wasn't a full serving like the one he had been offered the previous day. It was barely a couple of mouthfuls. It was just about enough to whet his appetite and would almost certainly leave him feeling hungrier than before. Besides, he didn't want to accept anything from Allan. Not after what he had done.

'It'll go to waste if you don't eat it and I'd rather not have to throw it away. Think of all the starving children in Africa.'

Victims of famine were the last thing on Joseph's mind right at that moment, his own yearning for food limiting his capacity for sympathy in relation to others. He weighed up the risks of turning the offer down again, considering Allan's reaction the previous time. Added to this, Allan had demonstrated that his willingness to hurt people knew no bounds. This situation was slightly different from the previous propitiatory offering, in that Allan appeared to have eaten most of the meal himself. Admittedly, there was nothing to have stopped him doing something to it after he had taken his fill.

'Ok, thank you. That's very kind of you.' Joseph decided gracious acceptance was the safest option.

Allan stepped forward and placed the plate on Joseph's lap. The food was already cut up into bite-sized pieces and a fork lay at the right-hand side of the plate, prongs partially hidden beneath a broccoli stalk. The knife had been removed. Joseph could see its handle jutting out of Allan's trouser pocket.

'I don't have time to stand here and spoon-feed you, so I'm going to undo one of your restraints. Don't even think about trying to escape. No matter how quickly you move, I assure you that I will move faster, and I swear that I will slaughter your girlfriend.'

'I won't do anything stupid. I promise I won't.'

'Just you remember that.'

He unshackled Joseph's right arm, alert all the time to any signs of an impending attack. None came, and soon the leather straps lay loose around Joseph's wrist, a shallow imprint remaining where they had once held his arm tight. Joseph waited patiently for the feeling to return to his arm. It felt like a dead weight at first, and he was afraid that he wouldn't be able to operate the cutlery unaided. But the freedom of movement slowly returned and he was soon able to bend his arm at the elbow, extending his fingers to their outmost reach.

Joseph grasped the handle of the fork as best he could. It was difficult because the strap around his neck limited his field of vision, restricting him to shapes but not details. The implement felt alien to him and he struggled to control it, the stiffness in his right shoulder proving a significant handicap. He managed to spear what he guessed to be a tree of broccoli and raised it up to his mouth. It was cold but tasted heavenly nonetheless. He only chewed it a couple of times before swallowing, eager to move on to the next tasty morsel. What little food there had been rapidly disappeared, with only one or two pieces rolling off the end of his fork and onto the floor.

Joseph laid the fork down on the empty plate and waited to see what would happen next.

'Nice?' asked Allan.

'Yes, thank you.'

Allan came back alongside him to refasten the restraints.

Now was his chance.

In one momentous movement, Joseph seized the fork and swung it at Allan with all his might. Both parties cried out in pain: Joseph as his shoulder blade ripped through swollen tissue to reach its new position; Allan as the spikes of the fork plunged inches deep into his leg.

Tears of agony streamed down Joseph's cheeks as the trauma in his shoulder blazed through his body, but he was able to yank out the fork and raise it high in the air before slamming it into the side of Allan's neck as he doubled over, clutching the initial stab wound. Allan collapsed to the deck in an instant, writhing about like a run-over cat, unable to compose himself enough to remove the object from his neck.

His blood was flooding out onto the floor, its flow restricted to a thin, lengthening, creeping oblong by the cracks in the boards.

Joseph unfastened his other arm and tore off the neck restraint with both hands. Free to bend down, he unfastened the belts around his legs, glancing up at Allan every couple of seconds to make sure he was still incapacitated. Joseph tried to stand but collapsed straight onto the floor, his legs unable to take the weight.

The fall momentarily stunned him, but seconds later his adrenaline kicked in. He crawled out of the room on his forearms, every inch of progress wracked with pain as his battered body groaned in protest. As he neared the door, his heart raced loud and hard in his chest, pounding in his temples at the thought of being free; at the terror of Allan's hands clutching at his ankles; of the blunt knife wedging into his vulnerable calves.

Suddenly, he was out of the room, escaped. He pulled himself up using the door, staggering towards Angela's room. She was there waiting for him, bruised but alive, her eyes lit up with hope, love and relief. He was untying her, helping her to her feet, holding her in his arms and ignoring the biting pain in his shoulder as she squeezed him tight.

Weeping tears of joy, they left together, helping each other down the stairs, taking Allan's car keys and driving straight to the police station.

Over.

Safe.

It would have been so easy. But what if it went wrong? What then? An inch this way or that and it would only have caused a flesh wound. Allan would have been up on his feet before Joseph could even unbuckle his other arm. He would have wheeled him next door and made him watch as he gutted Angela with the blunt instrument, splaying her insides all over the floor.

* * *

Allan tied Joseph's arm back up, took the plate and fork away, shut the door and returned downstairs to watch television for a while before retiring for another early night. The food had made him feel much better and, with a good night's sleep under his belt, he was confident that the following day would finally be the one when he got the chance to make a start on all the things he had to do. All those hundreds of important things.

* * *

The distant rumbles disturbed Allan's tormented slumber and he sat bolt upright in bed, his eyes crazed and his body enveloped in a film of sweat that covered every inch of his aching form. The sheets were crinkled and damp, cold against his burning skin. Heavy and humid, the air in the room stifled him, clouding his mind. It weighed down on him and combined with the fever to smother his sanity.

Another rumble followed and Allan flung himself back under the covers, pulling them tight over his head to shield himself from its malevolent roar. They offered little protection and the storm grew nearer, bounding across the sky on an unrelenting course of destruction. It was coming to punish him for his sins; to fire him into the underworld on a scorching dart of electricity. He cowered in the darkness, whimpering, shivering, longing for comfort and companionship. For the protective embrace of a woman. The feel of a woman. The taste.

He waited for the next rumble and, squealing, he tossed the covers to one side. He scurried across the landing towards the spare room, trousers hanging loosely about his hungry waist.

Two figures, motionless in a room. Man, woman. Captor, prisoner. Face to face, hate to hate.

The wind becomes the neutral spectator, looking in through the misted window, which does little to light up the stage. The beings watch each other, waiting, observing, looking for weaknesses, searching for flaws. And there are many.

He stares at her. She stares back at him. She is locked, condemned and trapped by his silent fury.

He opens her mouth by tightly gripping her cheeks, knocking her begging words back to their origin with a violent glance. This terrifies her, which pleases him. The wind cheers, causing the oak tree to rock in silence. She searches her mind for the words of condolence, the words of truce. He searches for the words of condemnation, the words of oppression.

The conflict darkens, and the support of the wind is joined by the applause of the rain. The savage drops beat against the tree, hurting her, weakening her. The woman recoils slightly in her chair. The man senses the advantage and draws one hand down to his pocket, waiting. The wind and rain welcome a new spectator: the storm. It is here. The tree retracts its branches, shielding itself from what is to come.

The woman finds the words she was pursuing, but the disgust in the man's gloat prevents her from expressing them and he stuffs her mouth full of tissues, suffocating her, gagging her, until she's unable to make a sound, even a single noise. The storm begins to brew, feeding off the emotions within.

Caught in a snare of vulnerability, the woman doesn't know what to do. The man does. He rips open her shirt, buttons scattering like hailstones. He brutally tears off her bra, grabbing her naked breasts and squeezing them hard. He digs in with his fingers, kneading them like dough. Tears ooze from her eyes and run unchecked over her cheeks, but she's unable to scream; trapped in a silent agony, helpless against his clenching claws. The man moves in closer and he's kissing her, licking her, biting her, savaging her. Her blood is warm, fresh, salty in his mouth.

In one powerful, intense, ferocious moment, the storm releases, hurling out a bolt of barbarous electricity. It collides with the tree, obliterates its defences, mangles, splinters and butchers its torso. It sends a limb thundering to the ground, ripping its branches until it is writhing in agony, sap leaking from its brutal wound while the rain drums its standing ovation.

A lone figure sits motionless in a room, the other having played his part and left the stage.

* * *

Allan had awoken at around seven o'clock with an optimism he hadn't experienced for some time; a shining light before his eyes that had been sadly absent over the past couple of bed-ridden days. It was hugely satisfying for him to be able to switch off the radio before it burst intrusively into life, as he had done not even a week ago when he had been fit, healthy and full of vivacity.

Shaking his head from side to side, Allan could sense the remnants of his flu still lurking deep in his sinuses and towards the back of his skull. Stretching his limbs further confirmed that he still wasn't one hundred percent, but the improvement on the previous day's state of health was so profound he felt like he could tackle anything the day might throw at him. Provided it wasn't raining. While he couldn't hear the pitter-patter of raindrops at that moment, he chose not to open the curtains in case the heavens were falling to earth in a silent drizzle. He wanted to hold on to this good mood for as long as possible.

The steam of the shower helped to clear his head further, loosening the mucus in his nostrils enough for him to be able to dispel it forever with one hard blow. It floated away along with the shampoo lather and the foaming shower gel. He had shaved so late the previous day that his chin wore only twelve hours' growth, but Allan removed it with the same care and precision as always, even replacing the razorblade for extra sharpness. A new blade for a new beginning.

He was pleased to see that the colour had begun to return to his cheeks, the heat of the shower adding a slight redness that gave his skin a healthy glow. Even the limitations of his wardrobe caused less misery than usual as he found it easier to clothe a healthy body. Allan wasn't sure whether he could stomach his usual breakfast, so he only removed two Weetabix from the packet, leaving the spare half biscuit in there for another day. Even the reduced portion proved to be a struggle, his mouth still playing home to a furriness that didn't mix well with the bland mush of the cereal. Nevertheless, he managed to finish the serving irrespective of the fact that he hadn't enjoyed it and, more importantly, he successfully kept it down for the next ten minutes, during which time he felt queasy and was forced to sit motionless on the sofa.

The feeling of sickness finally passed, and by the time Allan had brushed his teeth it could have been any other day.

The pivotal moment came when he was faced with the prospect of yet another vegetarian meal. He probably could have put up with one more protein-less feed using milk as a substitute, but there was little left in the four-pint carton and he certainly wouldn't be able to make it stretch to two meals' worth *and* breakfast the next day. He would have to go to the supermarket whether he liked it or not. Not wishing to expose himself to the bitter cold and invite back the illness that had plagued him for the last two days, Allan added an extra jumper to his outfit and donned a scarf, hat and gloves as well as his coat.

Upon opening the front door, he was greeted by a wonderfully crisp winter morning. The sun was blazing so brightly it made him squint and he had to raise a hand to shield his eyes before he could look upon the day's chilly splendour. Allan enjoyed his walk to the shops, the freshness of the atmosphere cooling and smoothing his face as he strolled down Lavender Hill. His breath condensed in the frigid air, so that he constantly passed through his own wispy white clouds.

Lit from behind, Asda had taken on the domineering appearance of an out-of-town superstore. As Allan approached it, he felt intimidated by its sheer size. Passing through the automatic doors at the entrance and catching a whiff of the hotdog stand dropped him firmly back into familiar territory and his previous state of well-being returned.

It had been so long since he was last there and he was pleasantly surprised to see that little had changed. As was always the case at this early time, Allan was given free rein of the supermarket without having to negotiate his way past crowds of shoppers. He set about his usual routine, slipping back into the mould as though the previous two days had never taken place.

He gathered together the various articles he required – milk, potatoes, vegetables and a salmon fillet – and made his way to the checkout, where he was immediately faced with a dilemma. He could see Becky at till number six looking more beautiful than ever now that he had sampled some of her delights. He didn't want to face her. Not yet. Not after the way he had treated her that night.

And in all probability, she wouldn't want to talk to *him* either. But Becky was as much a part of his daily routine as the supermarket itself. To block her out would be to break a habit and would require him to make a conscious choice about which queue to join whenever the time came to pay.

Allan swallowed his pride and took his place in the queue. Upon catching his eye as she served the customer in front, Becky gave Allan a nervous smile. She also felt slightly embarrassed about what had happened.

'Hey there, you,' she said, deciding that an informal greeting was the most appropriate kind given the circumstances.

'I wasn't avoiding you,' Allan blurted out. 'I've not been feeling too well lately.'

'That's ok. I think there's something going around.'

Becky was being surprisingly nice to him. He wondered why.

'What's on the menu today? It's a Tuesday, so it must be fish, right?'

Allan allowed himself a wry smile at Becky's recognition of his predictable routine.

'For me, yes. But today I'm entertaining a guest, so I'm making something special.'

'Oh really? What are you making?' There was a hint of jealousy in her voice.

'Pigeon.'

'Really? Where did you get *that* from? They don't sell it here, do they?'

'I found it,' grinned Allan, wearing the look of a schoolboy who had dug up a handful of worms.

A look of shocked revulsion crept across Becky's face, but she held on to her professionalism and nerve just long enough to continue the conversation.

'Surely not. They're like rats with wings, those things. You couldn't…'

'The very same,' Allan butted in proudly. 'I think he'll like it. He'll eat anything!'

'Remind me never to come to yours for dinner!' Becky quipped, albeit with a large degree of seriousness.

They both laughed as Allan handed over the money.

'See you soon, Becky.'

'Yeah, enjoy your dinner!'

He gathered up his bags and left the supermarket. His spirits were high and he felt more in love with Becky than ever before.

* * *

Joseph had heard the front door slam as Allan left the house, but he still hadn't dared make a sound. From his position next to the wall he could no longer look out over the street and had no way of telling whether Allan had left the building or not. On previous occasions, he had waited until Allan was far enough up the road – out of sight and earshot – before he started shouting for help. Now he couldn't see the road any more. For all he knew, Allan could have opened and shut the door without actually leaving the house, then tiptoed back to the lounge and lain in wait for Joseph to call for aid. At this point, he would almost certainly reappear with great excitement to punish him in the worst ways imaginable. This had also meant that he couldn't talk to Angela. He couldn't offer her any words of solace at the time when she needed them most.

So when the door had slammed a second time and Allan could be heard re-entering the house carrying plastic bags, Joseph cursed himself for letting a precious opportunity slip by, knowing they were few and far between. Deep down he knew that he couldn't have afforded to take the risk, not when he had witnessed the potential consequences of getting it wrong.

Joseph listened fixatedly as Allan cleaned the house, curious as to how it was possible that a man verging on being a recluse could generate enough mess to have to vacuum and mop on a daily basis. He speculated as to what Allan *did*, if anything, as he didn't appear to have any real sort of existence beyond those four walls. Joseph came to the conclusion that, somewhere along the line, this sick charade was being funded by Allan's rich and unknowing parents.

Lunchtime passed and Joseph listened to the news being read out on the television. He heard stories of the hardships taking place in the outside world; a world he no longer felt part of. The weather forecast promised more of the same for the next couple of days – cold, dry and bright – after which, a warm front would sweep across London, bringing with it a brief spell of wet weather. Not that it made too much difference to Joseph.

And then there was quiet as the television was switched off and Allan returned to the kitchen to wash up. Joseph knew what would happen next: the same thing that happened every day, apart from the last two days, when Allan had hardly left his room. Allan would come and clean upstairs, wiping and dusting everywhere apart from the room Joseph was in and the adjoining room, which was Angela's cell. He was like a machine. It came as a considerable shock when Allan entered Joseph's room at a time when he would usually be scrubbing the toilet.

In line with other days, Allan looked surprised to see him sitting there tied up. He stood in the doorway and stared at his prisoner with a glazed expression on his face, lips pursed in contemplation and eyes blinking heavily under the strain. Joseph observed a man deteriorating with every day that passed. Gone was the faultless efficiency. In its place, a vulnerability was beginning to show through.

'How long have *you* been here?' sighed Allan.

It was a straightforward question, but one to which Joseph didn't really know the answer. For all the time he had to think, he couldn't contemplate the duration of his imprisonment. He knew that it couldn't have been more than a week, but it felt like months.

'Five days or so?' he replied, his answer lacking any sort of conviction.

'You look starving. Are you hungry?'

'Yes,' Joseph found himself saying, 'I am quite hungry.'

'Ok,' Allan mumbled dreamily before heading back downstairs.

When he returned about half an hour later, he was carrying a full plate of food, all cut up into small pieces as if it had been prepared for a young child. As before, broccoli, carrots and potatoes covered the majority of the plate, except on this occasion there was meat of some description, unrecognisable in its butchered state.

Again, the plate was placed on Joseph's lap and his right arm was freed. Joseph noticed he had been given a spoon rather than a fork this time, partially removing the predicament of whether he should use the opportunity as a chance to stage a violent escape. He hesitantly took a spoonful of food, scooping up the whole spectrum of morsels on offer, and put it in his mouth. It tasted good, in a traditional kind of way. Having eaten more than half of the meal, Joseph still hadn't identified the origin of the meat, although it tasted a bit like pork.

'What is this?' he asked.

On hearing Allan's response, he wished he hadn't.

'I thought you'd never ask! Noticed any pigeons flying around lately?'

Joseph froze as Allan exploded into hoots of laughter. There had been something missing all day, something different, and now it had become clear what it was. The windowsill was empty, free from the three feathered musketeers that had made his life a misery over the past few days with their irksome strutting and insatiable cooing.

'Don't worry,' Allan spluttered through his guffaws, 'the meat is as fresh as it comes. I've got a whole load more of it in the freezer.'

Joseph retched, the food shooting back up his windpipe like porridge. If he hadn't been so famished it would almost certainly have ended up down the front of his jumper. He could feel it, thick and lumpy at the back of his throat, and he began to sweat profusely, overcome by queasiness. Joseph couldn't think of any other animal he would have preferred not

107

to eat; perhaps with the exception of the rats that infested the tracks of the London underground. Those pigeons were filthy, deformed even, and he hated to think what diseases and parasites they were carrying. He closed his eyes, unable to eat another strand of the repulsive meat.

Allan found his reaction a source of prolonged hilarity and tears of laughter were streaming down his face as he tied Joseph's limp arm back up. Thankfully, his good humour meant that he didn't insist on Joseph finishing every last bit.

He left his captive to sit alone and think about what he had just eaten, returning to his chores with a spring in his step.

* * *

Allan sat patiently in the lounge waiting for his pizza to arrive. He wasn't generally a great lover of junk food, believing it to be unhealthy and overpriced, but he was partial to takeout pizza from time to time and he felt he deserved it after the day's exploits.

While he hadn't even begun to think about any of the important tasks still waiting to be done, he had returned the house to its prim and proper state, which should, he felt, free up some time the next day for the big stuff. Despite all their natural goodness, the truth was he was sick to death of boiled vegetables.

* * *

The sound of the doorbell forced itself into Joseph's thoughts, destroying his visions of a better place. He had been trying to exercise a form of extreme concentration to draw his mind away from what was being digested in his stomach and consequently absorbed into his body. He was so preoccupied that he didn't recognise the sound at first. It could have been anything. It was shrill enough to be a bell on a clock and loud enough to be a fire alarm. It was the humanised rhythm of the ring that eventually convinced him a visitor had arrived at the house.

This was a unique occurrence. Joseph knew that Allan had entertained a female visitor the previous Saturday night, but she had been brought into the house *by* Allan. At the time, he had been desperate to call out to her for help, but what could the girl have done? Allan would have easily overpowered her and she would have ended up as another prisoner, if not dead. With Allan walking a psychological tightrope, which threatened to topple him into the depths of complete insanity at any time, the situation was too finely balanced to be taking uncalculated risks. It had been better to sit it out and wait for a better opportunity to emerge.

Like this one.

This latest visitor was *outside* the house, capable of evading capture and rushing off to raise the alarm. But how long would it take for help to come? No matter how efficient the reaction time of the police, it would leave Allan more than enough leeway to bring about his desired conclusion. And who knew what he would do if he were panicked into making a rash decision.

Joseph heard the sound of the front door opening and strained his ears to listen to the ensuing conversation. A closed door and a lot of empty space between them smothered the words, but Joseph could decipher just enough to ascertain that the caller was a pizza delivery boy.

His heart sank. The identity of the stranger made any potential attempts to attract his attention a lost cause. The man would undoubtedly have been victim to many pranks during his house visits and any screams of anguish from deep within the house would have been taken in jest. No alarms would have been raised; only smiles.

Joseph lent his head back against the wall. His Adam's apple jutted out and rested on the leather strap around his neck. He puffed out his cheeks in defeat.

There was no way out.

* * *

109

Wednesday morning saw Allan make a full recovery, so much so that he was on his way to Asda once again to make amends with Becky and, more importantly, to ask if she would give him a second chance.

Upon waking, he had lain in bed for ten minutes to see whether the headache or sore throat would show their faces, but they remained absent and it looked like things would stay that way. When he went to the bathroom, Allan blew his nose as hard as he could without causing internal haemorrhaging, but nothing came up aside from a slight wetness. Before getting in the shower, he performed stretches to test the strength and suppleness of his muscles and was delighted to find that he had made a return to full fitness.

So, walking along the road, Allan felt one hundred percent well. In fact, he felt better than one hundred percent, boosted by that post-recovery feeling when the body has fought so hard to push itself back to healthiness that it temporarily surpasses the level of health it was at prior to the illness, provoking a natural high.

It was a windy day and the breeze battered him from the front, slowing his progress. It gusted up under his coat and tried to rip it off his shoulders, so that he had to hug it against his body to avoid losing it altogether.

Allan had taken to using a slightly longer path into the supermarket, the detour coming towards the end of his route to avoid the assembly of tramps.

While meticulously combing each aisle of the supermarket, Allan agonised over his best approach with Becky. The only thing he could be sure of was that it wouldn't be easy. From his limited knowledge of women, he guessed it would be best to start with an apology, quickly followed by an excuse.

He ran over in his head what he was going to say as he selected the freshest-looking chicken thighs from the refrigerator and carried on silently practising as he filled his basket with the day's vegetables. Before he knew it, he had reached the final corner of the supermarket, having browsed every last inch of shelf space. He could put it off no longer. It was time to pay.

For once, Becky's till was free of people and Allan was able to unload his things immediately on arrival, throwing him straight into the firing line without another moment's preparation. Becky offered him a friendly smile and he returned it.

'Hi, Becky. Listen, I'm really, really sorry about the other night. I really hope you can forgive me.'

That was the apology out of the way, and now for the excuse.

'You see, the thing is, Becky, I wasn't feeling myself on Saturday. Maybe it was the flu or something. I'm not usually like that.'

'That's ok, Allan. I think we should just put Saturday night behind us,' Becky said comfortingly.

She scanned the barcode of the milk with her right hand and sent the carton sliding down the ramp with her left.

'I couldn't agree more! Still, let me make it up to you. How about I take you for a drink tonight?'

'Thanks, but I already have plans for tonight, I'm afraid,' she replied as she punched the code for carrots into the machine.

'Tomorrow?' he added hopefully.

Becky lowered her gaze and halted her duties, the bag of carrots resting on the scales between her hands.

'Allan, when I said we should put Saturday night behind us... I meant *really* behind us.'

'Oh,' said Allan dejectedly.

'I'm sorry,' she added.

Allan didn't hear her, his head having shrunk down into his body. No further words were uttered as he paid for the shopping and gathered up his bags. He smiled at her longingly and moped off in a daze, as if he had been diagnosed with a terminal illness.

Becky watched him leave, noticing how his feet shuffled across the floor as though his shoes didn't fit him properly. When he had finally disappeared through the automatic doors, she breathed a deep sigh that was a mixture of sadness and relief.

Allan needed a drink. It was too early for any of the pubs to be open and he had to settle for a caffeine fix. Unaware of the blossoming modern-day coffee culture, Allan found himself spoilt for choice when it came to choosing a café. After peering nervously through a number of windows, he settled for a commercialised chain store in the station, on account that it was the least intimate and intimidating.

To avoid having to translate the overwhelming menu, Allan ordered a tall black coffee and took the cardboard beaker over to one of the lofty stools by the window that looked out over the shopping area within the station. He felt a great feeling of calm wash over him as he watched the people stream past in their hundreds as they went about their daily business. The coffee was strong and bitter in his mouth, but the caffeine gave him a temporary lift and perked up his waning mood.

Allan watched as a glove fell from a woman's pocket and lay discarded on the floor. The woman carried on walking, oblivious to her loss. He continued to watch as each subsequent person proceeded to tread on the glove, too busy to notice it until it was too late, at which point they would glance back to see what they had stepped on before turning away nonchalantly when they realised what it was. He stared intently as the material became more and more soiled, every clumsy shoe adding an extra layer of dirt; the delicate beige fabric blackening until it was barely recognisable. The glove's fate was sealed. It would be swept up by the cleaner at any moment and disposed of in the bin, as would its more pristine companion at a later time, rendered odd and therefore superfluous.

But then the woman returned, scanning frantically for her lost accessory. When she found its filthy, crumpled form, there was a moment's hesitation when it looked as though she might have cut her losses and left it there. Yet she bent down and plucked it off the ground with her fingertips and slipped it back into her pocket, rescuing it from a lonesome end on the scrapheap. Allan watched the scene play out and wished somebody, or more specifically Becky, would come and lift him out of the gutter in the same way.

Maybe there was hope for everyone.

Not him. Not while he was just sitting there.

Allan knew that if he wanted Becky back he would have to be proactive. No amount of speculating and staring into his coffee cup could bring her any closer to him, and he turned to himself as the source of the problem.

His mother had always told him he was a good-looking lad, but what mother didn't say such things to her son? Yet, when faced with his reflection in the mirror, he was generally pleased with the person looking back. His nose was a little larger than he might have wished, but it was by no means a disfigurement. Besides, Becky had agreed to go out with him in the first place, so she must have liked the way he looked. Allan mused over what might have been different about him compared with when he had taken her out on Saturday. While he *had* been ill and was admittedly not looking his best, it was unlikely that he had deteriorated physically to such an extent that she could no longer consider touching him.

Allan tapped the side of his cup as he pondered the other possibilities, but, underestimating its lightness, he knocked it over. The contents splashed across his top, the droplets of black liquid clinging precariously to the wispy strands. It was during the process of dabbing the drab woollen knitwear with a paper napkin that he stumbled across the cause of his plight. On Saturday night he had been wearing the best clothes he could lay his hands on. While they hadn't been the most fashionable of garments by modern standards, they were a step up from the bland, unimaginative attire he was wearing that day. Thinking back to how long it had taken him to select the clothes on Saturday and how he would be unable to wear the same ones again for a second date, it dawned on him that he would have to invest in a new outfit. Allan cursed aloud as he consigned himself to a morning spent clothes shopping, the sudden four-letter outburst turning a few heads. When he declined to add to the impromptu rant, his fellow customers quickly turned back to their grande lattes and slices of carrot cake.

Allan got up and left, agitatedly gathering together his belongings. He hated shopping for clothes and would generally go to any lengths to avoid it. He didn't go clothes shopping, he went to buy things, and there was a big difference. Clothes shopping implied ambling around at a snail's pace, considering the merits of each individual item in turn: the fit, the stitching, the feel of the fabric. Going to buy things was far more efficient, the required item decided far in advance so that no browsing was necessary. There was just a matter of locating it and choosing the correct size. This trip would fall into the former category and he was already dreading it.

There was a boutique-style men's clothes shop on the main road, close to the station entrance. He stood outside and admired the athletic-looking mannequins gazing thoughtfully into the distance with hands on hips and chests puffed out. He dared not enter the pine-floored interior as he could see the shop assistants lurking around, ready to pounce as soon as he set foot in there. A man of Mediterranean descent left the shop carrying two large bags, each emblazoned with the shop's logo, and as he did so he released a blast of mind-blowing techno music that faded away as the door swung shut again. Allan took this as his cue to move on elsewhere.

His next stop was the area's main department store, the stately architecture of which marked the junction of St John's Road and Lavender Hill. This was never the easiest of roads to negotiate, and Allan had to wait for a sequence of three traffic-light changes before he was able to cross over to the multi-door entrance.

It occurred to Allan that he had never set foot in the place before and he immediately sought directions from one of the members of staff, of whom there was an abundance, all milling around trying to look as if they had something important to do.

The men's section was comfortingly compact and the absence of immaculately dressed youngsters with gelled hair and earrings made him feel less self-conscious than he had feared he might have been. He saw a mannequin dressed in an outfit that met with his approval and wasted no time in finding the items of clothing on the surrounding racks and shelves. A brief trip to the fitting room later and Allan was purchasing the clothes at the counter, where an elderly man complimented him on his selections.

Allan left the shop with renewed confidence and made one final stop at the flower stall outside the train station to pick out a bouquet for Becky. He didn't want anything too extravagant, opting for mostly pinks and whites. Embarrassed to be seen carrying such a feminine package and eager not to waste another minute of the day, Allan hurried back home.

* * *

'Angela refused to eat hers, so you get a double helping,' said Allan as he presented Joseph with a mountain of food.

Joseph didn't know whether this was a good or a bad thing, so he simply thanked Allan and started to eat. It was pigeon, the same as the day before. Having suffered no physical ill effects from the previous helping, Joseph was able to force the first couple of pieces past his lips. However, the psychological damage was harder to overcome and the very knowledge of what he was eating sent his stomach somersaulting in a bid to reject what he was trying to pass through. He picked around it as best he could, but the food was all mixed together and the meaty taste had contaminated the vegetables. Every single mouthful shared the same pungent, disgusting flavour.

'Angela doesn't say much these days, you know. Mind you, she was never as chatty as you to begin with,' said Allan in an attempt at mealtime conversation.

Joseph didn't hear the words as all of his efforts were concentrated on the task before him. He came to a halt, unable to eat any more of the filthy meat, and lay the fork to rest on the plate.

'Is that all you're having?' asked Allan.

'Yes, thanks,' replied Joseph.

It was a struggle for him to open his mouth without his insides gushing out.

'Go on, just a couple more mouthfuls,' insisted Allan as he scooped some meat up onto the fork and held it in front of Joseph's mouth, as if he were feeding a baby.

'Please,' implored Joseph. 'I really couldn't eat another mouthful.'

The smell of the meat made him feel dizzy as it wafted up his nostrils.

'Just *one* more then. Open wide.'

Allan pressed the fork between Joseph's lips and pushed it forward so that Joseph was forced to open his mouth or be stabbed in the teeth. His mind was flooded with images of tatty, grey feathers, lumpy legs like dripping candles, and flesh grown on a diet of garbage and rainwater. He swallowed without chewing and almost choked as the solid cube of meat made its way slowly and achingly down his throat.

'That wasn't so bad, was it?' asked Allan rhetorically.

But it was, and Joseph was left fighting to stop himself throwing up. He knew what a painful experience it would be. The body's natural reaction would be to double over with each convulsion, each retch, and the strap around his neck would choke him along with the vomit.

The relief was indescribable when Allan took the dish away and went to leave the room, but then he turned back and stood before Joseph once more.

'One more thing,' he started.

Joseph's resolve was crushed at what might be to come.

'How do I look?' Allan continued.

'What?' questioned Joseph, baffled by the new line of questioning.

'How do I look?' asked Allan again.

Joseph had been so distracted by the plight of trying to eat a plate of putrid pigeon he had failed to notice Allan's somewhat smarter apparel. Gone were the slacks and conservative cardigans. In their place were smarter, shinier trousers and a black, zip-necked jumper. They fitted better and Allan looked about fifteen years younger as a result; more like his actual age, which Joseph had guessed to be late thirties.

'You look good,' Joseph answered him truthfully.

'Thank you,' said Allan as he gleefully left the room.

* * *

'I'm sorry, she's not here,' said the woman impatiently.

Small, round and devoid of charm, she was a barrel on legs.

'But I need to give her these,' pleaded Allan, gesturing with the flowers.

'Well, that's unfortunate because she isn't here, as I just told you,' she snapped curtly, returning to studying a list of names on her clipboard.

'It's very important,' Allan started, but the woman stopped him dead with an impetuous stare.

'Now listen, young man. I have clearly explained to you that she isn't here. Her shift ended more than an hour ago. If you like, I can take the flowers and make sure Rebecca gets them first thing tomorrow morning, but that, I'm afraid, is the best I can do.'

'No, I'd rather give them to her in person.' Allan was undeterred. 'Does she work late any days?'

'Only Thursdays, until seven. Now, if you don't mind, I really don't have time to stand here and discuss the ins and outs of Rebecca's timetable with you.'

The woman picked up the phone with her sausage fingers and dialled what was probably a random number. She might as well have lifted her palm and held it up to Allan's face.

'Thank you for your help,' muttered Allan, but the woman wasn't listening. Or if she was, she was doing a good job of pretending that she wasn't.

* * *

That night, he could hold it in no longer and Joseph crapped himself. It didn't provide the same relief as when he had pissed himself a few days earlier.

* * *

117

When Allan's eyes opened on Thursday morning he was more eager to get up and kickstart the day than he had been for a long, long time. What made the day different from any other was that, in Becky, he had something to look forward to; a reason to exist other than the cleaning of the house and the looming commencement of all the really important tasks that had evaded him thus far and were becoming increasingly urgent with every day that passed.

He had a good feeling about this day, a *really* good feeling, and he bounded out of bed with such vitality the covers were sent sailing to the floor. Yet again, he had slept in his clothes. For once, he didn't mind. He decided to keep them on and go straight to the supermarket. It was only the fact it was just seven o'clock in the morning that forced him to stick to the usual routine.

His full appetite had returned and all two-and-a-half Weetabix slid effortlessly down his throat like a frictionless gunge. Before he knew it, Allan was ready to leave the house, ahead of schedule. A spare fifteen minutes was an unprecedented luxury and, determined to use it wisely, Allan zoomed around with the vacuum cleaner. On this occasion, he succeeded in doing a job he was sufficiently satisfied with not to have to do a second lap. Allan giggled excitedly as the chore was struck off his mental list. He skipped out the door and down the garden path, momentarily flummoxed by the sight of a plank of wood lying in the flowerbed. But it was unimportant. It had most likely been left there by the local kids, and seeing as he spent so little time in the front garden, he decided to leave it there until another day.

Faced with the distinct likelihood that he would finally have time to make a start on the specific chores that had been piling up like an errand mountain, Allan made a start on prioritising them. It took him eleven minutes to come up with a sensible order, by which time he was well on the way to Asda. The most crucial job was fairly easy to identify: getting rid of the smell in Angela's room that had been troubling him for the last couple of weeks.

Unsure as to the source, and almost reluctant to find out, he was confronted with the repellent, malodorous whiff every time he entered the room. It smelt like a cat had got stuck under the floorboards and was beginning to rot, and it was only a matter of time before the stench broke out from the confines of the room and engulfed the entire house like a noxious stink bomb. Maybe it already had and he had just grown used to it.

The ritualistic combing of the supermarket was one thing Allan would not compromise on and he spent his full quota of time diligently trawling the aisles, predictably ending up buying no more than he had originally come in for. Once this was completed, he wasted no time in tracking down Becky's checkout, patiently taking his place in the queue.

Thankfully, the frumpy fat woman and her judgmental attitude were nowhere to be seen and Allan was glad he hadn't let her take the flowers. The flowers! The surrender of the basket at the till had left him with two free hands and Allan realised that, in his haste to get there, he had neglected to pick up the flowers from the lounge on his way out. It was too late to go back now. Becky had already seen him standing there and might think he was running away from her.

Allan reprimanded himself for his short-sightedness. Flowers were not a usual item to take to the supermarket and he should have left them in a more obvious place. The one saving grace was that he *was* wearing his new outfit, and that, at least, ought to carry some weight.

'Oh, hello again.' Becky feigned surprised, even though she had seen him coming and had been expecting his visit all morning.

'Hi, Becky,' Allan greeted her in return.

He watched her yearningly as he loaded the items into plastic bags, adopting a posture that drew attention to his new clothes. Becky didn't seem to notice and deliberately spent more time focusing on the items that passed through her hands than she usually did as a way of avoiding eye contact.

'That's two pounds seventy-two, please,' said Becky when the last of the items had been scanned.

Allan sensed the coldness. The spark had gone. It was like they were strangers again. He handed over a five-pound note and simultaneously made a move to rectify the awkward situation.

'I know you're busy at the moment, so how about a drink tomorrow evening?' he asked humbly.

Far from appearing pleased by the invitation, Becky looked exasperatingly at him.

'Allan, please. You can't keep doing this.'

'No strings attached, just a friendly drink to say sorry.' He shrugged his shoulders and held up his hands while gazing at her with puppy-dog eyes.

'Allan, I'm sorry. I don't want to go for another drink with you. I thought I'd made that clear yesterday.'

Allan didn't answer as she handed him his change. He nodded to show that he understood and hurriedly left. This was a disaster way beyond anything he had anticipated. Not only had Becky turned him down, new outfit and all, but he had also managed to alienate himself from her in the process. Trips to the supermarket without some friendly conversation with the girl of his dreams just wouldn't be the same. He had to put things right somehow; to get things back to the way they were.

Accepting the fact there was no way she would agree to any further dates with him, Allan adjusted his aim to the reconstruction of their friendship. The flowers ought to help. All women adored receiving flowers and they would work equally well as an apologetic gift as they would have done a romantic gesture.

Allan rushed home to get the bouquet and returned to the supermarket. This was his fourth trip in two days and the second that had nothing to do with shopping. It took a conscious effort for him not to grab a basket and make his way to the farthest aisle, instead heading straight back to till thirteen, where Becky looked anything but pleased to see him, especially when she noticed that he was free of shopping and his motives became clear.

Allan didn't beat around the bush. He thrust the flowers towards her with an apologetic smile etched across his lips and a childlike terror shimmering in his eyes.

'Please don't do what I think you're about to do.'

'I-I got you these,' Allan stammered, pushing the bunch of flowers closer towards her.

'Allan, I don't want your flowers.' Becky's voice was quiet and low to avoid attracting attention, and it contained a sternness Allan hadn't heard before.

'They're just to say sorry. I don't want anything in return.'

'I think you should go, Allan.'

Her arms remained passively at her side as she spoke.

'Please, Becky, just take them. It would make me feel a whole lot better,' he pleaded.

'I'd really rather not.'

His hand tightened around the stems, the paper crumpling audibly beneath his fingers.

'I just want things to be back the way they were, that's all. Please take them.'

'Just go, Allan,' Becky persisted.

'Take them!'

He didn't raise the level of his voice, but he spat the words at her angrily and she flinched uncomfortably in her chair, raising her hands defensively.

'Look, Allan, either you leave right now or I'm calling security,' Becky ordered once she had regained composure.

By her tone and expression, he knew that she meant it. Allan scampered out of the supermarket and didn't stop running until he finally came to his senses some minutes later outside the local Woolworths.

Allan needed time to clear his head and, since he was heading in that direction anyway, he continued up the high street, carrying straight on over the crossroads and onto Northcote Road. It hadn't yet reached eleven o'clock and none of the bars, pubs and restaurants had opened, so the area resembled something of a ghost town. A handful of people could be seen milling about, sitting in darkened cafés or making their way back from the supermarket, but they were few and far between.

There had been a half-hearted attempt to erect a market, but the wares on offer – high-quality sweets, plants, continental breads and delicatessen-type meats – were the kind of specialist items people invariably chose to do without when the weather was as cold and dreary as it was. The stall owners showed dogged persistence, yet they appeared hunched and dejected.

Side streets criss-crossed the main road like stitching. Avenues lined with grand, multi-floored, bay-windowed Victorian houses provided exquisite locations for those who could afford it. The further up Northcote Road Allan strolled, the more residential it became, and eventually there was little more than the occasional pub or launderette and he was pleased to reach its end. At this point, he took a left down Broomwood Road and continued along this path until he reached Clapham Common West Side.

The wind hammered against him as he stood at the edge of the expanse of green and he felt tiny and insignificant at the sight of the acres of open turf. Overgrown, dirty and devoid of landmarks, this section of the common was not the most inviting of parks and Allan was unsure whether to walk through its centre or to pass around the edge. He chose to tackle it head-on and crossed over the busy road that acted as a hard, concrete perimeter. His only companions were joggers and dog-walkers, all silent like himself. He didn't take in much scenery as he trudged through the park, eyes focused on the path ahead, the traffic noise slowly dimming and lifting again as he reached the far side.

Upon exiting the park, he found himself within striking distance of Clapham Common underground station, thus stumbling across a part of Clapham he had never visited before. It was busier here, packed full of pedestrians all thickly wrapped from head to toe in protection against the elements; a swarm of zigzagging trench coats, browns, blacks and greys. Multicoloured scarves poked out from above the upturned collars, eyes peered out from beneath hoods and beanies, and mittened hands were plunged deep into pockets.

Allan meandered aimlessly around the streets for some time until he got bored of the scenery and decided to head back. His stomach growled at him, reminding him it was lunchtime in his old world, so he made a brief stop at Sainsbury's to pick up a sandwich, which he munched on as he made his way back towards Clapham Junction. For the sake of variety, he went around the common rather than through it, a longer route since it was equivalent to walking two sides of a triangle. Gigantic buildings, mainly blocks of converted flats, looked down on him as he walked, slow and stooped, lacking purpose and enthusiasm, the bouquet pinned to his chest by the oncoming wind.

Allan returned to Northcote Road, the subdued atmosphere of which was comforting and reflected his mood. Walking its length, he noted how everything had come to life. Blackened windows revealed glimpses of what lay within: moodily lit bars and empty restaurants, with staff standing around, impatient for something to do.

He checked his watch. 14:54. He had been walking around for hours without realising it, drifting aimlessly like a zombie, thinking about nothing but his next step; an empty vessel. And now his throat was parched, dried by the coffee, the sandwich, the wind and his own anxiety. His mind felt wilted, numbed by the morning's harsh rejection and further deadened by the emptiness of his senseless expedition. He needed a lift and the bars were there for him, enticing him in, welcoming him with open arms. Smiling faces stood behind the counters. 'Come on in,' they chirped, 'sit anywhere you like. We're here to help you!'

Allan pushed open the door of a spacious-looking bar with a strange name that sounded foreign, but that he suspected was probably made up. He entered, breathing in the warmth of the surroundings. The sweat came instantly and he frantically removed his coat and untucked his T-shirt to allow the air to circulate. He approached the bar and ordered a pint of lager.

The girl serving him was pretty and petite, with flowing blonde hair and huge, sparkling eyes, like a Japanese cartoon character. While she had nothing on Becky, Allan liked the posture she adopted as she pulled the pump, her back slightly arched, stomach tucked in, hips teasingly angled to one side and breasts thrust towards him like forbidden fruit. As the liquid flowed into the glass, she glanced up at him with those wonderful eyes to emphasise the fact that she was pouring it especially for *him*. It was a well-practised, contrived routine but Allan immediately succumbed to her charms. By the time the froth had dribbled over the rim, his head was already rammed full of carnal thoughts.

'That's two pounds and eighty pence, please,' she pouted.

Allan handed her a five-pound note.

It was an expensive pint, albeit worth every penny just to watch her pour it, so when she pushed his change towards him on a silver dish he pocketed the two pound coin and left the twenty pence piece for her.

'Thank you,' she said, smiling seductively. She had instantly recognised the telltale signs that this man had taken the bait and would be in for the long haul to unfailingly supplement her hourly wage.

Allan took a newspaper from the rack and took it over to one of the tables. He laid down his belongings on the chair next to him and sat down facing the bar so he could watch the barmaid performing her duties. He was eager to see whether all of the customers received such a flirtatious service or whether he had been a privileged recipient.

He had no interest in reading the paper. Its purpose was nothing more than a convenient prop, allowing him to sit quietly and think without appearing odd. Allan took a large gulp of beer and its chilled fizziness was indescribably refreshing, the coldness taking away much of the bitter taste he sometimes found off-putting. He took another lug, then another and another. Within two minutes of sitting down, he had already levelled half the pint and, glancing at his watch once more, Allan resolved to pace himself.

There were only two other customers in the bar: a young man and an older woman; mother and son, judging by their similar features. They lounged together on one of the sofas that formed the centrepiece of the bar's large floor area, and they sat in such a way that would deter other people from taking up the surrounding seats.

The floor of the bar was dark, polished wood and the decor was tastefully minimalist, adopting a considered use of metal, lighter wood and pools of colour to create a modernistic, stylish look. A brown, airbrushed mural depicting an open-air Parisian café and a waitress inexplicably flaunting her ample chest covered one of the walls, while the wall nearest Allan wore padded, fake leather and played home to a widescreen television that continuously bore the image of a blazing fire.

At the front of the bar was a row of French windows that were presumably folded back in the summer months to create an outdoor atmosphere like the one painted inside. If only the barmaid would be as shamelessly exhibitionist as the waitress in the picture, Allan would have made sure he worked a trip to the bar into his daily routine. Usually, he would have felt out of place in such an establishment, but his new clothes would allow him to blend into the crowd if one were ever to build up.

As he sipped his pint, Allan convinced himself that his best option was to confront Becky as she left work at seven o'clock and give her the flowers then. That way she would be free from the restrictions of professionalism and out from under the watchful eye of her superiors and customers. On neutral ground, the gesture would be gratefully accepted and he would be able to visit the supermarket the next morning and get the same enjoyment from it as he had done before that fateful night. Everything would be all right after all.

'Can I get you another?' asked the barmaid, the shock of her question instantly wiping the self-satisfied smile from Allan's face.

'Oh, yes. Same again, please.'

She took away the empty glass and gave the table a wipe. Allan caught an eyeful of flesh as she bent down and her chest threatened to spill out of her black, satin blouse, which was buttoned precariously low.

'Are those for me?' she asked sweetly as she returned with his drink.

Allan would have loved to have said yes, and possibly would have done if they had been bought for anyone other than Becky.

'I'm afraid not,' he replied, feeling his cheeks turn red and hoping the light was dim enough to hide it.

'That's a shame. Maybe next time, hey?'

She laughed and collected the money.

'Keep the change.'

'Thanks. You're too kind.'

Allan smiled and stared at her buttocks as she walked back to the bar, mesmerised by the way they quivered beneath the tight black material of her trousers.

The more he drank, the more attractive she became, and halfway through his fifth pint he was beginning to think he had done her an injustice by his initially unfavourable comparison with Becky. While Becky was taller and slightly slimmer, with a beauty born out of soft, innocent features, this new girl was pure sex. As well as possessing exaggerated features in all sex-related areas – mainly lips, breasts and bottom – she oozed it in everything she did: the way she walked, the way she held things, the constant pouting and posturing.

Allan's love for Becky was temporarily replaced with a lust for the barmaid, the power of which was no less intense. But the bar had begun to fill and Allan found himself losing her behind clusters of less attractive bodies. He grew increasingly frustrated at his obstructed vantage point. He knew the personal table service he had received over the past few hours would cease and he would have to order any further drinks at the bar like everyone else. He checked his watch and saw that it was ten minutes to seven, almost the end of Becky's shift. Despite having half a pint remaining, Allan left his drink, grabbed his things and dashed out onto the street.

It had been a number of years since he had last consumed such a quantity of alcohol and, combined with the early start, he found himself in a semi-drunken stupor. Night had fallen and the wind had sharpened itself into an icy lance, yet he no longer felt the cold. The light from the street lamps looked stretched and refracted, as if he were looking through a pinhole camera. Everything swam past too quickly for him to react.

Allan hurried towards Asda as quickly as he could without jeopardising his own safety, his footsteps clumsy and erratic as he lumbered down the street. Women moved aside for him as he came steaming towards them down the pavement, while men gave him aggressive, disapproving looks. It was only a short journey, but he had to lean against a lamppost at the zebra crossing as he panted and gasped for breath. He no longer knew what to say to Becky when he got there; only that he wanted to her to take the flowers more than anything else in the world. It was as if his future depended on it.

Asda was a hive of activity, teeming with people who had come straight from work to buy dinner or to do their weekly shop. Allan loitered on one of the benches outside the main exit, breathing deeply to calm himself down. He wished he had some chewing gum or anything strong-smelling to block out the reek of alcohol that must have been pouring from his mouth. He felt like a tramp, sitting there intoxicated on a cold iron bench, and he secretly vowed never to do it again.

And then there she was, more angelic and radiant than ever, trussed up in a thick parker jacket and lighting up a cigarette. But she was with someone else, another man. No, he was merely a youth, the lazy cleaner from the other day. There was a big grin on his face, happy to be walking alongside her, knowing she was too good for him. It didn't matter to Allan. This was a minor setback; one he could ignore and overcome. He got up, noticing Becky freeze in her tracks as she saw him. She stopped mid-sentence, the cigarette held redundantly at her side.

'Becky, I just want to say I'm sorry,' he slurred.

'I can't believe you're doing this!' exclaimed Becky, not quite able to believe he had waited outside for her.

'Please, just accept them and I'll leave.' He pushed the flowers towards her.

'No!' she shouted, batting them away. 'Are you drunk? For fuck's sake! You are, aren't you? What's wrong with you? Leave me alone!'

People had stopped to see what all the shouting was about and were watching from a safe distance.

'Is this the guy, Bex?' asked the cleaner.

Becky nodded.

The youth approached Allan and snatched the flowers from his hand.

'Give them back!' yelled Allan, reaching out like a baby who has lost his rattle. 'They're for Becky!'

The youth lifted a finger and pointed it at Allan's face.

'She doesn't want them. And she doesn't want you. Get the fucking message.'

'Please, Becky,' begged Allan, taking a step towards her.

The cleaner stepped between them, blocking his path.

'Just leave, mate, and don't come back. If I find out you've been hassling her again I'll fuck you up.'

He threw the flowers back at Allan, but they just bounced off his chest and onto the floor. There was a standoff as the youth stared at him. Allan didn't know whether to stare back or look at Becky, who had her head lowered and was openly weeping. Security guards began to gather by the door.

'I love you, Becky,' Allan said softly.

Then he ran off down the stairs and out through the car park exit.

Allan fled far from the scene, heading off down the street, past Boots, past the cut-price supermarket and under the railway bridge that crossed over Falcon Road. He stopped under the bridge to catch his breath, and at that moment a train thundered overhead and the whole world seemed to shake to its core. He covered his ears and cowered against the wall, expecting the bridge to come crashing down around him. But the train rumbled into the distance and he was safe once more.

Then something did fall from above: a feather, spiralling down through the air, rocking back and forth like a pendulum as it glided gracefully to the ground. Allan looked up and there they were, hundreds of them, bustling for space on the shit-covered rafters. An infestation of pigeons, clambering over one another like rats as they tried to get warm on their perch, squabbling and bickering selfishly among themselves. Allan shivered with repulsion and continued on his way, terrified of being bombed from above by the filthy, feathered freaks. He emerged out the other side and made his way around the overflowing recycling bins, finding himself in familiar territory, although he couldn't think of any reason why he would ever have been there.

Then an equally familiar face approached him.

'Excuse me, sir. I'm really sorry to bother you, but I don't suppose you could spare me some change. I'm trying to get to Oxford and I'm only a bit short.'

'What?' asked Allan in disbelief.

He assumed he had seen the last of the rodent-faced beggar, having crossed his palm with silver the other night.

'I'm trying to get to Oxford and I was hoping you might be able to spare me some change?' the man asked humbly.

Allan shook his head, remembering how helping this grubby waif of a man had denied him a taxi ride home and cost him two whole days in bed as a result; two vital days in which time his life had fallen apart and reduced him to a drunken wreck; two precious days in which he could have made a start on all those important tasks left unattended to for so long. Two whole days!

'Don't you remember me?' Allan asked.

The beggar began to back away as he recognised Allan's face and saw the rage pulsating beneath the surface. He smelt the alcohol on his breath and saw the tears in his eyes. Suddenly, it became clear that the situation wasn't safe and that he was in the vicinity of a man teetering on the edge of sanity, hanging on by the frailest of threads, liable to snap and explode at any second.

'It's ok, sir, I'm sorry to bother you,' he whispered.

He turned to run, but Allan was too quick, grabbing him by the coat and throwing him to the ground like a rag doll.

The man cowered helplessly on the tarmac, hands locked tightly over his head, knees brought up to his chest as a shield. He was a frail, feeble being, his limbs warped and shrunken like pipe-cleaners, weakened by drugs and malnourishment. He didn't know how to fight, only how to run, how to hide. It was too late for that.

Allan walked around him and aimed a kick at his exposed back. The attack was clumsy, thuggish, but it did the job. The man writhed in pain on the floor, his spine arched like a cat's, unable to scream as the blow had knocked all of the wind out of him. Allan walked around to the other side and grabbed him by the hair, the strands greasy and matted between his fingertips. He hauled the man up but he couldn't stand, the initial blow so severe that his legs hung limp and useless beneath him, like a puppet.

'Next time I give you money to go to Oxford, why don't you fucking stay there?!' Allan shouted into his face.

The man showed no sign of the words registering, a strand of saliva creeping from his mouth, so Allan slammed him face first into the pavement. His body lay motionless on the floor, knocked unconscious by the impact. Allan rolled him over onto his back using his foot and saw a stranger lying on the floor, unrecognisable due to the carnage. His nose had been obliterated on the pavement, blood gushing from his nostrils over his eyes and forehead, where it mixed with the discharge from the other bone-deep lacerations.

The awful face was so disfigured, so repulsive that Allan couldn't bear to look at it. He wanted to destroy it, so he kicked it with all his might, again and again, each blow accompanied by a sickening, deadened thud. The first kick took all the skin and tissue off one side, while the second snapped the neck so that the cheek was flush against the shoulder. Further kicks shattered bone and cartilage, the sound of splintering skull clear and crisp in the air. By the time he had finished, there was barely a head left at all, just a messy pulp of bone, flesh, blood and brain that was no longer identifiable as human.

* * *

Thinking back to the events of the previous night, Joseph could only wildly speculate as to what the day ahead might entail. The day before, Allan had left the house at his usual time in the morning but hadn't returned until late that evening. On his return, Joseph had heard two loud door slams. The first was the front door, banged shut with such ferocity the tremors could be felt through the whole house. The second was the door to Allan's room, hurled shut with similar force.

In the intervening period, Allan could be heard stomping up the stairs, the footsteps erratic and free of rhythm, suggesting some degree of difficulty on the part of their owner. Additionally, Allan had been making a series of strange whimpering noises that Joseph would have taken to be the sound of him crying had he not known better. And that had been the last he had heard of him until now, some twenty hours or so later.

Joseph squirmed uneasily in the chair. He could feel the shit drying between his buttocks and the sensation of it clinging stickily to the hair and caking his skin was revolting. His nostrils had largely become desensitised to the noxious malodour, but occasionally he would get a fresh whiff of the faeces that made him gag. He longed for a shower; to be able to wash away the blood, sweat and excrement. He hated to think how he must look and smell. Tramps sleeping in the street had better personal hygiene than he did. Even the pigeons were cleaner.

As he dwelt on the humiliation he would experience if he were ever to be rescued, Joseph suddenly became aware of movement somewhere else in the house. At first it was just muffled footsteps made by bare feet, soon drowned out by the scraping sound of someone dragging a hard object over the wooden floorboards. He heard the click of Allan's door opening and the grinding sound grew louder as Allan dragged the object over to the door of his own room.

Joseph held his breath as Allan unlocked the door and pushed it open, terrified as to what new instrument of torture he might be about to introduce. But as he entered the room dragging the thing behind him, Joseph could see that it was a chair. And not a modified chair like the one he himself was tied to, but a normal, wooden, dining room chair. Allan plonked it in the middle of the room and sat down facing Joseph, his hands resting on his knees.

Daylight was rapidly slipping away but, combined with the light flooding in from the hallway, it provided adequate illumination for Joseph to see that Allan's eyes were red and puffy, and that the skin immediately below them was dark, as though he had been up all night crying. His mouth hung slightly open and his cheeks seemed to droop down, as if the skin had lost all elasticity. He was a pale reflection of the man who had kidnapped him last week, breaking down from the inside, the effects starting to show themselves on his face.

Allan stared blankly at him, his lips forming the beginnings of words, but nothing materialised beyond mumblings and grunts, like those of a drunk. And then he remained silent, waiting for Joseph to say something.

Joseph just looked at him disparagingly.

'I've done some terrible things, Joseph,' he blurted out, his head falling into his hands. Allan wept, his body juddering, emitting howls like those of a hound.

Joseph could find no sympathy for the man before him, not after what he had done to him and Angela. He looked upon him with a degree of detachment, similar to the way he might observe an actor at a theatre.

'I-' Allan stuttered.

The rest of it was lost in a shudder. He removed his hands from his face and ran them through his hair.

'I'm sorry, Joseph, for everything.'

The apology, while heartfelt, meant nothing to Joseph. The belated show of remorse after all this time angered him in its absurdity. Tears still streaming down his face, Allan stood and climbed up on the chair, his head only a few inches from the ceiling, his hair almost brushing against the iron ring.

'Allan, don't,' said Joseph as he realised what was happening.

'I wish I could make things right, but I can't. It's too late.'

He began to remove the belt from his trousers and they started to slip down, clinging doggedly to his hips.

'Allan, you mustn't!' yelled Joseph. 'I forgive you! Everything will be all right!'

'It's too late, Joseph,' he wailed, looping the black leather belt through the ring and around his neck.

'Allan! Listen to me! It'll be ok! You can't do this! I'll die if you leave me here on my own!'

It was true. Without Allan to provide him with food and drink, he would perish in that very room, slowly and agonisingly starving to death.

'I'm sorry,' choked Allan as he pulled the belt taught and brought his arms down to his sides.

'Allan, don't! You can't leave us here like this! This is not the way! There are people who can help you!'

'Sorry,' Allan said for the last time.

He kicked the chair out from beneath himself and it clattered to the floor, his body plummeting half a foot before it was jerked back up by the belt.

He let out a panic-stricken yelp as the noose yanked tightly around his windpipe, violently halting his fall.

'Allan!' Joseph screamed, frantically fighting against his restraints.

He couldn't get free. He closed his eyes, not wanting to see Allan suffocating to death, but he had no way of covering his ears. He could make out every gasp, every choke, every scrape of fabric as Allan's limbs thrashed about, becoming more and more asphyxiated.

It took an age for all the life to be strangled out of him, and Joseph dared not open his eyes until he was sure that the lifeless corpse had stopped twitching. When at long last he plucked up the courage, he beheld a harrowing sight. Allan was suspended motionless before him, everything pointed towards the ground as though he had been hung out to dry. His face was dark and bulbous, golf-ball eyes bulging out of their sockets and threatening to pop out altogether. His neck looked stretched like that of an ostrich and was heavily marked with bruising and long lines of scratches from the clawing fingernails. It no longer looked like Allan; just a dead person.

Joseph stared at the body for a long time, waiting to feel any kind of emotion. None came. He felt empty. The initial fright of seeing a dead body had worn off, as had any pity or sadness he could muster. There was a brief spell of relief at the knowledge that his captor and tormentor was dead, but the relief soon turned into a fear of his own solitary abandonment. Even this eventually subsided, his head clearing itself of everything other than a planned method of escape.

His options were limited. Allan's untimely end didn't make it any more likely that he would be able to break free from his bonds. Joseph had spent hours trying to escape, varying between vigorous wrenching and calculated sliding. Neither method had offered him any leeway, only friction burns. He was reliant on the help of others. The present location of his chair was of no use to him, stuck up against an internal wall. He needed to manoeuvre himself over to the window to have any hope of attracting somebody's attention. After some experimentation, he discovered that, by perching on his toes, he was able to rock the chair back onto its hind wheels. His damaged ankle made this excruciatingly painful, yet he had little option other than to grit his teeth and push on through the pain. It reminded him of the willpower required when he went jogging with Iain. Joseph allowed himself a wry smile. It was likely to be a long time before he would be able to run again.

Once up on his toes, he attempted to tiptoe forward a couple of inches. It was already clear that, despite being less than five metres, the journey was to be torturously slow. The urge to scuttle forward in a few short bursts was strong, but Joseph knew he had to be controlled and measured in his progress.

The problem lay in the instability of his seat. While its steadiness wasn't in doubt when resting on all four legs, the moment he rolled onto his toes and the chair tilted back he was walking a tightrope. The slightest sudden movement and he risked leaning too far back. Once the centre of gravity went beyond the balancing point he would have no way of correcting it, the enforced rigidity of his body preventing him from creating any opposing momentum. Then the wheels would shoot out from beneath him and send him crashing to the floor, where he would be stuck forever, prostrate and helpless like an upturned tortoise. So, like a tortoise, he needed to take it slow and steady, creeping forward a little way at a time. He knew there was no particular urgency – whether he scaled the distance in one or two hours would be of little consequence – so he took his time, composing himself by taking deep breaths and allowing his ankles to rest between each attempt.

Two hours later, Joseph had moved only a couple of metres and was already exhausted by the effort. It wasn't so much the physical hardship – his calf muscles were tightening and he frequently had to stretch his toes upwards to avoid getting cramp – but the mental pressure that was slowing his progress. An incredible degree of concentration was required to keep the chair upright. Every time he rocked back the fear of falling gripped him, and there had been a number of occasions where he had almost passed the point of no return. His heart had skipped a beat as he braced himself for the fall.

He had somehow survived up to this point, the act of throwing his weight forward as best he could proving enough to tilt him forward again. Thankfully, he had negotiated his way past Allan's hanging body.

Out of sight, out of mind.

* * *

'Can you get that please, Jake? My hands are covered in flour.'

'Ok. You expecting anyone?' Jake called back.

Martha didn't answer. Her only response involved humming a tune from a West End musical from a past era. Jake couldn't remember her mentioning having guests over, so the identity of the caller was a mystery to him, particularly since they didn't know many people locally.

Using the armrests for leverage, Jake hauled himself to his feet, leaving a warm imprint of his body in the chair, which slowly rose and vanished as the air soaked back into the padding. The first few steps were tentative, allowing time for the feeling to return to his stiff, ageing joints. He shuffled towards the front door, which lay beyond the lounge and to the right, steadying himself against tables and walls where possible. Before he reached the door, the bell sounded again, loud and electronic, a grating jingle caused by the visitor's repeated pressing.

'Yes, yes, I'm coming,' mumbled Jake, upping the pace as much as his limbs would allow.

They had never got round to installing a peephole in the front door, so Jake left the chain on as he hesitantly opened it.

'Hi there,' greeted the caller, grinning unnervingly from ear to ear.

'Allan? What are you doing here?'

'I was just passing and I thought I'd pop by.'

Jake peered at him guardedly through the gap between the door and the frame, the chain not extended to its full length.

'Long time no see. Can I come in?'

Jake nodded and unhooked the chain, stepping back to allow the door to swing open. Allan stood before him, rubbing his hands together briskly against the cold. Coatless and clothed in garments of fairly thin material, he was dressed inappropriately for the weather. He kicked off his shoes and pushed them neatly up alongside the pairs already lying there.

'Good to see you again, Dad.'

Allan held out his hand and Jake took it, noticing the softness of his son's skin as well as its coldness. By contrast, Jake's hands bore the scars of many years as a labourer, with skin so rough he *could peel potatoes just by rubbing them. It was an empty handshake, devoid of feeling or friendliness.*

'Who is it, Jake?' Martha called from the kitchen.

'It's Allan.' His voice was flat, adopting a deliberate monotone as if purposefully trying to suppress any emotions he might have been feeling.

'Pardon, love?'

The sound of footsteps reached them and Martha emerged from the kitchen still clutching her rolling pin. An apron covered her clothes and her hands were caked in the pastry mixture she was in the process of preparing.

'Oh!' she exclaimed, upon seeing Allan standing in the hallway.

The rolling pin clattered to the floor, leaving a slight indent in the polished wooden panelling.

'Hi, Mum. You're looking well. Let me get that for you.'

Allan stepped forward and picked up the heavy cylinder, handing it back to Martha, who stood aghast, one hand raised to her mouth.

'Aren't you cold without a coat?' Her motherly instinct hadn't died, even after all this time.

'It's not too bad. Lovely and warm in here, though.'

Allan hugged his upper arms to emphasise his feeling of cosiness.

'You caught me in the middle of preparing dinner.'

Stating the obvious, the words were spoken to fill an awkward gap. It had been almost ten years since Allan had last graced their doorstep, and this was the first contact they had had with him since the day he walked out. There should have been so much to say, but time breeds uncertainty.

'My apologies. That's completely my fault, turning up unannounced. Tell you what, let me give you a hand.'

'Ok. Thank you.'

Martha returned to the kitchen and Allan followed close behind, a similarity of posture the only clue to their relationship.

'I'll be in here if you need me,' offered Jake, who returned to his chair in front of the television.

Although it was a genuine offer, Jake had long ago become accustomed to not receiving a response from Martha.

'What are you making?' asked Allan, confronted by a newspaper-sized slab of evenly rolled pastry.

'Cheese and mushroom flan,' replied Martha in a matter-of-fact tone.

'Fantastic. How I miss your home cooking,' said Allan with genuine enthusiasm.

Martha didn't answer, concentrating carefully on picking up the pastry blanket and placing it over a greased, circular baking dish, the pastry oozing over the sides like one of Dali's melting clocks. She gently pressed it into the edges, so that it sat right up against the sides of the dish, then removed the overhang using the pad of her thumb. The final touch was to prick the base with a fork to avoid any trapped air that might crack the pastry as it cooked.

Martha turned back to Allan.

'So, how have you been doing?'

What she really wanted to ask was, 'Why are you here?' but it was too early in the conversation for such a direct question.

'Not bad at all, really, all things considered.'

It was the typically vague answer a mother comes to expect from her son.

Martha turned away to cover the pastry with foil before placing it in the oven, the fan roaring a hot blast of air into the kitchen as the door opened.

'Are you well?'

It was essentially the same question, albeit worded differently.

'Yes, very much so. Apart from I'm not sleeping too well at the moment.'

Martha studied his face for any telltale signs of lack of sleep, but Allan looked fresh and healthy. Not sleeping well for Allan meant getting anything less than his usual nine hours. He had always taken the matter of sleeping very seriously, even as a teenager, and Martha had been able to tell exactly when it hit half-past ten just by looking at him, because after that time he became noticeably agitated. On the odd occasion he had stayed out late at *a party, he had calculated the time he would need to sleep until to achieve his full rest quota, and woe betide anybody who disturbed him before this hour was reached.*

'And why do you think that is? Have you got things on your mind?'

'It's probably the voices in my head keeping me awake.'

'That's not funny, Allan.'

The sternness of her voice cut short his chuckling.

'Sorry, Mum, that was in poor taste. To tell you the truth, I'm not really sure of the reason. Maybe it's the cold weather or something. I'm not a big fan of winter.'

'Maybe.' Martha had become noticeably subdued.

'Look, I feel useless standing here. Let me give you a hand with something. Tell you what, I'll slice the mushrooms. Where do you keep the knives?'

* * *

As the sunlight began to edge cautiously into the room like a creeping spotlight on the Saturday morning, it passed over the two bodies lying motionless on the dusty wooden floor. The first lay face down in the centre of the room, straight and stiff like a toppled statue. The second lay on its side just short of the window, still seated in a chair and held uncomfortably in position by a series of leather straps.

Joseph had taken one step too far and sent himself rocking backwards, the wheels sliding forward as he dropped like a domino, his head crashing off the floor so hard it had made his eyes water. Not wishing to be left with his legs up in the air and the blood flooding to his head, Joseph had succeeded in rocking the chair onto its side, so that he now lay in a semi-foetal position. He immediately regretted doing this when he discovered that the weight of his head caused the neck strap to dig sharply into his neck. He was unable to relieve the pressure as his head didn't quite reach the ground.

Stuck in this new position, Joseph began to holler and scream for help. Sometimes he would shout words, describing the basics of his predicament. Mainly he would just make noise, bawling like a lunatic. His throat soon became hoarse, and with no water to soothe it he had no option but to stop for fear of losing his voice altogether, an affliction that would rid him of his only hope of rescue. Given time to think while he couldn't shout, Joseph decided he would conserve his voice for the times of day when there would be most people about: early morning, lunchtime and early evening. These were the times when people would be going to and from work, assuming that anybody in the area was gainfully employed.

During the night, a deafening thud had almost given Joseph a heart attack as the ring holding Allan aloft gave way and the corpse came crashing to the ground. Thankfully, the body had fallen forward. If it had fallen backwards, the chances are it would have landed on top of him. As a result, the wooden boards played home to two bodies: one silent and the other a noisy siren. Joseph had screeched and roared until his blood vessels were on the verge of bursting, pausing at intervals to conserve his voice and to listen out for any responses or sounds of human life.

There were none. Nothing. Not a door slam, not a jangle of keys, not a call or a whistle.

He was alone.

As Allan had said, 'Why would anybody come here?'

* * *

'Oh Lord, no. Allan? What in God's name have you done? Allan!'
  'I'm sorry, Dad.'

Francis

'You're an idiot, Francis. A complete fucking cretin.'

The whole group roared with laughter, except for Francis, who smiled a fake smile; a meagre display of defiance against this ritual humiliation.

'You have got to be the worst estate agent ever,' Stuart continued. 'Your sales technique sucks donkey cock. You couldn't sell food to a fucking Ethiopian.'

The group laughed again, like the audience at a pub comedy night. Francis took a swig of his pint, swallowing his anger along with the bitter liquid. These Friday night drinking sessions after work invariably degenerated into a public mocking of Francis. Once the idle chit-chat about work, women and football had run its course – usually before the end of the third pint – they immediately looked for the easiest source of entertainment, which happened to be belittling Francis.

He was well aware that he was an easy target. It just infuriated him that the main antagonist was Stuart, a cocky little fucker who had recently joined the firm straight out of college. By hanging out with people who were stupid enough to always laugh at his terrible jokes, Stuart had gotten it into his swollen head that he was the funniest man alive. This meant he took every opportunity to share his drollness with his dim-witted entourage in the knowledge that he would always receive a favourable response. Every single fucking time. Why he had targeted Francis rather than any of the other monkeys he worked with was a mystery, but Francis was the chosen one, and so it had remained since Stuart's arrival.

There was some truth in what Stuart had said. The stock market boom had died a death and, as a result, the cartoon-rich city kids who populated the area had suddenly found themselves out of work or out of pocket, and the lofty rungs of the property ladder where they had once been sitting pretty were beginning to give them vertigo. Where they had once seen character and vigour, they now saw dirtiness and violence, and Clapham had finally begun to look overpriced. It provided a fitting welcome to the real world.

Demand for accommodation had dropped, and the sales and lettings business had slowed across the board. Sales were generally flagging for everyone. The situation seemed to have hit Francis the hardest, having not made a sale for weeks. There was an often quoted but unwritten rule that those who went more than a whole calendar month without making a sale would be told in no uncertain terms that it was about time they slung their hooks in someone else's pond. And Francis was getting close.

While he didn't believe management would actually push him out so ruthlessly, he nevertheless had the sensation of the sword of Damocles hanging over his head. He felt that this awareness of his own increasing desperation was undoubtedly visible to the outside world and affected his once-unflappable sales pitches. And although he recognised that his job wasn't realistically in imminent danger, the whole situation gave dickheads like Stuart ammunition to use against him and ruin the enjoyment of his pint.

It seemed like an eternity since he had been awarded the prestigious 'Salesman of the Month' title, and knocking back celebratory champagne rather than the cheap ale to which he had since become accustomed. Back then he had felt as though he ruled the estate agent kingdom. Tonight, the abuse had demoted him to the role of village idiot.

'So, Francis, you must be getting nervous now,' said Stuart with frustrating predictability. 'By my reckoning, you only have six working days left before, well, you know...'

He gestured towards the door with his thumb and whistled.

'Six days?' replied Francis, drawing himself upright on his stool to emphasise his height advantage. 'That's five more than I need. My position will be secure by the end of tomorrow.'

'Oh really?' responded Stuart with mock respect. 'Please share your secret with the class, Francis. What you got up your sleeve?'

'Lupton Road.'

The assembly degenerated into chimpanzee hooting and the scene suddenly started to resemble the PG Tips adverts of yesteryear. It took some time before Stuart eventually regained the ability to speak through the mirth.

'Lupton Road? *Pigeon Street?*'

'The very same,' Francis replied.

'And what makes tomorrow any different from all the other times you've tried to get rid of that property? You've shown people around that dump more times than I've slept with your gran!'

'Dug her up, did you?' said Francis in a humourless tone. 'Well, I've got a good feeling about tomorrow. The couple looking to rent the house were kicked out by their previous landlord when he sold the place. They need to find somewhere to live pretty sharpish and I have the perfect property for them.'

'Don't kid yourself, Fran,' – he often called Francis 'Fran' because he knew it was guaranteed to wind him up – 'That place will never be let. It certainly surpasses *your* abilities as a salesman. It's Pigeon Street, for fuck's sake.'

The name 'Pigeon Street' had been coined a few months earlier after Neil had parked his car there overnight and returned the next morning to find it graffitied with faeces, the red paintwork smeared like an oil painting with the bizarre browns, blacks and whites that could only have come from a bird's arse. The place was a pigeon magnet. They flocked there like swallows to warmer climates. It was as if there was a beacon that drew them in, like a residential Trafalgar Square. The endless supply of badly tied rubbish bags might have had something to do with it.

'Every property is lettable,' argued Francis. 'All it takes is finding the right tenants.'

'And what makes you think these people will be any different?' Stuart questioned. 'Are they blind? Do neither of them possess a sense of smell? Are they complete pikeys?'

'More to the point, they're fucking desperate. Speaking of which, I need to go for a Jayne Middlemiss.'

Francis had been needing the toilet for some time but hadn't wanted to go while he was so far on the back foot in the night's banter. He was also conscious that once he had taken his first piss of the night it would be the beginning of increasingly frequent trips as his body worked hard to reject the excessive amounts of liquid he was drinking. This wasn't the greatest of ploys, as the biting complaints from his bladder hindered his ability to concentrate on coming back with witty reposts. Plus it made him fidgety and he couldn't stop shaking his legs. However, he felt that his last comment had put him back on par. He could comfortably leave for the toilets knowing he would be returning to a level playing field.

Upon hoisting his considerable frame to his feet, Francis was intrigued to discover that the alcohol had already begun to take effect. A rushed lunch and a lack of dinner were never adequate preparations for a Friday night session. Leaving the hecklers behind, he ventured across the bar towards the toilets with a slight swagger, a semi-strut, which was subconsciously in time to the music.

It was barely eight o'clock, and the Slug and Lettuce was already getting packed; one of the advantages to being the closest drinking establishment to Britain's busiest railway station. Besides, it wasn't hard to create a 'trendy' bar these days with lots of wood, white walls, coloured lighting and a couple of sofas thrown in. The drunken, suited people who had come straight from work were joined by the soberer, more trendily dressed crowd who had been home to change and eat dinner, and were using the bar as a convenient meeting point before moving on elsewhere. Francis clearly fell into the former category, and right at that moment he felt he was probably drunker than most.

Making a trip to the toilet was never easy, especially for a man of his size. A forest of elbows greeted him, along with a whole host of drinks waiting to be released from hands at the slightest nudge. Alcohol and testosterone filled the air, a jungle of potential conflicts. All it would take was to spill someone's drink, step on the toe of someone's girlfriend or look at the wrong person for a second too long and the pathetic macho posturing would start. At a glance, violence would be the last thing an onlooker might expect to happen in such a place. The crowd was relatively old, affluent and supposedly intelligent. Yet the combination of alcohol and being smartly dressed seemed to make some people feel invincible, and the bouncers frequently had to pile in to break up the jousting fairies, much to everyone's relief, and particularly those involved. Francis had managed to avoid any trouble to date, but he was aware that he was clumsy at the best of times.

He crab-walked through the crowd, one arm outstretched like a probe, attempting to clear a path. The side-on stance made little difference to his manoeuvrability as his rotund belly meant he was approximately the same size from any angle, but it was certainly less confrontational. A combination of gentle pushing and repetition of the words, 'Excuse me,' saw Francis arrive at the other side of the crowd unscathed. The floor was crowded to the extent that people were huddled together like penguins and the edge of the crowd was so abrupt that escaping the mass of bodies was akin to emerging from a tightly packed cornfield.

Francis waited at the top of the stairs while a red-faced man with his tie flying at half-mast staggered to the top. He failed to acknowledge Francis's polite gesture and quickly vanished into the crowd. Francis went down the stairs, which snaked sharply to the right, keeping a hand on the banister at all times so he could steady himself in the event of slipping on one of the spillages from drinks people insisted on taking with them to the toilets. He always thought having to negotiate stairs in a drinking establishment was a bad design fault.

Even the toilet was crowded, with men lined up along the metallic urinal like feeding pigs. Francis waited for a sizeable gap to emerge before quickly slotting into the empty space.

It's funny how the presence of other people urinating can dispel even the most urgent need to go to the toilet. Invariably, those either side will already be in full flow, having overcome the psychological barrier that awaited Francis as he unzipped his trousers. When the torrents eventually came, they came fast, and Francis' relief was short-lived as he struggled to control the flow of liquid, spraying with the ferocious pressure of a fireman's hose. He muttered a couple of expletives as the urine bounced back off the flat, metallic surface of the urinal and onto his trousers. Luckily, the fine spray was quickly absorbed by the dark cotton threads and nobody looking at his crotch would be any the wiser. More importantly, his erratic watering had failed to journey as far as either of his neighbours. Even the sincerest of apologies carried little weight when a man pisses on another man's trousers. After peeing away what seemed like half his body weight, Francis zipped up and left the claustrophobic piss house, not bothering to wash his hands since he knew from experience that the dryer was broken.

Upon returning upstairs, Francis sighed at having to wade through the human labyrinth once again.

'Coming through. Excuse me. Watch yourself. Coming through.'

It seemed an easier trip than the inward journey, maybe because he wasn't in such a hurry. Their table by the window had been taken over by a group of women, who were presumably on a hen night. Francis scanned the vicinity. It wouldn't be the first time his colleagues had given up their table to the fairer sex in the expectation of receiving something in return. Fucking losers.

But they weren't there. The cunts had done a runner. He was left on his own with his hands in his pockets like a fucking gimp. Francis felt his cheeks flush, the capillaries expanding with anger as well as embarrassment. It was all Stuart's fault. Francis had a mind to go and look for the little shit and give him a good old-fashioned kicking. The cunt deserved it.

'Can ah have one of yer pubes?'

'What?'

An almost offensively plain woman stared up at him through a cheap-looking veil with tired, pinky eyes that oozed vodka. Her equally ordinary friends sniggered behind their hands like a gabble of imps.

'Please may I have one of your finest pubes?' said the woman in a faux-clarity that can only be spoken by drunks.

Francis screwed his face up and drew away in disbelief.

'For this,' she slurred, and turned her back on him to point at her T-shirt, which read like a poorly printed list of the lamest, crudest possible ways of humiliating the unfortunate wearer.

☐ Collect 10 different types of condom

☑ Snog a woman – must be a stranger

☑ Bare your naked buttocks on a crowded bus or tube

☐ Get a man to give you one of his pubes

☑ Dirty dance with 3 men who you find attractive

This was as far as he got, and Francis was disgusted to see that the majority of these tasks had been successfully completed, as indicated by the smudged lipstick ticks almost lost among the snakebite stains and general dirtiness of the T-shirt. Despite his red-blooded-male fascination with lesbianism, Francis was glad he hadn't been there to witness the completion of task two. Or task three for that matter. The fact that this woman had carried out these trials of her own free will made her all the more repulsive.

'Go on, mate,' came a call from the table.

'Yeah, go on. Don't be shy, darlin',' pestered the abhorrent hen, presenting her cupped hands like a beggar.

The women cheered as Francis slid his hand down the front of his trousers. They fell silent as his fingers paused among the dark mass of hair above his groin. Francis tugged and his hand emerged with an enormous bouquet of pubes, a handful of spiders, which he dumped unceremoniously into the unsuspecting woman's hands.

Presented with the blackened haystack, her expression quickly turned from one of gratitude to one of contempt.

'I only wanted *one*, you fuckin' weirdo,' she scorned. 'You could stuff a fuckin' mattress with all that shit.'

Her entourage giggled at her nerve and the woman calmly plucked out a single hair, which she placed on the corner of the table for safe keeping before throwing the remaining strands at Francis' chest.

Francis shook his head and brushed the hairs to the floor. Then he let rip.

'You're lucky you're a lady, otherwise you'd get a slap.' Francis spoke the words slowly and calmly to emphasise that he was in control. 'And I use the term "lady" in the broadest possible sense. Being a lady requires class and manners, of which you have neither. You repulse me. You and all your friends.'

The hen stared at him, mouth open in disbelief, her intoxicated brain unable to fully contemplate the dressing down she had received. Her companions exchanged uneasy glances as they waited for her response.

'Fuck you, you wanker,' came the reply, the expletives spat out with a confidence that could only have come from frequent rehearsal.

'Nice,' Francis commented. This woman made Stuart a comical genius by comparison. 'I really hope your fiancé comes to his senses. And I mean that sincerely. I pity the man who has to marry *you*.'

He turned and left, half expecting to be glassed from behind. Luckily, the hen decided to quit while she was ahead, her friends convincing her that, 'He's not worth it.' The victorious confrontation gave Francis a lift and he left the bar in high spirits, wishing the bouncers a good evening as he passed through the double doors, and leaving the music and loud chatter trailing in his wake.

Outside in the street the noise was just as invasive. In all directions, groups of drunks were shouting and singing as they walked the streets arm in arm, united in their quest to find the next watering hole. Traffic of the mechanical kind was also thick, the constant drone of vehicle engines awash with the liquid hissing of tyres sweeping through the rainwater, which lay across the road in a thin, glistening veneer. Buses thundered into view like colossal red spaceships coming out of hyperspace, decelerating so rapidly that the people on board could be seen surging forward, frantically grabbing at the nearest permanent fixture to avoid the unparalleled humiliation of being thrown to the floor on public transport. When the doors hissed open, the crowded bus stops quickly emptied as the travellers barged and shunted each other to gain a favourable position in the queue and a quicker escape from the cold. Passengers getting off the bus did so with some apprehension, many facing the prospect of a long walk home through this most unaccommodating of nights. The centre of the road played home to a line of black cabs, yet to be joined by their unlicensed competitors since the night was relatively young and the trains were still lumbering past with record-breaking frequency.

Francis waited for the green man to appear and headed across the road. The bastards had little imagination and there were only two places they might be. Kebab Feast was his first port of call. The fucking lightweights had most likely decided to call it a night and were busily stocking up on lamb doners with extra chilli to devour on the way home. But the kebab shop was empty apart from a lonesome old man eating his chips quietly in the corner and the staff on early shift who were making the most of the quiet time by standing around doing precisely nothing.

With one option defunct, he deduced that they must be in the other place: the Clapham Grand. The majority of their Friday nights ended up in that hellhole. There was an inevitability about it. They flocked there like pilgrims, usually at about ten thirty in order to avoid the queues that built up after kicking-out time from Clapham's various pubs and bars, none of which seemed to have a late license.

It was only just after ten, so the queue was almost non-existent, with only a group of tarted-up teenage girls and a young couple between him and the bouncers. Sodden red rope marked out the path to the entrance, where two bear-like brutes huddled in the doorway, warming their vast backs against the heat from inside while their thick fingers and weathered faces chilled in the winter air. Thankfully, the queue was whittled down quickly, the bouncers showing an appreciation of how the punters must be feeling standing out on the pavement.

'Just yourself, mate?' asked the first bouncer, giving Francis the once over to check that his attire was suitable to be granted entry.

Francis considered this to be an odd question, since he was the only one in the line, but glancing over his shoulder he noticed a group of five lads, all booted up in their Sunday best. The smell of aftershave and hair gel quickly drowned out the greasy waft of fatty lamb that emanated from the kebab shop, enticing the drunks to swarm towards it like flies to rotten meat. It was the strangest, most viscous of aromas, nauseating during the day yet almost irresistible while under the influence of alcohol; so oily it was almost touchable, pickled chillies adding a subtle, sharp twang that made the mouth orgasm with saliva at the very first whiff. They ought to bottle the smell and sell it to ugly women to wear when they're on the pull, thought Francis. Essence of kebab. Even the least desirable would soon have a man sucking on her neck if she were doused in such a scent.

'Yeah, I think my friends are inside already,' Francis responded.

Friends? Wankers, more like. Not one of them deserved the title of friend. But faced with the alternative of returning home early and alone, Francis was prepared to forgive, if not to forget.

Francis waited for the bouncer's reaction. They could be pretty anal on occasion. Confronted with a bouncer on a power-trip, the Queen would struggle to get in.

'Sorry, ma'am, no perms. And your husband's nose is too big.'

Fucking Neanderthals.

For a moment, it didn't look as though the bouncer was going to let him in. He waited with a morbid fascination as to what outlandish excuse the gorilla was about to come up with for refusing him entry. Francis was one of the few people who could look the bouncer in the eye when standing toe to toe. However, while their waists were of similar size, Francis was dwarfed in the shoulder department, and he wouldn't be able to refute the decision once it was made.

'In you go, then. Have a good night,' said the bouncer, waving him in.

The second bouncer frisked him, running his gigantic paws up each leg and around the torso. This was presumably to look for weapons, as the clumsy once-over would have been unlikely to throw up anything smaller than a mobile phone. Not that anybody would be taking drugs in the Clapham Grand. The place was strictly pissheads only.

Simultaneously to Francis being let past the last line of defence, the group of lads was being turned away for being a group of lads. They walked off in search of random women to escort them past the guards, constantly complaining to each other at having gotten all dressed up for nothing.

Francis handed fifteen quid over to a bored-looking woman in the ticket booth. Fifteen fucking quid to drink overpriced drinks and listen to DJ Dr Blitz playing shite music. It didn't exactly represent great value for money and it left his wallet looking a little light. The evening was all but over from a drinking point of view. In his rage, he had forgotten to go to the cashpoint and the minimum order at the bar for credit card users would mean getting in expensive rounds for people he didn't really like.

A dingy staircase led up to the cloakroom and the balcony. The scarlet décor gave the place the feel of a vintage horror movie set, a massacre waiting to happen. *Don't Leave Me This Way* by The Communards could be heard blasting through from the dancefloor. Surely it was too early for such a classic, he thought. No doubt Blitzy would be playing it again in a couple of hours.

The place was still fairly empty, but it wouldn't be long before the stairs were filled with a chain of people queuing up to leave their cumbersome coats and briefcases to be collected later. The balcony bar was also looking a bit bare. On the plus side, this made it easier to get served and Francis took the opportunity to get a drink in before the crowds arrived. There were four people behind the bar, an excessive number of pint-pullers while it was quiet, but still hopelessly understaffed during the busy hours between eleven and one, when it seemed to take about twenty-five minutes just to buy a fucking beer.

'Can I help you, mate?' asked the barman, an attractive young man sporting a heavily gelled, tufty, messed-up haircut that seemed to be part of the job description for people working behind nightclub bars.

'Just a sparkling water, thanks.'

The decision to stop drinking was an easy one to make. His head was already spinning, he was running low on cash and he had an important appointment in Pigeon Street the following morning.

The barman took a bottle from the fridge and poured it into a plastic cup, where it spat and fizzed like a hangover cure.

'That's two quid, please, mate.'

'Here you go,' said Francis, handing over a fiver. 'Can I have some ice in that?'

If he was going to part with two nuggets for a bit of water, the least they could do was give him some fucking ice. He waited for his change, which was shoved in front of him on a silver tray. Real classy this place. Francis shook his head as he pocketed the three dirty discs. Even not drinking was expensive around here.

Holding a cup in his hand gave him some comfort, as it meant he felt less self-conscious walking around on his own. With drink in hand he was one of many returning to his mates after a trip to the bar. Without one, he felt like a friendless loser. Billy-fucking-no-mates.

Opposite the intentionally claustrophobic bar area, the floor rapidly fell away, plunging down towards the dancefloor at a fairly steep angle. In their infinite wisdom, the designers had decided to leave the theatre seats in place, so the club offered the slightly bizarre capacity to sit down and watch the debauchery below. They should have left the classic red binoculars too, he mused, so all the voyeurs could get up close from afar and see every grope, every meeting of tongues.

Francis strutted down to the barriers, which were just about high enough to lean on without the fear of people toppling over the edge en mass like lagered-up lemmings. Shame in a way. The fall might bring some of the arrogant tossers that frequented this place down to earth with a bump. Literally.

He leant against the safety barrier, adopting a posture that said, 'I've temporarily lost my friends, but I know they're here somewhere.' Dr Shitz had progressed seamlessly on to the *Ghostbusters* theme tune. On the dance floor, where it seemed everybody in the place except Francis was presently standing, the crowd had regressed twenty years to relive their childhoods. They were eight years old again, back at their best mate's birthday party, full of jelly and ice-cream and fizzy pop. It was the ideal invitation to dance like a retard and one gladly taken up by the grown-up children, mainly made up of men at this point.

I ain't afraid of no ghost.

A real blast from the past, the dancefloor was a wonder to behold. Cutting-edge in the early eighties, the platform had withstood the test of time, and its uniform squares still winked with the same enthusiasm they had all those years ago, flashing out a chequered sequence of vibrant colours like a rebellious chessboard. Groups of girls were dotted around the dance area; the occasional pair but mostly threes and fours, as there was safety in numbers. They were invariably circled by rings upon rings of men, all facing inwards like compasses surrounding a magnet and the stronger magnets – the prettier girls – would attract bigger circles.

Stuck in a cluster between opposing forces were Stuart and the rest of the sorry group. They couldn't have been further away from any members of the opposite sex if they had tried, having just managed to slot between two groups of fans without knowing which way to face. Francis scoffed at their poor positioning. The losers had ditched him to do what? Dance with each other all night like a bunch of fucking gays, that's what. A smirk started to creep across his face and he knocked back a swig of fizzy water, swallowing with an ersatz hardness that implied he was drinking something far stronger.

A sudden surge of self-adulation prompted his head to start nodding to the music; slowly, controlled, and only acknowledging every other beat. The cool way.

Bustin' makes me feel good.

Here was a man too urbane to participate in the pantomime below. Here was a man that commanded an immense level of respect from those around him. A man who didn't feel the urge to twitch like a Tourette's sufferer just because some dickhead had put a song from his childhood on the CD changer. Here was a man...

'Hey, Francis.' The tap on his shoulder gave him such a start he flinched and spilt some of his overpriced water.

'Oh, hi Tony. You made me jump there,' said Francis, wiping his wet hand across the back of his trousers.

All the chic had left his body, spilled to the floor along with the Highland Spring. His aura had been shattered by the touch of this short-arsed gimp, Anthony, who stood before him wearing a pathetic, apologetic look on his imbecilic face. Anthony really *was* tiny. He was so small he made Francis feel like a building.

'You disappeared, mate,' started Tony. 'We didn't know where you were.'

'I was in the gents.'

What a fucking two-faced prick. They all knew where he had gone. That retard Stuart had suggested this juvenile prank and the others had gone along with it like a flock of fucking sheep. And here was Anthony playing the role of the innocent party. It made Francis sick.

'We thought you'd gone home.'

'I was *in* the gents,' Francis repeated, his voice containing a dash of aggression, like the kick of Tabasco in a Bloody Mary.

He had been quite happy looking down on the world from his vantage point on the balcony, but this cock had ruined his chances of making a dramatic arrival, denying him the opportunity to come back like a stubborn rash and force himself back into the group with a divine, blinding, heavenly light shining out from his cock and balls.

'Hey, no hard feelings. What are you drinking?' It was the voice of a guilty man.

Francis looked down at his sparkling mineral water and felt that the truth might damage his projected masculinity.

'Double G and T.'

'Let me get you another, for the mix-up an' all,' said Anthony.

'Cheers, Tony,' responded Francis. 'That would be good.'

The vertically challenged cunt deserved it. The fact Anthony was such a tight-arse made it all the more satisfying to take a drink off him.

'Ok, back in a minute.'

Hah! Take that, dwarf-boy.

Anthony waddled off, his legs moving in that faster-than-the-eye-can-see motion only available to the small in stature. Francis returned to his godlike role of judging the people below. In the short space of time that had elapsed since he had previously observed it, the dancefloor had reached new heights of crowdedness. The music lurched into the next track, Spandau Ballet's *Gold*, with a rhythmic ineptness that lacked any continuity or flow; a talent the DJ had no doubt spent years trying to perfect. Not that the revellers noticed. Hands were flung aloft, fists clenched, as the dancers cottoned on to the fact Dr Titz was spinning *yet another* phat tune.

Whoever was in charge of the lighting clearly enjoyed this particular number, as, come the chorus, the second shout of 'Gold!' would be met with every yellow light in the place being turned up to the max, the crowd of waving gimps flooded in an amber light as if Midas himself had entered the building with dangerously wandering hands.

To the left of the pit, a man could be seen ripping off his tie and swinging it round and round his head like a camp lasso, his pelvis grinding in a twisting, circular motion. A genuine Chippendale. Oddly, he proceeded to toss the tie over his head and into the bobbing mass of breasts and limbs, a ridiculous act he would no doubt regret in the morning when woke to discover that he had lost yet another expensive silk neckpiece at the Clapham Grand.

'Here you go, mate.'

Anthony had returned, somewhat sooner than expected. He usually took an age to get served at the bar, presumably because he was so damn short.

'Cheers, Tone,' Francis thanked him. 'You're a good man.'

Yeah right.

An awkward silence followed as Francis turned back to the precipice.

'You comin' down to the dancefloor?' asked Anthony, breaking the deadlock.

'Not right now. I'll catch you up.'

'See you later, then.'

The dejection at his shunned offer, which made his voice falter slightly, was music to Francis' ears, much more so than the vocals of Ballet frontman, Tony Hadley.

'Sure. And cheers for the drink.'

'No problem.'

Anthony moped off, quickly disappearing down the stairs, his diminutive frame sinking out of sight after what seemed to be only a few steps. Francis felt the coldness of the freshly poured beverage against his fingers, the contrast in temperatures between the liquid and the sweaty air that surrounded it turning the plastic moist against his skin. His fingertips would shrivel like pinky raisins if he held on to it for too long.

He took a sip. It tasted weak. There was no way it was a double. That fucking cheapskate! He should have known better than to trust that mothball-walleted twat. To drink the gin and tonic would mean mixing spirits with beer and Francis wasn't about to risk a hangover when he had such an important morning waiting for him in just a few hours' time. After a quick check that nobody was looking, Francis poured the contents of the cup onto the floor. He might as well have nicked a fiver from Anthony's wallet and thrown it away, cutting out the middle-man. The end result would have been the same. Five quid spent and no reward for either of them. Everyone was a loser.

Anthony rejoined the group and could be seen pointing up at the balcony in Francis' general direction.

'Fuck this,' muttered Francis, taking a couple of steps back into the aisle so they wouldn't be able to see him.

The seats suddenly looked so inviting. Like the first person through the doors at the cinema, he was blessed with a wealth of choice; a glut of dank material on which to park his bulk. He chose the seat directly in front of him in the second row. To sit anywhere else would mean either hurdling chairs or taking a long walk up the gangway and then down one of the rows, both of which would make him appear strange to anyone who might have been watching. After all, he was merely looking for somewhere to sit down, not a better vantage point.

It is a considerable challenge to look cool when seated alone in a place full of people in groups. To do so requires the exuberance of such a degree of self-confidence, such an air of popularity, that people will either assume you're alone out of choice or will come and talk to you with the notion that it will only be a matter of time before others follow. Posture was the key, so Francis slid forward in his seat to attain a position that looked relaxed without resorting to slouching. His legs were far enough apart to suggest large, well-stocked testicles, ready for action, but not so far as to look as though he was airing a sweaty, smelly undercarriage. He felt his chosen pose was a good one, the first and hardest part of the mission successfully accomplished.

What to do with the hands, however, was always tricky. Sitting still would appear rigid and intimidating, and it was always hard to find a comfortable position in which to rest the arms that looked natural and uncontrived. Francis settled for what he took to be the best option: left arm solid, stationary on the arm rest, right hand animated, tapping out the beat on the opposite side. He looked cool, he was pretty certain of that. This position was maintained for some time and Francis got quite into the whole hand-tapping thing, finding his ability to pat out increasingly complex rhythms improving by the minute.

Resurrecting the nodding of his head to the deep drong of the bass, he found himself becoming absorbed in the music. He felt like a giant carp, caught hook, line and sinker and being reeled into a world of crap eighties music and stupid dancing. Sitting down, the barrier blocked off everything that lay below. He might as well have been looking over the edge of the world, straight into hell, with Dr Squitz playing to the minions of the underworld.

The arrival of a pair of well-rounded arses put a new perspective on the scene. If this was what Hades looked like, it was time to start misbehaving. The hells angel on the left was by far the better specimen, from behind at least. Stretchy white material showed off a bum that must have taken endless gym hours to create. It was a joy to behold, the eighth wonder of the world. If God were to choose to redesign woman from scratch, he needn't have looked any further than this work of art. Obviously aware that she was in possession of such a wondrous asset, the girl struck a pose that emphasised the perfect curvature of her behind: one leg outstretched, a mind-blowingly silky path leading up to the promised land; the second slightly bent at the knee, sat astride the footrest in the classic model pose. The result was to stretch the material of her skirt even tighter, if that were possible, revealing every detail of what lay beneath, which, aside from fabulous female flesh, was very little.

The fabric clung to the padded globes, crept up high between the toned cheeks and framed the delectable rump as though it had been hand-painted directly onto the skin. The way it followed the form so closely suggested the girl must be wearing the most delicate of thongs, if not a G-string. When placed beside such an enchanting artefact, the legs were always going to be a disappointment. However, they made an admiral effort to gain equal billing; toned muscles suggesting suppleness and fitness without compromising on their alluring femininity. They were wrapped in a skin so soft it was hard not to imagine kissing them all over, starting at the feet and slowly, gently, working up higher to her exquisite behind. It was almost a misfortune this girl had been blessed with such a sensational arse *and* legs when so many others had neither. Such legs were wasted, as who would ever look at them when a couple of feet higher rested the most captivating of behinds.

Francis willed himself to be transported into another world, a place where he had no equal in the looks department. This pseudo-Francis would have stridden slowly up behind this beauty and clasped one giant hand firmly onto each buttock, kneading the flesh slightly to get better purchase, before tracing out their form with the palms of his hands, mapping out the contours of her hips and bringing them to a rest on her lower abdomen. Applying the gentlest of pressure, he would have brought her towards him, feeling the warm expanse of her bottom pressed up against his groin.

Initially startled by the contact, her alarm would have evaporated as she sensed the strength and sexuality of his touch, and the feeling of his hands pressed down so close to her clitoris would have filled her with excitement. She would have had no need to turn around; the power of the man would be felt through his presence, which smothered the area, blocking out her friend and the brashness of their surroundings. It would just be her and him.

She would feel the hugeness of his penis through his trousers and back herself further into him, making rhythmic movements from side to side, trying to arouse him. Francis would know what she was doing and it would make him feel even more powerful. He knew the rest was a mere formality. She would ask him back to her place, he would screw her, she would love it and then he would screw her again. And again. And each time she would plead for him to stop because she had never experienced such exhausting and draining sex, yet each time she would be unable to resist and love it even more than the previous time. And when she really *had* had enough, he would fuck her friend, who had been patiently waiting her turn, sitting there, watching, wet at the expectation of him inside her and fuelled by an intense jealousy of her friend who had got to him first. She would have sat there and waited all night if need be. He was *that* fucking good. And the best thing was that Francis knew he could afford to turn them both down. There was no shortage of nice arses in Clapham.

The end of his sordid reverie coincided with the well-put-together, albeit less impressive girl on the right turning her head to look at him, as if she had read his mind and wanted to catch him mid-letch. Francis quickly averted his lustful stare away from her friend's posterior and down to his watch, but not before getting a good look at the girl's face, which, even in the deadened lambency of the club was unmistakably at odds with her body. At that instant, he was doubly thankful for the gloominess of the surroundings as, not only did it mask his embarrassment at being caught having a perve, but it shielded him from the full brunt of her unsightliness.

The girl also looked hastily away, not having expected to meet the eye of this mysterious man sitting all alone. Curiosity soon got the better of her and she turned to look again, at the exact same moment Francis decided to look up to see if she was still watching him. When their eyes met again they had a longer visit, before both parties lowered their eyes coquettishly to the floor and took a round trip to some other point of interest. Francis found the encounter utterly vexing, as he had no obvious outlet for his gaze.

He had been in similar situations countless times before. It happened almost every time he travelled on the underground, where he was forced to sit opposite a whole row of strangers with very little else to look at, thus making unwanted eye contact almost inevitable. And once it's happened for the first time, both parties will inherently have to check the other isn't still looking at them, an act unfailingly precise in its synchronisation. With the wheels of paranoia set in motion, this disagreeable glancing continues until one of three things happens: one of the parties takes out some form of reading material; one of the parties dons sunglasses, a large hat or some other attire that hides the eyes; or either party leaves the train. There is a fourth option, a confrontational recognition that the other person is staring at you, but this almost certainly making matters worse and is therefore rarely used.

Francis's intermittent peeks saw the girl on the right lean across and whisper something into her resplendent companion's ear, the exchange causing her to take a gander at Francis, who was feeling more uncomfortable by the second. This girl's face, while not beautiful enough to draw attention away from her magnificent lower body, was pleasant nonetheless and Francis lost none of his libidinous feelings upon seeing it. Large, impenetrable eyes glittered above a nose almost measured in its straightness, save for a slightly bulbous tip, giving her face a childish cuteness that complimented her flawless body, which was undoubtedly all woman. Her lips sat in a permanent pout, ample and moist like a pair of pink slugs. She smiled slightly, more *at* him than *to* him, and whispered something back to her friend, causing them both to giggle.

Francis didn't really know how to react to this gesture. Stuck between two minds, he was unsure as to whether they were mocking him or sizing him up as a potential snog. He hoped it was the latter, but deep down suspected it was more likely to be the former. Not wishing to be seen as a figure of fun – he had already twice been an unwilling target that evening – Francis decided it was time to leave.

However, the girl on the left beat him to it. After a further light-hearted exchange with her appreciably less attractive friend, she sauntered off in the direction of the bar, her buttocks rising rhythmically and hypnotically with each step. The brilliance of her skirt caught the light, screaming, "Look at me!" as if a spotlight followed her every move. Francis couldn't help but watch her leave, trying his best not to let his jaw drop into his lap as she swayed her hips seductively in recognition of her audience. He was tempted to get up and follow her, but decided not to on two counts. Firstly, she was probably going to meet her boyfriend who, in all likelihood, would be a charmless, slick-haired, arrogant tosser who didn't deserve to be with such a beauty. The sight of his hands touching that exceptional arse would no doubt wind Francis up immensely and plunge the night into newfound lows. Secondly, he was sporting a massive erection and his loose-fitting trousers meant that if he were to stand it would look like he had a colossal dowsing rod shoved down his boxer shorts, deliberately designed to seek out arses.

When the heavenly butt cheeks had finally disappeared from view, Francis turned back to check the whereabouts of her friend and was somewhat surprised to be greeted by an empty space where they had once stood. Suddenly alerted by a movement to his right, Francis turned to see the ogress coming towards him, treading slowly and with considerable purpose between the rows of seats. Looking at her from the neck down, Francis could have been forgiven for thinking this was his lucky night. From behind, her figure had been more than acceptable, at least a seven out of ten. And her body was equally appealing from the front, if not more so. A clingy, low-cut, lilac vest top framed a voluptuous, if not overly large cleavage that showed no signs of sagging. While skimpy, her clothes left enough to the imagination to suggest this girl wasn't a complete slapper, something that, while viewed positively by many men, wasn't something that particularly appealed to Francis. Her breasts bounced as she walked and, while not quite as mesmerising as the previous goods on display, they were a mouth-watering sight, nonetheless.

The top ceased barely below her ribcage and her skirt didn't begin until about half a foot further down, exposing a slender midriff that emphasised the shapeliness of her hips. Her legs were slim and had a lissom quality to them that boded well for her likely bedroom performance. On reflection, Francis knew he couldn't realistically have hoped to be approached by a sexier body. It was undeniably more attractive than anything he had managed to get his hands on in the past. But the face. Oh, what a face. This girl had taken a walk through the ugly forest and bumped into every tree. In fact, she had taken numerous strolls through the woods, and maybe even got lost in there for a couple of days. She really was offensively ugly.

She sat down next to him, the whole movement a sexual show: hands placed delicately on the arm rests, arching her back as she slid her pert bottom into the seat. Wriggling back in the chair, she straightened her spine and pulled her shoulders back, puffing out her chest to emphasise her ample bosom and holding the pose long enough to guarantee Francis a proper look at the goods on offer. When she was sure she had his full attention, she leant in towards him, pushing her face in so close that her greasy blonde locks blocked out all that lay beyond them. Francis was left staring into that repulsive face.

'Mind if I join you?' she asked.

At least her voice was nice. Soft and deep, and naturally deep rather than a smoker's rasp.

'Looks like you already have,' replied Francis, before quickly adding, 'which is ok with me. What's your name?'

'Stacey,' she replied.

'That's a nice name,' said Francis genuinely. He had always liked the name Stacey.

'And what about you?' she asked. 'What's your name?'

'Francis,' he answered.

He waited for her reaction.

'Francis? Isn't that a girl's name?'

'If spelt differently, yes. Otherwise, no.'

Stupid as well as ugly. He was going off her by the second.

'Oh,' she said blankly.

There was an awkward pause as she calculated whether she had offended him to the extent that it was pointless continuing the conversation. She figured he must be used to the response and carried on regardless.

'So, what do you do, Francis?'

'I'm in finance.'

It was his usual lie; one that implied he had lots of money but wasn't really interesting enough to prompt further questioning, especially by the likes of Stacey, who presumably didn't know anything about the financial world. It wasn't that Francis was ashamed of his present employment. On the contrary, he was proud of his position and could see himself staying in the business for many years to come. Unfortunately, the title 'estate agent' seemed to conjure up a multitude of negative emotions within the majority of the general public and he had learnt from experience that it rarely cut the mustard with the opposite sex.

This nationwide denouncement of his chosen profession was a mystery to Francis. He saw himself as someone who provided a helpful and much-needed service to the community and it was a constant source of annoyance that he was viewed as the scum of the working population. Even accountants had it easy by comparison. They were merely labelled as dull, while, upon stating what he did to earn a living, Francis was more often than not assumed to be a bit of a wanker.

'Oh,' she said again, before describing her own working background. 'I'm a beautician.'

Francis couldn't help but allow himself a faint smile at this admission.

'I work down in Wimbledon, on the Broadway,' she continued. 'Nails are my speciality. Look.'

She raised her hands in front of him, wrists bent forward, fingers spread wide apart. They were indeed nice nails and Francis nodded his approval.

'My boss says I got a big future in the beauty business,' she said, buoyed by his display of appreciation. 'Says I'm his best worker.'

Francis looked away, not really sure how to respond to this naïve self-adulation. The DJ had progressed to *YMCA* by the Village People and, while Francis hated the song with a passion, part of him wished he was on the dancefloor spelling out letters with his arms alongside all the other revellers. Anything to get away from what he could see was about to happen. Turning back towards her, he focused on her eyes. They looked ok if taken out of their unfortunate context. They held each other's gaze for a moment and her eyes wrinkled into a smile.

'I think you're gorgeous,' she said, rolling her eyes up into their sockets in a clumsy attempt at seduction.

Francis wished he could say the same for her. Every time she opened her mouth she displayed a set of yellowed teeth that jutted haphazardly in all directions like a coastal rock formation, the sight of which was enough to make him wince.

'Er, thanks,' said Francis, choosing not to return the compliment. He really didn't want to have to lie to her more than he needed to.

'Do you think I'm attractive?'

Unfortunately, Stacey was quite persistent.

'Well...' Francis began, but he was quickly interrupted.

'Most blokes don't even look at me,' she said, the low self-esteem beginning to ooze to the surface. 'They all fancy my mate.'

'What? The girl you were talking to before?' Suddenly, Francis was interested in what she had to say.

'Yeah, but Becky's off men after a bad experience with a right weird one the other day, so they won't get nothin' from her.'

Dressed like that? A likely story, Francis thought.

'She's good lookin' though, don't you reckon?'

'Didn't really notice,' Francis lied again, almost sounding convincing.

He was a well-practised liar – it was part of his job – but he still didn't like doing it.

'Nobody takes a second look at me.'

Francis hated this blatant fishing for compliments, but she came across as so fragile that he feared she might burst into tears if he said anything even mildly derogatory. There's nothing worse than seeing a woman cry, especially when the tears are of your own making, so he took the bait.

'I'm sure you have your fair share of admirers.'

Stacey said nothing, clearly wanting him to continue, so he did.

'I mean, you've got a fit body. I...'

It was hardly an amorous remark. A stronger-minded woman might even have found the comment disparaging, but it proved to be all the invitation Stacey needed. The rest of the words were stifled as she plugged his mouth with her monstrous, cow-like tongue.

One of the best things about kissing is that it's acceptable to close your eyes while you indulge and, as a result, with a bit of imagination, you could essentially be kissing anyone. So Francis did the natural thing and imagined he was snogging her infinitely more attractive mate, Becky, whether she was off men or not. This was made more difficult by the fact he could feel the craggy ridges of Stacey's teeth as his tongue thrashed about like a fish out of water in her cavernous mouth. Plus, every time he opened his eyes he was reminded of his involvement in an exchange of bodily fluids with Joseph Merrick's mutant offspring. It really wasn't a very pleasurable kiss; just the coming together of two drunken and desperate individuals, devoid of any emotion or respect for the other.

She took him by the hands, which, until now, had been lying dormant on the armrests in exactly the same position they had been before her arrival. She placed his left hand on her bare waist, giving him the freedom to move up to her breasts or down to her arse, a fairly difficult choice and an important one since the wrong decision could earn him a violent reprimand. Smooth and cushiony, her skin gave off a comforting warmth, like a cup of tea that has been sitting on the side for ten minutes.

Stacey guided his right hand to her face and held it there, clenched tightly against her cheek; so tightly, in fact, that he could feel the individual nodes of her acne that the industrially applied make-up couldn't mask. Hot, dank breath blustered from her mouth with each exhalation; a sickening, smoky sweetness concocted by a marriage of cigarettes and alcopops. The whole experience made Francis feel slightly nauseous, but he soldiered on regardless since it was so long since he had last had a snog. That said, if he had known this was what it was going to be like, he would happily have gone without.

Pulling away for a second and giving Francis the chance to get his breath back, Stacey drew his hand away from her cheek and began to kiss his fingertips. The kisses soon became nibbles, which, in turn, evolved into licking, and it wasn't long before she had all four of his fingers in her mouth. His thumb was the only survivor, serving as an anchor lest she should swallow his hand right up to the elbow. Far from being erotic, her zealous sucking only stimulated feelings of disgust within

Francis as her putrid saliva coated his skin like a suffocating glue. His mind returned to how he had neglected to wash his hands the last time he went to the toilet and how, if she knew they had been touching his nob, she wouldn't have been so enthusiastic about putting them in her mouth. Or maybe she would. Francis began to wish he had drunk Anthony's peace offering, as some extra-thick lenses on his beer goggles would have come in useful at that moment.

After what seemed like an eternity, she decided his fingers weren't really edible and removed them from her jaws. Francis resisted the urge to sniff his hand when it was returned to him, opting instead to wipe it discretely against the back of her chair, where she couldn't see what he was doing. Without taking her eyes off him, she leant forward and placed both of her hands on his right leg, those elegant nails of hers pointing towards his groin.

'Would you like to come back to my place?' she asked, licking the residue from Francis' fat fingers away from the sides of her mouth.

He was slightly taken aback by the proposition, and he stammered slightly as his blundering brain frantically foraged for excuses.

'I really don't think that would be a good idea, you know.'

It was the best he could manage under the circumstances.

'But if we both want the same thing...'

Francis was less than convinced that they did want the same thing, especially as he wanted to go home, alone, as soon as possible.

'I'd love to, really I would, but I've got to go into work early tomorrow.'

'That's ok,' she replied. 'I'm workin' tomorrow as well.'

He really didn't know why he was making such an effort to preserve this girl's feelings, but he found himself fumbling for ways to let her down gently.

'I mean *really* early. I've got this important project to finish off.'

'Oh,' she said dejectedly.

The guilt enveloped his body.

'Look, I'll tell you what, give me your phone number' – smooth, he thought to himself – 'and I'll give you a call when I'm less busy. We can meet up and go somewhere where we can hear each other speak.'

And somewhere darker, preferably.

Stacey's eyes lit up. It had been months since a bloke had asked for her phone number. She eagerly gave him her mobile number, watching attentively as he keyed the digits into his phone.

'I really should go now,' said Francis. He kissed her on the forehead, the least spotty part of her face.

'Thanks, Frank.'

'Francis.'

'What?'

'Forget it. It doesn't matter.'

He smiled at her, then got up to leave. He was pleased he had got her number. It meant that, for once, there would be a girl out there waiting expectantly for his call. And it meant that he had a fall-back plan in case he was ever in desperate need of a shag.

Francis decided not to go and find the others. Instead, he went to pick up his coat from the cloakroom so that he could leave promptly. It was getting quite late and the queue was long, not to mention wide. It was at least two bodies deep at every point, except for the space that Francis occupied alone. It is never particularly easy to leave a nightclub, and Francis had timed his exit badly. If it hadn't been so Siberian outside, he might well have left his jacket there and picked it up the next day during his lunch break, claiming to have forgotten to take it home the night before. It probably would have been easier.

As it was, it would be almost suicidal to travel home without it, so Francis had to wait patiently in line with everyone else. In a way, this was a good thing as it allowed him time to think about the night's events rather than doing so later when he was lying in bed trying to sleep. Questions shot into his head with the regularity and ferocity of rocks in a meteor shower. They slammed into his consciousness, smashing through any barriers his mind had set up to protect the well-being of his inner self.

Why had he tongued Stacey when he didn't find her even remotely attractive? She had a nice body, but this hadn't been to his benefit and he hadn't even been able to see it most of the time as his face had been attached to hers. Maybe it was because he was such a nice guy and it would have been rude not to. But she was *so* ugly. Was he really that desperate? No more than any other bloke, he supposed. Most blokes he knew would have done the same, wouldn't they? In fact, most blokes he knew would have taken her up on her offer. Why had he turned down a definite shag when it had been gifted to him on a plate? He could have got his hands on that gorgeous body.

Francis would have given almost anything for even a couple minutes with those breasts. Why had he said no? Was he scared? No, he just wasn't a slag. He was a man of high moral fibre and an example to the rest of the male population. He respected women, even the ugly ones. But to caress those beautiful, naked breasts. In all probability, some other bloke was trying to slime his way in there while he was wasting time queuing for his coat. Should he go back for her? No, it would be almost impossible to find her again, like searching for a specific turd in a London sewer. He would get a good night's sleep and contact her in the morning. That's what he would do.

Breasts were the last thing on Francis' mind as he was buffeted by the arctic blast that gusted up towards St Johns Hill. It was the type of wind that was almost liquid in the way it would leak through the minutest of gaps in your clothing and bite at your skin in places you thought safe from its icy tongue. Francis checked his wallet and found four nuggets, enough for a large shish kebab and change for his bus fare. He had to press into the chilling zephyr to get to the kebab shop, which was always the final port of call before home.

Wrapping his arms around his chest for extra protection against the cold, he marched the short distance down the hill to the takeaway shop, where the elephant leg of lamb spun triumphantly on its gigantic skewer. It was like a meaty trophy, illuminated from behind by the gas fire; a drunken man's holy grail. Kebabs were an essential part of a Friday night. A Clapham drinking session that wasn't capped off with a trip to Kebab Feast was like visiting the Louvre and not going to see the Mona Lisa.

Kebabs are notoriously hard to eat without making a mess, especially when on the move, and during the short walk to the bus stop Francis managed to leave a trail of lettuce behind him like a modern-day Hansel and Gretel. He had finished eating by the time the bus had arrived, discretely letting the wrapper fall from his hand and into the road, where it sat miserably like a pasty iceberg in a puddle of filthy water. The number 39 bus arrived at the scene in spectacular fashion, its gargantuan frame ploughing through the puddles, creating a tidal wave that soaked the feet and ankles of all who didn't possess the foresight to see what was about to happen. The watering was taken in good spirit by most, the victims able to laugh at their own misfortune.

It was the last regular bus before the irregular 'N'-labelled counterparts took over, and it was packed as a result. Despite a good number of passengers stepping off into the commuter heaven that is Clapham Junction, the bus remained full enough to dictate that Francis had to stand next to the luggage shelf at the front. He would have got a seat if he had been more assertive in the queue, but he didn't have the energy to argue with drunks, so he had allowed his fellow travellers to push and shove at will. If it meant that much to them. they could have a bloody seat.

Standing opposite Francis with his arms held behind his back and an eternally entertained expression on his face was a short, foreign man whose accent Francis deduced to be South African. Browned, weathered skin and hair so dark it was almost a uniform colour like a hat or helmet made the man's origin even more difficult to place. Already having pestered Francis in the queue with numerous questions about the intricacies of the bus' destination, the man appeared dissatisfied with Francis as a source of amusement and spent the journey looking at each person in turn, ever hopeful of a reaction.

'It's hot on this bus. Please can you turn the air conditioning on, sir?' he asked the driver, who had already had his fill of weirdos for the night and told the man to step back behind the line and out of earshot.

'Aye aye, captain,' saluted the man. He returned to his space opposite Francis, grinning like a maniac.

It came as some relief to Francis when the foreigner got off, as crazy people can be hard to get rid of once you have made the mistake of being helpful to them.

* * *

Francis awoke the next morning with a clear head and congratulated himself on his purchase of mineral water rather than alcohol at the club. No doubt Stuart and the rest of the wretched crew would be simultaneously waking to considerable pain right now. Bunch of amateurs. It would all contribute to their downfall in the end and he would be left to rise like a phoenix from the flames of a struggling property rental business. He had made a special effort to get in early to draw attention to his superior professionalism. His co-workers would look slack in comparison and the seeds of doubt about their commitment to the firm would be sewn into his boss' brain where, over time, they would germinate and grow into fully-fledged resentment.

A mouth that felt like he had stuck the nozzle of a vacuum cleaner into it and sucked out all the moisture, replacing it with dust, was his only physical reminder of the night before, and this was easily remedied by downing the glass of water beside his bed that he had cleverly left there for this very eventuality.

A shit, shower and shave later, Francis was donning his lucky pants, which he saved for the most critical days of his life. The claret-and-blue briefs bearing the crest of his beloved Aston Villa had seen him through his A-level exams, driving test, various job interviews and a number of important sales pitches. Admittedly, they had brought him little joy when it came to nights on the pull, but he knew when he was on to a good thing and retained his faith in their luck-providing power.

While he didn't hold any of his suits, shirts or ties in the same regard as his sacred underwear, he still had his favourites and this day called for white collars and pinstripes. The man he saw in the mirror wouldn't have looked out of place chairing top-level meetings at a large American bank and this image of hard-hitting corporate sophistication would be too much for any average home-seekers. who would be falling over each other to put pen to paper on the most dubious of properties just to have the privilege of doing business with this exceptionally dapper individual.

Francis brushed his teeth twice after breakfast in case his breath gave away any indication of his activities from the night before. This reminded him of Stacey. He called up her number in his contacts list, but, glancing at his watch, decided that trying to contact her before nine would be to stoop to unparalleled levels of keenness. He would wait until eleven at least.

Curiosity had got the better of him by 10:23. Everyone was out of the office on house visits, apart from himself and Lisa, the Saturday secretary, who was as annoying as she was incompetent. Francis had only one viewing that morning – the house on Lupton Road – and the phones were eerily quiet for a Saturday. He took the opportunity to carry on where he had left off with Stacey the night before. Text messages were the best method of attack in these uncertain situations, as they avoided the embarrassment of the other person um-ing and ah-ing on the other end of the phone as they tried their best to reject you in a nice way, if they even remembered who you were.

It took a number of attempts to produce a message he was happy with. Francis was no literary genius and he didn't want to fluff his lines at such an early stage of the relationship. He opted to avoid the comic route, as he had some doubts about his own funniness and had absolutely no idea what sort of sense of humour she had. In the end, he opted for a succinct message that he felt got his point across effectively while limiting the likelihood of a loss of face.

> hi. there is light at the end of the tunnel in terms of the project. r u free 2 meet up in the near future?

The display flashed ✔ **Message Sent,** and then all he could do was wait.

Eight minutes had passed and the suspense was getting to him. Francis spent more time looking at the tiny LCD display on his handset than he did examining the new properties list, the details of which he was supposed to be inputting into his computer. Three minutes later he phoned his own number to check it was working properly. Five minutes after that, Francis was in the middle of writing a test text message to himself when a dark shadow passed over his desk, indicating the arrival of some potential clients. Visibly flustered, Francis quickly threw his phone into a drawer and slammed it shut.

'Yes.'

He was greeted by two girls, one tall and one short, who couldn't have been much older than twenty. Students. His embarrassment at being caught frantically texting vanished as he realised he was dealing with the underclass.

'How can I help you?' he added, his voice adopting a smarmy, patronising tone that boiled the blood of the two ladies.

They explained they were looking for a two-bedroom flat within ten minutes' walk of the station that would cost no more than one hundred pounds each a week. Francis shook his head.

'I'm afraid you'll find your budget will severely limit the options available to you. Let me see...'

He fanned through the rental listings brochure, skipping quickly towards the back pages to the cheaper properties. Suddenly, from the depths of his desk emerged a strident beep that echoed around the wooden cavity so loudly that it made all three of them jump. A text message had arrived and Francis had to get rid of these two layabouts before he could read it.

'I'm afraid all I have is a seventh-floor flat in the Winstanley Estate, which is...' he pointed at a large, black-and-white ordinance survey map that hung proudly on the wall, 'about there. Over the other side of the station.'

'Isn't that a council estate?' asked one of the girls, turning her nose up slightly at the very suggestion.

'Yes it is, although the number of privately owned properties is increasing all the time. As I said, you'll struggle to get anything better for a hundred pounds a week.'

The girls looked concerned as their misguided dream of finding an affordable palace was shattered. This was precisely the reaction Francis was looking for. They were most likely from wealthy families, and to this day had lived their lives wrapped in cotton wool paid for by their stinking rich fathers. They would go and look elsewhere and he would be free to check Stacey's response.

'We'd like to look at it, please,' requested the taller girl, who had been the sole spokesperson up to this point.

This frustrated Francis, as he knew it would be a waste of time. There was no way these delicate daddy's girls would be willing to live in Clapham Junction's equivalent to the ghetto, and it would be a fruitless trip for all concerned.

'Are you sure?' questioned Francis. 'What I mean is, it can be quite rough around there. Burnt-out cars and stuff. Well, I exaggerate a bit, but you get my point. Two young girls, *attractive* young girls, living alone. To be completely honest with you, I wouldn't live there myself, so I doubt you'd feel safe.'

'I think *we'll* be the judge of that,' snapped the previously mute friend, sick of this arrogant, sleazy, patronising man who was sitting there dressed like a wannabe stockbroker.

'That's fine. Indeed. Right,' grovelled Francis, begrudgingly booking them in for an afternoon viewing.

Before they were even out of the door he was excitedly opening his drawer, his face like that of a child on Christmas morning as he noticed the graphic that signalled a text message had been received.

Unfortunately, the content of the text wasn't particularly uplifting. It read:

I'M SORRY, I HAVE NO IDEA WHO YOU ARE

Francis slumped back dejectedly in his chair, then sprung forward again with rejuvenated hope. His original message had given no indication of his identity, and his little white lie about working on an important project obviously hadn't struck a chord. Add to this the fact that she didn't possess *his* mobile number and it explained the confusion. From Stacey's point of view, the message could have been from anyone. He sent a follow-up message:

```
whoops! sorry Stacey, it's Francis
from last night. just wanted to know
if you fancied going for a drink?
```

✓ **Message Sent**

That ought to clarify things. Allowing for a delay in delivery, plus an assumption of the average person's text-writing speed, her response was almost immediate. She must be keen. Francis checked nobody was watching, then eagerly opened the message.

```
STACEY??? MY NAMES DAVE. THINK YOU'VE
GOT THE WRONG NUMBER MATE. FRANCIS?!?
YOU A BIRD OR A GUY?
```

The parting comment was the nail in the coffin for Francis, who had sunk lower and lower with every word. It was a blatant dig at his name, unlikely as it was that 'Dave' seriously thought he had stumbled across a lesbian.

Francis sent a final message back, a one-word note that simply read:

```
dickhead
```

Dave's response was instantaneous.

```
YOU'LL REGRET THAT
```

Francis doubted this very much, but he wasn't about to waste another ten pence sharing this fact with his persecutor. To be on the safe side, Francis kept the phone number stored in his address book under the name 'Dangerous Dave' in case he were to phone him at work, in which case Francis' always professional manner of answering his phone would give away his location and he didn't want to be faced with a disgruntled Dave coming into the office all loaded up with testosterone.

It then occurred to him that Dave could call him from a different phone to the same effect and he began to wish he had never sent the message at all. Nevertheless, the anxiety caused by the infinitesimally small chance Dave might carry out his threat paled in comparison to the fact the stupid bint had given him the wrong number. The most irritating thing was that the brainless wench was likely clutching her phone tight against her improbably wonderful breasts right now, wondering why he hadn't called. He should have given her his number instead. Not that it would have made much difference as the dense cow would doubtless have managed to lose it anyway.

The arrival of Stuart bounding gleefully into the office with no evidence of a hangover was the last thing Francis needed. The little prick had been out on visits all morning, so Francis had yet to have the pleasure of his company until now.

'Gee, Fran, I think the tradin' floor is thataway,' crowed Stuart in a corny American accent.

'Morning Stuart,' sighed Francis, ignoring the joke at his attire's expense.

He knew he looked good, especially when compared to Stuart. The padded shoulders of Stuart's cheap, charcoal suit hung loosely from him as if he had chosen it to allow for growth.

'Yeah, morning Francis. What happened to you last night?'

Francis was amazed he had the gall to ask this.

'I felt a bit knackered, so I went back on the last bus.' He didn't look up from his screen as he spoke.

A long silence followed as both pretended to do some work.

It was Stuart who broke the ice.

'Rumour has it, you pulled.'

'That is correct.'

'Was he a good kisser?'

'You're a funny man, Stuart. Her name was Stacey and yes, *she* was.'

'Did you shag her?'

'No.'

'Did you get her number?'

'Yes.'

'Have you called her yet?'

'No, and I don't think I will either.'

'Why not?'

Stuart wasn't taking the hint.

'It was a drunken thing. I'm happy to leave it at that.'

'You mean she was a munter,' Stuart assumed, correctly.

'Not at all. She was pretty damn fine. A bit young for me, though.' He hoped nobody had seen her up close.

'Cradle-snatcher.'

Predictable.

'Not *that* young.'

'Well, you'll have to point her out next time.'

'Will do.'

It was the end of the conversation and one of their more civil ones. Without an audience, Stuart was bearable, albeit only in small doses, but Francis hadn't forgiven him for instigating the mass desertion the night before. They continued pretending to work in silence.

It was just before eleven; not long until his career-saving appointment.

'I'll see you later,' he said.

There was no harm in getting there early.

'Yeah, good luck. You know you're gonna need it. Pigeon Street...' Stuart chuckled and shook his head.

Francis puffed out his chest and strode over to the door.

'Bye, Francis,' smiled Lisa.

'See ya,' he said, without turning back.

His car was still parked around the corner, where it had been sitting since the day before. It nearly always spent Friday

181

nights away from home, unless Francis wasn't drinking for some reason, such as illness or a lack of drinking partners. It took a couple of attempts to get it started. The winter months seemed to give it asthma, and the engine coughed and wheezed into action. It was a sick motor, deteriorating with each month that passed. He would buy a new car as soon as he had the money. One that matched his suit.

Lupton Road was only a five-minute drive away, but it was vital that he turned up before his clients, as this would allow him to interrupt, control and, most importantly, limit their examination of the area. Unquestionably, the less they saw of the street the better. Intercepting them as they arrived would allow him to quickly point out some of the neighbourhood's more positive features, such as the lack of traffic. And the trees. That would pretty much be the extent of the niceties.

* * *

Clapham basked in the apathetic December sunshine, while Lupton Road sat brooding in a sullen shadow like a great concrete vampire longing for the return of darkness, where it could thrive and feed. Hung low in a sky unspoilt by cloud, the dazzling ochre disc gave off a lustrous blaze but no warmth, peeking out from above the rooftops and casting long, distorted shadows that stretched for miles. This created an elaborate network of black, in stark contrast to the pockets of light that leapt off the puddles as though the floor was sprinkled with polished glass. Yesterday's wind had been replaced with a deadened tranquillity, the cul-de-sac sprawling uncomfortably in the languor.

Crouching low like a mutant beetle, a skip squatted, idle and rusting; a permanent resident in the parking space outside number 17. Its contents were piled high like a mountain of history, each layer a snapshot of someone's past existence; a sodden, lifeless semblance of a time gone by when they all had a purpose. Now all that remained was a tarnished reflection of their former glory. A once-regal wooden chair slumped upside down in one corner, its protruding limbs saturated, bloated, twisted by the weather, the intricate work of a craftsman wasted away by a cycle of watering and freezing. Crisp packets, fish-and-chip wrappers and discarded magazines added some variety to the refuse, with pictures of the celebrity flavour of the week grinning up at the sky with transparent smiles that revealed the pages underneath.

Made prominent solely by its macabre form was a headless doll; a cheap, crude replica of a baby. Arms and legs moulded into a fixed position, it was constantly reaching out for an embrace that would never come. The skin, a repulsive pale red that befitted no race, was smeared with filth, its patches of greys and browns like bruises. The decapitated head lay some five feet down the road, too big to wash down into the gutter, into which it had been carried by the wind and rain. Sitting atop the grill like a meatball on a griddle pan, it stared upwards through its one remaining eye; still bright and full of life, the eyelid never blinking; constantly observing the everyday lives of the street's inhabitants.

No longer fighting against the blustering wind, the trees stood tall and rigid like a military display, their brittle arms finding a sinewy strength in the calmness. The rain had brought the smog to earth and the air was left fresh and crisp. Gone was the aroma, the texture, the taste. Now there was nothing. A void.

A vehicle slid in at the base of the mushroom-shaped road, simultaneously entering and shattering the torpor. As the single animate object, it instantly became the point of focus. Everything was so quiet that the sound of tyres passing over the tarmac was distinct, a low scraping sound interspersed with the occasional scrunch of a piece of litter or fallen twig. An alien intruder, the car endangered itself by its mere presence, the street doing its utmost to reject it, engulf it, suffocate it; threatening to swallow it up and spit it back in the direction from which it came.

The car pulled up behind the skip; two rusty hunks of metal in an unattractive juxtaposition. The body of the car partially obscured the skip from the view of anybody turning in from the main road, which was a deliberate ploy on the part of the driver. The engine died and once again the scene was an unstirring plateau. It remained thus for some time, the wind occasionally mustering up enough puff to tickle a branch or rustle a newspaper, but there was nothing noticeable without having to look hard for it.

The next notable development was a young couple entering the scene from stage left. Their introduction prompted the driver to step out of his car. He remained at its side and waited for the couple to come to him rather than going to meet them, ensuring all parties were aware that his was the position of power.

The costumes the players wore for the occasion were varied. The couple wore modern dress, adopting the urban look of dark greys and blues that oozed off their legs. Their boot-cut trousers bunched around their ankles, almost touching the floor. Their attire made them look younger than their years, maintaining their grip on youth through fashion.

The woman sported a knitted cardigan, which was purposefully frayed around the edges as though it had been stolen from a charity clothes bin; a concoction of green, grey and pink that shouldn't have worked but somehow did, the garment giving the illusion of being six inches deep and suitable for arctic exploration. Its stylish scruffiness was in stark contrast to the neatness of her hair, which was tied back with impeccable precision. There wasn't a strand out of place and the bun was so tight it provided a natural facelift, pulling her skin taught over her sculptured features, not a line or sag in sight. Her skin glowed in the frosty freshness, so smooth it looked almost polished, carrying a healthy shine that could dazzle the gaze of anyone who lingered on it for too long.

Her partner's features were as rugged as hers were immaculate. His chin and cheeks wore a soft stubble, the result of a number of days' growth, while his neck had that slightly scalded appearance that comes from frequent shaving. His hair was no longer than his beard, but it was denser and more uniform, as though it had been coloured onto his scalp with an HB pencil. He wore a navy hoody that sat kindly across his broad shoulders, the hood only partially disguising the angular muscularity of his thick neck.

By comparison, the estate agent's clothing was formal. The combination of white collar and black suit meant that, from above or behind, and at a distance where the pinstripes weren't apparent, he could have been mistaken for a man of the cloth. He was a man of considerable physical stature, possessing a size that came naturally rather than manufactured in a gym, a protuberant belly lurking within the confines of the suit, which was a decent enough fit to hide it well.

The couple seemed to slow down hesitantly as they drew near to the lone figure, taking smaller and smaller steps that would never fully take them to their destination. Sensing their uncertainty, the man moved towards them, one hand outstretched in offer of an introductory handshake, which was accepted with gratitude.

'You must be Francis,' said the man as he enthusiastically shook his hand. 'I'm Dale,' he continued, without waiting for a response, 'and this is Andrea.'

He gestured towards the girl and Francis shook her hand, noting how cold it was compared with Dale's.

'Nice to meet you both. I believe we spoke on the phone, Dale.'

'Yes, on Thursday.'

It hardly had the makings of a great conversation.

'Lovely morning,' commented Francis, moving swiftly to the trusted topic of the weather.

'It's wonderful, isn't it?' replied Andrea in a voice too powerful and too deep for a woman of her build. 'Especially when you think what it was like yesterday.'

Francis chuckled, even though the comment wasn't supposed to be humorous. A bit of laughter always helped to relax the punters. Now that the weather had been discussed, it was time to move on to business.

'Right then, let's get to it!'

Francis rubbed his hands together and marched off down the road, bypassing the skip and hoping the couple would follow closely behind. The couple exchanged a raise of eyebrows in reference to Francis' attempt at power dressing, but followed him all the same. They were there to rent a house and if that meant having to deal with somebody dressed like an idiot, so be it.

'Here we are, then,' announced Francis, holding his arms aloft to signal that they had arrived at their destination.

It was hardly a glorious sight. The whole area needed disinfecting. It was only distinguishable from other similar dead-end roads by the vast amount of rubbish and muck. The garbage formed a rainbow perimeter that traced the shape of the estate, pushed as far back as the wind could manage, but halted by walls, gates and trees. It was almost artistic; a broken, multicoloured arc of distorted shapes, some transparent, some insipid; a varied border to the uniformity of the buildings themselves.

The house itself, number 21, had been split vertically in half, forming two properties rather than one, which would have substantially increased the rental income for the owner. If they were occupied, that was. Dale and Andrea were there to view the upper flat. There was no garden, but then again there would be no noise coming through the ceiling. And it was also cheaper.

'A little bit about the area first,' said Francis, psyching himself up for the hard sell. 'Do you know Clapham at all?'

'I... we've a couple of friends who live on the Falcon estate,' said Dale, 'but I've never really come to this part of town.'

This was good news.

'Ok then, well I'll give you a brief rundown.' Francis took a deep breath. 'You're less than fifteen minutes' walk from Clapham Junction Station, and Queenstown Road Station is also within walking distance.'

He paused to make sure they were still listening. They were.

'There's a regular, reliable bus service that runs into town, and the bus stop is at the end of the road. You have an allocated parking space at the front of the house, so you just need to contact the council to obtain a permit. Do either of you have a car?'

They shook their heads.

'Sensible, living in London. Well, anyway, it'll be useful for when you have guests. The nearest supermarket is Asda.' Francis subconsciously tapped his back pocket to simulate the 'Asda Price' advert. 'Plus you have a range of shops, pubs and bars in both directions.'

'Does this place ever get cleaned?' Andrea interrupted, looking at the rubbish in disdain.

Cut off in full flow, Francis stammered as he was forced to think on the spot.

'Th-the council are supposed to come fortnightly.' This was true, even if the words sounded like a work of fiction.

'Supposed?'

'Hmmm, I see your point. I'm sure the recent weather has plenty to do with the present state. I've never seen it anywhere near this bad before.'

They didn't look too convinced. Francis needed to act quickly.

'On the plus side, you're a long way from the main road, and being a cul-de-sac, traffic flow is minimal. The area is generally quiet, as you can see.'

Francis gestured behind them and they turned to look onto the deserted street, which was as still and silent as when they had first arrived. The general state of disrepair and the deluge of rubbish and debris meant they could have been forgiven for thinking they had stumbled across the aftermath of a nuclear apocalypse and that the only other survivor, an inexplicably overdressed man, was still intent on carrying out his duties by trying to lease them a property in a place whose only other inhabitants were cockroaches.

Their puzzled expressions didn't go unnoticed by Francis, who thought it best to move them indoors as quickly as possible. He didn't really want them to see what their neighbours-to-be were like. And the pigeons, conspicuous by their absence up to this point, wouldn't stay away forever.

'Right then, I'll show you around the inside.'

For one awful second, Francis panicked that he had forgotten to bring the keys to the flat. However, they were hiding in the very depths of his left-hand jacket pocket, the fifth place he checked. Even then he only found them at the second attempt.

'Phew,' he said to the couple, pretending to mop his brow, a strong element of truth behind his theatrical anxiety.

They all squeezed into the tiny entrance porch at the base of the stairs like sardines in a tin. Francis fumbled for the light switch and thankfully it worked.

'I don't know if you noticed as we came in, but the main door has a double letterbox so your mail doesn't get mixed up. They feed through into the two bins behind you. The key to the cage is kept in the flat,' he added, 'which is right this way.'

As he led them upstairs, a stale, damp aroma seeped out of the walls and kicked up from the carpet with every step. It was the smell of emptiness, of abandonment. One could only guess how long it was since anyone had trodden this path.

After the stinking staircase, the flat itself was something of a revelation. Sullied carpet was replaced by polished wood, which, although in need of a thorough sweep, was nonetheless pleasing to the eye and reassuringly firm. Here the smell had nowhere to rest or linger, so it stayed away, an invisible barrier preventing it from entering. And it was warm; an inborn warmth not due to the heating, as if the walls were three feet deep and had captured and held the summer sunshine, holding it long enough to last through the winter and into the spring.

'The door to the right leads into the lounge.'

Francis darted through the double doorway, temporarily vanishing from view. They found him standing in the middle of a small, adequate sitting room, furnished with two sofas: a two-seater and an armchair, both blue and covered by a crass, textureless material that spoke volumes of their cheapness. The colour sat uncomfortably next to the industrial grey of the carpet, a conservative choice designed to complement any choice of upholstery, but failing in this case. The carpet wore the scars of cigarette burns and liquid spillages, detailing the carelessness of previous tenants. The furniture had no doubt been tactically placed to hide the worst of it from view, as it was neither an obvious arrangement nor one that worked from a Feng Shui perspective. The only other pieces of furniture were a pine bookshelf and an austere dining-room table surrounded by four equally unnoteworthy chairs. The room was a step up from the staircase – comparatively as well as literally – but disappointing after the minimalist splendour of the corridor.

'And the kitchen is through there.'

A further door lay just out of sight on the wall adjacent to the front of the house. Behind the door was a kitchen so small that it would struggle to accommodate two grown adults at the same time. Unfortunately, the kitchen was already in use. Two large cockroaches stood confidently on the work surface, motionless except for their bobbing antennae, which rotated like radars. Sensing the movement, they turned towards the door, unperturbed by their giant alien guests and soon returning to whatever it was they were doing; namely eating, laying eggs and socialising.

Dale froze at the sight of the bugs, rooted to the spot, utterly immobilised. Andrea acted quickly. In one movement, she stepped towards them, drew a tissue from her pocket and swept them into her open palm, the tissue holding them in place. The roaches didn't even have enough time to raise one of their six legs.

'Could you open the window, please?'

Francis obliged, the window sticking slightly from the dried-in dirt. Andrea threw the pests out and they plummeted to the ground. They landed dazed but unscathed, gathering their consciousness before scuttling back to the asylum of the house. The whole flat seemed to shudder and shrink at the influx of cold air, and it was a relief when Francis slammed the window shut again. The abrupt change in air pressure and the loud crack of the window pane as it slotted back into position left all three of them temporarily deaf and disorientated.

Andrea was the first come to her senses.

'It's safe to come in now, Dale.'

Dale entered warily, eyes scanning for evidence of more cockroaches. He smiled wryly at his irrational fear.

'Man, I hate those things.'

'There are plenty of them in London, I'm afraid,' said Francis. 'Gives you an incentive to keep the place clean, right?'

He chuckled and gave Andrea a wink. She smiled back out of politeness.

'Everything you see in the flat will be here when you move in. Except for the cockroaches,' he added quickly. 'I'll get an exterminator in to sort that out. What I mean is, the washing machine, microwave and furniture all come with the flat.'

'Ok,' said Andrea, washing away the remnants of the insects under the tap.

Dale nodded in fake approval, eager to leave the kitchen.

The bathroom was the next destination. It was functional, albeit somewhat spoilt by some tasteless lino that didn't stretch far enough across the floor, leaving an unsightly barren patch of exposed floorboards that were not designed to be on show.

The bedroom was similar in its mediocrity: a reasonable size, sparsely decorated and only the bare necessities in terms of furniture.

'Well, that concludes the tour,' said Francis. 'That's pretty much all I can show you.'

'Can we have a minute?' asked Dale.

'Sure, sure. I'll wait for you in the lounge.'

'Thanks.'

Francis loped off down the corridor, leaving Dale and Andrea to contemplate the magnitude of what they were letting themselves in for. At least they were thinking about it. The bathroom had hardly been inspiring and the cockroaches had definitely been the low point. That they were even considering renting the place was a minor miracle. Francis felt satisfied with the part he had played in the proceedings. He had been charming, witty, informative and, above all, he had been professional.

If they decided against taking the flat, it would be through no fault of his own. Conversely, if they put pen to paper, he would be elevated to the status of lettings guru. All of his colleagues had taken numerous stabs at offloading the flat, but the suspect location always proved too much of an obstacle. It had become the red-hot coal of the office, passed around like a bag of rats with nobody wanting it on their books for too long in case it became a permanent stain. So, when Francis had agreed to take it on for what must have been the fifth time and keep it until he had leased it out, the others had breathed a collective sigh of relief. His repeated failure to rent it out, rolling up time and time again to meet prospective tenants like some kind of Trojan donkey, made their unproductive days seem less so.

Francis saw it differently. To him, 21a Lupton Road had become something of an obsession; his own personal holy grail. He had quit at too many things in his life, and it was time to make a stand. This one wasn't going to get the better of him. He saw the flat as his chance of redemption; an opportunity to gain the respect of those he worked with; a means by which to silence the doubters.

'We've come to a decision,' said Dale, as he and Andrea entered the room.

'Wow, that was quick,' exclaimed Francis, fearing that the hastily made resolution was to be a negative one.

'We'd like to take it,' said Andrea, her words devoid of conviction or enthusiasm.

Dale's words gave a reason for her indifferent demeanour: 'While it's hardly our dream home, it'll do for the moment, until we've had a chance to find somewhere better.'

'Sure, sure,' said Francis sincerely.

'I understand it's possible to get a six-month contract,' he said, more as a statement than as a question.

'Yes, that would be absolutely fine.' Francis tried his best not to sound too eager.

'Ok then, I guess it's a deal.'

He had done it. Francis the king. Francis the legend. He had leased the unleaseable. What a way to end the barren streak, to banish the fiend that had clung to his back for so long! Stuart, Tony, Neil and the rest of them would be forced to go down on bended knee and praise his superiority. How he looked forward to returning to the office.

Dale held out his right hand to forge a gentleman's agreement, withdrawing it before Francis had time to shake it as a muffled cry bled through from the neighbouring house.

'What the fuck was that?' asked Dale, more out of amusement than anything else.

'What was what?' replied Francis, pretending not to have heard.

'It sounded like a man screaming,' said Andrea, wearing an expression of concern.

'I must've missed it,' Francis said agitatedly. 'Look, let's get going. I can give you a lift back to the office and we can go through the paperwork.'

Holding open the front door with one hand, Francis waved them through with the other. Dale shrugged his broad shoulders and left without further prompting, while Andrea hung back for a moment in the hope of discovering further indiscretions. Beginning to feel foolish for standing there, listening out for the daytime equivalent of a bump in the night, Andrea eventually followed suit and Francis was relieved to be able to close the door on 21a Lupton Road, hoping he wouldn't have to return for at least another six months.

Back on the pavement, Dale and Andrea waited among the litter while Francis double-locked the main door of the house. Swapping the keys in his hand for his car keys, Francis skipped gaily towards them along the garden path, twirling the jangling bundle of metal around and around on his index finger, the bronzes and silvers scattering the sunlight into a metallic Catherine wheel. A five-minute drive was all that separated him from his moment of crowning glory.

He was halted in his tracks by a second howl from the neighbouring house. This time the sound was more pronounced, partially stifled by the walls and windows, but still distinct. It rang out audibly and eerily, slicing through the silence, the turbulent wail piercing and spreading like a shotgun cartridge filled with pellets of dread. It was enough to stop Francis dead in his tracks, giving him such a start that the keys leapt from his hand, tumbling gracefully through the air before crashing in a heap on the lawn. He went to retrieve them, and as he bent down he was disturbed by a third cry. This time they were all listening out for it, and the words were unmistakeable.

'Help me!'

'I'm sorry about this, it's most unexpected,' Francis apologised.

They weren't listening. Dale had placed a comforting arm around Andrea's shoulders and they were sharing a whole range of concerned looks.

'Help me, please!' Another desperate plea.

Francis could feel the sale slipping away from him due to events beyond his control.

It was Dale who compounded his fears: 'Look, Francis, we're going to need more time to think about it.'

The words shattered his resolve, tearing through his self-assurance, deflating him so much that they might as well have left him in the skip with all the other unwanted, useless junk.

'But...'

Francis couldn't find the words to convince them otherwise. His confidence had left the building. He had nothing left to offer.

'We're sorry,' said Andrea compassionately. 'We'll get back to you later on when we've reached a final decision.'

They all knew this decision had already been made. Why prolong the agony? The words were analogous to a girl saying, "I'll let you know." Bloody women and their mind games. They think they're being nice by not giving a straight rejection, when all they're doing is promoting false hope.

'Ok,' muttered Francis, doing the typical bloke thing and clinging to that very same false hope.

At least they had the courtesy to tell him now rather than scabbing a lift back into town and springing it on him at the office in front of everyone else. However, this was small consolation and Francis sulkingly stretched his hands towards the brick wall bordering the front garden, found it and sat down, the stones so cold they chilled his buttocks through his jacket, trousers and pants. The lucky pants that had failed him again.

The exit of Dale and Andrea had left him in a state of despair. The greatest sale in estate agent history had vanished, plucked from his grasp at the eleventh hour. He was back where he had started, and the fear for his employment returned stronger than ever now that his saving grace was all but dead. Looking down at his clothes, he saw himself for what he really was. A failure. It was all a facade. Beneath the spurious bravado of the suit cowered a bumbling fool, an oaf, another of life's losers, hopeless at the job *he* loved and everybody else loathed.

'Help. Please, help me.'

That fucking lunatic! It was probably some scally kid mucking about to stop him leasing the house.

'Shut the fuck up!' Francis hollered back.

Tears of anger welled up in his eyes and he didn't care who heard him; not Dale, not Andrea. The fickle bastards. In a way, he wished they *could* hear him to see what their petty standards had reduced him to.

'I beg you, please,' the voice replied, coarse and weakened.

Francis stormed over to the door of number 20 and pounded on it with both fists.

'Fuck off!' he roared. Then he stooped down to yell through the letterbox: 'You could've cost me my fucking job!'

He was well aware that he was losing it, but the events of the last two days – the pub walkout; the hideous hen night; the traumatic kiss; Stacey's wrong number; the threat from Dave and now this – it was all too much for him.

'Call the police,' came the voice.

It was a pleading, begging request. To Francis' ears, it sounded sarcastic and mocking.

'Too right I'm gonna call the fucking police!' bellowed Francis. 'I'm gonna have you arrested for disturbing the peace!'

'Thank you! Thank you so much.'

Sarcastic fucker, thought Francis as he punched the numbers into his phone. *Well, I'll show that wanker not to mess.*

'Which service do you require?'

Francis steadied himself before he answered.

'Police, please.' A pause followed. 'Hello, yes, I'd like to report a disturbance at 20 Lupton Road.'

* * *

When the police arrived, they found a man who was farcically overdressed for his stated occupation. The man was so insistent on having a rant to anyone who would listen that, after taking his details, he was told in no uncertain terms to return to his place of work to calm down, and to stay there until he heard otherwise, at which point he would have to come down to the station to make a statement. It was a relief to all those present when he begrudgingly left. However, the moans from within the house did not cease and the police made the decision to enter by force.

* * *

A search of the house turned up four people: one alive and three dead. The survivor, a man in his late twenties, identified himself as Joseph Peters. Mr Peters was found in what was a largely empty spare bedroom, tied by his hands, ankles and neck to a wooden chair that had toppled onto its side, so that he was effectively lying on the floor in a seated position. The chair was distinguishable, in that it had been modified to enable it to be easily moved about while a person was seated in it.

Mr. Peters' body showed signs of torture and neglect. There were visible cuts and bruising to his face and neck, friction burns around his wrists from the rope, and closer examination revealed possible fractures to his left shoulder and ribcage. Also evident were signs of sleep deprivation and malnutrition. At first glance, it seemed that the man had been tied in this position for some time as he was covered in his own excrement.

A further body was found in the same room and identified as that of Allan Thompson. Mr Thompson had been dead for a number of days with the cause of death recorded as suicide by hanging. There were no other signs of injury to his person.

The adjoining bedroom contained another two bodies. Both had been carefully wrapped in plastic sheeting and stored in a large antique wardrobe. This had done little to mask the smell. They were identified as Jack and Martha Thompson, owners of the house and the parents of Allan Thompson. They had been dead for up to two weeks. Mr Thompson had been killed by repeated blows to the head with a blunt, heavy object, possibly a hammer, while

Mrs Thompson had been the victim of multiple stab wounds. Initial investigations suggested that both murders had been carried out by Allan Thompson.

Nothing else unusual was found within the house, which had otherwise been kept in an immaculate condition. However, a modified plank of wood that could only be described as a home-made, miniature bed of nails, was found face down in the flowerbed of the front garden. This was thought to have been used to prevent birds from landing on the windowsill of the master bedroom. It was likely that it had been knocked down during the recent storm.

* * *

Untying the shackles and granting Joseph freedom of movement for the first time in ten days brought little relief. A paramedic slid the chair away from his emaciated body and, after a check for visible bleeding, placed a blanket over him. The natural impulse was to stretch, to work the fatigue from his joints, yet no amount of willpower could overcome the enervation of his muscles, which had suffered badly due to their inactivity. He felt like he was thawing out, having been frozen for years in suspended animation. It was a bleak condition to be in.

Joseph feared he may never move again, that he would be paralysed for eternity in a rigid, seated position. The lassitude affected his mind as well as his body, the sleepless nights and emotional distress traumatising his brain to such an extent that he couldn't cope with the commotion around him or the incessant questions, 'Are you able to move?' 'Are you in pain?' 'Are you able to speak?' There were so many questions, too many to comprehend, the voices merging into one. 'You, You, You.' Every word was a pejorative, a revilement.

He closed his eyes, but the voices remained, 'You, You, You.' Rusty nails in his legs prevented him from kicking out at his tormentors, his arms too decrepit to raise to his ears. 'You, You, You.' Allan lay next to him, rising to his feet, stiff and strong, his face dark, puffy and black. 'You, You, You.' Can't breathe. Must stop panicking. Here to rescue you. To help you, to laugh at you, to piss on you, to shit on you.

'GIVE HIM SOME SPACE!'

Now there is light. Quiet.

Two men dressed in green carefully lift Joseph onto a stretcher, where he lies in the same crooked position. They lift him with ease as he is nothing more than skin and bone, gaunt. And he smells. It's written on everybody's faces. They swan around him wearing expressions of revulsion. Nobody wants to breathe. He can't smell it, he's used to it. He can only smell the freshness of the air when they leave the room and the sterile, synthetic smell of the blanket.

Why do they scorn?

His is a natural smell, a dirty mix of blood, sweat and excrement, the most natural smell there is.

They carry the stretcher down the stairs. Although they move slowly and deliberately, he's bumped around. He should be in pain, but there's nothing, only numbness.

Angela. *Angela?*

Outside, the sun was shining brightly and the air was pricked with a retreating frost that promised to return in the dead of night and cast a silver sheet over anything that stayed still for too long. The street had undergone a complete transformation and was unrecognisably busy. Its residents had crawled out onto the street, disturbed by the sounds of sirens. They emerged from the houses like goblins from their caves, pale and stooped, squinting at the brightness. They congregated in a silent huddle, drawn by the flashing blue lights, facing number 20 like a crowd of zombies.

Joseph was unaware of their presence as he was being carried head first, although the attendance of yet more people would have brought little reaction. He was thankful for the blanket, which he clung to doggedly with what little strength he could muster. Its comfort came not from its warmth but from its role as a shield, concealing his twisted, soiled body from the intrusive, pitying stare of the outside world. It preserved what little dignity remained.

At the moment the doors of the ambulance were opened, Joseph was aware of something landing on his stomach, a sudden instance of pressure, over as quickly as it had arrived, as though somebody had prodded him with a stick. Looking down, he noticed a wet, brown stain on the blanket, interlaced with a mixture of white and black, like oil paint on an artist's easel.

He looked up at the skies for the provider of the present. It could have been one of three, as the trio of pigeons swooped overhead in a flash of grey before coming to rest at their favourite spot on the upstairs windowsill. Joseph lowered his gaze to the lump of crap on the blanket and his focus remained there as he was lifted into the ambulance and the doors slammed shut.

Shat on by a bird. It's good luck, apparently.

Leila

Sitting there in the Royal Albert Hall for close to three hours seemed like a monumental waste of time. Not that I had anything better to do with my afternoon. Far from it. Today had been just like any other day; a complete non-event. Life had become so mundane that each day merged into the next with seamless regularity. There was no longer such a thing as a weekend. To be so, there would have to be weeks. Yet, with no job and little motivation to find one, every day was exactly the same. The only thing that signalled the arrival of what the working population termed the weekend was that the pub would be a bit more crowded and what followed was two days of nothing on television, unless you were a fan of minority-interest sports or a lover of variety shows, of which I'm neither. Still, there existed within me a masochistic urge to bemoan the fact that this phenomenally dull ceremony was depriving me of non-existent social engagements with friends I didn't have.

As always, it was my parents' fault. They were the ones who had wanted to come to this intellectual beauty parade, to watch their beloved Leila stroll across the stage while the melodious throngs of the college orchestra danced through the air before ungraciously dying due to the hall's infamously bad acoustics. And they hadn't even come. They had simply booked tickets. Indeed, I had spotted a pair of empty seats where my parents maybe *should* have been sitting. It was a terrible shame the ceremony clashed with the store-card-holders' sale at Harrods.

'Don't worry, Leils,' my mother had said. 'We can go to Harrods in the morning and come to your graduation in the afternoon.'

'Whatever,' I had replied.

I knew Harrods. It was a huge, monstrous black hole of a shop. It sucked you in, wallet first, and once beyond the principle it was impossible to get back out. The only way to avoid its gravitational pull was to wear ripped jeans or a rucksack.

I knew my mother wouldn't be able to spend a mere morning doing sales shopping. Therefore, the 'personal' invitation from Mr Al Fayed had been like a blessing in disguise. Since my father would have to accompany my mother for the sake of our future financial stability, I had assumed this would mean my own attendance at the graduation ceremony would no longer be necessary. Unfortunately not. All this meant was that I had to attend alone. It made me smile looking at those empty seats, and at the same time imagining my mother riding up the Egyptian escalator like a poor man's Cleopatra, while a couple of steps down would be my father, weighed down like a bell-boy, wishing that an asp would slide from the cracks in the moving stairway and sink its poison into her bloodstream before she could spend any more precious money.

To me, the ceremony was meaningless. Of the hundreds, or even thousands of graduates on show, the number I knew was miniscule. One of the few exceptions was the idiot I had to sit next to, Luke Hinton, or 'dickhead', as I preferred to think of him. It was a constant source of annoyance that something as trivial as having the same surname meant that I always ended up sitting next to this moron.

'Hey, we've got the same surname,' he had said when we first met. 'Maybe we're related.'

'I doubt it,' I had replied, quickly scanning the room for somebody, anybody else, to talk to.

Even the suggestion that we might be genetically linked was utterly offensive. And he couldn't take the hint. He was a relentless pest, a giant wasp; always there, sitting behind me in the lecture theatre making imbecilic comments.

'Hey, we should get married. You wouldn't have to change your name or anything.'

When I had entered the hall earlier that day, I had seen him waiting there, grinning like a fool in anticipation of my arrival. The sight of him was almost enough to make me turn and flee. My parents would have been none the wiser if I hadn't had stuck around.

As it was, I had done everything properly. I had patiently queued for my gown and had allowed one of those appalling graduation photos to be taken. It was originally going to be a family shot, which would almost have been acceptable, but since my parents had deserted me I was forced into a cheesy solo effort. Modern technology meant that I was able to view the photograph on a computer before it was developed. It was awful.

Not because it was a particularly bad picture of me; in fact, I had been caught in good light and had almost carried it off. It was the robe, the hat and the ridiculous scroll. Had I been challenged to dress more like a ponce I would have struggled to do so.

'You look very distinguished,' the photographer had said.

I had smiled sarcastically as the flash hit the room, my defiance captured for eternity. The worst thing about it was that I would have to look at that photo every time I visited any member of the goddam family. I could see it now: holding a prominent place on the mantelpiece at my grandparents', sitting on top of the television at Great-aunt Charlotte's, watching people taking a leak from atop the cistern at Uncle Matthew's.

I had spent the rest of the day fighting an ongoing battle with my cumbersome robe, the parachute design of which was faultlessly efficient in catching the shrill October breeze, wrapping itself around my neck like a wrestler's stranglehold at even the slightest blow. All around me I was confronted by the smiling faces of proud parents and friends reunited. It made me feel lonely because I had neither, and I resented that. I liked to think I would always be content with merely myself for company and most of the time this was true, but not at times like this. This was an artificial situation; it wasn't real life. It had been created purely to identify my insecurities and throw them back in my face at every turn. Everybody was in their little groups, discussing how great their new jobs were, how great it was to be earning so much money, how great it was to see everyone again. Everything was so fucking great.

I walked anonymously through the masses, weaving between the padded, suited shoulders that jutted out from all sides; purpose-built make-up smudgers. This wasn't my year. It was everybody else's year. Three years of chemistry had been more than enough and I had left with all the other dossers and underachievers. A trip to Thailand had meant that my graduation was put back a year.

Much as it pains me to admit it, my solitary existence since leaving university had been entirely of my own making. Only a few months into my first year, I had already severed all links with my school friends. These 'new' people, my fellow freshers, were so much more interesting: untouched and varied, unfailingly friendly. These were *my* people, London people, not the small-town-mentality crowd from back home.

What had I been thinking? It was a science college! The workload soon kicked in and the exciting new crowd had withdrawn to their rooms. The once-partisan atmosphere of the halls of residence, which had begun with all the energy, verve and shallowness of a Butlin's holiday village, had become stagnant. The corridors had contained long stretches of shut doors, behind which the would-be professors studied and masturbated in roughly equal measures. Where people had previously gone to great lengths to be pleasant and inoffensive, their real personalities had eventually seeped out and the halls had resembled a Pandora's box of antisocial personality traits. The spoilt only-children, those from overprotected backgrounds, the drunken tossers, the bitching girls and the perverts had scuttled forward one by one and overtaken the ugly, seventies-style dormitory like an embodiment of social screw-ups.

I had hated it so much that I had decided to stay there for a second year, where I witnessed the same circle of events happening all over again: the initial optimism, the rapid decline and the culminating falseness of the final day, when everyone acted like they were upset and would really miss everyone. I hadn't bothered to pretend, which was partly why nobody was making any effort to talk to me now. Glances showed recognition but were quickly averted. I'm not the sort of person you particularly want to talk to in front of your parents.

'So what did you get in the end?' Luke asked, loud enough so that those around us would hear.

'I got a first. I was really shocked when I found out,' I replied, mimicking his volume of speech.

'Really?' Luke was shocked, not anticipating this answer at all.

'I guess I must have pulled it together in the final year. Shows what a difference a bit of hard work can make.'

'But you...' Luke started, cutting himself short.

He knew I hadn't done any work. I had hardly been to any lectures, let alone the library, at least not as far as he could remember.

'How about you?' I responded, sensing I had already crushed his resolve.

'I got a 2:1. A high 2:1, mind,' he quickly added. 'I think I fell down on synthetic condensation polymers.'

'Really? That exam was my highest mark. I got ninety-four percent or something,' I said, sinking my heel in further.

'Ninety-four percent?' Luke repeated, looking down. 'That must have been the highest mark in the year.'

'I thought that at first myself.' I was in full flow now. 'Then I figured somebody *must* have got a higher grade than me. I mean, it was such an easy paper. I bet there were a few who got a hundred.'

'Maybe,' said Luke, slumping back in his chair.

He had given everything for that 2:1, and the waster sitting next to him had quashed his achievement with ease. I smiled, knowing I had completely ruined Luke's day. He wouldn't be speaking to me again. Never. Ever. Again.

I was, of course, lying. I had got a third, not a first. A third. Three boring, unenjoyable years at a university I hated for a poxy third. But it was such an easy lie to tell. I had practised it on my parents, much to their delight. Plus the deal was, if I got a first, I got a car, and my doting parents were too easy a target, eager as they were to have a high-flying angel of a daughter.

'*My* daughter, a first-class student,' my mother would say, over and over again, whether there was anybody listening or not.

I was always *her* daughter if there was an achievement involved, so she could bask in my reflected glory. Otherwise, I was just plain old Leila.

The lie didn't even take much looking after. All it required was the disposal of my official degree classification when it arrived in the post and a couple of additional stories about administrative foul-ups at the university. Once my mother had begun telling every person she came across that her daughter was a genius, the rumour mill was set in motion and the lie became a virtual reality.

It remained a mystery to her how her daughter, armed with such an accolade, couldn't seem to find any sort of job.

'You'd think they'd be lining up to hire someone with your academic ability,' she used to say in bemusement at the sight of yet another rejection letter. I had left them lying about to let my parents know that I was still trying.

The closest I came to being caught out was when my overly keen mother got me an interview via 'one of Daddy's contacts'. With 'Daddy's' considerable influence, it should have been a formality, requiring only that I turn up with a pleasant smile on my face and the relevant documentation. The latter was obviously the problem. Even on my most rebellious of days I can smile for England provided there's something in it for me. But a display of pearly teeth and healthy gums would have gotten me nowhere without a piece of paper bearing the words 'First class honours', so I had been forced to decline the interview with the reasoning of wanting to make it off the back of my own abilities. Yeah right.

'Richard Colby, who has been awarded the Neil Arnott Prize, the Sondheimer Prize, the Nyholm Prize and the Chemistry Award for Excellence.'

The crowd gasped a collective 'Ooh' in awe of this young Avogadro on the stage before breaking into rapturous, respectful applause. Here was a model student: well-presented, slim and healthy, with an exceptional brain to match.

'Tosser,' Luke and I muttered in unison. At least there was one thing we agreed on.

From my distant vantage point, everybody looked the same. A gaggle of crows. All dressed in black, they crossed the stage like a trail of ants, different shapes and sizes but essentially all insects. Every now and then I would recognise a name; someone I hadn't spoken to since the first year or had regrettably snogged while intoxicated at the student union. These were in the minority, though. Most were anonymous entities, nobodies, insignificant Imperial College clones. Watching these strangers parading past reminded me of the time I had sat and watched the scores of the *Eurovision Song Contest* coming in without having seen any of the musical acts. Entirely meaningless. On that occasion, television had simply been preferable to study, as it always was, no matter what was showing. This time I was here against my own free will, which made it all the worse.

The usher signalled and my row stood up in turn, like a one-line Mexican wave. It was time. We made our way awkwardly down the steps to the pit, fiddling with each other's gowns, which were creased and crumpled from spending more than two hours beneath warm, sweaty behinds. I concentrated hard on every step. My worst fear was stumbling in front of all these people. That would really cap off what was already turning out to be a rubbish day. Two ushers blocked my way to the stage, their arms held across my path like nightclub bouncers.

'Are you Leila Hinton?' the man asked, while the woman looked down her finger at the never-ending list of names.

I nodded silently.

'Are you two related?' asked the woman quietly, gesturing towards Luke with a twitch of her head.

'Fuck you,' I whispered, recognising Becky, Little Miss Perfect, who I had had the misfortune of sharing a floor with in the first year.

Becky looked different in her formal wear – chic, refined, even *more* beautiful – and my dislike for her exploded to new heights. I marched defiantly through them and up the stairs, sensing the smug smile sitting proudly across Becky's sculpted lips behind me. A further person stood between me and the stage, which was empty apart from the rector who stood at its centre.

'Leila Hinton,' bellowed the announcer in a tone of voice that suggested I was about to receive the highest attainable military accolade.

The usher tapped me on the back and the stage opened out before me, imaginary curtains drifting apart to reveal a lawn of crimson felt. It was as if I was standing on the surface of an inflating balloon, and everything seemed to expand away from me. At the centre of the red abyss stood the rector: grey, rotund, a beardless St Nicholas. He looked swamped by the extravagant robes that burdened his stately shoulders like a patterned milkmaid's yoke. It was impossible to judge the size of his frame because the regal garments looked to have been layered upon him like a material pass-the-parcel.

As I approached him, I found myself pitying the old man, who might well not have been in a fit state to stand there for three hours in all those clothes. I had been determined not to bow to him. Why should I? I didn't know who he was or what the hell he had ever done for a third-rate student like myself. But as I drew closer, I saw his eyes. I saw through them to the turmoil within. It dawned on me that he didn't want to be there any more than I did, falsely smiling at the stream of arrogant youth, most of whom believed their achievement was a unique one; that their degree in mechanical engineering would set them up for a life of continual employment at London's finest financial establishments.

None of these people respected him. None of them knew of his work. To them, he was just another old man they were forced to show the utmost respect to, like he was royalty. He was well aware that most of the graduates would have preferred to receive their award from a D-list celebrity. His was a thankless task. And hard on the knees. He knew nobody would remember what he looked like, let alone his name, by the time they had left the stage. He was a fleeting novelty, and an acceptance of this was written in his eyes.

So, despite my preconceptions of how I would react at this point, I found myself stooping into a long and genuine bow as I came to a standstill opposite him. The corners of his mouth rose for a second and that faint smile, that display of appreciation from this bizarrely dressed old man, gave me far more pleasure than receiving a meaningless third for chemistry.

And then it was over, or at least my part in the proceedings was. The path back to my seat seemed to take an eternity, snaking through the maze of seated black beetles who were still and stuffed. Bugs on display. Eyes pressed into me from all directions as I moved, gravity gaining strength with each step and the floor becoming more and more liquid. By the time I got back to my seat I was drowning.

'Are you all right?' whispered the girl sitting next to me, noticing my distress.

'Yeah, I think so.'

'You look like you're about to faint.' She gave me a sympathetic smile.

'I'm probably just dehydrated,' I said, smiling back. 'It's pretty hot in here.'

'Here.' She began rummaging around in the rucksack stored under her chair.

She had come well prepared with fruit, chocolate, make-up and magazines. If only I had known this earlier. I could have done with something to read. The girl found what she was looking for, a bottle of water, which she unscrewed and offered to me.

'Thanks.'

I could see traces of her lipstick around the rim; a breeding ground for germs and bacteria. Who knew what she had put in her mouth since the last time she brushed her teeth. I checked her out before taking a sip to make sure she appeared to be of reasonable personal hygiene. She seemed clean enough – no cold sores or excessive acne – so I took a lug of the water, knowing that, once in my mouth, it was past the point of no return. I could hardly spit it out while I was sitting right there. While the water had once been refreshingly chilled, the overzealous heating meant it certainly wasn't now, and one of the problems with tepid water is that you can taste it. This stuff was unmistakably straight from the tap and the supplier had gone overboard on the chlorine. It must have been really dirty where she lived.

'Thanks,' I said again, handing her back the bottle.

'Please, have some more,' she insisted.

'No, thanks all the same. I feel much better now.'

Pushy cow. I'd had enough of drinking her swimming pool water.

The girl gave me a look. Maybe she could read my thoughts. I'm getting cynical in my old age. Negative. I really ought to do something about it. She was only being nice. I just find nice people hard to trust. I always suspect ulterior motives. I've never met a genuinely nice person, and I'm sceptical that such a thing even exists.

The rest of the ceremony passed without incident. Further highlights were largely restricted to the announcer's inability to pronounce foreign names. Anything that consisted of more than two syllables provided too great a challenge and the bumbled words would be met with joyous delight by the majority of the audience who, like myself, were rapidly losing the will to live. However, the loudest sniggers were reserved for the unfortunate students whose innocently chosen names had since taken on a whole new relevance due to the coming to the fore of a similarly named person in the public arena. An aeronautics student by the name of Robyn Cook was rewarded with the day's heartiest bellow of laughter, her make-up failing to hide her embarrassment. It must be pretty bad to have more than a thousand people laughing at your name. On the bright side, at least she didn't have to sit next to Luke Hinton. Every cloud.

It was something of a miracle that the seats remained filled for the duration of the ceremony. I pitied the parents whose children had walked up in the first passing. They would have recognised even fewer faces during the rest of the ceremony than I had. Then again, parents love this sort of tradition stuff. Well, most parents do. Others prefer shopping. It's testimony to the politeness of the British that bums stayed on seats until the final whistle. Maybe they were expecting a grand finale of sorts. Or maybe it was because they were paying to be there.

It was almost four o'clock by the time the ceremony ended and everybody rushed for the exits like the place was about to explode. The toroidal corridor that encircled the arena was suddenly a river of shiny black silk, heads bobbing up and down above the murky, oleaginous flow. People became overwhelmed by the number of exits as it dawned on them that their designated meeting places were ambiguous. They were confused, taking random walks; heading this way, that way, and stopping in awkward places like tourists on the London underground. I, on the other hand, knew exactly where I was going: exit 6, the main exit that led out onto Kensington Gore, the road that runs alongside Kensington Gardens. This was the same route used by the stars at award ceremonies and the only suitable place for my parents to wait. Around the back would have been more convenient for all of us, but it would have meant standing next to a building site and Mum would have complained about the increased possibility of getting dust on her clothes.

At five foot four, I'm only a couple of inches below average height for a girl, but this is enough to make me invisible in crowd situations. And it means that I'm armpit height to most men, which can make using public transport an unpleasant experience, especially during the summer months when temperatures on the tube can hit forty degrees. By law, cattle aren't allowed to be transported in such conditions. Afforded no adequate alternative, us Londoners just have to grin and bear it. And there's only so long you can hold your breath for. It wasn't quite that bad in the hallway, but I found it vexatious nonetheless. My bulldozer approach was proving unsuccessful, so I eventually consigned myself to the fact that I was going to have to be patient. After three hours of wasted time, another few minutes wasn't going to make a whole lot of difference. My parents would probably be late anyway.

For some reason, I expected it to be dark when I eventually made it outside, even though it had scarcely turned four. I think this was a throwback to my childhood, when cinema and theatre trips would always take place in the evening, so we would enter in daylight and leave in the dark. Here, the October sun was still shining as brightly as it been when I arrived, albeit much lower in the sky. There was no sign of my parents, so I waited in a spot where I was at least partly sheltered from the wind and still able to see them or be seen by them if they ever decided to show up.

It was pretty cold. The breeze had developed a sharper edge to it as the day went on and while I had resented my superhero cape earlier in the day, I was now appreciative of its warmth, hugging it close to my body like a gigantic scarf. I had my suspicions about where my parents were, but I was prepared to give them the benefit of the doubt for the time being. One day they might surprise me.

It felt like hours that I stood there waiting. I observed as my contemporaries and their families were reunited with open arms.

Some women were so proud they were crying. It makes me sick. They only got a degree, not a Nobel prize. It's really not that big of a deal. I would have hated for my Mum to cry about something so trivial. Not that there was much chance of that happening, mind you.

I switched my attention to the traffic instead. Traffic is calming, reassuring. It comes and it goes, relentlessly, one vehicle after another, sometimes stopping at the zebra crossing but otherwise emphatically racing through. Every car was different, every driver was different, but they were all doing the same thing. Passing by. Occasionally I saw an interesting vehicle and it became my focus for the whole time it was in view, everything else merely the supporting cast. Once gone, it was completely forgotten, with no memory of what was special about it, and I returned to watching *all* of the traffic again, alternating between those going east and those travelling west. I can watch traffic for hours if I'm in the right frame of mind.

Right at that moment, I was categorically not. A glance at my watch showed that it had only been thirteen minutes and I was already bored. Time passes so slowly when you're waiting on your own. The Gucci watch was a present from my Dad, and apparently it was worth a fair amount. I quite like it. It isn't too garish and the way the numbers are set out is quite funky. I tell everybody it's a fake, partly because I'm not particularly materialistic and don't want people to assume I am just because my dad can afford to buy me decent stuff, and partly so that people aren't tempted to nick it. More importantly, it keeps time well and right then it told me my parents were late. I phoned Dad's mobile but it was switched off, so I tried Mum's instead. It rang for some time before she answered.

'Oh, hi Leila. Are you finished already?' Her voice was quiet, muffled.

'Yeah, obviously *you* aren't.'

There was a pause. She was pretending to look at her watch or something, I suspected.

'Gosh! Is that the time? Sorry, Leils, I had no idea it was that late.'

She should be an actress, my mum. She really should.

'You're still in Harrods then, I take it?'

'Yes. Look, darling, you're not really allowed to use mobile phones in here. I'd better go.'

Charming.

'Fine. Listen, I'll come and meet you. Whereabouts are you?'

'We're in the food hall, darling.'

'Ok, well don't stray too far from there. I'll meet you in about fifteen minutes. By the cheese,' I added.

'Ok, Leils. See you later. Bye bye!'

She hung up.

The food hall? They had stood me up for the sake of browsing around a glorified supermarket! It was nice to know that I ranked below perfectly poached salmon and the finest foie gras. The truth was, I had already known this would happen, and when I left them at Harrods earlier I had already accepted deep down that it was likely to be me coming to meet them rather than the other way around.

Quite frankly, I wasn't too bothered. It saved me the hassle of having to take them to the post-ceremony chemistry drinks being held in the senior common room, where we would have been surrounded by some of the finest young minds in Great Britain. Geeks, in other words. And it would have quickly become apparent that I didn't know anybody there and, despite it not being my academic year, my parents would have got all concerned and tried to start up cringeworthy conversations with other parents in an attempt to push me into being sociable. So, in a way, it was a relief to ditch my robe and walk alone to Knightsbridge.

Having frequented this part of the city for three years, my local knowledge stretched as far as knowing a route to Harrods that wasn't only shorter, but more scenic. I left the phoney happiness of the student union and took a left down Prince Consort Road, passing the College of Music and the Royal School of Mines. The route took me onto Exhibition Road, so called because it plays home to the Science Museum, Natural History Museum and the V&A. My way avoided all of these, however, cutting through the small patch of green and trees that is Princes Gardens, a place where I lived for two of my three student years.

It didn't hold many happy memories for me. A few, but not many. For both of my resident years I was in the seventies monstrosity that is Southside Hall, a charmless, looming mixture of grey stone, windows and walkways. It isn't all that bad inside, it just doesn't sit well in the extravagance of SW6; Britain's costliest postcode. I was fortunate enough to have a room overlooking the gardens both years, which, apart from the nice view, had the advantage of being north-facing. So while those on the south side were literally sweating about their finals, I could relax and study in comfort. Or relax in comfort, as was the case. Their clammy fates were sealed when a potato-throwing incident resulted in locks being placed on all of the windows, plunging half of the hall into an airless greenhouse that reeked of BO and stale spunk.

Hands deep in my pockets, I walked past Southside Bar, a place where I had spent many an evening trying to forget where I was and who I was with. It's a good thing the drinks were cheap in that place as the rudimentary décor had all the allure and elegance of a multistorey car park. Seeing it again brought back memories of lethal birthday cocktails and the hockey team trying to fill a dustbin with vomit. They even had a brass band that played there every Wednesday. If I remembered correctly, it was a completely pointless addition to the entertainment roster, as all it did was spoil people's enjoyment of the European football. It's a shame I didn't have more time or I might have popped in for a quick browse around the place purely for the sake of nostalgia, but I had a dinner appointment to make, which was bound to be more fulfilling than a trip down a lager-scented memory lane.

Just beyond the halls of residence lay a quaint, cobble-stoned street that could have been lifted straight out of a small village in the south of France with its white-washed walls and hanging flower baskets, with an adjoining path that traced the perimeter of a peaceful churchyard. The residents must have been gutted when the powers that be decided to erect an unsightly student accommodation complex right next to their Gallic paradise, blocking out the sun and pumping the area full of an endless stream of marauding scientists and engineers.

A huddle of blokes was gathered at the oak tree that marked the turning point in the path. By the looks of their baby faces, I guessed they were freshers, which would make them about eighteen years old, although their messy hair, baggy trousers, chains and T-shirts emblazoned with the names of their favourite rock bands made them appear a couple of years younger. They thought they were dressed pretty damn slick, but without their skateboards they looked a bit lost, like they had been stranded on their way to a fancy dress party or something. The air was heavily fragrant with the unmistakeable smell of skunk and I noticed they were handing around a spliff, taking it in turns to sneak a puff or two while pulling ridiculous facial expressions in an attempt to look cool.

The kid facing me muttered something to the rest of the group as I approached and they all stopped what they were doing and turned to look at me. All conversation had ceased and they were staring at me, eyes tracing over my body, then back up to my face. I stared right back at them because I wasn't intimidated and I wanted them to know it. As I drew nearer, their expressions turned to sleazy smirks as they checked me out.

Blokes are such cowards. If any of them had been on their own they wouldn't have dared to take a second look but, surrounded by their mates, they reckoned they had a right to perve at me as I walked by. They were blocking the path and I was going to have to drive a wedge between them if I was to get past. I could have turned back and gone around the other way, which would only have cost me an extra couple of minutes, but I didn't see why I should have to make a diversion because some juvenile pricks couldn't control their hormones.

I stuck to my route, keeping the same pace and focus, and strolled on towards them in an undeviating path. It's a good thing they parted, otherwise I would have blundered straight into them. Not even granting them an acknowledgement of their presence, I passed slowly between them, aware all the time of their lustful eyes undressing me from high above as they towered over me like buildings. One of them wolf-whistled as I emerged from their circle and I gave him the finger, holding it defiantly aloft without looking back.

'Suck my dick, bitch,' someone called out, presumably the same guy.

I clenched my raised hand into a loose fist and waved it back and forth to signify what I thought of him and his mates. That's the problem with most blokes at Imperial. They were so used to being surrounded by other blokes that on the odd occasion they come across a pretty girl they didn't know how to react. The caveman approach may have worked in the backward places *they* came from, but it didn't cut the mustard around here. And the students at this university were supposed to be intelligent. Trust me, most of the time you wouldn't know it.

I tried not to let the encounter wind me up too much as I knew my parents would no doubt do a great job of that later, and by the time the path had brought me out onto Knightsbridge the encounter was all but forgotten. This road must have been a grand sight back in the day. It still is, to an extent. The six lanes provide a production line of traffic, giving the place a busy feel that makes it impossible to relax, no matter how plush the décor in the numerous cafes that adorn either side of the road might be. What amazes me is that the class of car that roars by is so consistently high, as if it were an exclusive street guarded by a pedantic doorman at either end.

I took a left and saw Harrods towering in the distance, an ostentatious building that sits and laughs at all those that surround it, a great display of power and a visual warning to the boutiques that squat beside it like foothills.

It took an age to cross the road and I had to stop at the island in the middle. I noticed that the cold weather had given the women around me the opportunity they had been waiting for since last winter and the Burberry scarves were out in their hundreds, some real, some fake; a generous smattering of beige cheque warming the necks of the fashion-conscious. They all knew there would be a new trend this Christmas and wanted to squeeze every bit of use out of the garment before it became 'so last year'.

I walked into Harrods through one of the side doors and headed towards the food hall, my route taking me through the synthetic wonderland of make-up and designer fragrances. The counters were manned by ageing Barbie dolls who smiled sweetly, although not too sweetly in case their faces cracked and fell apart under the strain. Women who sell make-up wear more of the stuff than anybody else; a grotesque, living, breathing advertisement for the product. Fast food chains would quickly go out of business if everyone who worked at their outlets was covered in ketchup stains and weighed twenty stone, but the world of foundation, lipstick and mascara seemed impervious to this type of negative association. I felt like a bug as people tried to spray me from all sides with the latest perfumes and body sprays, and I was lucky to escape from the section without smelling like I had been in an explosion at a fragrance factory.

Entering the food hall, I could see my parents seated on stools at the coffee bar on the left-hand side. They made for a comical sight. Mum had her eyes closed, hands tightly gripping the sides of the seat and her head hung back at an angle that couldn't be comfortable. She was breathing deeply while Dad used a napkin to frantically fan air into her flared nostrils. Meeting by the cheese had been a deliberate ploy as I knew Mum couldn't stand the smell, and the punishment had taken the desired effect. I tried not to laugh as I approached them.

'Hi, Dad. What's wrong with Mum?' I asked innocently.

'Oh, hi darling. Thank God you're here. Your mother's feeling nauseous.'

Dad let out a sigh that suggested he had been to hell and back. He looked physically drained and it was clear why. There were so many bags and boxes around his feet that he might as well have been a Christmas tree.

'You know I hate cheese, Leila. Isn't there anywhere else we could've met?' snapped my mother, without opening her eyes to acknowledge me.

'Oh, sorry Mum, I completely forgot about that. Well, you appear to have survived, so it's not the end of the world.'

'Bloody feels like it,' muttered Dad under his breath.

'What was that, Charles?' accused my mother, instantaneously regaining full consciousness.

'Nothing, darling. Look, can I stop fanning you now? My wrists are beginning to hurt.'

'Yes, please do. Your clumsy flapping is beginning to get on my nerves anyway.'

Dad settled the bill while Mum fussed about, straightening her clothes and examining her make-up in the small mirror she kept in her handbag. She didn't step down from the stool until Dad was free to help her do so in a regal manner.

'Come on, let's get out of this godforsaken place,' she demanded. 'Leila, give your father a hand with some of those bags. It'll be the death of him if he has to carry the whole lot.'

She marched off empty-handed while Dad and I shared the load between us.

'This way, Mum!' I called after her, signalling with my head towards the way I had come in.

She pretended not to hear me but changed her route all the same, and we followed her out of the store.

It wasn't until we were tucking into the main course that either of my parents mentioned the graduation ceremony. The original reason for their trip to London and the explanation for my unusually smart attire had been pushed to the backs of their minds by the pleasure or trauma of the shopping trip. Of course, the question was delivered by my mother in a form that went little way to disguising the real angle of her enquiry. Tact isn't one of her strong points; a hereditary weakness that I myself am trying to conquer. Being told that I sound just like my mother is something I could really do without.

'So, now your graduation is all official, I suppose you'll be starting to seriously think about getting a job. How was it, by the way?'

It was too much to ask to expect my Mum to be genuinely concerned that she might have missed an important occasion in my life, and this marked the low point of the meal up to that point. It had taken an age for us to get through the first course as Mum had her heart set on taking me through each of her purchases in turn, explaining in each case the original price as well as the 'bargain' price she had paid for it. Added to the inconsequentially dull anecdotes that seemed to be attached to so many of the items, the story of how the contents of her numerous bags came about was stretched out over a whole hour. It had taken only a fraction of this time for Dad and I to suck and slurp our way through the mounds of mussels we had ordered, and we were left to listen to her wittering on and on. It wasn't until every last purchase had been accounted for that she had made a proper start on her own food, which by this time had gone cold and, accordingly, she hadn't enjoyed it. This had given me a chance to make significant inroads into the wine, the alcohol proving quite effective at anaesthetising me against my garrulous mother.

'It was ok.' I always gave her the standard answer to questions concerning anything to do with my education.

'Good, good.'

I could sense her dissatisfaction at my uninformative answer and waited for the follow-up question.

'So, did you meet lots of your old friends?'

I felt like I was ten years old again the way she was talking.

'Not really, no. That's the downfall of putting back your graduation by a year, I suppose.'

'And what are they all up to?' responded my mother, having taken absolutely no notice of what I had said.

'I expect they're all working in highly paid jobs in the city, just like I should be doing,' I said, saving her the bother of trying to say it nicely herself.

'There's no need to be like that, Leila. Your mother was only asking you a question.'

Typical Dad, jumping to her defence. It makes me sick.

'Sorry.' I tried my best to sound like I meant it. 'If you must know, I'm still considering my options. From what I understand, most people are fearing for their jobs at the moment and are working seventy-hour weeks just to try and stop themselves getting the sack. I'm not sure I'm prepared to do that.'

'You have to start working hard at some point, Leila. This is the real world.'

'Is it?'

Neither of them answered. They knew there was little point arguing with me when I was in this kind of mood. Dad changed the subject to more mundane matters, such as my plans for the weekend, and conversation was hard work for the remainder of the meal, which was a shame as the food was really very good.

* * *

It never ceases to amaze me how quickly time passes when you're doing absolutely nothing. It was already December and in the two months since my graduation ceremony I hadn't achieved anything worthy of mention. The days dragged by torturously, minutes strung out like hours, yet the weeks flashed past so rapidly I felt my youth slipping through my fingers like a falling chain. I knew that if I didn't make a grab at it soon and start yanking it back it would run out of links and I would be left to ponder where all the missing years had gone.

I was supposed to be in my wonder years, back from my post-university, spirit-cleansing travels and straight into a highly sought-after graduate position that would pay me enough to afford a newly converted studio flat in Clapham or Islington, where I could snort coke and drink cocktails at trendy wine bars with my equally hip and affluent friends; play squash every Tuesday and Thursday; learn to play the guitar; go on skiing holidays; eat out at exclusive restaurants charged to corporate hospitality; join a health spa and be tanned all year round; learn Japanese; and enter the London marathon. I would do all this and work a sixty-five-hour week without batting an eyelid, kept alive by Marks & Spencer ready meals, effervescent vitamin cocktails and gallons of mineral water bottled at source from the volcanic regions of southern Italy.

That's every graduate's dream, is it not? Work hard, play hard, the superhero lifestyle of the pinstripe-suited young professional. Something we should all aspire to. 'Lunch is for wimps, I'm going to the gym to pump some iron.' Success was judged by the size of your bank balance, the level of your resting pulse rate and the length of time until the next free evening in your calendar. Sound of body, sound of mind.

What a load of tripe. I don't know who created this blueprint for the ideal lifestyle for high-flyers in their early twenties, but people had jumped onto it like the latest miracle weight-loss diet as if to do anything less was a sign of laziness, loneliness or lack of ambition. The cogs had started turning during my final year at university when word got around that a couple of people had already landed obscenely well-paid jobs in the city and everyone started to think they should be doing the same, applying at random to firms they had never heard of for positions they knew nothing about, brainwashed by guest speakers into thinking the streets of London *were* paved with gold.

It was like jumping onto a moving walkway that took you along the journey of working life, a journey with only one route: forward, full speed ahead. There was no emergency stop button on *this* travellator. It took you past the first few years – the probation periods, the professional qualifications, the rise up the ranks, the changes of job, the share options, the management positions, the directorships – and delivered you at the other end, aged forty-five, for a long and comfortable retirement. Some got to the end quicker than others, picking their way past their fellow travellers who chose to lean against the handrail and let the momentum carry them along.

My problem was that I never got on it in the first place. I couldn't have graduated at a better time. The IT boom and the merger and acquisition culture meant companies were employing at a scale that had not been seen for many years. In my infinite wisdom, I had decided it was all too easy, so I had jetted off to Thailand to lie on a beach for six months. I had returned to find that the stock market bubble had burst and that firms were downsizing rather than recruiting, the moving walkway switching to reverse and dumping people back where they had started. Only the very fittest had been able to overcome its inertia, still moving forward despite the adversity, leaping over the bodies of their colleagues, who were merely impedimenta to their rise to the top. I found myself stuck in a mob of crazed lunatics, champing at the bit to get back on before their student debts caught up with them, eagerly applying within twenty-four hours for every vacancy that appeared in the papers or on the net. The problem was, they were all a lot keener than me and the majority had experience. They were no more intelligent, though. My problem was idleness, not stupidity.

The truth is, a fat salary would have been useful right now, even if I had to work quite hard for it. It would mean I could move out of West Brompton, for a start. I was only living there because my dad owned a poky two-bedroom flat in Ongar Road and had allowed me to live there rent-free until I found my feet. This would have been good, except that I had lived around there in my final year and seeing the students wandering to and from college with their rucksacks slung across both shoulders served as a constant reminder that I hadn't moved on since university.

I was living alone, the spare room sitting idle and dusty. It had crossed my mind to get somebody in as a source of income, but tolerable housemates – let alone good housemates – were almost impossible to find, so I had traded prosperity for sanity and made do with solely myself for company.

You have to appreciate that I've had bad experiences in the past with housemates. Living in student halls had the advantage of being large enough so that people had no idea whether you were in or out, and it was easy to keep yourself to yourself just by refusing to answer knocks on the door. This wasn't so straightforward in the third year when I lived in Telephone Place, a grotty back street close to the junction of Lillie Road and North End Road. I should have known that expecting to get on well with six other girls in a house with only one bathroom would be too much to ask. The arguments started on the day we moved in. With only four large rooms and three box rooms, it was inevitable. Understandably, nobody wanted to pay ninety quid a week for a prison cell, so the pitiful excuses came pouring in as we all sat fuming in the minimalist lounge.

'I can't sleep unless I'm in a double bed.'

'I'm not used to traffic noise, it'll keep me awake all night.'

'I need to be able to spread out my lecture notes.'

It makes me ashamed to be female when I hear this kind of whingeing. We ended up pulling names out of a saucepan, which was the fairest way any of us could think of, but those who ended up with the smallest rooms still weren't happy and harboured petty grudges against their more fortunate occupants for the rest of the year.

The arguments started off small: trivial disagreements about cleaning rotas, queues for the shower and washing up not being done. Next, people started getting overprotective about their belongings and there was plenty of finger-pointing and accusations about scratched saucepans and shampoo stealing. Where we had once shared stuff like milk, bread and margarine, some of the girls had announced they were going solo and didn't want to partake in communal food any more.

The problems escalated when boyfriends were brought back to the flat and, once the alcohol was flowing and inhibitions were drunk away, the flirting would begin and one of the insecure girls I lived with couldn't handle it. I don't think I'm a particularly flirtatious person, even if many people have suggested otherwise. Apparently, I have this way of looking at a guy when I'm talking to him that gives off a whole host of signals. The wrong signals, I might add. I'm usually happy if a guy looks me in the eye at all when I'm speaking to him. Most of them just stare at my chest. I swear, some blokes have had a ten-minute conversation with my cleavage and it isn't until it gets up and walks away that they remember there's a person behind the bulges, by which time it's too late.

That's essentially why, at the moment, I'm happy living alone. Housemates only complicate matters, and trying to come up with ways of getting even with people is both mentally taxing and time-consuming.

* * *

Drifting between the various aisles of the store, Joseph found himself baffled by the layout. It was a maze of shelves pointing in all directions, alleys turning into dead-ends, gaps in the units appearing like passageways where he least expected them. Hundreds upon hundreds of identical items were piled high like multicoloured buildings, the whole place swaying, disorientating, like the duty-free section of a cross-channel ferry. There was no order to the produce; rows of groceries transforming abruptly into stationary, large electrical items stacked neatly among canned foods and toiletries. Customers seemed to come and go like apparitions, the store brimming one minute and barren the next, shape-shifting shoppers brushing silently passed him, every stranger's face so familiar, yet entirely anonymous. Close friends from an alternative existence. The chaos bewildered him and, without a shopping list, he didn't know what he had come in for or why he was there.

He felt a woman's hand on his shoulder. He couldn't feel it, but he knew it was there. He turned to face her and there she was, beautiful and pure, an angel.

'Have you got the carrots?' asked Angela.

'Yes, right here.' Joseph picked up the basket and sifted through its contents.

But there were no carrots, only feathers.

'Come on,' Angela said with a smile. 'Let's go and pay.'

She took him by his spare hand, gently, as if she were holding a snowflake. Her skin was so soft it was almost frictionless. No matter how hard he squeezed, the form of her fingers seemed elusive, like clutching at mist, but the contact was real and it filled him with happiness.

'The queues are so long,' commented Joseph. 'It's going to take forever.'

'Down there.' Angela pointed to an empty checkout at the end of the row and they made their way over to it.

While shoppers at the neighbouring till queued like waxworks, Joseph unpacked his basket onto the conveyor belt, carefully lifting out the socks, light bulbs and orange juice in turn. The checkout girl scanned the items through and Angela stuffed them into yellow plastic bags while Joseph paid.

'Thanks,' said the server, waving him through.

Joseph took Angela by the arm. She had an expression of amused embarrassment on her face, a shy, self-conscious smile.

226

'That woman keeps looking at me funny,' she whispered into his ear. *'Tell her you're dead. Then she really will think you're weird.'*

The weight of reality was crushing. You can never fully appreciate something until it's gone forever.

* * *

You join me approximately halfway through a job interview for some nondescript financial consultancy firm. I'm sorry to say that I can't tell you any more about the company because I'm unsure myself, having completely lost track of who or what I've applied for. Over the last few weeks, my inexorable campaign to find myself worthy employment has seen me become a machine, churning out application forms, CVs and covering letters at a phenomenal rate. And, like a machine, my output is both consistent and dull, but I figure if you push a product hard enough, fill enough shelves, then somebody out there's eventually going to buy it. And besides, I'm a pretty good product. I just need picking up and looking at.

When I started out on my job-hunting mission I was thorough and selective, diligently researching companies and positions on the internet before deciding whether or not to apply. Initially, I narrowed down the universe of employers to a shortlist of four and spent a great deal of time and effort getting the wording right on the application forms, making sure I had included a satisfactory amount of corporate clichés and business bullshit to convince the reader they were looking at the real deal. I sent these off and waited, and it was only a matter of days before the first of the replies came back.

I've learnt that you can tell what the letter is going to say based purely on the size and weight of the envelope. If the envelope is small, it's hardly worth opening it. These big companies don't beat around the bush when it comes to telling you you're not good enough.

> Dear Leila
>
> Thank you for your application for the Graduate Training Programme.
>
> We have reviewed your qualifications and experience and have concluded that other candidates match our requirements more closely. We would like to thank you for your

> interest and wish you success in your future
> career.
>
> Yours sincerely

Another couple of small envelopes arrived the next day with similarly blunt rebuffs. The wording varied slightly and one of the firms even threw in some statistics to soften the blow.

> I do hope you are not too disappointed and can understand that there is a very high pressure on places. You may find it interesting to know that we receive approximately 8,000 applications each year for only 600 places.

Yes, that's extremely interesting. Knowing I'm just one of many losers makes me feel a whole lot better. And I don't see it as a barefaced declaration of your own popularity at all, not one bit. I'm sure you genuinely care that I might be upset that you've boxed me in with all the other muppets who didn't make the grade. And as for not being too disappointed, well, I'm finding it quite hard at the moment, but the counselling is helping and one day I hope I may be able to look at myself in the mirror again without seeing a pitiable failure.

The fourth company didn't even bother to acknowledge my application because that would have taken five minutes of someone's precious time, and time is money in their business.

Not to be deterred by this early setback, I worked my way further down my preference list and rattled off another half-dozen applications. This batch took far less time than the initial four, as I could simply lift most of the answers from the previous forms. Plus I spent far less time on neatness, figuring that if they wanted perfectly parallel sentences they should have printed some lines. A week later I had received six rejection letters, much to my frustration. I guess when they said they required a minimum of a 2:1 in any numerate discipline, they really meant it. My third-class degree was proving a greater handicap than I had first expected, so I had to aim lower and lower until I felt I was really scraping the barrel. However, even the paltriest firms seemed reluctant to give me a chance to prove my worth at interview, and the ever-expanding pile of rejection letters quickly grew big enough to require its own folder, perched on my desk as a constant reminder of my unemployment and failure.

Even the thickest-skinned, most self-confident individual will start to undergo some form of self-doubt when faced with more than thirty letters stating, in black and white, that they aren't good enough, and it got me down for a while. But grief and depression, they're an indulgence. They are of no use whatsoever to society and are of no benefit to my cause. Sitting around and moping about it wasn't going to find me a princely pay packet. So I scoured recruitment websites and employment supplements from newspapers and found a host of new positions to pursue.

By now, I had honed my application technique to an art form and the final submissions were a collection of my finest works. At the back of my mind, I knew this really was the last-chance saloon. If they didn't turn up the goods I was going to have to recast my career goals with a more pessimistic – or perhaps a more realistic – slant.

The truth was, I was slightly disappointed when I finally received my first positive response. Rather than taking the invitation to an assessment day as a recognition of the quality of my application form, I found myself doubting the merits of the company and asking myself why they were willing to grant me the time of day when so many others had balked at the offer of my services. I pictured one of their HR people agonising over whether or not to grant all four candidates an interview when only one of them was of remotely employable standard and concluding that desperate times called for desperate measures. That said, beggars can't be choosers and I wasn't in a position to turn the opportunity down due to what was, essentially, my own paranoia. So I had given them the benefit of the doubt and that's how I came to be sitting here now.

When I first arrived at their offices in the West End – the location was certainly one of the more attractive things about the firm – I discovered that I was the only candidate to be assessed on that particular day. I was informed that it was a one-stage selection process and if I proved my worth over the course of the day there was a good chance I would receive an offer of employment. A tour of the office followed, the number of fake plastic plants and rounded edges a deliberate attempt to fashion a reassuringly modern informality. It was so contrived that the space resembled a cross between one of the neighbouring Soho bars and an internet café. Staff subconsciously put on a show for the tourist, with exaggerated laughs, chiselled smiles and overstated facial expressions adopted by the majority, the remainder opting for looks of such disinterested nonchalance that I might as well have been the new cleaner.

Next came the numerical aptitude test. I hold no fear of these stupid examinations, thinking of them as 'monkey tests' since they were so straightforward they must have been designed purely to weed out the chimps rather than to identify the high-flyers. It was nothing more than adding and subtracting. Even so, many faltered at this first stage, their degrees in advanced mathematics inhibiting their understanding of the basics. Intelligence and common sense don't always go hand in hand. The wheel is turning but the hamster is dead, if you know what I mean.

The examination room took the term minimalist to extreme lengths. The walls were bare and there was only one desk and chair at its centre, plus one further chair in the corner where my guide, Clayton, sat and watched me like a hunter as I punched figures into my calculator and coloured in the boxes on the multiple-choice answer sheet. It reminded me of being in detention.

I finished well before the time limit and declined the opportunity to check through my answers again, stating that I had checked them as I went along. Clayton took my paper and disappeared from the room, presumably to get one of his assistants to mark it. When he returned, he announced that the company president, Faye McGarland – the lady who had been named as my interviewer in the letter – had been called away to a world-saving meeting and that he would be conducting the interview himself.

This was music to my ears as, given the choice, I would always prefer to be interviewed by a man. Women have a tendency to feel threatened when presented with either a younger, more attractive or potentially smarter model, and these insecurities are heightened in the workplace, where everybody is considered as competition of sorts. This creates an intense rivalry among women that leads to backstabbing and bitchiness, making it very difficult for them to become friends in situations where they're both aiming for the same goal. The phrase, "May the best man win", is specific to men, as its wording suggests, and there is no similar expression for the fairer sex.

Therefore, had the interview been conducted by Faye, it would likely have been far tougher. She would have entered the room determined not to like me and I would have had to walk a personality tightrope, balancing my approach to appearing competent without coming across as a whiz kid; sophisticated but not too sexy, throwing in a bit of dappiness to make her feel better. That sort of thing.

A man was a whole different proposition altogether. Being interviewed by a man would allow me to flirt, pout and relax, knowing full well that any weaknesses would be viewed as a vulnerability that could be overcome with a bit of gentle coaxing. And there is nothing men like more than to help a damsel in distress. It was slightly unfortunate that Clayton, as with most men working in human resources, was almost certainly gay. Never mind. A homosexual man was still undoubtedly preferable to a heterosexual woman.

I'm conscious that it isn't easy to judge these things, particularly as I have no basis for comparison, but the interview seemed to be flowing forward comfortably, with no hiccups of note at the halfway stage. The interview was principally a verbal extension of the application form, an exercise to see whether I could relate the stories using spoken word rather than on paper. And they *were* stories; elaborate works of fiction that were no more *my* achievements than anybody else's.

'Describe an occasion outside your academic studies when you had to persuade somebody to perform a task against their will.'

The answers that immediately sprung to mind all related to the bedroom. Cunnilingus, for example, as I don't think my ex-boyfriend would have done it out of choice. He eventually conceded and made a passable attempt that prolonged our relationship for a further couple of weeks when the end had seemed inevitable. Unable to share this fine example of my powers of persuasion with Clayton, I instead regurgitated one of my many carefully concocted lies prepared solely for the situation.

This kind of thing degenerates interviews into the realms of farce; a lesson in lie detection. Never one for joining clubs or societies, my extracurricular activities didn't stretch any further than socialising and watching television; pastimes every student indulged in to various degrees. I think more credit should be given to those candidates who leave the Other Interests box on application forms blank. Which lifestyle reflects the more balanced individual? The one in which free time is used to stage third-rate theatrical performances, to join societies that mean you can hang out with strangers exclusively from your own culture, and to participate in a sport you detest purely for the purpose of some sadistic self-gratification, or the one where time away from studying is spent with people you genuinely like or relaxing in front of *Trisha*?

It's a frustrating misconception that if you're not out there trying to make the next Commonwealth Games, launching your own internet company or finding a solution to world poverty, you must be a shallow and lazy individual. Unfortunately, this mistaken belief is held nationwide and it leaves people like me with two options. The first is the one adopted by the majority of students, whose extracurricular calendars are organised purely for the sake of their CVs, doing things they would rather not so they have something to talk about during future interviews. The second, more efficient option – and the one I adopted – is to lie.

It doesn't take much effort or imagination to turn another person's achievements into your own. And if you tell the lie enough times, you can become so convincing you'll almost believe it yourself. The material is all there already, kindly supplied by the moralistic fools choosing option one. Of course, there's always a danger the *actual* captain of the Imperial College second hockey team or the *real* entertainments representative of the Chemistry Society may be going for the same job. However, the chances of this are extremely slim, especially if the roles don't even exist. So I can easily paint the picture of a student whose grades suffered as a result of having tried to gain the most out of my university experience. I was making some deliberate strokes with my brush now.

'What do you see as your main strength, Leila, and how do you think this will transfer to the workplace?'

This was all too easy, all too predictable. I fed him some spiel about being able to look at a problem in great depth, to analyse things in detail and come up with a unique and creative solution. I said I relished the challenge of becoming an expert in a particular field; to take my knowledge to unparalleled depths. I could tell by the look on his face that this wasn't the answer Clayton was looking for.

'Hmm. While detailed analysis is certainly part of the process, the work we do here is more to do with tailoring broad solutions to individual clients.'

I didn't like his outright rejection of my answer, and all of a sudden his patronising human resources tone was beginning to annoy me.

'Selling the same advice to different people for different prices, you mean?' I quipped.

Now it was Clayton's turn to be displeased by *my* attitude. Taking the comment personally, his voice developed a sharper edge that had certainly *not* been taught in business school.

'I think you misunderstood my comment, Leila,' he said firmly. 'What I mean is that much of consultancy work involves delivering consistent information to clients in a form that is best-suited to their needs.'

I know what consultancy entails, you moron!

'Ah, I see what you mean now. Apologies, my mistake. You mean coming up with a solution that an eight-year-old could have come up with and presenting it in such a way that the client is prepared to pay for it.'

This was meant to be a semi-light-hearted comment and I smiled as I said it to hint that this was the case, but the humour was lost on Clayton, whose face had noticeably reddened.

'How can I put this?' he muttered under his breath, tapping his pen on the tabletop as his feeble mind searched for words of professionalism while countless swear words were leaping forth in derogatory droves to the tip of his tongue.

He reached for a sheet of blank paper.

'I like to think of consultancy as the letter T,' he started. 'You have one area of specialist knowledge...' he drew a vertical line down the centre of the page, 'and a broad understanding of all other areas...', the latter represented by the cross of the "T".

'You, Leila,' he drew what looked to be the beginnings of a game of hangman after two incorrect guesses. 'You're more like the letter L.'

The letter L? What kind of ridiculous corporate speak was that? L for Lazy? *L for Loser?*

'Oh, I see what you're saying,' I replied, with a distaste I usually reserve for my parents. 'And you, Clayton, you're like the number eight. You go round and round in circles but never actually get anywhere.'

Clayton slowly put his pen down, placed his hands on the table and leant back in his chair. He let out a sigh of defeat and gazed up at the ceiling in exasperation.

'I really don't think there's any point in continuing this interview. I thank you for your time.'

He stood up and offered his hand to shake, withdrawing it when it was clear that I wasn't about to return the gesture. 'Somebody will contact you within the next couple of days.'

I was silenced by the abrupt end to the proceedings. And, if in any way I hadn't realised that my attitude had cost me a golden opportunity, Clayton was ready to fill me in.

'A word of advice, Leila. Speaking off the record, I'm sure it will come as no surprise to you that you have been unsuccessful. I meet people like you every day. You come here straight out of university thinking you're something special. Do you think I didn't notice the way you looked down on me from the moment we met? That you thought yourself to be superior just because I work in human resources?'

This was clearly a rhetorical question.

'A bit of arrogance isn't necessarily a bad thing, but it only works if you have something to be arrogant about, and a brief study of your CV suggests you have ideas way above your station. To tell you the truth, your application was due to be binned, as we generally only accept people with a 2:1 or higher. But I could see from your written responses that you were perhaps more intelligent than your degree class suggested and I persuaded Faye to give you a chance. You've thrown this back in my face with your sarcasm and your rudeness. Many people would do anything for the opportunity you have *wasted* today. To be honest, your attitude appals me.'

'Have you finished?' I asked him.

I hadn't been lectured like this since secondary school.

He nodded and ushered me towards the door. We walked in silence to the main reception area, where I relinquished my security pass at the desk. I wanted to have the last word, to leave him with a biting final comment, but nothing came to the fore. My mind was preoccupied, thoughts muddled. Deep down, I knew he was right, and the acceptance was damning.

* * *

Many people tell me they can't understand why anybody would choose to live in London. Personally, I love it. It's not so much the dirtiness, crowdedness and absurdly high cost of living that puts people off; more the size and the attitude. People complain that in London you're a nobody and it's easy to become lost amongst the ocean of faces that fill the pavements and the underground for fourteen hours a day.

These people are missing the point. London anonymity is a self-imposed state its inhabitants choose to adopt. It's a mistaken belief that London is so big and vastly populated that you'll never bump into anyone you know. I see familiar faces every time I leave the house. The difference is that in London you're allowed, even *expected*, not to acknowledge them. Of course, if you lived in a remote village it would be unjustifiably rude to ignore the elderly couple from three doors down as you passed them on a deserted street, but in London there are no such pressures on courtesy and this allows everyone the luxury of being able to save their greetings for friends rather than mere acquaintances.

If I bump into a familiar face from university, I don't want to have to make superficial chitchat with them and pretend I'm interested in what they're doing. The big smoke allows me not to do this. I can walk straight past them with nothing more than prolonged eye contact. And it's nice not feeling obliged to get to know your neighbours. Outsiders see all of this as arrogance; an example of Londoners possessing a superiority complex that they believe gives them the right to ignore each other. It isn't really like that.

This is what fills my head as I step out of Bayswater station and onto Queensway. I often come to this neck of the woods to wander around the shops when I'm bored. Of the surfeit of options, none is particularly to my taste, this being a good thing. My dad might be extremely generous, but my resources are by no means limitless. Just a few stops up on the District line, it provides me with a cheap way of wasting a few hours on days when time crawls by so slowly that lunchtime seems like a week away and I get concerned that I might suddenly get old if I don't do something about it.

I take a left out of the station and head north, following the downward slope of the road towards Ladbroke Grove. I rarely go in the other direction because there's little there before you hit Kensington Gardens; only an endless row of Chinese restaurants interspersed with the occasional overpriced convenience store. It's always busy down Queensway, right up until the pubs shut. I like it because it's a genuinely multicultural area, which makes it good for people-watching. Whereas Earls Court is full of Australians, Bayswater plays home to a lot of Greeks, Egyptians and Chinese, the food outlets reflecting the ethnic diversity. You're never more than a stone's throw from a kebab shop around here. That's one of the reasons why the students seem to love it so much, I guess.

There are people on the street handing out leaflets for all-you-can-eat buffets, but I ignore their intrusive thrusts and keep my eyes on the floor, where most of the leaflets end up anyway. Postcard racks sit awkwardly outside the souvenir shops, the windows of which are adorned with tacky ornaments of Big Ben and the Tower of London. The cards bore pictures of the royal family alongside breasts painted to look like piglets and cats with nipples for noses.

As I walk past Harts I catch a whiff of the £1.99 roast chickens, which smoulder and turn at the back of the shop like carriages on a Ferris wheel. The smell makes me hungry, but I'm not about to devour a whole greasy chicken by myself, so I beat a hasty retreat to the scentless sanctuary of the Whiteleys shopping complex. Whiteleys is pretty plush inside, with a lot of brass and marble, and it's a shame the shops within it aren't more befitting of the surroundings, otherwise it would save me having to make trips to the more varied, busier (and therefore more traumatic) stores on Oxford Street.

I tackle the ground floor first, then the first floor. I don't venture any further up because there are only eating places and a cinema up there. I must have been around these shops about a hundred times in the last two years and I know the produce so well I can instantly tell when the new season's designs have been added to the shelves. There's nothing new today, however hard I look, so I'm left to browse the garments I've seen many times before. But today, more than any other day, I feel like treating myself, so I buy a top. It's nothing special: tight, pale blue and short-sleeved, with a simple logo across the front. I have to try it on a couple of times before I make the decision, but the fit is good, limiting my waist while enhancing my chest. As I said, it's nothing special and I doubt I'll wear it much, and it'll most likely be half the price in a few weeks' time when the January sales start, but I want to buy something and this is as good as it gets. I pay for it and it's worth the money to have the comfort of holding the bag in my hand.

I forget how cold it is outside and have to hurriedly button my coat against the chill. I'm not good when it comes to cold weather and I tell myself I really ought to consider moving to a hotter country. It's not as if I have anything to stay around for. My pace slows as I realise there's nothing waiting for me when I return home; only my own thoughts and the television. I'm a lady of leisure, for God's sake. It *should* be fun. But free time isn't the same when it's been forced upon you; when it isn't your own choice. My life needs some focus, otherwise I'll end up wasting it.

* * *

Today, the two flights of stairs seemed like an insurmountable summit, yet it was one Joseph had to conquer time and time again. Moving out of the flat was proving to be far harder work than moving in had been. This was mainly to do with his state of mind rather than any increased physical hardship. While he still didn't have a full range of movement in his right shoulder, his physical rehabilitation had been a success up to this point and no anticipated long-term problems had been diagnosed. But the weight of his emotions remained a considerable burden, weakening him far more than carrying the multitude of boxes and all the awkward bits of furniture. The chore of moving in had been dramatically diminished by the knowledge that he and Angela had been about to undertake a significant step in forging a life together, a dual existence, and both had been filled with excited expectations that were more than enough to take their minds off the task. Now the opposite was true.

Angela was gone, probably forever. Although her body had yet to be recovered, deep down Joseph had consigned himself to the fact he would never see her again, and the act of having to pack away her things was the final stage in a harsh acceptance of the reality. The last few months had been torrid times. With Allan dead, the police had little to go on in terms of tracing her whereabouts. She could literally be anywhere. Joseph was left in a state of limbo, not knowing whether to mourn her death or keep things ready for her return.

During this time, he had sunk to unfathomable lows, unable to eat or sleep, and, on the isolated occasions when his body collapsed through emotional exhaustion he found his dreams plagued by confused messages, cameo appearances by Angela, alive and well, mixed with visions of mutilated corpses discovered in the woods. Every night he watched the news with a fear of what might be announced, and as time went by he almost wanted to hear confirmation of her death so he could know for certain.

Angela's parents had come earlier that week to pick up the majority of her belongings and, while they were sympathetic in their grief, Joseph sensed they were looking at him as if *he* were to blame, as though *he* had failed their daughter and brought about her disappearance. He had been glad when they left. Joseph kept back her most precious possessions and stored them with his own, so that if she were ever to walk back through the door she would be able to see that he hadn't forgotten about her. Not even for a second.

Iain had come to assist him in loading the van and to help lighten the mood. Few words were spoken over the course of the morning, aside from practical conversations, such as, 'Is this box ready to go?' Nevertheless, Joseph welcomed the company as the presence of another person meant his pride prevented him from breaking down. He had been doing that far too often of late.

The move itself had come as quickly as Joseph had been able to bring it about. He had craved a change of scenery, desperate to get away from all the constant reminders of his solitude. Returning home from work to the empty flat he and Angela had once shared and climbing into a vacant bed at night was too much to take.

Work had also proved too much for him. Joseph had thrown himself back into it as soon as his body was strong enough to do so. Initially, it had helped to take his mind off things, but once the renaissance period had passed he had begun to slip back into a state of depression that deprived him of the power of logical thought. It had never been the most sociable of jobs and, left to his own devices, he found himself completely unable to focus his attention on the task in hand. Noticing his dwindling productivity, Joseph's boss had offered him the option of a sabbatical. Instead, he had chosen to resign altogether in an attempt to make a fresh start.

Joseph loaded the last of the boxes into the van and slammed the door shut, taking a couple of attempts to convince himself that it was securely locked.

'That's the lot, then,' he announced. 'Thanks a lot for helping out, Iain.'

'No problem, mate. Are you sure you don't want a hand unloading at the other end?'

'Thanks for the offer, but I'll be ok. There's a lift at the new place.' Joseph smiled. 'Hey, let me give you a lift back.'

'Don't be silly, it's only a short walk.'

'It's be the least I can do,' insisted Joseph.

'No, really, it's ok,' replied Iain. 'It's out of your way. Besides, it's a nice enough day and I could do with the walk to cool me down.'

He puffed out his cheeks and shook the front of his top to get some air circulation going. Moving all that stuff had been hard work.

'If you say so. Thanks again. I'll see you soon.'

'Yeah, see you, Joseph,' said Iain, heading off towards the gate.

Joseph got into the van and sat for a couple of minutes in the driver's seat, the inflated interior alien due to its size. He took one last look at the old flat and reflected on what could have been. Snapping himself out of it, he started the engine, which roared into life and sent a cloud of stinking smoke bellowing from the exhaust. Eager to get out of the place, Joseph was frustrated by the time it took for the electric gate to swing open. As soon as the gap was large enough, he lurched through it and took a left towards Falcon Road. When he reached the junction, he turned right and passed under the railway bridge for what he hoped would be the last time.

* * *

Spring has quietly crept up on me, quite unlike the proverbial lion it's sometimes compared to. However, it does bring some degree of change, as it's seen me come out of my employment hibernation. My job is nothing to shout about, and I won't try to claim I've outdone myself in any way or fulfilled my potential to any stretch of the imagination. Still, things could be a lot worse and I'm pleased to no longer be sitting on my backside all day pretending I'm leading a busy and fulfilling life.

Basically, I've got a job at Selfridges. And not a fast-track, gateway to greater things graduate position such as a trainee manager or anything as remotely glamorous, but as a lowly style consultant. At least my degree counted for something in the end and I can be thankful I'm one step above the standard floor staff and a whole two steps above cleaner. My role is essentially that of personal shopper; 'style consultant' is a term I coined to make myself sound more important in social situations and when talking to my parents.

To be honest, it suits me down to the ground as it allows me to shop on a grossly exorbitant budget, albeit on behalf of somebody else, which is something I'm used to and extremely good at. It also allows me to be critical of people's outfits and I can assure you it's immensely satisfying telling other women that their present outfit makes them look fat, in the politest possible way. Research for the job comes in the form of keeping up to date with all of the latest fashions and styles, which entails flicking through the pages of various magazines, many of which I read from time to time anyway. And the people I work with are quite nice, in a limp-wristed, air-headed kind of way.

'Hey, Leila. What we doing for lunch?' asks Roxanne, my main work buddy.

'Same as always, I guess,' I reply.

She asks me the same question every day. I don't know why she bothers because we never do anything different. She's a creature of habit and if I suggest anything other than Pret she complains about it or refuses to eat anything once we get there, so I've learnt it's best to stick to her routine. It's a bit annoying, to tell you the truth, because I'm sick to death of their bloody sandwiches.

'Ok. If it ain't broke, don't fix it!' says Roxanne with a wink. 'I'm going for a fag, so I'll meet you outside in a bit.'

I wave to dismiss her and smile to myself as she walks away. She's wearing her favourite jeans, the ones she claims give her 'a fit arse'. This basically means they're tight. Her arse still looks just as big and wobbly as usual, just with extra attention drawn to it.

I potter around tidying the place up for a while and then join her outside. Roxanne has only been out there for about a minute, but the cigarette is burnt almost down to the filter. She must have been sucking on it like a freeze-pop. Her main purpose of being outside is to check out the blokes, and she has adopted her usual posture in an attempt to look sexy as she stares at each man she likes the look of as they stroll by, oblivious to the attention. One day somebody might stop and talk to her, or even just look at her. I really hope so, for her sake.

'We going, then?' I ask her.

'Sure,' she replies, taking one final look around before throwing her cigarette to the floor and crushing it to death with the toe of her right boot, like a fat version of Sandy in *Grease*.

It's my turn to reserve seats while Roxanne queues up to pay. I've opted for couscous salad because this saves me having to trawl through all the different flavours of sandwich on display. Normally, I don't mind this too much, but for some reason there seem to be more people in here than usual and they're all clustered along the refrigerator, peering at the contents, heads bobbing back and forth like chickens. I don't have the patience to join them. There are certain days when I can't stand being surrounded by people, all bustling and nudging me. I would be liable to kick someone or launch into a verbal assault, so it's safer if I sit here and wait.

Roxanne takes an age to purchase the food. As usual, her choice of queue is poor and she manages to stand behind a man who is buying coffee for the whole office and decides to swap queues, which ends up taking her longer than if she had stayed put in the first place. Her faffing about doesn't bother me too much as an hour's lunch break is more than enough to allow for this kind of holdup.

Eventually, she returns to me with a tray containing the food and two tall coffees; hers a mocha and mine a cappuccino.

'Man, what a mission!' she exclaims. 'I thought I'd never get served.'

'Yeah, it's packed in here today,' I reply, when what I really want to say is, 'You and me both.'

'It's all these fucking French tourists,' she complains, rather too loudly for my liking.

Not that anybody would have taken offence, given that the 'French' tourists she was referring to were actually Spanish.

'They should all piss off back to France,' she continues.

'Not him, though,' she adds, gesturing towards a bloke at the back of the queue, who could only be described as average, at best. 'He can stay as long as he wants.'

'What, with you, you mean?' I chuckle. 'Why don't you ask him?'

'Nah, he's way too hot for the likes of me,' she says forlornly.

'Don't be stupid.'

I shouldn't really say things like that around Roxanne, because sometimes she takes them to heart, as she is fully aware that she isn't the brightest. But these things have a tendency to slip out and it's not my fault if she has apartments to let. Having said that, I don't want to unnecessarily hurt her feelings, as I like the girl. Luckily for the both of us, the comment breezes over unnoticed.

'How's your love life these days, Leila?'

I really wish she wouldn't keep asking me this question as it's the one area of my life I'm really not content with at the moment. Having to say it out loud doesn't make things any easier.

'Completely non-existent,' I moan. 'I haven't seen any action in about eighteen months. Not even a snog.'

'You must be going to the wrong places,' she says supportively. 'I meet guys all the time. In fact, I met a guy just the other night.'

I had a sneaking suspicion this might have been the motivation for her initial question.

'What's he like then, Rox?'

I'm content to humour her for the time being.

Roxanne does about seventy percent of the talking in our conversations and I'm more than happy with this arrangement, it being a form of free entertainment that requires very little effort on my part.

Roxanne went on to describe the guy, Paul, in an incredibly superficial way that suggested not much talking took place when she met him. Apparently, he was an investment consultant, but she couldn't elaborate further on what this was, only that it meant he earned a lot of money. When I queried her on his surname, she was only able to tell me it matched that of a famous business school in America. Unsurprisingly, it wasn't one she had heard of herself. But he was a good kisser, apparently, and they had exchanged numbers, although he hadn't called her yet.

'Why don't you call him?'

It seemed like an obvious question.

'I'm playing hard to get,' she replies with confidence.

'Too hard by the sounds of it. What if he's doing the same? It could go on for weeks.'

'I know, I know. I just don't want to seem desperate.'

'Rox, you met him on Friday and it's now Tuesday. He'd hardly think you were desperate if you called him now.'

There is a glimmer of light as Roxanne processes what I've said.

'Nah,' she says eventually. 'I'd rather stick with playing hard to get.'

'Your loss,' I inform her.

'If it's meant to be, it will be,' she sighs dreamily. 'Anyway, what about you?'

'What about me?' I try to drop the hint that I'm not keen on talking about romance, but I know she's unlikely to take it.

'How are you going to overcome your situation?'

'So it's a *situation* now, is it?' I say defensively.

'You know what I mean. I know, let's see what your stars say.'

'Do we have to? I really don't believe in any of that stuff.'

Roxanne isn't listening. She's too busy wrestling a copy of *Cosmopolitan* out of her bag. She finds the correct page with worrying ease.

'What star sign are you?'

'It's all a load of rubbish. They just write stuff that's vague enough to apply to anyone.'

'You'd be surprised how much truth there is in it, Leila. I know a girl who can guess people's star signs nine times out of ten after talking to them for less than five minutes.'

'Fascinating.'

'What's your star sign?'

'Taurus.'

'Taurus, Taurus,' she mutters as she scans over the page. 'Ah, here we go. *"Mercury's move into your sign on the ninth could see you break free from the murky waters where relationships are concerned. Self-confidence is what's holding you back against the competition. And maybe if you don't take steps to bridge the gap, they'll zoom off without you to the other side of the Cosmos. Venus's sexy link with Pluto on the twenty-ninth encourages you to stop looking for what you believe to be the man of your dreams, and by the end of the month a new relationship may beckon".* Hey, that's you in a nutshell! You see, there's a lot of truth in this stuff. Point proven.'

'Except that I'm not a Taurus. I'm a Capricorn. As I said, it's a load of rubbish.'

Roxanne looks a bit hurt by my deception, but I can tell by her face that it will take more than this to waver her belief in the predictive power of the stars. She reads out the Capricorn section a bit more hesitantly and less matter-of-factly than before, as if she's scared I'm lying to her again. It comes as no surprise to either of us that this passage can be seen to describe my life if interpreted in a certain way. Neither of us comment on the findings and there's a period of uneasy silence before Roxanne's face develops a puzzled expression as she chews on her crayfish and rocket sandwich.

'Leila, can I ask you a question?'

'Sure, fire away.'

Roxanne appears unsure of herself, like she's about to ask me something really deep and personal and isn't sure whether she should be asking it at all. For a moment, I think she's going to withdraw the question, then it comes out and she asks me, with all seriousness:

'What do prawns grow into?'

I always envisaged myself as a lady who lunches. Admittedly, this isn't quite what I'd had in mind.

* * *

It's almost ten thirty by the time we get to the bar, and judging by the number of people there we must have been among the last to arrive. It's typical of my luck that I had been lumbered with a selection of the slowest eaters I've ever come across earlier in the evening. While I'm not particularly a scoffer myself, it had almost been painful to watch some of these people eating. By the time they had eventually finished, I was almost ready to eat again.

There were varying reasons why they had taken so long. One of the girls talked so much she hadn't had time to eat as her mouth was never closed for more than a couple of seconds. Another had struggled so much to cut her food that I guessed she must have somebody to do it for her at home. Either that or she lives on a diet of soup. And one of the guys chewed each mouthful so many times he had developed such highly visible jaw muscles that, combined with his long face, made him closely resemble a horse.

The evening had been organised for charity, but I couldn't tell you which. The theme was 'a single's night'. Basically, everyone invited had to bring along their most eligible friend of the opposite sex. Roxanne had desperately wanted to go and demanded that I accompany her. We had invited a couple of the single guys at work and made it a foursome. Roxanne had tried to claim we were going mainly for my benefit and that she was simply there to lend moral support. As it was, we both knew she was creaming herself at the prospect of spending a night in a bar full of single men.

I had been dubious about the whole thing as I could all too easily imagine the calibre of man that would be attending: socially challenged, bespectacled IT geeks with centre partings and pale, blotchy skin from a lack of sunlight and basic personal hygiene. Then again, maybe there would be the male equivalent of me; someone deserving of a decent partner but unswervingly unlucky in love.

My hopes had been dashed as early as the pre-bar dinner. The idea was that you and your platonic partner would join three other couples at a mystery restaurant and that each singleton would find a potential date out of one of the other people at the table. And even if you didn't, you still got a second bite at the cherry as all of the diners would congregate at a particular bar afterwards, giving everyone the opportunity to see what else was on offer. I must admit it was a good idea in theory, and one I wouldn't have minded coming up with myself. The only problem was that, while it created the perfect pulling scenario, it added a certain pressure to the evening, as not to at least get asked out by its conclusion would suggest you maybe had something wrong with you.

My dinner companions had been a strange bunch. All of the girls had gone to considerably more effort than I had to make themselves look glamorous and, despite being a good deal smarter-dressed than I usually am, I had still felt a little underdressed when I first arrived. More importantly, the blokes had been aesthetically pleasing, even if none of them had shown any imagination when it came to their outfits. Each had opted for the tried and tested 'jerk in a shirt' look of loafers, dark trousers and uniform-coloured, branded shirts. I had been sandwiched between my 'date', David, and a charmless Australian called Bruce, who was under the impression that simply being from another country made him a novelty and therefore far sexier than he actually was.

I had done my best to disassociate myself from David, who spent most of the meal cracking jokes nobody found funny. I didn't want people to think we were friends, which we weren't. He had only been invited along because attendance without a date was strictly forbidden. This had meant having to put up with Bruce's crassness, which, admittedly, became more amusing as I got increasingly drunk.

I had been pretty withdrawn over dinner. If I decide early on I don't particularly like a person, either men or women, I generally make little effort to get to know them better. And while the other girls were pleasant enough, they weren't really my kind of people. They were real girlie girls, all into make-up, jewellery and Shania Twain.

So once it had become apparent that neither my future husband nor a friend for life was sitting at the table, I had become impatient for the dinner to end. I had been at my most furtive and the others must have thought I was a right sulky cow, but this didn't bother me in the slightest as I knew I would be ditching them as soon as we got to the bar and found more interesting people to hang around with. Still, the dinner had been a partial success in that David and Michelle had seemed to hit it off and had left the venue holding hands. Good luck to them. He had found the one woman on this earth who found his anecdotes amusing, and she had found herself some arm candy.

I had secretly given them a couple of months, if they even made it through the night. It wouldn't take long for him to realise that the reason she found him funny was because she's dumb, and it was only a matter of time before she realised David ain't that good-looking. As I said, good luck to them. It meant one less piece of competition for me and one less idiot I had no interest in hampering my search for the good ones.

The tube is never the easiest place to try and hold a conversation and, although we had all shared a carriage, little was said for the duration of the journey. All of us had been clustered in the main standing area between the sliding doors, except for David and Michelle, who had snuggled up in the only two seats available. The chemistry between them was on the verge of causing a small explosion and I wished they would hurry up and snog rather than gazing sickeningly into each other's eyes as they were at present. It was as if they were restraining themselves purely for our benefit. As if any of us gave a damn. Except for Carl, maybe, who had also inexplicably developed a minor crush on Michelle and was constantly making jealous sideways glances at them to check nothing was happening.

I couldn't see the attraction myself. Maybe it was the 'come get some' top she was wearing, which left little to the imagination. You know, it's amazing how much attention you can get by showing a bit of flesh. I think this has something to do with there being a lot more desperate men out there than there are desperate women. Half of them went to my university. Men don't seem to relish a challenge, which is why even the plainest of girls could find herself a string of willing suitors simply by implying that she's 'up for it'. Any woman who dresses trashily develops a 'dirtiness' that's appealing to desperate men. And let me tell you, there are plenty of men out there with low enough self-esteem to sleep with pretty much anything, so there's no real reason why any girl need be single provided that she doesn't have very high standards.

The short walk to the bar from Oxford Circus tube station had been briefly interrupted by Carl making a stop at the cashpoint. He withdrew far more money than he could possibly need and I suspected that this flash of cash was mainly for Michelle's benefit, although she hadn't appeared to notice. The ceiling of cloud meant the day's warmth was locked in with a muggy closeness and a lot of people were mingling in and around the large paved area at the front of the bar, making the most of the fleeting opportunity to enjoy a drink out in the open at this time of year by sipping on champagne and continental beers.

'Anybody want a drink?' asked Carl.

He promptly began to take orders from the group, mine being a double vodka and tonic. I decided that if he was seriously going to go through with his costly charade, I might as well benefit from it. I figured the least I could do was accompany him to the bar, so I followed him inside, showing my invite to the bouncer, who grunted his approval and waved me past. The serving area was tiny and the crowd of people around it was three rows deep, but the bar staff – all dressed in black and seemingly plucked from the catwalk – worked quickly and efficiently, so it didn't take nearly as long to get served as I had anticipated. The bill came to more than fifty quid and I felt a momentary twang of guilt. I needn't have, as Carl looked almost pleased that it had come to such a large amount. He handed over three twenties with such arrogance that any sympathy I had held for him vanished in an instant.

I took three drinks, including my own, which was as many as I could carry without the fear of dropping them, and made my way outside. I handed them to the appropriate people and went off in search of Roxanne, who I had no doubt would be wrapped around some random bloke by now. She was nowhere to be seen in the small, overcrowded ground-level area, so I journeyed down to the basement. The music – a vibrant mixture of Latino, jazz and hip-hop – grew increasingly louder as I approached the double doors, and when I heaved them open I was hit by a blast of clarity and presented with a churning mass of bodies, all dipping, bobbing and busting shapes. They formed one huge, sweaty mass, like a many-limbed, multiple-headed monster.

I stood at the side for a few seconds as I scanned the floor for Roxanne. This was always going to be an uphill struggle; one short person looking for another. Instead, I traced the perimeter of the dancefloor, sideling my way past the dancers, who filled the space from wall to wall. Body heat overwhelmed the chilling breath of the air conditioning and I felt damp clothes against my bare arms as people brushed against me. I felt eyes peering at me from all angles, as though I were being watched by hundreds of spiders. I made a point of never looking in the same direction for any period of time, making sure I avoided lingering eye contact with the rows of smiling faces; big, red and beaming like an arrangement of tulips, all thinking *they* were the one I was searching for.

Roxanne wasn't among them and I began to think she wasn't actually at the bar yet. Either that or she had arrived early, snared a man and already taken him home. Just as I was about to give up hope of finding her, I abruptly reached the end of the dancefloor, which led on to a number of large tables straddled by long benches, almost like the ones you might find in a modernised prison canteen. Low arches rolled overhead like sandstone anacondas and beneath one of them sat Roxanne and, unsurprisingly, an accompanying man. I turned to leave, not wishing to disturb her when she was so close to succeeding in her aim for the evening, but she had already spotted me.

'Leila!' She waved me over excitedly and I obliged, relief spreading over me at the promise of familiar company.

'Hi, Leila. Where have *you* been all this time?' she asked in an exaggerated nudge-nudge, wink-wink tone.

'Nowhere exciting. I was stuck at the restaurant for ages. I only got here about five minutes ago.'

'We've been here ages, haven't we, Francis?'

'Pardon?' said her new friend.

'I was just saying that we'd been here for quite a while.'

'Yes, quite a while,' he echoed.

'Francis, this is my friend Leila. Leila, this is Francis. He's involved in finance.'

'Pleased to meet you,' I said politely. 'What area of finance are you in?'

'Banking.'

'That's cool. Which bank do you work for?'

Francis seemed to shift uncomfortably.

'Er... One of the big ones. American one. Really big.'

'Which one?'

'Excuse me for a moment, I'm just going for some fresh air, but I'll be back in a bit. It was nice to meet you.'

Francis awkwardly edged his way along the bench and vanished as he was eaten by the monster on the dancefloor.

'Something I said? He's a bit of an oddball! Where did you find him?' I questioned.

'I sat next to him at dinner.'

'And the rest is history, I suppose.'

A long pause followed.

'Met anyone that takes your fancy?'

'Not yet. As I said, I only just got here.'

There was another pause.

'It's pretty cool this place, don't you reckon?'

'Yeah, it's not bad at all.'

'Listen, Leila, Francis has been gone a while.'

Yeah, all of two minutes, I thought.

'I'm gonna go and check he's ok,' she said.

'Sure.'

And then I was alone again.

It wasn't the greatest conversation we had ever had, and it had hardly been worth the trip down there to see her. However, I wasn't without company for long, as no sooner had Roxanne gone than Bruce swept into the space she had vacated. He was wearing the broadest of grins. In fact, if his smile had grown any wider he would have been in danger of swallowing his own face.

'You stalking me, Bruce?'

'Who was *that*?' He cut straight to the chase, which seemed to be his general approach.

'I assume you're referring to the girl I was just talking to?'

He nodded eagerly, like an expectant puppy. I half expected his tongue to loll out of his mouth at any second.

'Her name's Roxanne. She's a friend from work.'

'Is she single?'

Don't beat around the bush do you, Brucey boy?

'She wouldn't be here if she wasn't.'

'How do you rate my chances?' he asked.

'Judging by her track record, I'd say you were in with a chance.'

'You mean she's a walk-up fuck?'

Nobody can be crude like an Australian.

'Excuse me?'

'A walk-up fuck,' he repeated. 'Meaning, I just have to walk up and ask her, and she'll fuck me.'

I had guessed that was what he meant. The answer was almost certainly a resounding yes, but she was my friend and I felt some obligation to uphold her reputation.

'I wouldn't put it quite like that, and if you approach her with that attitude you're liable to get a slap; if not from her, then from me. Roxy is... How can I put this...? Currently open to offers.'

That hadn't come out exactly as I had planned. Not that it mattered, as Bruce would have grasped whichever end of the stick he wanted to anyway, irrespective of how I packaged it.

'Thank you, Leila, that's all I needed to know. See you around.'

Bruce disappeared as abruptly as he had arrived. I hoped Roxanne had managed to find Francis, who, despite coming across as a little odd, was likely to be a safer proposition than the walking sack of testosterone from down under.

The bench seemed so much bigger with only me sitting on it and I felt like a kid, banished to the corner of the classroom while all of the other children were allowed to run about and enjoy themselves. I noticed I was sitting directly under a light, which was heating the top of my head, so I shuffled over to the left to escape the uncomfortable warmth and its attention-grabbing glare. I really didn't want to advertise the fact I was sitting there alone and desperate like a middle-aged spinster. I couldn't remember the last time I had felt like this at a party. It wasn't as if everybody else knew each other and I was an outsider. Most people were meeting each other for the first time. Yet that's how I felt; like an *outsider*. I used to be able to talk about anything to anybody. Right at that moment, I felt like I would struggle to hold a decent conversation with my best friend in the world, whoever that might be.

I was filled with anxiety: the fear of introducing myself and quickly running out of things to say; the fear of those awkward exchanges consisting of superficial questions and hesitant, one-word answers. Had the last six months really dented my confidence *that* much? No, they couldn't have. It wasn't me, it was *them*. Why should I bother to make an effort to speak to people who had nothing to say? I could if I wanted to, but it would have been a waste of time.

Who was I trying to kid? I had fallen into a social hole, and by making little or no effort to get out I was beginning to sink in the mud at the bottom. Part of the problem was that I hadn't done anything over the past six months. At university, there had always been the common ground of being at university to fall back on when conversations were flagging. Faced with strangers from unknown backgrounds, I was left doubting my own ability to come across as interesting enough to make them want to talk to me for more than a couple of minutes.

I looked down at the expensive drink I had barely touched. Alcohol usually helped this type of problem. Maybe I should drink a bit faster. I took out the two little black straws, dropped them onto the table and necked the drink in one go, grimacing in disgust as the vodka lurking unmixed at the base of the glass burnt the back of my throat. I put the glass down hard and pushed it away from me with the back of my hand.

'One of those nights?' came a friendly voice.

Before I could answer, the same voice asked, 'Mind if I join you?'

I felt my cheeks redden at having been seen downing my drink.

'Not at all, although I'm not sure how long I'm sticking around.'

'Not quite what you were expecting?' he asked as he sat down next to me.

'Not really, no,' I said truthfully.

'Me neither. To be honest, I'm not exactly sure what I *was* expecting.' He smiled.

It was a nice, genuine smile.

'I've never been to a singles night before,' I informed him.

'Neither have I.'

'I kind of thought the place would be full of desperate losers, but it doesn't seem to be like that at all. It's a pity in a way!' I really hoped he realised I was joking.

'Makes you feel better, doesn't it, that there are loads of other *normal* single people? It's kind of reassuring.'

'I guess so.'

'Makes you feel like less of a leper.'

It was my turn to smile.

'Before we continue this conversation, there's something *really* important I need to know about you,' I demanded.

The statement caused him to back away slightly, shifting uncomfortably in his seat.

'What's your name?'

'Oh, right,' he chuckled. 'Sorry, you had me worried there for a second.'

'Why? Got something to hide?' I pried.

'No,' he said defensively, 'but it's always a bit worrying when someone tells you they *really* need to know something about you.'

'Maybe you're right. Look, stop avoiding the question. It's not that difficult, you know!'

'Phil.'

'Leila. Pleased to meet you, Phil.'

'Pleased to meet you too, Leila.'

We shook hands with mock formality.

'So, what brings you to such a night, Leila?' he asked.

'I'm here for moral support,' I replied.

'That's what they all say. Obviously, my role for the evening is merely that of chaperone.'

'Ok then, if that's not good enough for you, I'm here to support the charity.'

'Nope, heard that one before as well. I don't buy it.'

'What do you want me to say?'

'The truth. That, like me, you came here hoping to meet someone special and having failed to do so are now trying to justify why you came at all.'

'You shouldn't assume everyone shares your insecurities!' I said with a laugh.

'You'd be surprised.'

'Would I now?'

I used the pause in conversation to check him out. It was the natural thing to do and I was sure he was doing the same thing. When you meet somebody of the opposite sex for the first time it's an automatic reaction to assess whether or not they're boyfriend material. I try to ignore the immediate opinion based on looks because, judging by experience, men often shatter any decent first impressions as soon as they open their mouths. Once it's evident that they might be one of the few blokes that isn't a complete wanker, you make a second assessment of their looks. After all, he might be the kindest, funniest man in the world, but if he doesn't double up as eye candy I don't want to know. It's not too much to expect the full package.

I would say that, based on what little I had seen, Phil had passed the looks test. He was by no means stunning, not model material or anything, but he was fairly handsome in a straight-nosed, firm-jawed, thoroughbred English kind of way. His hair – dark brown and thick – looked free of product, hanging nicely all the same in a no-nonsense, minimal-effort style. There was something about his eyes that demanded further attention, but to identify what it was would require me staring into them for a reasonable length of time and I wasn't prepared to do that at this early juncture. Dark and piercing, they harboured a timid vulnerability and it occurred to me that we had barely held each other's gaze since he sat down, which is slightly odd seeing as we had been talking to one another. I tried not to dwell on this too long for fear of gawping at him like a goldfish, so I made a move to restart the conversation.

'So, what do you do with yourself, Phil?'

These 'getting to know you' conversations always start off in the same way.

'I work in a homeware shop, which is about as exciting as it sounds.'

At least he was honest.

'Whereabouts?' I asked, trying to sound interested.

'In Whiteleys, in…'

'…Bayswater.'

'You know the area, then?'

'I've been there a couple of times.' A couple of hundred, more like. 'How do you find it?'

'Bayswater or the job?'

'The job.'

'It's not bad, to be honest. I've only been doing it a few months, but I kind of like it. Set hours, minimum stress. Makes a change from working in the city.'

'You used to work in the city?' I questioned.

It seemed strange to me that somebody who used to be involved in the financial world would choose to work in a shop selling cute candle holders, stainless-steel saucepan sets and fancy photo frames.

'We all have things in our past we'd rather forget!' he said with a laugh. 'There's only so long you can work for the devil before you start wanting your soul back.'

'Do you get the same sort of satisfaction?'

I was intrigued by this. Here was a man who had secured the kind of job I had been striving for all those months ago and he had supposedly given it up in favour of menial work.

'Satisfaction?' he asked with great amusement. 'Put it this way. Neither job is mentally taxing, neither job is of any benefit to the greater good, and neither job entails anything you might call exciting. So it boils down to a toss-up between sociability and ambition, comfort and prestige. And right now, I'm quite happy to take it easy.'

'Well, when you put it like that it makes a lot of sense.'

'Or maybe I'm just trying to convince myself,' he says, smiling. 'One thing's for sure, and it's that I'm happy for the moment.'

There was a brief lull in the conversation before he picked it up again.

'And what about yourself, Leila? How do you pay your way?'

Part of me wanted to tell him that I didn't pay my own way at all; that my dad paid it for me. However, the image of a spoilt little rich kid hardly endears me to people, so I told him how I spent my weekdays.

'I tell people what to buy. In terms of clothes,' I add.

'Sounds cool. Tell me more.'

'There's not a great deal more to tell. I work at Selfridges. People come in, they tell me their budget and I go and find them things to wear.'

'Ok,' Phil nods, deep in concentration, like the concept of a personal shopper is something completely alien to him. 'So, you're kind of like a clothes hound, sniffing out suitable outfits for people whose money can't buy taste.'

'If depicting things with animals instead of people makes it easier for you to understand, then yes, I'm a clothes hound.'

We both laughed. It really wasn't that funny, but the alcohol was beginning to make itself known. I noticed there was more eye contact by this time and our bodies were pointing towards each other. I'm always a big observer of body language because it's an instant messaging service as to what people are really thinking. And right then things were looking positive. Thinking back, I couldn't remember either of us moving positions, but we had done. It was almost as if an unseen force had rotated us as we sat unawares, twisting us and pushing us closer together.

'Tell me, Leila. The outfit I'm wearing now, would you have picked it out for me if I came into Selfridges with my hard-earned, fairly limited cash?'

'Hmm, now let me see,' I mused as I tugged at his jumper, then his jeans. 'You don't know much about clothes, do you, Phil?'

'No,' he chuckled. 'Is it *that* obvious?'

'Not to the untrained eye. You have to remember you're dealing with an expert here. The jeans are the giveaway. They're Levi's, are they not?'

'That is correct.' Phil looked impressed, and at the same time slightly baffled that I could tell this merely by touching them.

'Well, in the same way that people who know nothing about music but want to appear as though they do listen to David Gray, people who know nothing about clothes but want to look trendy wear Levi's jeans.'

'Who's David Gray?' asked Phil, looking utterly perplexed.

I was about to give him a different example involving dinner parties and spaghetti bolognese when he told me he saw the point I was making.

'Well, for somebody who knows nothing about clothes, you have made a valiant effort. It's to your great credit that you haven't turned up in a uniformly coloured shirt and dark trousers like all the other clones in this place.'

I waved my arm in the direction of the dancefloor and we laughed together at the cluster of men who conveniently supported my statement.

'And do you find *your* job satisfying?'

'Immensely.'

'Thought as much,' he said, grinning cheekily.

'What's that supposed to mean?'

'Nothing.'

Things started to get tricky from this point on because I had it in my head that I liked him and, once this has happened, what had once been an easy-going conversation takes on increased importance. There was an added incentive to impress. Every pause, every miscalculated comment played on the mind. In a way, this takes the fun out of it, but the challenge certainly makes things more interesting, and sometimes you can even surprise yourself with what you can come out with.

'You know, Leila, we must be pretty much the only people in here who aren't in powerful jobs. We're the working equivalent of the underclass.'

'Speak for yourself!' I argued. 'How many of these spods can claim to change the way people look?'

'I guess so. And how many of them can claim to have furnished the houses of the majority of people in West London?'

'Exactly,' I agreed. 'It's all about perspective. As someone who is *older*, you should know these things.'

'Hey, how do you know I'm older? Actually, don't answer that.'

'Pardon?'

The music had been cranked up and I couldn't quite hear what he was saying. This had its advantages, because it meant we were going to have to get closer to each other if we were to continue the conversation. I turned my head to offer him my ear and Phil leant forward to repeat what he had said. It made me tingle having his face so close to mine and when I replied I put my hand on his shoulder to test the water and he didn't flinch or back away.

Once I had finished speaking, I withdrew my hand and we moved apart again. Neither of us spoke for the next few seconds, but I knew that he had also felt it. We just looked at each other, not knowing whether to smile or not, our lips nervously twitching at the corners, unwilling to broaden.

'Leila, I've got to go soon, but I'd like to meet up again.'

He spoke softly, and although I could barely hear the words I was concentrating so intently that they made sense nonetheless.

I was gutted he was leaving so soon. In a way, it could be for the best that both of us departed without having given too much away; with both left wanting to know more. He reached into his pocket and pulled out his mobile phone.

'Can I take your number?' he asked.

'Sure. You ready? It's 07968501129.' I read out the numbers in robotic monotone.

'I'll try and call you now to check I've got it right.'

There was a short pause before I felt my phone vibrating in my pocket. I pulled it out and held it up so he could see his own mobile number flashing on the screen.

'Well, you've got it now, so no excuses for not calling,' I said, nudging him in the arm with the point of my elbow.

'I'll do my best,' he replied, acting like he was playing it cool.

'Hopefully see you soon, then, Phil.'

'Yeah, see you soon.'

I'm not exactly sure what happened next. I went to give him a hug but our heads got caught on the same side. We performed an inelegant dance, not too dissimilar to when you're trying unsuccessfully to dodge an oncoming pedestrian on a narrow pavement. We were stuck for a good few seconds with our heads darting from side to side like chickens in an attempt to break away from the mirror image display we were involuntarily creating.

In the end, our faces just move closer together and we kissed. Don't ask me who instigated it, as I really didn't know. It was a strange kiss, almost carried out for the sake of politeness since it would have been quite a rejection to withdraw one's face just because we couldn't coordinate a hug. But it was a nice kiss. No tongues or slobbering, just a gentle bringing together of our lips. It didn't last long, and when we pulled away we both looked down in embarrassment.

'See you soon,' Phil said again, making a fairly hasty exit.

'Hope so,' I whispered to his back as he walked away.

I sat there alone for some time longer, gathering my thoughts. For the first time in months, I felt genuinely happy. And all because of an accidental kiss.

* * *

Early April brought tragic news for the nation with the passing away of the previously indestructible Queen Mother. Now, I've never been one to take a strong stance on whether the monarchy plays an important role in today's society but, at times like this, the cringe-worthy reaction of the British public always makes me wish we could do away with tradition in order to save face.

In typical fashion, I chose to expose myself to those who annoy me most and decided to go and sign the book of remembrance. I'm not sure what possessed me to do such a thing. It seemed like a great idea when I woke up for work on the Tuesday morning; so great, in fact, that I phoned my supervisor and told her I had been struck down with a mysterious virus and was unable to go in to work. The lie was a necessary one. I wasn't going to waste a precious day's holiday on paying my respects. I took the opportunity to catch up on some much-needed sleep and then made my way across to Westminster midway through the morning, almost looking forward to being involved in a slice of British history.

My enthusiasm was chased away by the sight of a queue that vanished into the distance as I stepped out of the station. I had clearly underestimated the popularity of England's most famous great-grandmother. The sheer size of it should have been enough to bring me to my senses, it being a clear signal that I should do something a little more constructive with my day off. Yet I found myself marching to the back with a dogged stubbornness I'm pretty sure I inherited from my mother. Plus it couldn't take that long to sign a poxy book, so the queue ought to move fairly quickly.

It's lucky I don't suffer from vertigo, as the point at which I joined the line was about halfway across a bridge, offering a somewhat hair-raising view over the murky milkshake that is the River Thames. Within ten minutes of my arrival, the queue had grown with the rapidity of a magic beanstalk and I consoled myself with the belief that, as was usually the case, things could be a lot worse. I guess you shouldn't really need reminding of that at a funeral.

I had to constantly keep my eyes peeled for television cameras and people I knew. It would have been of considerable inconvenience, not to mention embarrassing, to be caught pulling a sicky to go and see the boxed-up Queen Mum. Fortunately, the cameramen were only interested in those who thought Union Jack flags and silly hats were appropriate things to bring to a funeral. And there was always the saving grace of an overemotional housewife who took the event as a deeply personal tragedy, as though she had lost one of her oldest and dearest friends. When these sentimental freaks are broadcast to other countries, their words should be accompanied by a disclaimer saying, "The views of this disturbed individual are by no means representative of Britain as a whole", so they are clear that not everybody cries when a famous person bites the dust. At least we can be thankful that, on this occasion, the death was wholly expected and natural, meaning there was little chance of Elton John releasing a single.

Newspaper sellers were handing out free memorial posters with every issue sold; a reflective Queen Mother pasted onto a black background with a few well-considered words of solace. I can't imagine anyone actually putting one up on their wall and, like nightclub flyers, they would pave the streets by the end of the day, hundreds of people treading dirt into her face as they hurried home from work. The whole thing had a distinctly touristy air about it, and the only missing link was provided by the people selling T-shirts bearing her picture. Those gathered immediately in front of and behind me were all foreign. Aside from the accents, I could tell merely by the way they were dressed. Only Americans wore those awful cream-sleeved sports jackets and only a Frenchman would wear tight, bleached jeans. I would have liked to ask them what the hell they were doing there, were it not for the fact that they could justifiably ask me the same question.

A drinks seller walked past, offering me his wares. I politely declined. Recognising my accent, the father of the American family behind me seized the opportunity to get the views of a real-life Brit.

'Hey, you're English, right?'

'I am indeed.'

His powers of observation were truly sensational.

'We're over here from the US and thought we'd pay our respects.'

'That's nice.' I really couldn't think of anything else to say.

'Gee, would you look at all these people! You guys must really love the Queen Mother.'

I wanted to explain to him that this queue was nothing compared to the ones I had seen outside the various branches of William Hill following the news of her death, but it wasn't the time and it certainly wasn't the place.

'She was a wonderful lady,' I said, biting my lip.

He nodded thoughtfully, gazing out over the Thames, as though he were wistfully recalling a happier time. He put an arm around his son's slender shoulders and drew his wife closer to him. I turned away in the nick of time, just before the smirk spread across my face. Weirdo Americans.

It was a pretty pleasant day, which was lucky for everyone, especially the Queen Mother, since the weatherman had granted the public no excuses for not turning up. My stomach began to murmur. I wished I had done the sensible thing and picked up a sandwich en route. I didn't really want to leave the queue and risk losing my place as a five-minute trip to the shops could end up costing me a few hours. I looked up and down the line and noticed most people had come prepared with packed lunches and thermos flasks. I don't know why I never think of these things myself. I guess planning ahead has never been one of my strong points.

As if to reassure me that I hadn't missed out, the aroma of fried onions carried past me on the spring breeze. I briefly stepped out of the line and followed my nose in the direction of the scent and, sure enough, a man had set up a hotdog stall about fifty yards down the bank. I wasn't so famished that I couldn't wait a bit longer, so I stepped back into the queue and waited for it to take me there naturally. A couple of years ago I had sworn never to buy a hotdog from one of these portable stands for fear of what it might do to my insides, but right at that moment the smell of burnt onions and smouldering fat couldn't have been more tempting.

It was hardly a bargain at three quid, but it was money well spent and I enjoyed every last bit of it, right down to the last bite of the stale bread roll. Time always passes more quickly when you've got something in your stomach.

Just as Westminster Abbey came into sight, I was disturbed by an incoming call on my phone. It was a relief to see the name 'Phil' blinking on the screen as I took it out of my handbag.

'Hi, babe. How's things?' His daily lunchtime call always brightened up my day.

'Pretty good. I was thinking, it's fairly quiet here today. Would you like to meet for lunch?'

'Er, I can't, I'm afraid. I'm kind of busy,' I replied hesitantly.

'Why? What are you up to?' he asked suspiciously.

'It's kind of embarrassing.'

'Embarrassing? You have to tell me now!' he said with a laugh.

'Ok, if I must. I've taken the day off to sign the Queen Mother's book of remembrance.'

There was no response at the other end of the line, probably because he was too busy laughing.

'It's not *that* funny!' I protested.

'I'm not laughing,' he replied, although I can tell he blatantly is. 'I never knew you were a fan.'

'I'm *not* a fan.' I hated to admit it, but his mocking had me flustered. 'I'm just along for the ride. I couldn't give a damn about the senile old bat.'

'Well, I had a bit of a soft spot for her myself, so write her something nice from me.'

'Like what?'

'I'm sure you'll think of something. From the heart. Anyway, I'll leave you to it. Can't let you have too much excitement in one day. Speak to you later.'

'Maybe,' I said grumpily, hanging up.

Once he had gone, I allowed myself a smile. In a way, it made a nice change to have someone making fun of me, it usually being the other way around.

Glancing around, I could see that I had become the subject of many a disapproving glare and I realised my senile old bat comment had been an unacceptable show of disrespect, so I did my best to look repentant. It wasn't as if any of us *knew* her, for God's sake, and it was generally accepted that you're allowed to freely criticise people you don't know, particularly those hounded by the media.

It didn't take too long for people to get over my outburst, except for one sour-faced old woman whose focus hadn't moved from me for a good five minutes. I hate it when old people get like that, waiting for an opportunity to pour scorn on the younger generation. I was determined not to rise to the bait, but I could feel her wrinkly stare drilling into my head and it made my blood boil until I was engulfed in a cloud of red. I looked up and fixed her back with a stare of such intense ferocity it ought to have made her avert her gaze. She didn't even blink.

'I'm sorry, I was only messing about. I take it back,' I said, holding up my hands submissively.

'You should be ashamed of yourself!' spat the old biddy.

'You're right, I should be,' I agreed in a patronising manner.

'She was a wonderful lady. An example to us all. You young people should take a leaf out of her book.'

'Yes, we should all aspire to be just like the Queen Mother,' I said with a sigh.

'Your lot won't last to her age, young lady. Not the way you're going.'

I wanted to tell her that I didn't expect to live to such an age, as I didn't have an entourage of people around me whose sole purpose in life was to tend to my every need. I wouldn't be kept alive by daily transfusions using the blood of poor people, or have my decrepit joints replaced with those of the homeless. I knew I was grossly outnumbered, so I kept my mouth firmly shut and hoped the stupid old cow would hurry up and say her bit before shutting the hell up. Either that or have a heart attack. Then we might have another funeral to celebrate.

'She's ignoring me now,' I heard her say to her companion.

Nothing winds me up like a grumpy pensioner. Nothing. Hopefully I had ruined *her* day sufficiently that she wouldn't enjoy it as much as she had expected to, and she would go home looking forward to the next royal funeral instead, running through the remaining members in her head and trying to anticipate who would be the next one to pop their clogs. And hopefully she would feel guilty about it. They all should. Every one of them. They had all been waiting for this day for the last ten years so they could come and sign a book and feel good about themselves. It made me sick.

I didn't enjoy the rest of the wait one bit. Every time anybody opened their mouths I was forced to wince. They had all been standing there too long and had run out of things to say. People had resorted to saying what they could see; that and pathetic anecdotes. If only I had brought my minidisc player with me I could have shut them all out. Some people couldn't hack the wait and left early, muttering audibly so everybody around them could hear that they were going to post their best wishes on the internet instead.

Yeah, nice one. If only you'd thought of that this morning you wouldn't have spent half the day queuing for nothing.

I was caught in two minds as to whether I should follow suit. Part of me thought I should cut my losses and go home. Then again, if I had waited that long, what difference would another couple of hours make? It's like when your bus has been delayed and you've been waiting at the bus stop for about forty minutes. You could have walked it in that time if you had known, but once you've waited for a certain length of time you have to continue waiting, because imagine how you would feel if you started walking only to see the bus drive past. So I waited, determined to do what I had come to do and sign that goddam book.

The act of finally setting foot in the chapel was met with considerable relief. The feeling of having at last made it outweighed any emotions I otherwise might have felt, which is a shame as the atmosphere was enthralling. It always moves me to some extent to be in the presence of so many people obediently adhering to a request for voluntary silence, in addition to the solemn splendour and that churchy mustiness that's impossible to recreate. Everyone who entered the room found themselves unable to utter a single sound and had to stoop low as they walked, as if feeling a great weight on their foreheads.

The coffin sat, huge and menacing, in the hall's centre, large enough to sleep five Queen Mothers. It was guarded by four beefeaters, whose vibrant robes provided the only splash of colour in an otherwise lustreless space. The line formed a human cage around this sepulchral scene, and we all stared at it, as we would an exhibit in a museum. That's what it felt like; as though we were in a museum, the notion that there was a person inside the box almost lost amid the surrounding attention to detail.

In the same way that queues for rollercoasters at theme parks never seem to end, getting inside the abbey was only the start of about another half an hour of waiting. By the time my turn had almost come to put pen to paper, I felt sick to death of the whole grotesque affair and would have happily gone home. While initially humbling, the atmosphere had become really depressing and I had had enough of looking at the statuesque beefeaters with their waxwork, emotionless faces and the way people were pacing around with their hands clasped together behind their backs as though that was the only way you were allowed to walk in such a place.

I had been so eager to step up to that great big book, but when I eventually did I realised I hadn't decided what the hell I was going to write. I had been gifted about five hours to think about it and, as always, I had left it to the last minute. I stood there, mind completely blank, pen hovering over the page like a pin waiting to be stuck into a map. Nothing came to mind. Zilch. Nada. I looked at what other people had written as a source of inspiration. It didn't help. It was all dull and clichéd, as if they hadn't been given enough time to decide what they were going to say either.

And then I sensed it; the condemning stare of that miserable old cow from earlier in the day arrowing into the back of my head. The Americans had called it a day a couple of hours earlier and I had been forced to endure her moaning in my ear ever since. If she hadn't been so old I would have told her to shut the hell up, but unfortunately in today's society you're supposed to respect your elders whether they deserve it or not. I imagined her muttering and complaining about me taking too long, and it wound me up so much I needed to get back at her in some way; to offend her so deeply she would be rendered speechless with anger and shock. And then it occurred to me how I could do it.

In large, clear letters, and set out in such a way that I knew she was guaranteed to read it, I wrote the following words:

> Her death should act as a warning to others who think it's cool to experiment with drugs.

I left hurriedly, half expecting to be reprimanded at any second; to feel a firm hand on my shoulder. It never came and I made it safely to the station without incident. I didn't look back once, but the picture of horror I imagined on the sagging witch's face filled me with an overwhelming joy that still makes me smile every time I think about it.

* * *

Summer in London is great. Well, summer in most places is pretty good, but there's something special about being in London when the sun is blazing overhead and everybody manages to relax a little for once. I accept that you have to turn a blind eye to those occasional days when it hasn't rained for weeks and the smog makes the air so thick you struggle to breathe, so that when you blow your nose it comes out black. And that you have to avoid the West End on Saturday and Sunday mornings unless you want to choke on the smell of stale urine. But this is a small price to pay.

While arguably a waste of space during the winter, the royal parks come into their own between June and September, when they're transformed into London's playgrounds, awash with sunbathers, picnickers and frisbee players; a patchwork of glinting sunglasses and smiling faces. The most prudent of people strip down to their bathing costumes or even their underwear as they try to rid themselves of their pasty complexions, a collection of pearly flesh baking brown like biscuits over the course of the day. Scenically, the parks are nothing compared to the countryside. It's the act of them being *in* London that makes them special, like dollops of nature in the concrete jungle. It's almost as if they shouldn't be there, and you experience a unique sensation emerging from the grey overhanging buildings into an open emerald space. That's why everyone flocks to them at the first suggestion of summer sun. I guess it's like London's equivalent of the beach, only here you don't get sand between your toes.

Hyde Park is very conveniently placed, it being situated in the middle ground between my workplace and Phil's. Before the weather became so agreeable, we had met for lunch about once a week, with either him travelling east to Oxford Street for a sandwich or me journeying west to Queensway for a Chinese. Now the sun appears to be here for an extended stay, our rendezvous have become more frequent and Phil will often come and meet me near Speaker's Corner. This regular choice of location is a lot handier for me than for him. I only have to walk the short distance between Selfridges and Marble Arch to reach it, whereas he has to sweat it out on the tube or bus. That said, it's more acceptable for a man to have sweat patches than a girl, so it's a necessary compromise on his part. Not that Phil particularly suffers from sweat patches, I might add.

Occasionally, I'll bring Roxanne along because she gets long-faced if I go too many days without lunching with her. Phil doesn't seem to mind her company, since, like me, he finds her dappiness entertaining. What we do when we get to the park is heavily dependent on how hot it is. On the cooler days, we stroll around scoffing Mr Whippy ice-creams before they melt over our hands. We make our way down to the Serpentine to see the ducks, or sometimes we even go and gaze longingly through the windows of the exclusive car showrooms that line the north end of Park Lane.

Other days, the heat gets so intense the only thing it's bearable to do is lie on our backs under the shade of a tree, sitting up occasionally to take a sip of our fruit smoothies or Frappucinos. Some days it's too hot even to talk and we lie in silence, stroking each other's hands every now and then to remind each other we're still there. Going back to work afterwards is always a monumental struggle, and we always joke about not bothering and lying there together all afternoon instead, even though neither of us has the courage to carry it through. It's the prospect of not going back to work that makes the idea so appealing. Lying in the park all day at the weekend just isn't the same. One day we might actually do it, although I doubt it. I imagine half the people in the park are contemplating the same thing and, like them, we're all empty talk.

But it would be nice to spend more time with Phil. Up to this point, it's all been fairly casual. Not casual in that we aren't fully committed to each other. Casual in the sense that our relationship so far has consisted of a long series of dates. I've enjoyed every minute of his company, and I know I'm lucky to be with him, but it leaves me feeling empty sometimes when we've been out and had a great evening only to have to say goodbye to each other at the tube station and go our separate ways. It's some consolation that he always calls me when he gets home and constantly texts to see how I'm doing and to tell me what he's up to, but it's just not the same as snuggling up under the covers or waking up next to each other in the mornings.

Phil made it clear right at the beginning that he wanted to take things slowly, and back then it suited me fine. Now the more time we spend together the more I want to be with him, and it's reached the stage now when I wouldn't mind being with him twenty-four-seven. I know I may have to wait, unfortunately. You can't push these things.

It gives me something to think about in that dead time between work and home, when the trains are too crowded for you to even open a newspaper. Travelling is the one and only thing I really dislike about the summer. The transport system is ill-equipped to cope with the weather when it gets *really* hot. Unwilling to spend money on installing air conditioning in the underground, the government condemns the average Londoner to about an hour of hell every single day. Mine is a relatively short journey, taking me across to Notting Hill Gate on the Central Line, then a quick change to the District Line to get me down to West Brompton. Yet it's still enough to reduce me to a state of grumpiness that takes a shower and a clean change of clothes to fix.

Today is pretty bad by any standards. Being at work is fine because the management recognises nobody is going to buy anything if they have to enter a sauna to get it, so they maintain the temperature at a comfortable level. But as soon as I step outside onto the street I can tell the journey home is going to be a bad one. It's a windless day and the air is blue with exhaust fumes. Some days in London you can almost taste it. There's that horrible, humid closeness you get before a thunderstorm, although there aren't enough clouds to grant us an atmosphere-cleansing downpour.

And I know things will get worse when I enter Bond Street station. Walking through the shopping centre offers me my last few seconds of comfort before I begin my descent into the airlessness of the underground. It's rush hour and the tunnels are busy; full of flustered, impatient people who want to keep their time down there as brief as possible and consequently don't give a damn whose heels they tread on, while tourists congregate in inappropriate places and make a general nuisance of themselves.

There must be delays, because the first train that pulls up is so full hardly anyone can get on it. Many people try anyway in a bid to escape the crowded platform, and they squeeze their way into every last inch of space and have to duck their heads to avoid being decapitated by the closing doors. I wait for the next one, and the next one again, and it's worth it because I manage to grab the seat of a lady who is stopping off to do some shopping. You get used to where to stand in order to maximise your chances of getting on the train. The inexperienced traveller stands directly in front of the doors, and when they open they're forced to step back to let the people out. Slightly to the side is where you want to be. A seat carries greater importance on a day like this as it spares you the unpleasantness of being thrust up against the sweaty body of a stranger. You're guaranteed a small amount of breathing space, rather than having your face inches away from an armpit.

I'm lacking reading material today and have to look to my surroundings for entertainment. Directly in front of me is a man of about Phil's age wearing an expensive-looking suit and a modern briefcase alternative slung over his shoulders like a record bag. He's also wearing sunglasses, and by the arrogant expression on his face he believes that doing so makes him some sort of minor celebrity. Now, wearing sunglasses indoors is bad enough. Wearing them on the underground is plain ridiculous, so I smirk at him in a way that ought to deflate his ego, but I don't think he notices.

The gentleman sitting to my right is a man of considerable size and he's finding the conditions harder to cope with than most, a ring of dark sweat creeping out from his collar. That's not to say he's the only one perspiring. The majority of men have beaded temples and the general smell suggests most people are sweating somewhere or other. My seat is at the end of the row, so I don't have anybody sitting to my left. Instead, I have a woman's buttocks squashed hard up against the glass, so much so that her flimsy underwear is clearly visible through her white skirt, which doesn't leave a great deal to the imagination. And there's not even the suggestion of cellulite. I wish she had tied a top around her waist or something, as I can do without having a flawless behind shoved in my face when I'm on my way home. It reminds me I should really start thinking about going to the gym. Call me bitter, if you like.

The parading of her assets puts me off people-watching and I switch my attentions to the adverts that line the top of the wall, bridging the gap between window and ceiling like a garish cummerbund. The subject matter of the adverts is markedly different from those seen twelve months ago. Back when the employment market was buoyant, every other advert was for an online recruitment agency telling you your present job was rubbish and promising you dream jobs with fat salaries instead. Now the focus has switched to hanging on to the job you have at any cost. They tell us that something as trivial as serious illness should not prevent us from completing a day's work and that we should do the honourable British thing and go to the office drugged up like zombies. It's a strange society we live in; one where illness is a sign of weakness, whereas it's fashionable to develop allergies to entire food groups we've eaten unperturbed for most of our lives. I feel left out at work sometimes because I'm about the only girl there who isn't gluten-intolerant.

We get to Notting Hill Gate and I give up my seat for an old lady. To be honest, I ought to have let her sit there in the first place as she's certainly 'less fortunate' than I am. However, she didn't die or anything, so I don't feel that guilty, and besides, none of the other selfish passengers stepped forward either. The Notting Hill section of the District Line track isn't really underground, meaning the wait at this station is just about bearable. I rarely get a seat on this stretch of the journey and I make do with a spot by the pole next to the door. If I'm lucky, I'll be able to grab a seat when we get to Earls Court, where the turnover of passengers is greatest. I'm well-positioned to do so.

Sod's Law means I get stuck behind a lady who dallies so much that all the vacated seats are taken by people coming the other way. I swear at her under my breath. It's all very well being polite, but you shouldn't let your politeness hinder the people behind you. So I'm stuck with my position by the pole. It doesn't matter too much as it's only one stop. A seat would have been nice, all the same, and what really grates on me is that I would have got one had it not been for Mother Theresa.

The doors slide shut and we are back in the airless gas chamber. All the windows are open, but the outside air is so muggy it does little to aid the situation. The train clunks loudly as it jerks away from the platform and everybody inside is shunted backwards as one; those who anticipated it carried by the weight of those who didn't. The scenery around us vanishes as the train tunnels into the darkness. And then it stops.

People raise their eyebrows in acknowledgement of yet another delay. The driver's voice rings out over the tannoy system to inform us the train in front is stuck at the platform and we will be held where we are for the time being. There's a collective sigh, even if most people are able to see the funny side. These things don't usually last for more than a couple of minutes.

Ten minutes later, we still haven't moved. The driver pipes up every now and then to ensure us they're doing everything they can, but all he achieves by doing this is to put the idea into people's heads that this may be something serious. My fellow passengers start to fidget uncomfortably, shifting positions and readjusting their clothing to allow more airflow. It's understandable. The carriage is holding more bodies than it's designed for and nobody possesses the luxury of personal space. The interior is like an oven, the body heat adding to the already simmering air, and I can feel myself beginning to overheat. Already down to a top and trousers, I can't remove any further items of clothing, so I look to my drink to cool me down. The bottle is empty. I hadn't bothered filling it up before I left work because I'm usually home within half an hour. I never account for situations like this.

I sense the sweat coming. It starts at my head and within seconds it covers my body and I can feel a thin film of liquid covering every section of my clothed skin, my face and arms the only dry parts. The more conscious of it I become the worse it gets, and I feel my top sticking to my stomach and back. And as my body heats up I feel my head getting lighter, my vision wavering vertiginously and my heart beating so hard it resonates around my temples like somebody is jabbing me in the head with their fingers. I start to feel nauseous, and herein lies my greatest fear: the fear of throwing up on a crowded train. I start to panic and it makes things worse. The sweat flows faster and my heart beats louder. I crave fresh air, but there's no way out. I slump back against the rail and my vision darkens, like the driver is dimming the lights, and I begin to black out. I try to fight it, but my body is too weak and I feel myself sinking, sliding down the rail like a pole dancer.

It's the movement of the train rather than the hands of a fellow passenger that shakes me back into consciousness. I'm sprawled crookedly on the floor, surrounded by a forest of legs. As I sit up I still feel a little woozy, but I manage to haul myself upright. We are still in the darkness of the tunnel. Who knows how long I was lying there. My head is still pounding, but my vision has returned and I look around in disbelief at the other travellers. Not one of them had come to my aid. They had simply stepped aside so they weren't treading on me and deemed that to be enough. Londoners! You've got to hand it to us.

* * *

'You're no fun any more, Leila,' complains Roxanne.

'Just because I don't share your taste in men doesn't mean I'm boring!' I argue back. I think I've made a fair point.

This minor altercation is a consequence of me acting with indifference to a guy Roxanne had pointed out to me a few seconds earlier. I really don't know how she expected me to react to being shown a plain-looking man who displayed neither unique looks nor style. In my eyes, she could have been drawing my attention to pretty much anybody.

'But he's *well* fit!'

I need more convincing than that. The more I look at him, the less attractive he becomes and he's in danger of sliding down the scale from average to ugly. He doesn't look too bad from the front, but in profile he is hardly an Adonis. His arms are unnaturally long and his 'trendy' haircut doesn't work from the side. He also hunches too much when he walks. And then I notice that he doesn't walk, rather he waddles, his toes pointed outwards in a comical strut. I feel like grabbing Roxanne and shaking some sense into her.

'You have to be kidding me,' I say, not wanting to go into detail. 'And keep your voice down!'

'Whoops!' she whispers, bringing her hand up to her mouth to hide her giggles.

I assumed this would be the end of the discussion, but she hasn't finished yet.

'It's true though, Leila. You're not as fun as you used to be.'

'Please elaborate.'

I'm interested to hear her reasons, as ridiculous as they may be.

'Ok, so *that* guy isn't the best.'

She points in his direction and he happens to turn around at the exact same moment, so we have to turn our backs sharply to avoid being spotted. He probably thinks we fancy him now, God forbid.

'Still, when was the last time *you* pointed out a fit bloke?' she continues.

'I don't know...'

'Ages ago, that's when.'

'Is that right?' I try to think of an example so I can disprove her argument, but there isn't one.

'Yes it is. I can't remember the last time you said, "Hey, Roxy, check *him* out."'

'Well, maybe there haven't been any good-looking blokes about.' This is a poor excuse, but I'm only arguing with Roxanne so I should be able to get away with it.

'Oh, come on, Leila. It's the summer. There are always good-looking blokes about in the summer.'

She's right. A bit of sunshine makes everybody look healthier and it gives them a chance to wear tight T-shirts so they can show off the biceps and pecs they've been working on in the gym for the last six months. In fact, even if I scan the area now there are a few potential studs drifting about the place with their chins held high and their chests puffed out. Maybe I haven't been looking hard enough.

'It's ever since you met that Phil,' she sulks. 'Nobody else exists any more.'

'That's a bit harsh!' I protest.

'You've gone all serious. It's probably because he's so old.'

'He's *thirty-one*! He isn't *that* old. It's not as if he's old enough to be my father!' I say with a laugh.

'Almost.'

I could have explained to her that seven years is hardly a generational gap, but I hoped she realised this anyway.

'Maybe it's about time I grew up a bit,' I say, taking the other side of the argument.

'Nah,' she sighs. 'I like you the way you are.'

'Thanks, Roxy,' I chirp. 'Well, don't worry yourself too much about it. I still have a few young years in me yet.' And then, to prove my point, I add, 'Hey, check out the arse on that guy over there.'

'Wow,' she swoons. 'I wouldn't mind getting my hands on that!'

Simple things entertain simple minds.

* * *

There is no need for Phil to come and meet me at the station because I know the area so well already. It all feels slightly odd. Of all the times I have visited him in Bayswater, this is the first I have been invited over to his flat. My frequent, persistent dropping of hints had previously fallen on deaf ears and I had been beginning to think he might have something to hide. Then, out of the blue, he had invited me over for dinner one Friday after work. Maybe he had been perfecting his culinary skills all this time and I was in for an extravagant feast. Or maybe he felt that, after going out for almost four months, it was about time I saw where he lived.

I walk on the side of the road that attracts the sun as it's slightly chilly in the shade. It seems like summer has only just started, but in truth it will be over before we know it and the coldness will soon return. It's a short walk, less than five minutes, the block situated just beyond the tip of Queensway. Location-wise, it's pretty idyllic; a stone's throw from the high street, but on a road few cars ever use, so the residents get the best of both worlds.

The doorman is outside polishing the glass of the main entrance. There are few men short enough for me to be able to stand eye to eye with, but he's one of them.

'Good evening,' he says by way of greeting, then steps aside to let me through.

In doing so, he blocks off the panel of buzzers via which I was planning to call Phil. It doesn't matter, I'll surprise him instead. Having finished his cleaning duties to a level he is satisfied with, the doorman follows me inside. I press the 'Up' button to call the lift, and as the doors slide open to reveal the mirrored interior I catch a glimpse of the doorman looking at my arse with a quite revolting expression on his face. I pretend not to notice him. A confrontation would only be embarrassing for the both of us. And besides, he's essentially only doing what Roxanne and I do at work, although we're slightly less crude about it. You can't stop people from looking. Plus, in a way, it's almost flattering. Almost.

I get off at the fourth floor and follow the signs to number 43, which is about halfway down the corridor to the left. All of the doors are a repulsive shade of grey, which leads me to believe they found the paint rather than chose it. I press the doorbell and its loudness makes me jump. It must have been installed by an electrician who was hard of hearing. Phil appears at the door within seconds, a good sign as it shows he must have been eagerly waiting for me. He gives me a massive hug and invites me in. A quick tour ensues.

The flat is tidy in a way that suggests it's always tidy rather than Phil having done it especially for my visit. And it's fairly spacious for a one-bedroom flat, with a largish lounge leading into the kitchen, and the bedroom and bathroom on the other side as you walk in the front door. You can tell a man lives here, in that there's something very functional about the place, although I won't insult him by calling it a bachelor pad.

'What do you think?' he asks, concluding the tour by ushering me towards the sofa in the lounge.

'It's really nice,' I reply, shuffling to make myself comfortable. 'You've made good use of the space.'

'Needs a woman's touch, right?'

'Got it in one.'

Judging by the smell, dinner is already in the oven. And nearly done.

'Is there anything you don't eat?' queries Phil.

'Isn't it a bit late in the day to be asking that? Luckily for you, the answer is no!'

'Excellent.'

He disappears into the kitchen.

'Need a hand with anything?' I holler after him.

'No, it's all under control. Make yourself at home,' Phil calls back, his voice muffled by the sounds of cooking.

I feel at a loss as to what to do with myself while I'm waiting for him to return. I can't spot the television remote, so I'm forced to go for a newspaper, which I find in a rack by the side of the couch. It's a few days out of date, but I fan through it regardless. I've got as far as page twelve when the kitchen door opens again and I can hear the roar of the extractor fan and bubbling pots.

'Just need to wait for the vegetables,' Phil informs me. 'Are you comfortable?'

'Yeah, thanks. What's cooking?'

'Lasagne, carrots and green beans.'

'Smells good. Homemade or bought?'

'Bought, I'm afraid.'

'Thought as much.'

'What do you expect? I only got back from work about an hour ago!'

This is true. It's hard to make lasagne in less than an hour.

'If you were really organised you would've prepared it last night so you'd only have to reheat it now,' I point out with annoying sensibility.

'Well, let's just say I'm playing it safe,' he smiles. 'I'm no chef and I'd like for you to come again.'

With this, he returns to the kitchen and I to my old newspaper. It's a while before he returns with the finished product, all neatly laid out on the plates, vegetables and all. He puts them down on the table, which is already set, and goes back to the kitchen once more. He emerges brandishing a bottle of wine, which he pours into the glasses on the table.

'Take a seat,' he says.

'Looks great, Phil, I'm impressed. Let's make a toast.'

'Sure, to what?'

'To Marks & Spencer.'

'Very funny.'

We clink glasses and drink. It all seems a bit weird. We've had dinner together countless times before, but always on neutral ground. It makes quite a difference to be in Phil's territory. As always, the wine helps and we get through the bottle alarmingly quickly.

'Do you want to retire to the sofa while I clear these dishes away?'

'Let me give you a hand,' I offer.

'No, it's ok. You put your feet up.'

I'm not about to argue about being waited upon hand and foot, so I do as I'm told and go back to the sofa. Judging by the sounds coming from the kitchen, Phil is loading the dishwasher rather than washing up the old-fashioned way, and sure enough he returns after a couple of minutes and snuggles up next to me on the sofa. We have a long-overdue welcome kiss that ends up developing into a passionate snog, involving wandering hands and the rubbing together of bodies to such an extent that it's surprising we don't create sparks of static electricity. By the time it's over, I'm lying with my head on his shoulder and my body resting half on his torso and half in the gap between his body and arm. I'm sure I must be more comfortable than he is because his feet are stretched clumsily over the end of the armrest, but he assures me he's fine. I feel like one of those leopards you see on nature programmes relaxing across the branches of a tree.

Once in this position, we talk for ages without realising it. You know how it is when you're chatting to your partner for what seems like a few minutes and when you look at the clock you learn you've been chewing the fat for hours. And it's always impossible to remember what the hell you talked about for all that time.

Phil has this habit of discovering what he's saying as he goes along, so he starts reticently and then suddenly goes off on one, jumping from topic to topic with the randomness of rolling dice. If I want to say something that relates to the subject he's on I have to get in there quickly before he moves on to something else and the opportunity is gone. Nonetheless, this is far preferable to one of my previous boyfriends, who would get so bogged down in a subject that he would be unable to talk about anything else for days on end.

Even though it's been a wonderful evening, lying with each other doing nothing, there's a lingering doubt in my mind that we've yet to reach its pivotal point. There is an inevitability about it that both of us are trying to avoid, but as time passes and it gets later and later, we know we're going to have to make a decision. I know deep down it's up to Phil, being the host, and I expect him to announce any minute that it was about time I left if I was to catch the last train.

'Leila, how would you feel about staying the night?'

I was quite taken aback by his question, having fully anticipated him taking the other route. I rack my brains for an appropriate way to accept the offer gracefully.

'I would love to, if that's ok.'

'Of course it's ok.' He hugs me tighter as he tells me. 'I even have a spare toothbrush you can borrow.'

'To tell you the truth, Phil...' I'm not sure whether I should admit to this, but I've started now so it's too late. 'I was kind of hoping you'd ask me to stay, so I brought my own.'

'Even better,' he replies.

With this mental obstacle overcome, we go back to chatting about life, the universe and everything else that comes to mind. It isn't until about two in the morning that we eventually think about going to bed, both of us subconsciously delaying the decision. And when the time comes, neither of us instigates it. We just happen to yawn at the same time and take that as our cue. It doesn't take long to get ready for bed as neither I nor Phil have any overly laborious bedtime rituals we need to go through. We venture to the bedroom and stand there for a bit as both of us are unsure what to do next. I'm not sure I'm even supposed to be here. For all I know, when he invited me to stay over he might have meant for me to sleep on the couch.

'Do you have a spare T-shirt I can borrow?'

My advance organisation had only stretched as far as bringing a toothbrush.

'Sure.'

He rummages around in the drawer, digs out a plain, white T-shirt from the depths of one of them and hands it to me with both hands.

'I'm just going to go and check I've turned the dishwasher on,' announces Phil.

I know for a fact that he has. He knows it too, I suspect, but he's just giving himself an excuse to leave the room so I can get changed in private. My suspicions are confirmed when he closes the door behind him as he leaves. I take off my top and slip on the T-shirt he has leant me. It's huge, more like a dress, and it smells slightly of wood varnish, like it's been sitting unworn and forgotten at the bottom of the drawer for months. The sleeves come down almost as far as my elbows and I feel a bit like a little girl dressing up in her dad's clothes. Once I've put it on properly, I wriggle out of my trousers and socks and leave them in a neat pile along with my top. Then I slip off my bra and add that to the pile, folding it up so its shape is obscured and less bra-like.

Climbing into someone else's vacant bed is never going to feel particularly natural, and this occasion is no exception. It's like clambering into deeply personal terrain, entering into an unknown part of their life you would otherwise have no contact with. I shift myself across to the far side of the bed, where the materials are equally as cold and alien. The door handle slowly turns and there's a deliberately long pause before Phil hesitantly pushes the door open.

'It's ok, you can come in,' I say softly.

Suitably reassured, he wastes no time in entering the room. His expression and body language insinuate a significant degree of relief to find me already tucked up under the duvet. He walks over and switches on the bedside light, then returns to the door to turn off the main light. It isn't until he's bathed in this newly subdued lighting that he begins to get undressed, stripping down to his underwear. Now it's my turn to feel uneasy, unsure of whether to look or not. I want to, so I glance over at times when I know he won't catch me in the act: as he's pulling his T-shirt over his head or bending down to remove his socks. As he approaches the bed, I look only at his face, and he at mine. He climbs in to join me, leans over and flicks the light off. For a time I see nothing, the sudden darkness as effective a cloak as a blanket over the head.

Slowly, my vision returns and Phil develops an outline, becoming a silhouette in the inky indistinctness. I can feel the heat of his body creeping towards me under the blankets, a coming together of our inner warmth. I search for his hand and, finding it, give it a gentle squeeze, and he pulls me in close so my body is pressed up against his own. We kiss, and he ties me up in his arms, our bare legs tangled up in each other's. It's a novelty to feel my naked flesh against his, the texture a combination of frictionless skin and soft, wispy hairs that makes it difficult to maintain a fixed position, our legs slipping and sliding off each other like writhing snakes. I dig my fingers into his back, following the contours of the muscles with my thumbs. It isn't as if I haven't touched his back before, but it's a different sensation altogether when my hands aren't fumbling blindly under a T-shirt. He mimics my movements, his hands gliding underneath my top and massaging my back. I'm surprised by the size of the handfuls he's able to grab and I realise I must have put on weight over the past few months. It's amazing how the pounds can pile on when you're relaxed and happy.

Then he moves one of his hands around to the front and gently cups my breasts, kissing me more passionately as he does so and sending a shiver of exhilaration through my body. I pull him in closer and I can feel his penis hard against my thigh, so I slowly and firmly rub myself against him until he lets out a short gasp. He lifts my T-shirt up over my head – the T-shirt I've only been wearing for about five minutes – and squeezes me tight so that our chests are squashed tightly together. As we kiss, he's more forceful than he has been before, his tongue filling my mouth and overpowering my own, which is forced further and further back as he presses forward. I feel a little suffocated, so I roll him over and lie on top of him. I don't last long before he flips me off onto my back and clambers on top, so I'm pinned down against the mattress by his weight.

Supporting himself on his left arm, which he places above my head, Phil caresses my breasts with his spare hand, playfully tracing circles around my nipples with his fingers, bringing me out in goose-bumps that break out over my body like a rash. His mouth shares its time between my lips and my bosom, both areas bringing me a pleasure he seems to share. All the time, I can feel his groin rubbing against my own, the dividing material adding a restrictive elusiveness that frustrates me but at the same time makes me want him even more.

'Phil,' I whisper in his ear, 'do you have any protection?'

I know this is very forward and I'm treading a tightrope by asking, but I long to feel him inside me.

He doesn't answer, rolling off me to the side he had come from and I hear him opening the drawer of the bedside table. His fingers scramble around for a bit and emerge with a condom wrapper. Neither of us says anything as we remove the last of our clothes and he works the condom on under the duvet. Then he turns back to me and holds my head in both hands, the unmistakeable smell of rubber on his fingertips as they glide past my cheeks. He kisses me once again, more tenderly this time, like he's trying to subdue the ferocious lust he had displayed earlier.

He climbs back on top of me and thrusts slowly between my legs. His initial aim is wayward, so I use my hand to guide him in, gently gripping the shaft and working it in the right direction. I feel the tip of his penis entering me and I close my eyes as he leans forward. But then it melts, shrinking and softening between my fingers and falling out of me before it's fully entered. Phil collapses on top of me and buries his head in the pillow. He remains in this position for what seems like an age, with me squashed underneath him, a dead weight.

'I'm sorry, Leila,' he says dejectedly. 'I thought I was ready, but I'm not.'

'Don't worry, Phil. It's my fault. I shouldn't have rushed us into it.'

I try to be as supportive as possible, since I understand this must be one of the most humiliating things for a bloke to go through. Let me tell you, it's not too great for the girl on the receiving end either, left wondering whether it's her fault in some way or whether the bloke fancies her enough to do it.

'No, Leila. I really wanted to make love to you, more than anything. But something happened and I panicked.'

'What kind of something?' I ask.

'I don't know. It just didn't seem right.'

'Is it anything I can help with? Something you want to talk about?'

I don't want to push it too hard because I can sense his embarrassment, but I think he at least owes me some form of explanation.

'Leila, I promise you, it has absolutely nothing to do with you. You know I think you're amazing. It's something I need to deal with myself. I hope you understand.'

I nod, although how he expects me to understand anything based on the vagueness of what he has said is beyond me. He gives me a hug and a peck on the cheek, then turns away so I'm left facing his back. There's a small gap between us, but it feels like the widest chasm in the world.

* * *

The sun was at a height that blinded us as we walked down a gentle incline into the ancient ornamental beauty of the Marlborough Gate, a place of serenity between the hectic hustle of Oxford Street and the pretentious sophistication of Notting Hill. Four stretched octagonal ponds sit within a paved area framed on two sides by a black iron fence, the basic modernity of which is broken up by old-fashioned stone pillars, each bearing a family crest of sorts. Balanced firmly atop each granite cuboid is a finely crafted vase, each unique and all displaying an inward-looking face, most commonly a ram or cherub. At one end of the area is a building, a myriad of archways holding up a turreted roof. At the other end is an ornate stone wall, built at a time when masonry was a valued art form, water nymphs framing a magnificent fountain, the centrepiece of a vast balcony overlooking the tip of the Serpentine, which seeps under the road that dissects Hyde Park and Kensington Gardens.

Phil and I stop at a bench next to a statue of Jenner, a man I know nothing of, but who looks to have been someone of aged wisdom. Jenner sits tall on a truncated church pew, a scroll in his right hand, the left propped up his chin in a state of eternal contemplation. If I were him, I would try thinking about a way to halt the oxidisation that would eventually disfigure him, the turquoise corrosion already creeping over his iron body.

The sky is blue apart from a single bank of cloud that has stubbornly moved across the sun. Suddenly it's cold and I snuggle closer to Phil, nestling in beneath the arm he has outstretched as he reclines. I'm still not warm, but I feel safe, at ease, and there's no place I would rather be.

The noise of the traffic can be shut out if you concentrate hard enough. I choose instead to listen to the gentle sound of the spray as it falls into the water. It's windy, and the ponds are a dazzling sea of tiny waves, while the jets of water are blown across the horizon in a drifting mist needled with cold. Every now and then, the wind swirls and we feel the droplets of water against our hands and faces, the sensation refreshing rather than chilling.

It's a Wednesday and the park is quiet. There are people dotted around in couples or alone, but no groups, not even tourists, and no benches seating more than one or two.

Everything is unhurried. Even the joggers seem to glide past silently and unnoticed, the sound of the wind carrying away the tinny beats of their personal stereos and their wheezing breath. Most people are reading, resting or just thinking. The ducks, usually so raucous and chatty, are going about their lives in a state of hush, politely taking it in turns to dive into the depths of the pond.

Sometimes it's nice to sit in silence with the one you love. Did I say *love*? If you add up all the time Phil and I have spent together since we first met, it would barely equate to a full waking month. Yet I feel so comfortable with him, so at ease to be myself. That ill-fated first night together is a distant memory and everything feels right now. It's hard to pinpoint why, but times like this, cuddled up in his arms on a fresh summer afternoon, push me closer to him than I ever thought possible. My inner barrier, the psychological forcefield that prevents me from getting close to people so they can't hurt me, was penetrated the very first time we kissed. I had let him in, granting him unrestricted access to my cynical world. And now that he was there, walking about in my mind, I couldn't see a way of getting him out. Not that I wanted to.

My mushy musing was interrupted by the sensation of Phil's body suddenly seizing up so that he was as rigid as the seated statue to our right.

'What's wrong, Phil?'

He didn't answer, his mouth caught in a half-open, half-closed stutter, nostrils flared and breathing ceased.

'What's the matter?' I ask with greater urgency. 'You're scaring me!'

I give him a gentle shake to try and snap him out of his trance, the physical approach no more effective than my words. He remains rooted to the spot like a waxwork model. At a loss as to the cause of the seizure, I follow his line of sight and see that he is transfixed by a pigeon pecking about near our feet. There is nothing particularly special about the bird. One of its legs has been melted like a candle and it is hopping around like Long-John Silver, this kind of deformity fairly common among London pigeons. It had wandered over from an almighty flock that smothered the ground on the opposing side of the plot, where birds had been attracted in their hundreds by an elderly lady who was dishing out the entire contents of a bakery from a plastic bag.

Not sure as to whether this is the source of the problem, I swing a foot at the pigeon anyway, causing it to jump back a few feet. It tenaciously comes back, thrusting its neck back and forth in a cocky strut. I have to admit this winds me up a bit. Pigeons should know their place, but they've become too tame for their own good. This one is about to suffer as a result. Jumping up, I take a couple of steps forward and aim a kick at its head. I'm no footballer, or martial artist for that matter, so the attack is clumsy and frustratingly it takes to the sky unscathed, the pointed toe of my boot merely clipping its tail feathers. It does the trick, though, and the pigeon returns to the rest of the flock, disappearing among the twitching gathering of greasy grey feathers.

The colour quickly washes back into Phil's face and the softness returns to his muscles as they relax.

'Thanks,' he mutters, regaining his breath.

'You never told me you were scared of pigeons,' I say, digging him playfully in the ribs.

'What do you expect?' he replies, not drawing any humour from my nudges. 'I mean, it's not the sort of thing you shout about, is it?'

His cheeks had turned scarlet. It's never easy to admit you're scared of something, especially for a bloke. Particularly when the thing you're afraid of is as harmless as a pigeon.

'Well, you've picked a great place to live for steering clear of pigeons.' I know sarcasm is the lowest form of wit, but sometimes nothing else will do.

'I survive.'

'Yeah, looks like it!'

'I'd rather not talk about it. Come on, Leila, let's go. It's getting cold.'

Phil stands up and hauls me to my feet, my hands like a child's compared to his great paws. We walk the long way around the enclosure in order to avoid the swarm of winged rats the old lady is so insistent on feeding. Personally, I think feeding the pigeons should be punishable by law. An on-the-spot fine seems a reasonable deterrent. Any pensioners found carrying stale bread in plastic bags should have them confiscated immediately.

One of the nice things about Kensington Gardens is that it's large enough and plays host to enough trees that you can't see the far boundary when looking from one side to the other. Therefore, if you don't look too high up on the horizon, where the distant hotels and office blocks tower above the foliage, it's possible to completely forget that you're in London. It provided a means of escape for me when I was at university; big enough to lose unwanted company and pretend I was someplace else.

The footpaths within the park form an intricate web, with a number of focal points where the various paths meet, so that, from above, it looks like stones have been dropped onto an enormous sheet of green glass. The path we're on takes us towards a statue of a man battling to gain control of a powerfully built, rearing horse. I have always remembered what this statue is called, ever since some German tourists stopped to ask me what the title meant when I was walking back from college one day. *You* try and explain the meaning of the words 'Physical Energy' to someone who doesn't speak English.

Phil and I had said little more to each other by the time we reached the sculpture. The only things that sprang to my mind were ways to ridicule him about his phobia. Eventually, I submitted to my evil streak.

'I was thinking...' My sensible side warns that this might not be a good idea, but I press on regardless. 'We could get a DVD out on the way back. How about that Hitchcock film, *The Birds*?'

'I've seen it already, if you must know. And before you ask, I didn't find it particularly frightening. Did it really take you that long to think it up?'

He smiles at me and squeezes my hand. This is a good sign, as I hadn't been sure how he was going to respond. He seems to take the comment in good humour, giving me the incentive to carry on.

'So, tell me, *Philip*,' I only ever use his full name when I'm taking the piss. 'Does this pigeon phobia stretch to other bird life? Sparrows? Chickens? Flamingos?'

This was a semi-serious question. I wanted to know what I was dealing with here.

'Fortunately not.'

'And what about flightless birds? Are you scared of them? I could understand why you might find an ostrich menacing.'

'Now you're being stupid.'

He had a point.

'How long have you had this fear of these terrifying beasts?'

'Leila, I've had enough of your *wit*. The subject is closed. If you continue with your present line of questioning I'll be forced to throw you into the round pond.'

'I doubt it,' I scoff. 'You wouldn't be able to get near enough… too many pigeons.'

This is the last thing I managed to say before Phil attacks me. Half expecting the assault, I was already on the move, but he was too quick, grabbing me around the waist and hauling me back towards him. He keeps his hands around my midriff, squeezing his strong fingers into the sides of my waist in pulsing movements that cause me to reel with laughter. I'm ticklish even during my most sombre of moods and this onslaught, provoked by my own mockery, is almost too much to bear. Being a great deal smaller than him, my only form of defence is to pester him further with bad pigeon impressions while pecking at him with beaks formed out of my hands.

However, the hilarity caused by his groping swiftly renders me powerless and he easily overcomes me, wrestling me onto a nearby bench, where he pins me down with his body, my hand movements reduced to a futile chasing of his wriggling fingers as they scuttle over me like crabs. I squirm beneath him, squealing in a mixture of pleasure and frustration, my cooing lost in the giggles as I struggle to draw breath. And then he stops, satisfied he has proved his point, the point being that I was helpless against him when push came to shove, or tickling in this case.

The few people milling around have all stopped to look at the pair of loons fighting on the park bench. They could have been forgiven for thinking he was trying to molest me, I had screamed so loud. Once we have halted and started to sheepishly peer around, they soon return to their business, heads hung low as if embarrassed to have been caught watching.

We are still laughing to ourselves as we climb off the bench and set off arm-in-arm towards the garish splendour of the rejuvenated Albert Memorial. Every now and then, Phil nudges my lower back in case I'm considering resurrecting some sort of pigeon joke.

* * *

After our walk in the park, we ventured back in the direction of the flat. It's some feat to walk from one end of Queensway to the other without purchasing food of some description and we didn't even make it as far down as Bayswater station before temptation got the better of us and we ducked into a small Chinese restaurant on our left. The combination of the glistening red ducks hanging in the window and the mouth-watering aroma of monosodium glutamate proved too much for our feeble determination to cook for ourselves. We only had to look at each other as we strolled past our usual haunt and the decision was made.

Displaying a complete lack of imagination, we ordered our usual array of dishes: mine a special ho-fun, his a beef in black bean sauce with egg-fried rice and a plate of quick-fried salt and pepper squid for the two of us to share. As always, he eats most of this. This is what we order every time, yet we still give the menu a thorough read because there's always a chance something else will catch our eye. But once you've found something you know you enjoy, it's difficult to persuade yourself to try anything else in case the new dish pales in comparison. I think it would have taken a severe case of food poisoning to divert us from our usual selection.

After wolfing down the complimentary oranges and picking the bits of pith out of our teeth with the toothpicks supplied, we made our way back to the flat, patting our bulging bellies in smug satisfaction. When we got back, we collapsed onto the sofa with that feeling of exhaustion you sometimes get after eating too much. We lay there for a bit and I felt like I could go to bed right then and sleep through until morning, despite it being only about six o'clock.

In a bid to overcome our lethargy, Phil nipped off to the kitchen to make a couple of strong, sugary coffees. When he came back we still didn't have the energy to talk and instead we loudly slurped our coffees to break up the silence. The caffeine kicked in after a while and my mind rediscovered itself amid an agitated, drug-assisted high.

'You never did tell me, Phil. How come you're so scared of pigeons?'

The question had been digging away in my mind ever since the incident at the park. I knew he had been deliberately avoiding telling me the answer, but he couldn't seriously expect me just to let it go.

'You don't want to know,' he replied in a stand-offish manner.

'Yeah, I do,' I said.

It's true, I really did want to know. If I didn't find out right then it would bug me every minute of the day and I wouldn't be able to sleep for weeks.

'Trust me, you don't,' he said with equal seriousness.

'Look, Phil, you might as well tell me, because otherwise I'm only going to think the reason is something far worse than it actually is.'

'I don't think that's possible,' Phil responded without humour.

I looked at him with pleading, puppy dog eyes and let my mouth droop down at the corners. I often employ this tactic when I want something and it usually works. This time, Phil looked back at me with an expression of indifference and suddenly we were locked in a staring competition neither of us was in a hurry to lose. His aura implied a far greater degree of stubbornness than I had ever experienced in an opponent before and I caved in quickly, throwing my arms around his waist and burying my head deep in the fibres of his jumper.

'Please, please, *please* tell me,' I begged like a child. 'I'll be your best mate.'

I found my own whining annoying, so for him it must have been hell.

'Ok, I'll tell you. But you have to promise to keep quiet until I've finished, because if I tell you this I'll have to tell you everything.'

'Sounds ominous,' I commented.

'I'm serious, Leila.'

He was. I could tell by the tone of his voice.

'Ok, I promise.' I pulled my fingers across my mouth to indicate a zip.

'I'm not sure where the easiest place to start is,' he said thoughtfully, stroking my hair with his fingertips.

I could tell he was nervous because his skin had become slightly clammy.

'Ok. Four years ago, I was engaged to be married...'

'What?' I interrupted, sitting bolt upright like he had stabbed me with a pin.

'Hear me out,' he demanded, pulling me back down on top of him.

I lay there like I had been before, except that my eyes were wide open and my ears were pricked to his every word. *Engaged to be married?* To say that alarm bells were sounding would be a huge understatement.

'Four years ago, I was engaged to be married,' he repeated.

It felt as if he was reading from a script, like what he was about to say could only be said in one way.

'If it hadn't happened, I'd probably be married now.'

Nice to know. I felt like leaving there and then, but I decided I should at least hear him out, for my own peace of mind if nothing else.

'One night I returned to my flat to find that my fiancé, Angela, was gone. I thought nothing of it at the time, but a few minutes later I was assaulted. Attacked in my own home,' he emphasised, in case I hadn't understood the first time. 'He broke my shoulder, fractured my ankle and pretty much beat the shit out of me.'

His body quivered as he recalled the blows one by one, and I found myself squeezing him tighter. A weaker part of me wanted to scream at him.

'He took me to a house. He drove me there in his car. When we got there, he tied me to a chair in an empty room. By the wrists and ankles. And around the neck.'

He swallowed uncomfortably and I began to wish I had listened to him in the first place and ceased my questioning.

'And Angela was there. Not in the same room. Next door. He'd beaten her like he had me. He let me see her so he could show me what he'd done.'

Phil's shudders became more regular, more pronounced, and it dawned on me that he was fighting to hold back the tears. I felt awful knowing I had pushed him into recalling all of this.

'He kept us there for ten days. *Ten* fucking days!'

The tears came down and he stopped speaking for a while as he silently wept, the convulsions of his body pushing me up and down.

'And he forced me to eat pigeon; stuff he'd found lying around. I didn't want to eat it, but I had no choice. He *made* me. It was disgusting. The most disgusting thing I've ever tasted.'

He was becoming more and more worked up. I wanted to tell him to stop, but to cut him off now would be to leave whatever it was brewing up inside him and I feared he might go insane if he didn't let it all out.

'Do you know what it's like to consign yourself to the fact you're going to die? And I don't mean eventually; everybody accepts that. I mean *now*, in the foreseeable future. Do you know what that feels like?'

I shook my head.

'Every one of those ten days I thought I wouldn't live to see the next. And on the ninth day, he hung himself. The *sick fuck* who had put us through all of that hung himself in front of me. And when he'd done it, I thought that was it. I had no way of escaping. The street was deserted. I thought I'd waste away in that room like an abandoned pet. That was the worst bit, waiting to die.

Wishing for it to be quick and painless, but knowing it wouldn't be.'

'How did you escape?' I asked, my curiosity getting the better of me.

'I was just coming to that.' He sounded annoyed that I had interrupted his flow after promising to keep my mouth shut. 'Some people came to look around the flat next door and they heard me shouting and called the police. They broke in and found me, and sent for an ambulance to take me away.'

Describing his rescue seemed to have had a therapeutic effect on him and he began to calm down, his breathing slowing to a normal rate and the tightness leaving his voice.

'And now I can't bear to look at pigeons. It's not that I have anything against them, as such. They just bring back too many painful memories.'

'I understand,' I reassured him, patting his shoulder comfortingly.

But I didn't really understand. How could I? I had never been in a situation that was anything like that. I hadn't even dreamt about being in a situation like that. Phil appeared to have finished his story, but he had left a pretty major question unanswered.

'What about Angela?'

'She was never found. Vanished without a trace. The police did their best to locate her, but to be honest they had little to go on. It's got to the stage now when I don't want them to find her. I've accepted she's dead now and come to terms with it. Any other outcome would make things complicated.'

'Do you think about her much?'

I knew it was irrational to be jealous of a dead person, yet I found myself fighting it.

'Now and then. To begin with I couldn't think of anything else. Whenever I returned to the house I half expected her to be waiting for me like nothing had happened. It took a while to accept she wasn't coming back. And when I eventually did, it destroyed me. I was even suicidal for a time. Letting go of hope is one of the hardest things to do, but I had to in order to move on. I still think about her from time to time. Less so, with every day that passes. And when I think of her now it's different from before. She's a memory; a part of my life that's gone and I can never get back. I don't wish for her to be here any more. Only that, wherever she is, she's happy.'

It's strange. What Phil had said was an admission of a pretty major secret he had been keeping from me all this time. Suddenly finding out that you're only in your present relationship due to the death of another doesn't exactly fill you with happiness. But what sort of person would it have made me if I had walked out on him then? I find out he isn't quite as perfect as I first imagined, and all of a sudden I get cold feet? I told myself it was part of his past, something neither of us could change; something we could only overcome. Maybe I ought to have felt hurt or betrayed in some way, but once the initial shock passed I realised I didn't.

'And you know what the funniest thing is?' he asked.

'What's that?' I hated to think what he was about to say next.

'My name's not Philip. Well, it is, in a way. Philip's my middle name. My real name's Joseph.'

'Joseph,' I mimicked. 'Suits you.'

'Thanks,' he said with a smile. 'I don't even like the name Philip.'

'Neither do I,' I admitted. 'So why did you change it?'

'To get away from my past. You know, a new beginning and all that. When I moved here I cut off all ties with my old existence and became a new person. Nobody knew what had happened to me and I wanted to keep it that way. You're the first person I've told.'

'Thanks… I think.'

It's always flattering when someone confides in you even if, more often than not, you wish they hadn't.

'And you're probably questioning why I've been lying to you all this time. I don't see it like that. When you met me, Joseph didn't exist. There was only Philip. My mind had pushed what had happened as far back as it would go. Maybe that's why I got so upset when I was telling you about it. It was like reliving it for the first time.'

I didn't say anything at this point. I was trying to take in everything he had told me and make some sense of it all. I acknowledge that I may not always think this, but right at that moment I felt like what he had said to me didn't change a thing. If anything, I felt closer to him now that he had spilled his heart to me.

'So what should I call you now?'

It was a reasonable question.

'It's really up to you,' he said unhelpfully.

I deliberated over it for a bit longer before coming to my decision.

'I think I'll call you Joseph. Or Joe. Seeing as neither of us like the name Philip.'

'Ok,' he said, smiling again.

'Pleased to meet you then, Joe,' I said, greeting him the continental way by kissing him on both cheeks.

'Pleased to meet you too, Leila,' Joe replied. 'Do you know anyone who likes their middle name?'

I was sure I must have known someone, but if I did I couldn't remember who. And then the kissing started. We filled most gaps in conversation this way, and I was pleased to find that Joe was every bit as good a kisser as Phil had been.

That night we try to make love again and this time it is successful. Very successful.

* * *

302

I spend many a night at Joe's flat these days. Sometimes it feels like the only time I ever visit my old place is to pick up more clothes or for a general check that the flat is still ticking over without me there to look after it. Every now and then I feel like I need a good night's sleep or some time to myself, so I venture to West Brompton to sleep alone. These solitary visits only serve to convince me that it's much more pleasurable to spend the night with someone else. That's not to say I don't miss my flat when I'm not there, regardless of Bayswater being more convenient for the both of us when it comes to commuting to work, not to mention it being a nicer area generally. Joe comes to stay with me every now and then, which partially overcomes the problem. It's only fair. Plus it would be criminal to leave a flat empty in London when you can make so much money renting it out to desperate people.

* * *

My parents have requested my company, so I've taken the afternoon off work and dragged myself over to Wimbledon Village. It's typical of them to choose a location without a tube station just to make it really inconvenient for me, and I have to struggle up Wimbledon Hill Road, a fair old climb given that I never do anything remotely resembling exercise. Especially in this heat, for today is a sweltering day; one of the hottest I can remember this year. You always get a couple of days like this towards the end of the summer, and of all the days they could have chosen they had to choose this one.

You can tell how posh this place is by the number of antique shops and designer boutiques that line the high street. They leave little room for anything else, namely a few pubs and restaurants, and a branch of each of the main four retail banks, aggressively competing for the custom of the area's wealthy inhabitants. What I find striking is the number of ladies of leisure. It's mid-afternoon on a weekday and the pavements are suffocated with women who are all of an age at which they should be at work. And most of them seem to be attractive, the younger ones particularly. Those who haven't been blessed with natural beauty still possess immaculate clothes, professionally styled hair and bodies that bear testament to a healthy diet and the benefits of having their own personal trainer. I suppose when you're *this* wealthy there's little excuse for not looking half decent.

I'm looking for an establishment called The Dog and Fox. It's not like my parents to go to pubs, so I guessed it wouldn't be your average local. Luckily, they had provided me with some vague directions on the phone that proved to be more than sufficient, and I find them with comparative ease. They're sitting outside on one of the many benches that adorn the paved area out the front. My mother is facing out over the road, a deliberate ploy since it allows her to watch and study all the people drifting by; the same people she aspires to be. I'm sure my dad has already been forcibly hauled before every estate agent window in the entire area. In fact, there was one next door. Mum had undoubtedly made him sit where he was so he was forced to look at it. She's clever that way, my mum.

304

I sit down next to her, partly so I can also people-watch and partly so she has to turn around if she wants to talk to me. Hopefully, this will be too much effort and she simply won't bother.

'Would you like a drink, Leila?' my dad asks.

'Not especially. I'm ok at the moment thanks,' I reply.

'Can I not interest you in a Pimms?'

'Oh, go on then.'

I cave in easily. I haven't had Pimms in ages and you can't beat it on a day like this. And Dad seems very eager to get me one. Maybe he fancies the barmaid.

'One Pimms it is,' he announces, disappearing inside the pub without a moment's hesitation.

'Your father and I have been discussing a possible move here.'

What a surprise. Although I doubt the word 'discussing' is an accurate description.

'What would you think if we moved here?'

'It's up to you, really. It's all right round here, I suppose.'

I really couldn't care less if they moved. I hardly ever go to their place anyway, so it wouldn't make a great deal of difference.

'As long as it meets with your approval, darling,' says my mother, as if it would make any difference if it didn't.

It's a bit more pleasant up here on the hill, and now I'm sitting down I don't feel so hot. The wind carries with it a refreshing breeze that takes the edge off the sun. It also carries something else. The smell of manure. Not all the time; only when the wind blows in a certain direction. It occurs infrequently enough to forget about it for a while, but then you happen to take a deep breath and get a lungful of it when you least expect it. I crane my neck in the direction of the smell and the cause of the offending aroma quickly becomes apparent. There's a side road that runs off behind where we're sitting and there's a large sign depicting a horse and rider on the wall. Stables.

'Here you go, darling.'

Dad has returned with my Pimms. It's a big glass, filled to the brim. And there's a fair amount of fruit sitting at the bottom. The server was pretty generous with this particular drink.

'Thanks, Dad.'

'So, Leila, how are things with you?' he asks.

It occurs to me that this is the first time I've spoken to them for quite a while. It's not that we haven't *tried* to contact each other. There are various messages on one another's answerphones as proof of this. It's just that neither party has made a great deal of effort and, as a result, we always end up missing each other.

'Things are going well. For the first time in about five years I actually feel settled.'

'That's good to hear,' comments Dad. 'And how's work?'

'You know. Work's work. I never expected much out of it and so far it hasn't surprised me.'

'Then shouldn't you think about doing something more challenging?' asks Mum, the question bordering on the rhetorical.

'Maybe, but I'm enjoying what I do at the moment. And if by "challenging", you basically mean something with longer hours and higher pay, the answer is no.'

I'm fairly sure that's what she *did* mean. She doesn't respond either way.

'And how's the house?'

Dad is checking up on his investment, as he does every time I speak to him.

'It's fine. No problems to report.'

He looks relieved.

I take a sip of my Pimms. It's delicious, so I take a bigger sip.

'Mum tells me you're moving here,' I say, purely for the purpose of amusement.

Dad gives Mum a quick glance for some sort of signal and, judging by his flustered expression, I don't think he receives a clear one.

'It's... been mentioned,' he stammers. 'I really don't think now is a good time to buy, though. You should see the prices.'

Mum doesn't say anything, but I can tell she's not happy.

'So what have you been up to, besides working?' enquires Dad. 'You never seem to be in.'

I had kind of hoped this line of questioning would never materialise. In a way, it was good that it had because I would have to tell them eventually and it might as well be now.

'I've got a boyfriend.'

This provided the cue for Mum to spring into life.

'And how long has *this* been going on for?' she squawks, turning right round to confront me.

'Mum, please. You make it sound like some sordid affair,' I protest. 'We've been together since March, so about six months.'

'And what does he do?'

The important questions always come first.

'Don't you even want to know his name? *Joe* works in a shop.'

'Oh, Leila...'

She cuts the sentence short, but she's already said enough. Too much. I shake my head but don't reply. She's so bloody materialistic. In her eyes, I should be dating a lawyer or a surgeon; somebody with a title she could brag about to her equally shallow friends at their pathetic coffee mornings. It makes me so angry.

'Where did you meet him?' asks Dad, doing his best to salvage the situation.

I don't know why he puts up with her, I really don't. He could do so much better.

'At a singles party...'

'God forbid!' exclaims my mother.

'Oh, shut up, Mum! You have *no* idea what you're talking about!'

All conversation within fifty yards ceases and we become the centre of attention. Loaded cutlery freezes en route to mouths as the world waits to see what will happen next. Mum hides her face with her hands, not wanting to be recognised by what could be her future community. I glance around nervously while Dad takes a sip of his pint and acts like everything is normal.

While it is by no means the first time this has happened, it *is* the first time since my teenage years and I feel a little foolish for letting my temper get the better of me. I try to think of something to say, but the knowledge that there are about thirty people all hanging on to my next word prevents me from doing so. One option would be for us to all get up and leave with our tails between our legs, but this would be difficult to coordinate in silence.

Mercifully, we're saved by a procession of horses parading out of the riding school. The clip-clop of their hooves breaks the unnatural languor and everybody breathes a collective sigh of relief.

Riders always make me laugh. They always sit so goddamn straight, like it's physically impossible to slouch on a horse. And it's pretty much impossible not to look stuck up when you're in the saddle. Even if you wear your scruffiest clothes you still look like a toff and it's all down to the posture. If you ever feel intimidated by someone, picture them riding a horse. It works every time for me. Just to prove my point that horse riding is a ridiculous pastime for city folk, one of the animals takes a gigantic crap on the pavement. You could tell it was going to happen. The tail went up and out it came, absolutely loads of it. Enough to take a bath in. And nobody is going to clear it up. That would mean them getting off their mounts and stepping down to our level. So we'll all have to put up with a stinking pile of excrement while we finish our drinks. If there's any justice in this world, one of them will fall in it on their way back. Wishful thinking.

The good news is that it directs people's disdain away from me, and now we're out of the spotlight we can comfortably talk to each other again.

'Sorry about that,' I murmur.

Apologising is one of the hardest things in the world for me, especially when it's to my parents.

'That's ok, Leila. Nobody's *perfect*,' Mum says in a matter-of-fact tone.

I quickly learn my lesson from the last time and don't rise to it, taking a sulky sip of my Pimms.

'It was a *charity* event.' I don't know why I'm bothering to justify myself, but I am. 'Not some get-together for desperate people.'

'There's no need to be so defensive all the time, Leila. It's not healthy,' says my dad, the eternal voice of reason. 'Tell us more about Joe.'

'Like what?'

'I don't know. Tell us what he looks like, what he's into. Paint us a picture so it doesn't come as a complete surprise when we meet him.'

Meet him? You've got to be kidding me. Maybe when marriage is on the cards and it's absolutely essential he meets the future in-laws I might start to think about introducing him to them. Until that day, not a chance.

'I'm not sure what to say, really. He's about your height, dark hair, slim. Nice eyes. More importantly, he's good fun. And considerate.'

'Well, if he makes you smile just by talking about him, he can't be too bad,' says Dad.

I hadn't been aware that I was smiling. In fact, smiling was the last thing on my mind following my earlier outburst. Dad's right, though. Thinking about Joe *does* make me happy. That I'm meeting him later this evening helps me overcome my issues with my present company.

'He's great.'

I stop myself from saying more because I know there's nothing worse than listening to someone banging on about how fantastic their boyfriend is.

A silver-haired lady who has the 'just stepped out of a salon' look about her is greeted by a smartly dressed man who takes her shopping bags from her and loads them into the boot of his Jaguar. He drives away alone and she's left to enjoy the rest of her afternoon without the hassle of carrying around her cumbersome purchases. Mum glances down at the bags sitting by her feet and glows green like a traffic light.

'Can we go now please, darling? The sun is giving me a headache,' she complains.

'Not yet, darling. Leila hasn't finished her drink.'

I savoured the last couple of mouthfuls more than I had savoured any other drink in my life. I might as well have let it evaporate at the speed I was drinking.

* * *

Watching Leila sleep was one of life's truly pleasurable pastimes. She was turned away from him so that her face, completely perfect and at ease, remained elusive. Leila was the world. The epitome of everything wonderful and important. All other existence ground to a halt to look upon the sleeping beauty. And to listen. Far from traffic noise and birdsong, the air was pricked only with the gentle whisper of Leila's slow, rhythmic breathing and, if an ear was held to her pillow, the soft grinding of the material as her body rose and fell.

Gaudily patterned sheets lay crumpled across her legs, their sharp creases forming an abstract work of art that rested over her like a Picasso canvas. Brilliant white sheets covered the rest of her body, the lie of the fabric springing up into a snow-covered mountain range that plunged into the deep valley of her lower back before rising swiftly to the rounded heights of her behind. The linen stretched out across her shoulders, creating the perfect background for her hair, which, in contrast to the pure, delicate shine of the bed sheet, was dark and richly exotic. Intertwined, almost black locks writhed across her neck and down over the pillow like the waves of a midnight sea, while streaks of colour, ambers and reds, caught the sun that arrowed through the window.

Her upper arm, the rest of its length curled beneath the pillow, was the only visible flesh. Wrapped in a skin so immaculate and soft, it cried out to be touched, stroked, caressed, although he knew that to do so would disturb the owner from her slumber and shatter the scene.

Occasions like this were limited and unique to him, and Joseph wasn't about to spoil it. Watching Leila sleep made it worth waking up in the morning.

At first, Joseph was content to gaze for as long as it took her to emerge from her restful state. Impatience soon set in and he wanted to hold her in his arms as he had the night before. However, he was well aware of how annoying it was to be woken while in a deep sleep, and he had to be subtle about disturbing her.

He pretended that he was still asleep, granting himself a restlessness that allowed him to toss and turn and sigh heavily, tugging hard at the duvet every time he moved. It had the desired effect and Leila woke momentarily and shifted position, turning onto her side so she was facing him. Her eyes remained closed, a clear sign of her desire to continue sleeping.

Leila could hardly be described as a morning person. She always had to be dragged out of bed, sometimes forcibly, and Joseph was thankful he had to leave for work later than she did as it meant he could make sure she made it out of the door each day. Otherwise he was sure she would have lain in bed until lunchtime.

At this time in the morning, Leila's face always had a subtle swell to it, her cheeks and lips possessing a chubbiness that disappeared after she had showered and woken up properly. Joseph found it irresistible, and he reached out and stroked her face, the flesh plump and spongy to the touch. Leila breathed hard through closed lips, as though she were trying to blow his hand away from her face, and turned away from him again. Joseph followed her and, leaning over, stroked her face once more. This time her eyelids fluttered and she reached up and grasped his hand, pulling it down beneath her body so he was forced to hug her.

'What time is it?' she mumbled, her puffy lips unable to form the words properly.

'It's about half nine,' Joseph answered.

'Why did you wake me up so early?'

'I didn't.'

'Yes you did. You disturbed me.'

'Sorry, I couldn't resist.'

'Try harder next time.'

Joseph gave her a hug and moved his hand up from her chest to under her chin. He pulled her face towards him and gave her a kiss on the lips. Leila recoiled in revulsion and thrashed about as she tried to avoid the barrage of follow-up kisses peppering her forehead and cheeks.

'Get off me! Your breath still smells of last night's kebab. And your fingers,' she added after sniffing his hands.

Joseph did as he was told and rolled back over to his side of the bed. After lying there motionless for a bit, he threw off the duvet and walked towards the bedroom door.

'I'm going to go and brush my teeth,' he announced.

'Good. Wash your hands as well,' demanded Leila. 'And make sure you use warm water. I'm not having your freezing cold hands all over me.'

Leila could hardly be described as a morning person.

* * *

Joe gestured to attract my attention as I walked into the bar about twenty minutes late. It wasn't really my fault. He had only requested my company late in the day and I had already agreed to go shopping with Roxanne. Besides, shopping trips have a tendency to overrun quite unlike anything else I can think of. One minute you have all the time in the world, then you start trying things on and before you know it it's time to leave, but you still have to find the right size and pay for the stuff.

So I had texted Joe to warn him I wouldn't be there at the time I had said I would be, leaving the message suitably vague so he wouldn't be left with any unrealistic expectations. I turned up laden with bags, quickly dumping them under the table before taking a seat. He had already ordered himself a drink, an orange juice by the looks of it, and had almost finished it. It was good to see he hadn't gone straight for the hard stuff in my absence. He stood up to greet me and I gave him a big hug and a quick kiss, little more than a meeting of our lips. We don't show much affection towards one another in public.

'Have you been waiting long?' I asked him as I sat down.

'Not really. When I got your text message I decided to go for a wander rather than waiting for you here.'

'Where'd you go?'

'Just down Wardour Street to Leicester Square. There were these buskers doing breakdancing and stuff. It was pretty cool. Almost makes me want to learn myself.'

'I can't imagine you breakdancing.'

'Neither can I, to be honest,' said Joe, smiling. 'What would you like to drink?'

'It's ok, I'll get them. You stay there,' I insisted, about to stand up.

'No need,' said Joe, grabbing my arm.

He gestured with his hand and, sure enough, a petite blonde waitress started making her way over. I say petite. She was actually fairly tall, but she was so thin around the waist she seemed tiny.

'Table service, eh? Very classy,' I commented while she was still out of earshot.

'Can I get you anything to drink?' Her accent was European.

I ordered a vodka tonic and Joe got himself a bottle of Corona. The waitress went away again and wasted no time in bringing us our drinks, leaving them on the table along with a small silver tray that harboured a folded piece of white paper. I picked it up and read the contents.

'Remind me never to come here for a drinking session,' I said, handing it to Joe for him to read.

'Wow,' he responded, his expression mirroring my own surprise. 'That's expensive, even by Soho standards. Maybe I should've stuck to orange juice.'

I placed a ten-pound note on the tray and didn't expect to see a lot of change. One disadvantage of table service was that the waitress would no doubt be expecting a tip.

I suppose it's fair to say that you get what you pay for in these places, and this bar was pretty slick. The predominantly black and white décor had been brought to life with the rainbow lighting, and the walls displayed funky, original artworks, all of which were for sale. Plasma television screens showing footage of a Kylie Minogue concert were a throwback to the bar's gay beginnings and the crowd still reflected this to some extent; a mixture of the colourful and liberal-minded creating a vibrant, friendly atmosphere. That's the great thing about places like this. Lagered-up rugby lads would take one look at the trendily dressed clientele and beat a hasty retreat with their backs to the wall. And by repelling the jerks in shirts, you lose the Essex girls as well. Two for the price of one.

I tried my vodka tonic and it was delicious. The quality of both elements shone through, although the difference didn't *really* justify paying so much over the going rate. As I said, you're paying for the full package, not just the drink. Joe's beer came with a wedge of lime sitting in the neck of the bottle and he shoved it down so that it floated in the liquid, the initial impact causing a controlled eruption of fizz and froth.

'So what was so important it couldn't wait until tomorrow?' I asked. 'Or are you getting withdrawal symptoms from not having seen me for a whole two days?'

'I've been thinking,' he started.

My heart sank. When a sentence begins with, "I've been thinking", it usually means there's bad news to follow.

'We've been together for about eight months now, and seeing as we spend most nights together anyway, how would you like to move in?'

His words sounded slightly unnatural, like he had rehearsed them one too many times in his head.

'What, move in to your place properly?' I don't know why I asked this question, because I knew exactly what he meant.

'Yeah. It'd only mean spending an extra couple of nights there anyway.'

He was right. From a practical point of view it made no odds, but from a commitment point of view it made a massive difference.

'I'm not sure, Joe. I'll have to think about it. It's not that I don't want to, but it's a big step.'

He looked a little disappointed. I was only being honest with him.

'That's ok. It was just an idea.'

'I haven't said no yet,' I reassured him. 'When I said I'd think about it, I meant it. The last eight months have been fantastic and being with you has turned my life around. I just don't want to rush into anything.'

'That's fair enough. I had to think about it for a fair while before asking you, so I can't expect you to make a snap decision.'

Joe always sees sense. It's one of his many qualities. You don't have to spend hours reasoning with him about things. He takes on board your point of view and if it's reasonable he'll generally accept it.

'So, what have you bought then?' he asked, changing the subject. 'Quite a lot, by the looks of it.'

'It's all clothes.'

'Surprise, surprise.'

'Old habits die hard. How about we go and get something to eat and I'll model them for you when we get back?'

Joe looked at my shopping bags again and his eyes lit up as he recognised the logos of various underwear shops.

'Hell yeah!'

He dramatically downed his drink, then mine. Then he scooped up the bags, grabbed me by the arm and dragged me out of the bar.

* * *

'Come in, quickly. Trust you to be late!'

I usher Roxanne into the flat as she pours out the excuses, blaming her unpunctual arrival on everything from her inability to find an agreeable pair of shoes to my supposedly incorrect directions. Even the pigeons stand accused, one of them having taken a crap on her coat so that she had been forced to return to the house to wash it off. Or so the story went. I had to promise not to tell any of the other guests about it.

Even after I've got her in the door, it still takes an age before she's ready to be introduced to everyone. I have to help her remove her scarf, her hat, her coat, her gloves and her extra layer, taking the opportunity to reassure her she's presentable and that the journey hasn't rendered all the time she has spent labouring on her make-up obsolete. I lead her through to the lounge, where everybody else is sitting. I have some sympathy for Roxanne, knowing full well how awkward it can feel when you're the last to arrive and have to endure a very public introduction. I do my best to make it easy for her.

'Everyone, this is Roxanne. Roxanne, this is everyone,' I announce, making sweeping gestures with my arms.

I glance over at Roxanne, who is smiling nervously, and realise I ought to be slightly more specific.

'Sorry, that was a really unhelpful introduction. This is Roxanne, who has the pleasure of working with me.' Then, going round the circle, I say, 'This is Joe, who you already know. This is Iain, a former colleague of Joe's. And this is Paul and Abi, our next-door neighbours.'

'Hi, everyone,' says Roxanne, raising a hand in a self-conscious wave.

She sits down on the vacant cushion of the two-seater sofa, hands clasped together defensively in her lap. Conversation has momentarily ceased, its flow interrupted by the addition of an unknown entity. I needn't have worried, since Roxanne was never going to keep her mouth shut for long.

'You would not *believe* the journey I just had,' she starts. She goes on to describe how she had made it home from work, then from home to where she was sitting now.

Good old bucket mouth. The only break in the narration occurs when Joe butts in to offer her a drink, which she gratefully accepts before diving straight back into her story. It isn't a particularly interesting tale, devoid of humour or noteworthy incident, yet she tells it with such enthusiasm we all listen intently until she has finished, at which point her hands return to her lap once more.

I feel sorry for Iain. As the only single male in the room, he'll be lucky to escape the attentions of Roxanne. He probably suspects that Joe and I are trying to set them up. This couldn't be further from the truth, as Roxanne was supposed to have brought her boyfriend. In hindsight, it had been wishful thinking to believe they would manage to sustain their relationship between the time of the invitation and the date of the actual event. So, instead, we get a lonesome Roxanne who, to make matters worse, is on the rebound.

Looking around the room, it occurs to me that it's a strange mix of people; one that, if you were to look upon it as an outsider, you would wonder how the hell such a group ever came together.

Abi is a really sweet girl, but she happens to be a damn sight better-looking than the rest of us. The fact is, she would stand out in most groups of people and I'm convinced Joe fancies her; an accusation he refutes wholeheartedly. I wouldn't really blame him if he did. If I were a man, she would be at the top of my list. Paul is an unquestionably nice guy, but he's all too aware of how lucky he is to be with Abi and lives his life in a state of permanent paranoia that a richer, smarter, better-looking man will come and whisk her away. Plus he has this habit of talking in questions that I find pretty annoying at times.

Iain is one of those people who is good at everything, and if he wasn't such a sound bloke I would be hard-pressed not to hate him. Roxanne is Roxanne, loud and garish. And then there's me and Joe, little and large. It's always risky bringing together different groups of friends because they might not get on and that leaves you stuck in the middle of their hostility. Nobody here is particularly confrontational, mind you, so they ought to be ok.

They have all been invited round for an early Christmas dinner. It's only mid-December, but social calendars get hectic at this time of year and it was the only night when everyone was available. Ideally, I would have liked to have included a couple more people if the flat had been big enough to accommodate them, although I'm not sure I would have known how to cater for more than six. It was hard enough work with the present turnout.

Considering all the things that could've gone wrong, the food had turned out pretty well. The turkey wasn't too dry, the gravy was free of lumps and the potatoes were so crisp you could almost crack them like eggs.

'Isn't this the greatest Christmas dinner you've ever tasted?' said Paul, which was his way of saying that it was the greatest Christmas dinner *he* had ever tasted.

'It *is* fantastic,' agreed Iain. 'It even rivals my mum's, and she's had about forty years extra practice. We'll make a housewife out of you yet, Leila.'

I stuck my tongue out at him playfully.

'Even the sprouts taste good,' praised Abi, 'and that takes some doing.'

I've never received so many compliments about my culinary skills before and I'm not sure I like it.

'That reminds me of a Christmas joke,' I piped up. 'Why is a Brussels sprout like a pubic hair?'

I paused for effect before delivering the punchline.

'Because you push it to the side of the plate and then carry on eating.'

It was met with a mixture of shock and disgust. I've never been much good at judging my audience. Roxanne saved my blushes by erupting into fits of laughter, albeit a good few seconds after the joke was finished.

'I like that. That's a good one,' she giggled, taking a sip of wine. 'I can never remember jokes.'

'Just as well, if Leila's is anything to go by,' said Joe.

I sneered at him in retaliation.

'So, what's it like living with Joe?' asked Iain, changing the subject but somehow still managing to keep the spotlight on me.

I sensed that, after my misjudged gag, everybody was looking to me to provide them with amusement, like some kind of wise-cracking monkey.

'He has his moments,' I replied, adopting a deadpan expression.

'No embarrassing habits you'd like to share with us?' probed Paul.

'Not that I can think of. Apart from... no, nothing.'

They all looked a bit surprised that I had refused to dish the dirt. I would never have aired his dirty laundry in public, but even so there's really nothing to say. Apart from the initial stress of trying to find space for all my extra stuff, it had been a smooth and enjoyable ride to this point.

'Some of us are just perfect,' said Joe in a mock gloat.

'Hey, I never said you were *perfect*.'

'What about Leila, then?' Iain asked Joe.

'Don't answer that,' I snapped, and he sensibly kept his mouth shut.

'Are you spending Christmas here, Leila?' asked Abi in her usual punctilious tone.

'Unfortunately not. I'm going back to see my parents, as I do every year. I need a pretty good excuse not to go home for Christmas. I've only ever been absent for one, and that was when I was in Thailand.'

'It must be nice, a family Christmas,' Abi continued.

'The theory is better than the reality.' I didn't wish to say any more than that.

'Are you joining her, Joe?' Iain asked.

'Not this year. I'm going to see my parents as well. Christmas at my house is usually pretty good.'

My family had been invited to spend Christmas with Joe's parents, but it would all have been a bit full-on for this stage of the relationship. Besides, there would be many other Christmases.

'What about you, Iain?' I turned the tables back on him for a change.

'Same as you guys. Back home to see the folks.'

'No special lady to spend it with?'

'Only my mum,' he joked.

'Why is it that you're permanently single?' I pried. 'You're knocking on a bit. Don't you think you should get yourself a girlfriend while you still have your looks, your figure and your hair?'

I sensed Roxanne's eyes lighting up at the mention of the word single and kicked her under the table.

'He's too picky,' Joe explained. 'Whenever he meets anyone he always finds something bizarre to dislike about them, like their hands being too big or the way they pronounce certain words being annoying.'

'These things are very important,' Iain said with a laugh. 'It's the way I approach everything. It's not that I'm looking for perfection. Maybe I'm scared of finding what I'm looking for because I won't know what to aim for next.'

'How do you mean?' asked Roxanne, fluttering her eyelids.

'It's hard to explain. Basically, I believe we all need our fantasies to live. And I don't think it's always a good thing to realise them.'

Roxanne looked puzzled, but I knew what he meant. And he was right.

* * *

Such is the extent of the rain that, even in the thirty seconds it takes us to get from the taxi to the restaurant entrance, we still receive a sizeable soaking. We wouldn't even be there if I had gotten my way. I had taken one look out of the window at the monsoon and begged Joe to get a takeaway delivered instead. The downpour was so heavy it had partially obscured from view the opposing block of flats, and I had thought I might get swept away by the floodwaters if I went outside.

Apparently, we were going somewhere posh so he had wanted me to wear a dress. I had really felt like I couldn't be bothered because that would mean having to do my hair properly as well. Joe had remained adamant that we went out. He had reserved us a table at some new restaurant where vacancies were hard to come by and he didn't want to have to wait another couple of months before we got the opportunity to go again. Still, it had taken the promise of a taxi ride both there and back to convince me to leave the flat, and even then I had done so with a stubborn reluctance.

The weather meant the traffic had been heavier than you might expect for a Tuesday night, and it had quickly become apparent that we were going to be late. Joe had spent the journey in a state of bewildering stress, fearing our table would be given to somebody of greater importance and that we would be politely turned away at the door. I had done my best to calm him down, my reassurances carrying little weight since he knew I would have been more than satisfied with that particular outcome. Still, even when you're in no hurry to get to your destination, there's nothing more frustrating than sitting in traffic watching the taxi meter ticking upwards, paying money to wait while people on the pavements strolled past for free. On the other hand, at least we had been warm and dry.

We arrived at the restaurant about fifteen minutes late, and for once it wasn't my fault. To my amusement, it was far from full. I couldn't have been the only one who hadn't wanted to get drenched for the sake of some fancy food.

Once we were there, I got an inkling of why Joe might have been so eager to come. Even in the partial emptiness there was a buzz about the place. The level of noise and the constant skating about of the waiters created an atmosphere you wouldn't seek if it was relaxation you desired. There was a marked impatience beneath the surface; an expectation that something monumental was about to take place. This lingering tension encouraged people to talk and the air was filled with the monotonous drone of a hundred conversations and the clinking chimes of cutlery colliding with plates.

A waitress led us to our table, taking a long route that prevented us from having to squeeze between closely seated chairs, steering us clear of hot food in transit and generally keeping us out of harm's way. Ours was one of the snug circular tables to the left of the vast dining area, a couple of positions in from the elongated counterparts that dotted the perimeter of the room like tacking stitching. The waitress pulled the chairs out for us so we could be seated and helped us employ our napkins. She supplied us with the wine list and a menu apiece and did an unnervingly efficient job of making herself scarce so we could study them at our leisure.

The table was tiny. Our knees were almost on top of each other and it was barely possible to rest our forearms on the table without touching hands, promoting a kind of forced intimacy. I glanced around to see if all the tables were like this and notice that the other tables accommodating couples were equally cramped, while those hosting single-sex couples or small groups were more spacious. It seemed like a strange system to me.

Closing his eyes, the waiter drew in a deep and prolonged breath, making the most of this moment of serenity amid the evening's laborious clamour. He wiped his hands firmly across the front of his trousers, the action providing only temporary relief from the moist, sweaty palms that added extra complications to an already difficult task. The waiter always savoured times like these, since he had quickly discovered from his short time at the establishment that they were few and far between.

We ordered the least expensive bottle of Chardonnay available to assist us in tackling the menu. It read like a poem. It was one of those occasions where everything sounds irresistible and you want to try it all, only your finite stomach capacity and the crippling prices prevent you from doing so. To make the choice even harder, a constant stream of mouth-watering dishes were being carried out from the kitchen, each leaving a trail of ambrosial scent that reached right down into my voracious stomach. I must have changed my mind about twenty times, and that was just for the starter.

'This all looks fantastic,' I complained. 'How can they possibly expect you to decide?'

Joe shook his head, also at a loss as to what to order.

'I almost wish I was a vegetarian. That would limit my choices down to about three things. But then I wouldn't be able to have the duck... Or the lamb. Or the lemon sole. This is too hard!'

'We can always go somewhere else if it's all too much for you,' smirked Joe.

'No way! I'll come to a decision eventually. It may take me a while, that's all. What's the occasion, anyway? This place is way upmarket from our usual haunts.'

Joe shrugged his shoulders. 'No particular reason.'

Without warning, he sniffed loudly and swiftly brought his finger up to his nose to stem the flow.

'I think I'm getting a cold. I don't suppose you brought any tissues, did you?'

I clicked my tongue in disapproval.

'Typical. A few drops of rain and you get sick.'

'Sorry.'

One of the many disadvantages of wearing a dress is that you don't have any pockets and I was forced to rummage around in my handbag. I didn't want to be seen scrabbling around beneath the table, so I brought the bag up onto my lap, allowing me to see what I was doing. I couldn't find any tissues, despite being sure I had packed some. But there *was* an alien item in there that I had never seen before.

A small, black velvety box.

'Where did this come from?' I asked, looking up at Joe.

His hand was no longer covering his face and his runny nose had miraculously cured itself.

And then it sunk in.

'Oh. My. God.'

Joe reached forward and took the box from me. He flipped open the lid and pulled out the diamond ring that sat inside. He took me by the hands and stared intensely into my eyes.

'Leila, being with you has made what should have been a difficult time into one of the best years of my life, and I want to stay with you forever. Will you marry me?'

His proposal left me shell-shocked. It was *so* soon and I hadn't expected it for a second. Now it was all too clear why he had been so keen to come out tonight. Something tickled my cheek and I reached up to brush it away. My wet fingertips told me I was crying. I went back to my bag to search for tissues, forgetting that there weren't any.

'Here,' Joe said softly, passing me some tissues from his pocket. The same tissues he had removed earlier in the evening.

I dabbed gently at my face, not wanting to spoil the make-up I had spent so much longer than usual putting on. Wiping away my tears served to wipe away my fear, and I gave him my answer.

'Joe, I am *way* too young to get married. Despite this, and against my better judgement, the answer is yes. Nothing would make me happier.'

He slid the ring onto my finger and we leant forward to kiss. We didn't have to lean very far. I kind of expected a round of applause from neighbouring tables, like you see in the movies, but everybody was too engrossed in their own little worlds to notice the couple next door getting engaged. Not that I minded. This was our moment.

We held our grip on one another's hands and looked at each other. There was no need to say anything. I could feel the joy spreading around my body, working its way down to my fingers and toes, which tingled excitedly. I was aware of the ring pressing lightly against my skin, my finger not yet used to bearing its subtle weight. Just thinking about wearing it made me want to yell with delight.

'Phew!' I exclaimed as the silence became too much for me. 'Choosing a starter has got to be easy compared to that.'

We were interrupted by the return of the waitress, who sprang out from nowhere to appear dutifully at our sides.

'Sir, madam, are you ready to order?'

'I think I'm ready. Leila, do you need a bit more time?' asked Joe.

'No, it's ok. I'm just about ready. You go first.'

It was a blessing in disguise. Her arrival forced me into making a decision or I might have stared at the menu for hours.

'Could I have the pigeon for starter, please, and the John Dory for main course?' he said.

'Certainly. And you, madam?'

'Er… please could I have the… the carpaccio of swordfish for starter and the duck for main course?'

'Ok. Would you like anything else?'

'Just a side salad to accompany the main course and I think that'll do, thanks,' replied Joe confidently.

You would think he dined at these places all the time, the way he was acting.

'Pigeon? Are you sure?' I questioned him after the waitress had gone.

'Positive. Tonight is a new beginning, Leila. Eating pigeon again will be the final stage of my rehabilitation. A chance to put everything that happened behind me, once and for all.'

'That's quite a rousing speech, Joe. I seriously hope you don't throw up.'

'So do I,' he agreed. 'Anyway, we're close to halfway through the wine and we haven't even had a toast yet. So, here's to us.'

Joe raised his glass and I lifted mine to meet it.

'You know, with modern etiquette it's considered vulgar to clink glasses,' said Joe.

'Who gives a shit?' I replied, knocking my glass against his with a loud chime.

We both took a large gulp and Joe topped up the glasses.

'I still can't quite believe we're engaged,' he said, grinning from ear to ear.

'Neither can I. My parents are going to kill me!'

It was true. They hadn't been happy about me moving in with Joe, and this latest news might just push them over the edge.

It didn't take long for our food to arrive. Perhaps they had clocked that we weren't likely to spend a lot of money and were hurrying us out so they could give our table to some wealthier customers.

The food looked as good as it had sounded on the menu. Sometimes when your food arrives you feel disappointed before it's even entered your mouth, but this stuff looked fabulous. Whoever had prepared it obviously took pride in their work as the presentation was flawless. There wasn't a leaf or even a dribble of sauce lying out of place. The waitress wished us an enjoyable meal before vanishing again.

I didn't quite know where to start with mine. It was so carefully stacked it seemed a shame to spoil it. Were you supposed to eat it layer by layer or all together; to savour the ingredients individually or in combination? It would almost certainly taste nice either way. Joe appeared far from impressed by his choice, although it looked delicious to me. He sat there prodding it with his fork, as though he wasn't sure whether it was actually dead.

'What's up, Joe?'

'It looks different from when I had it before.'

'I'm not surprised. I doubt Psycho Allan was quite as skilled in the kitchen as the person who prepared *that*.'

'True,' replied Joe, taking a mouthful.

I watched intently as he chewed, grimaced, swallowed uncomfortably, grimaced a bit more, took a few deep breaths and washed the taste away with a sip of wine.

'What was it like?' I asked curiously.

'I'm not sure. Hold on one second. Excuse me!'

Joe attracted the attention of the waitress as she marched passed with a precarious stack of dirty plates. She raised her eyebrows in acknowledgement.

'Are you sure this is the pigeon?' he queried.

'Yes, sir. Is there something wrong with it?'

'No, nothing's wrong. Thanks.'

She continued on her way and Joe looked down at his food once again. He sliced off a bigger piece this time. Free from sauce or any other kind of garnish, it was just a big, plain slice of meat. He put it in his mouth as he had the previous piece, chewing it more slowly this time, letting the juices swirl around his teeth and gums. He chewed it for ages, like he was afraid to swallow, grinding it down into a mushy pulp that bore no resemblance to its initial form; a messy mixture of muscle and blood.

And then he finally swallowed, closing his eyes as he did so and wincing like it was burning his throat. His knuckles turned white as he squeezed the cutlery tightly in his hands, the grooves in the bones visible through the taut skin. And then he retched. The movement started with a tensing of his stomach and caused him to rock forward as his mouth opened in a dry heave. Tears trickled from his eyes as he slumped back in his chair with one hand over his mouth.

'Joe?'

He raised the napkin from his lap with his other hand and stood up, placing it on the chair, which creaked at the sudden release of weight.

'Excuse me for a second,' he said, his voice quiet and emotionless.

Joe shuffled away from the table. He swayed uneasily on his feet as he timorously moved forward in the direction of the toilets. The colour had left his face and a thin layer of sweat had crept over his brow, as though he had risen from his deathbed and was taking one final stroll before retiring forever.

The way he looked, I feared he might not even make it as far as the toilets. I pictured him collapsing to the floor, spouting a fountain of vomit over the other diners, whose astonishment would soon turn to disgust as their evenings were ruined in one of the worst ways imaginable. But he did make it, disappearing from sight behind the door, which swung violently back and forth until it finally came to rest in its original position.

Safe in the knowledge that Joe was in a position to throw up discretely and in private, I turned back to my dinner, which was sitting, neglected, in front of me. It was a cold dish, so it wasn't as if it would spoil if I left it sitting there a bit longer and waited for Joe to return. But the way it lay there, tantalizingly glistening under the spotlights, made me think that it deserved to be eaten. The second mouthful was equally delectable, better even, as my taste buds were now attuned to the flavours. After the third and fourth mouthfuls, there was very little left and I made myself stop eating so there would at least be enough for Joe to try some when he got back, provided his stomach was up to it, of course.

I sat there and twiddled my thumbs for another five minutes or so, but still there was no movement from the men's toilets. Nobody passed in or out. Even the heaviest vomiting session couldn't last this long. It occurred to me that Joe had maybe managed to get some on himself, in which case he would be doing his best to make himself look presentable again, something that was bound to take a little time.

After a further five minutes I began to worry that something was wrong. He had looked fairly shaken and it was possible he had fallen and hit his head, or something worse still. I couldn't really enter the men's toilets myself, so I scanned the room for someone who could help.

The waiter's short period of rest was prematurely ended, as his attention was drawn to the gesturing motions of a young lady. He acknowledged her signals and promptly made his way over to her table. Even from a distance, her manner suggested some degree of distress.

Although the lady had been seated alone for some time, the presence of another plate of food indicated that this hadn't always been the case. Little of the meal she had ordered remained on the plate. In contrast, the plate of her absent companion was almost untouched; the cutlery lying crudely across its contents. The waiter offered a well-rehearsed smile.

'Yes, madam. How can I be of assistance?'

The lady paused before answering, glancing down to avoid his inquisitive gaze. When she raised her head, he noticed that her cheeks were flushed with colour.

'I'm sorry to bother you,' she said, her voice timid and embarrassed. 'It's my boyfr... er, fiancé. He left abruptly, I think to the bathroom.'

The waiter raised his eyebrows, prompting her to elaborate further.

'I-I know this sounds stupid,' she stammered, 'and I'm probably just being paranoid, but could you possibly check to see he's all right?'

The waiter nodded. This certainly wasn't the first time such a request had been made.

'Certainly, madam.'

The woman looked momentarily relieved, her shoulders lowering and relaxing, but only for a second.

'It's just for my peace of mind,' she added. 'I'm really sorry for all the bother.'

'Not at all.' The waiter smiled again. This one seemed genuine.

He strode away from the table and towards the washrooms, swanning between the chairs of other diners with great dexterity. The lady watched from afar as he pushed open the door bearing a picture of a stately gentleman and disappeared from sight.

A short interval elapsed before the waiter re-emerged, one hand passing agitatedly through his hair. Such was his demeanour that the lady was out of her seat and heading towards him before he could even raise his hand to deter her.

'I'm sorry, madam, you can't go...' the waiter appealed but she shoved past him and through the swinging door.

Leila barged into an empty room, the blend of gleaming chrome and frosted glass surfaces conveying an unblemished sterility. The surroundings were foreign to her and she momentarily floundered in the centre of the floor space, shuffling disconcertedly on the tiles before dashing towards the cubicles that lay to her right.

Of the three cubicles, only the one in the far corner was occupied, and it was towards this that she headed. She reached *forward to open the door but was yanked back by the waiter, who grabbed her around the waist and hauled her back, her fingertips flailing helplessly in the air as they stretched out into the emptiness in front of her.*

She thrashed about like a snared animal, throwing her body from side to side in an attempt to break free from his grasp. His grip was too strong and he overpowered her, dragging her backwards towards the exit, her arms and legs lashing out like those of a fitting child.

Changing tactics, she dug her nails deep into the backs of his hands and he yelped in pain as he was forced to let go. Surging forward again, she got one hand on the door before the waiter pounced again, this time dragging her to the floor and trying to pull one of his hands over her eyes. She kicked out violently with her flailing legs and one of them made contact, the door of the cubicle flying open and slamming firmly against the inner wall before careering shut again with a crack that echoed around the room's hard, claustrophobic confines.

It had swung shut sharply, but not so quickly that it had failed to reveal what lay behind it, and she caught a glimpse through the waiter's fingers, which were scrabbling desperately across her face.

She saw the leather belt slung into a noose, the rigid body, the lolling tongue.

The antecedent serenity of the restaurant was shattered by the commotion that followed.

And the screaming.

The resounding, nauseating shrieking.

Acknowledgements

Thanks you to Joy Tibbs for your fantastic editing skills and encouragement. Thank you to my parents and Amanda for being unfailingly wonderful. Thank you to Jenny, Olivia and Katie for making my world.

And thank you to you, the reader, for reading *Pigeon Street*. Gaining exposure as an independent author relies mostly on word-of-mouth, so if you have the time and inclination, please consider leaving a short review wherever you can.

Coming soon from Mark Fieldsend

Nightmare Slammers
Out of Mind